**DO NOT REMOVE
CARDS FROM POCKET**

DEMCO

CONTROL

JACK ANDERSON

CONTROL

A NOVEL

ZEBRA BOOKS
KENSINGTON PUBLISHING CORP.

ZEBRA BOOKS

are published by

Kensington Publishing Corp.
475 Park Avenue South
New York, NY 10016

Library of Congress Catalogue Card Number: 88-50952

First printing: October, 1988

Printed in the United States of America

CONTROL

ONE

1986

Four guards in dark blue uniforms saluted military-style as the elongated black Mercedes rounded the last turn in the long driveway and drew up to the gate. The chauffeur ran down the windows. It was security procedure at VWH for outgoing vehicles to be examined as thoroughly as incoming ones, and the guards had learned from experience that they were to extend no courtesies—beyond their respectful salutes—to the black executive limousine. Indeed, they were to examine it more closely than they would another automobile.

They looked inside the car and satisfied themselves as to the identity of each occupant—the two passengers in the rear, the driver and plainclothes guard in the front seat. They opened the rear and examined the baggage space. When they were finished, they stepped back and saluted again. The limousine rolled through the gate and turned left on the highway to Frankfurt.

The passenger directly behind the driver was the founder, principal stockholder, and chief executive officer of Verlagsgruppe (Publishing Group)—Wilhelm Hildebrandt. He was sixty-seven years old but looked fifteen years younger, a tall, erect, ruddy-faced man whose blond hair was now reduced to wisps combed from side to side across his high liver-spotted dome. He had served as a *Leutnant* on a U-boat in the North Atlantic during World War II, and he still carried himself with the disciplined bearing of a naval officer, yet with the informal affability imposed by the cramped confines of the crew quarters in a U-boat. He was reading *Stern* as the limousine passed out of the corporate compound and entered the highway.

Sitting behind the guard, Friederich Hoffman gazed thoughtfully at the traffic and checked his watch. Herr Hildebrandt had a disconcerting habit of leaving for the airport with barely enough time to catch his flight. Their flight for Rome was scheduled to depart at 11:20 hours; heavier-than-usual traffic might cause them to miss it. Although Herr Hildebrandt would accept responsibility and would not blame him, Hoffman could never avoid feeling a missed plane would be his fault. It was his responsibility, after all, to arrange travel. At age forty and climbing, he was acutely conscious that he had served for six years as personal aide to Herr Hildebrandt, and he wanted, with quiet desperation, to please *der Chef.* Despite Herr Hildebrandt's genial assurances that he would not be upset over missing the plane, Hoffman was sure that secretly he must mind and secretly he must blame someone.

The driver, Hans Valentin, was twenty-nine years old. He regarded it a privilege to drive this man and this car. If he had one nagging concern, it was that Herr Hildebrandt, encountering him on the street and out of his chauffeur's uniform, probably would not recognize him. Herr Hildebrandt was that kind of man; a natural aristocrat. He would see to it that Hans received appropriate increases in his wages as the years went by, and each time Frau

Valentin bore a child, there would be flowers at the hospital, followed by a routine bonus. Still, *der Chef* seemed to look through a man who held so menial a job as chauffeur.

The guard, Sepp Krueger, was relaxed and impassive. The biggest thing on his mind was the beer he hoped to share with Hans after they dropped Herr Hildebrandt at the airport. Krueger was thirty-five. He had been a uniformed guard for seven years before he was promoted to this job. He carried a small automatic pistol under his jacket, and in a rack under the dashboard he had a Schmeisser submachine gun. His main function, he had learned, was to give the appearance of being rigidly alert, as if he expected an attack at any moment. Although he could not appear to be, he was, nevertheless, relaxed, for the limousine was a mobile fortress, superpowered and heavily armored, and Hans had been trained in defensive driving tactics.

For security reasons, Sepp still did not like to be passed on the highway. When he glanced back and saw a BMW overtaking them at high speed, he muttered to Hans to be alert. The BMW was followed by a Volkswagen van; it, too, was moving up fast—too fast for a VW van.

Hans's rules of the road were simple and logical: You did not try to outspeed every vehicle that overtook you on the highway. What sense would it make, after all, to drive an armored limousine into a high-speed crash? The BMW was signalling to pass, and he would let it.

As the BMW breezed by—both cars travelling at speeds above 140 kph—the man at the wheel focused intently on his driving, staring straight ahead. In the Mercedes, Hans tossed a nervous glance at the speeding BMW, but Sepp Krueger gave it a full laserlike stare. He thought it odd that the man kept his eyes glued on the road ahead, without so much as a curious glance at the long black limousine.

"Vorsicht!" yelled Krueger.

The BMW had cut in front of the limousine, and its driver was braking. The brake lights glared an ominous red, and the BMW swerved and fishtailed as its brakes locked and the car skidded. Hans jammed down on his brakes but too late, the Mercedes slamming hard into the rear of the BMW.

The face of Wilhelm Hildebrandt smashed against the glass that separated the passenger compartment from the driver's compartment of the limousine. Krueger gaped in horror at the bloody caricature that stared at him through the cracked glass. Damn! was his thought. Why wouldn't the man ever wear his seat belt? The rest, who had, were not injured.

Krueger started to climb out and open the rear door. . . .

Hans shrieked. The van had stopped abruptly beside them. Hans yelled something incomprehensible. Then the van sped forward, and Krueger saw the driver of the BMW limp up to it and reach out to be pulled inside. Now he understood.

The flash was white. All the witnesses agreed to that. The yellow flame that followed the flash was seen only for an instant before it was swallowed by a rolling cloud of black smoke and red fire.

"I would have supposed this is not quite your beat," said Stan Ross.

"In that supposition you would be entirely correct," said Bert Stouffer. "Except . . ."

"Except?"

Stouffer sipped from his glass of cold white Rhine wine and sampled the crumbly white cheese the waiter had just placed on the table. "I've been on this story for a long time," he said.

"Are you suggesting you had some reason to *expect* the murder of Wilhelm Hildebrandt?" asked Ross.

"No, no. It's a total surprise to me. In fact, it may have screwed up my story."

"Well . . . if I'm going to cooperate with you, you can cooperate with me."

"Of course," said Stouffer. He winced over the cheese. It had an odd, sour taste, and he didn't like it. He bit off a mouthful of bread to suffocate the taste. "Let me ask you one question first. Do you have any sense at all that the Federal Republic is not being entirely forthcoming about how Hildebrandt happened to be blown up?"

"You've seen the reports," said Ross.

"Yes. 'Another victim of terrorism, the killers motivated by Hildebrandt's editorial policies.' Do you agree with those reports?"

"I have to, since I haven't seen anything to the contrary."

"I called on the functionaries of BFV in Bonn," said Stouffer. He was talking about the Bundesamt für Verfassenschutz, the counter-terrorist agency of the Federal Republic. "What I got mostly was apologies that people don't speak English."

"What kind of credentials did you show?" asked Ross.

"Well, I don't have a Reuters card like you," said Stouffer. "I free-lance mostly, you know. My relationship with the *Wall Street Journal* doesn't provide credentials."

"Maybe you could show them your Pulitzer," suggested Ross dryly.

Stouffer gave him an exasperated look.

"I can tell you," said Ross, "that the Federal Republic is embarrassed."

"I would think so."

"There is talk that Hildebrandt was done in by the MfS," said Ross. "You know what MfS means?"

"Nope," said Stouffer as he picked up his menu and began to frown over the German. "I have enough difficulty with the *American* alphabet soup."

"It means Ministerium für Staats-Sicherheit," said Ross. "It's the East German version of the KGB. They've carried off assassinations before."

"Does it make any sense that they would murder Wilhelm Hildebrandt?" Stouffer asked.

"About as much sense as finding Bert Stouffer in West Germany asking questions about the Hildebrandt assassination," said Ross. "It's off your beat, we agreed, and you said you'd tell me why you're interested."

Stouffer nodded. "What do you recommend here?" he asked, scowling at his menu.

Stan Ross was the Reuters bureau chief for Bonn and Frankfurt; he had been assigned there for three years. Earlier, he had worked in the Washington and New York bureaus. He had studied French and German and had asked for a European assignment. Two years after he arrived in Germany, his bureau chief had been murdered—a crime that remained unsolved—and Ross was promoted into the vacuum. The bureau usually produced three-paragraph stories for the inside pages, but an event like the assassination of Wilhelm Hildebrandt projected Ross's byline onto the front pages. He had been flattered by the call from Bert Stouffer. They had met in Washington six or eight years ago, but he was surprised Stouffer remembered his name.

Bert Stouffer was forty-two, maybe forty-three years old by Ross's best guess. He had been an athlete once, as Ross remembered, a collegiate football player—a wide receiver—which was reflected in his wiry build and bent nose that had once been crushed against his face and kneaded back into shape by a surgeon. His light step and shoulders-back posture gave an intimation of the physical. He had steady, piercing light blue eyes, the lid of his right eye drooping slightly. His brown hair was highlighted with gray, not just on the sides but on the top as well, and tonight it appeared uncombed since morning, tumbling over his forehead and bushing out over his ears. He wore a professional gray tweed jacket with leather patches on the elbows—a holdover, Ross supposed, of his preppie days.

Stouffer was a dogged investigative reporter who had won his Pulitzer Prize by looking under some luxurious rugs; he had exposed insider trading by partners and employees of major New York law firms. His usual beat was Big Business, and though he was a free-lancer, his byline appeared so often in the *Wall Street Journal* that many readers believed he was a staff correspondent.

He was a graduate of Brown University, with a proper Ivy-League partiality for his fellow Ivy Leaguers—except Yalies, whom he did not like for attending a university which, all too recently, had enforced a strict quota on the admission of Jews. He was unmarried, though it was whispered that he contributed to the support of a teenaged child in Arlington, Virginia. He was also known for occasionally getting roaring drunk.

Ross recommended the veal, and Stouffer pushed back his chair and sat pensively sipping his wine while the bureau chief summoned the waiter.

"It was professionally done," said Stouffer when the waiter had left their table. "I mean, the assassination."

"I'm not so sure," said Ross. "They got away without being identified. I suppose that was skillful. But when you consider that two of the men in the car survived . . . I mean, most of the limousine remained intact, and it is possible Hildebrandt would have survived, too, if he had been wearing a seat belt. In fact, it's possible his neck was broken when the limo crashed into the BMW, not by the explosion."

"It was plastique, hmm?"

"Yes. Very common. It was thrown from the van. That's something else not very professional. It skidded across the pavement. Two or three feet more, and it would have exploded off the side of the limousine, not under it. As it happened, it went off directly under the right front seat where the bodyguard was sitting. That killed him. Hildebrandt was thrown up and back, crushed against the roof of the car. But the driver and Hoffman survived."

"A hundred witnesses," said Stouffer.

"Two hundred," said Ross. "Three hundred. But not one had the wits or the courage to chase after the van. The police found it abandoned about five kilometers away."

"All of which I have read in your wire stories," said Stouffer. "Now tell me what you know that you haven't reported."

"I don't know anything more, really. Anyway, you haven't told me why you're interested. As I said, it's not exactly on your usual beat."

Bert grunted. "All right. Strictly *entre nous*, Stan."

"Okay, I won't steal your story."

"I may not have a story. If I do, I want to publish it all at once, in my own way. Understood?"

"Of course."

Bert glanced around and lowered his voice. Clearly, no one was listening; he had acted instinctively. "Did you know, Stan," he asked, "that Verlagsgruppe Wilhelm Hildebrandt is a major stockholder in Catlett Communications?"

Ross's jaw slumped. "Hildebrandt . . . and *Catlett*?"

"I've been watching Catlett Communications Enterprises for more than a year," said Bert. "In the last eighteen months, CCE has acquired ten television stations—or nine, if you want to count the WYRK stations as one. Television outlets don't come cheap, even if you buy marginal ones. Catlett's newspapers aren't making the kind of money he's spending. And try—just try, if you will—to find out where he's getting all the cash. CCE is closely held. They report only what they are absolutely compelled to. They—"

"I know," Ross interrupted. "I've heard rumors . . . speculation about where the capital comes from. He owns a lot of properties, you know. He has a damned good credit record. He's borrowed many millions over the years and never failed to pay what he owed when it came due—or earlier."

"You've been out of the country, Stan. Maybe you don't know the latest."

"That he's going after States Broadcasting? That's no secret even here in the outback."

"What do you think it will take to buy a controlling interest in States?"

Ross shrugged. "You tell me."

"Half a billion," said Stouffer, picking up his wine glass. "Catlett Communications owns seven newspapers, of which only five make money. He loses a bundle every year on the *Sentinel-American*, and he's had the *Register-Herald* for what—fifteen years?—and it has never broke even a single year. I grant you the man is a multi-millionaire, but—"

"All those stations must make money."

"Sure they do," said Bert. "But not enough to mount an assault on States Broadcasting. Stan, we're talking about half a *billion*. Probably more."

"They'll fight him hard," said Ross. "My God! He's taking on the Christian right!"

"Sure they will. The evangelical crowd will fight tooth and nail to prevent their stations being taken over by the man they call America's chief pornographer. States management is already looking for a deep pocket."

Ross shook his head. "Catlett and Hildebrandt. Are you sure?"

"Oh, there are more twists to the plot," said Stouffer. "Half a billion is a lot of bucks. I doubt even Hildebrandt could have come up with that much loose change. I've got a feeling there're more snakes in the grass."

Ross glanced around the room as his mind turned, as he tried to assimilate the significance of what Stouffer was telling him. Suddenly, his eyes widened, and he turned on Stouffer with a hard stare. "Hey, just a minute! You aren't suggesting Catlett had anything to do with the murder of Hildebrandt?"

"No," said Bert firmly. "Catlett's a bastard, but no; he would stop short of murder. No. But I would like to find out if there is some link between the death of Hildebrandt and the Catlett-Hildebrandt connection."

"What link?" Ross asked. "What connection?"

"I don't know," Stouffer said to Ross. "Maybe there is no connection. But I'd like to know."

"Is there any evidence of a connection?"

"Yes," said Bert. "The same kind of evidence that Jesus Christ was an actual, historical reality—if you know what I mean."

"I'm afraid you've lost me," said Ross.

"Aside from religious faith," said Bert, "there is no first-century evidence that such a person as Christ really lived. There is contemporary documentation of the life of Caesar Augustus and Tiberius. There is even contemporary documentary evidence of the life of Pontius Pilate; but not one document survives from the time of Christ that mentions him. Yet . . . within a few years, Christianity was a powerful, if a controversial, force. No one in the first century, though, protested that no such person as Christ ever lived, that Christianity was based on a myth. Ergo, Christ must have existed, on the basis of the *negative* evidence."

"And the negative evidence of—"

"Catlett publishes the *Washington Register-Herald*, the *New York Sentinel-American*, and four other big-city newspapers, besides his damned *Terrier*. Hildebrandt was a major stockholder in the company that owns them. Yet, when he was assassinated, those papers ran the wire-service stories only. Not one of them mentioned his stock ownership."

"Doesn't prove anything," said Ross.

"No. But it raises suspicions."

"What's the thrust of your story?" Ross asked.

"Not the death of Hildebrandt," said Bert. "That's a sideshow. I'm looking at a bigger issue."

"Which is?"

Bert lifted his wine glass, then glanced around the room. He was looking for the waiter, for his dinner. As Ross had already observed, Bert Stouffer valued his time, had little patience, and seemed unable to relax. Even though they were in no rush to eat dinner, Bert wanted it served.

He sighed. "Stan . . . the most valuable commodity in our complex society in this final quarter of the twentieth century is *information*. I mean, I'm not a disciple of McLuhan, but the prime product is information, how we disseminate it, who controls it. . . . I think Thad Catlett anticipated McLuhan and did something very practical about it. He had money behind him; he could have gone into any business. But he chose to go into publishing. There is no end to his ambition. I mean, he wants to out-Luce Luce, out-Chandler Chandler, out-Murdoch Murdoch. And so, I bet, did Hildebrandt. The two of them, combining their resources, might have—"

"—monopolized . . ."

"Short of monopolized," Bert interrupted. "But grandly influenced public opinion . . . by controlling too large a share of the public's means of accessing information."

"And now somebody kills Hildebrandt," said Ross.

"Who wanted him dead? Who planned the assassination? Who carried it out? And why? Why? Why? Damn! It does raise interesting speculation."

"So you came over here to see if you can find out what's not been reported about the death of Hildebrandt."

"There might be a break in it," said Bert. "I've got an enlarged curiosity."

"I don't have any answers," said Ross. "But I can help you look for them. Do you want to see the scene of the crime?"

Bert smiled for the first time. "If you haven't anything better to show me," he said.

Stouffer was registered at the Frankfurter Hof. After his dinner with Ross, he checked into his room at about ten. He showered and rolled into bed. He set his clock to wake him at 3:00 A.M. When the alarm went off, he got up, rubbed the sleep out of his eyes, brushed his teeth, and placed a transatlantic call to New York.

Kathy answered the telephone. He had expected that and had instructed the operator to explain there was a call from Frankfurt for Mr. Johnson. After a moment, Charles Lodge Johnson came on the line.

"Who's calling?"

"Bert Stouffer, Charles."

"From Frankfurt?"

"From Frankfurt. Right. Sorry to call you at home at night, but you're not the easiest man in the world to reach. If you weren't an old friend, I'd think you've been trying to avoid me."

"To be altogether honest with you, Bert, I have," said the cool, precise Boston voice of Charles Lodge Johnson.

"I'm not an easy man to shake."

"What is it, Bert, three in the morning in Frankfurt? Is this something urgent, or have you been drinking again?"

"I figured you'd take the call when the operator said it was from Frankfurt. That's a bit revealing, Charles."

"You didn't fly the Atlantic just so you could place a telephone call to me from Frankfurt."

Bert smiled, as if Johnson could see his visual reaction, and quickly realized the error of the instinct, which broadened his smile. "No, I didn't," he said. "I'm over here looking into the assassination of Wilhelm Hildebrandt."

Johnson was silent for a significantly long moment. "I'd be surprised to learn the *Wall Street Journal* has much interest in that," he said cautiously.

"Thad Catlett's partner," said Bert.

"No. You exaggerate if you characterize the man as Thad's partner."

"Then what *was* the relationship?"

"Nothing that had anything to do with the man's death, if that's the connection you're looking for."

"I don't expect to solve the murder," Bert said. "That's not what I'm looking for and not why I called."

"May I then inquire what possessed you to arise at three in the morning and place a transatlantic call to me at home?"

"I am trying to write a story, Charles, and I've been constantly frustrated by the receptionists and secretaries at CCE. They won't put me through to you. Even Kathy tells me you're not at home, when I know you are. You used to be a reporter. You should remember how that feels."

Bert knew he had touched a sensitive nerve. Charles Lodge Johnson did not like to be reminded that he *used to be* a reporter. He had been, in fact, a great reporter. He had won a Pulitzer Prize for his exposure of corruption in Boston politics twenty-five years earlier. Bert had never understood why a talented and scrupulous journalist like Johnson had accepted a job with Catlett in the first

18

place, let alone adjust to his organization so well that he had risen to the number two position. Worse, he had become a loyal Catlett defender.

"Just what did you want to talk about, Bert?"

"States Broadcasting."

"What about States Broadcasting?"

"What I want to know is where in the hell F. Thad Catlett is going to raise half a billion or six hundred million to buy control of States?"

"That is a subject I am not at liberty to discuss," said Johnson with cold corporate precision.

"On the public record, without anyone betraying any confidences, Charles, I can find something like four *billion* dollars that your boss has scattered around. He isn't good for ten percent of it. CCE never had that kind of money."

"Thad has a remarkable talent for capitalizing his ventures," said Johnson blandly.

"I'm in Frankfurt," Bert persisted, "where the records show CCE has a fifty-million-dollar line of credit at Frankfurter Landesbank. Why would a Frankfurt bank make that kind of money available to Thad Catlett? Also a Japanese bank—"

"Bert," Johnson interrupted, "you can't expect me to violate confidences. I will tell you this much: It's all perfectly legal and perfectly honest."

"Then why is it all such a deep, dark secret?"

"A great deal of the world's legitimate business is conducted in secret," said Johnson.

"You're stonewalling, Charles. So be it. But let me point out, for your own sake, that secret financing hangs like a miasma over the whole deal. That's going to poison the atmosphere. Quite a coalition is building to defeat the CCE raid on States. Congress may actually legislate to stop you. And the FCC—"

"We're aware of that, Bert."

"Quite a coalition," said Bert. "A lot of power. Money power. Political power. Media power. They—"

19

"I am reminded," Johnson interrupted, "of something an old-time Boston ward heeler told me many years ago. He was talking about a local election, and he said, 'With what we got on our side, there ain't no way we can lose. We got the money guys, the labor guys, and the rackets guys.' And you know what, Bert? They lost."

"You and I are friends, Charles, from many years back. For what it's worth, here's my advice: Take this matter seriously. Your boss may finally have bitten off more than he can chew. He's stepped on too many toes over the years. His enemies are ganging up on him. And he's not invincible. He's vulnerable."

"Thank you, Bert," said Johnson distantly.

"I'll be objective," said Bert.

"What else? You're a professional journalist. You should be able to be objective, even about Thad Catlett."

"It won't be easy," said Bert. "Someday I'll tell you why. But you have my word that I will be objective. Between you and me, I hope they beat him. I hope he takes his lumps. And if honest reporting of the facts contributes to that, I hope I can contribute."

"Very well, Bert. If you want to reach me at home again, I'll tell Kathy to call me to the telephone."

Stan Ross had apologized for a heavy morning schedule and had promised to pick Stouffer up after lunch, to drive him out to the scene of the explosion that had killed Wilhelm Hildebrandt. Ross was on time, at one-thirty; not long afterward Stouffer drove up in a rented black BMW.

"Sorry I couldn't join you this morning," said Ross cheerfully. "Did you have a productive morning just the same?"

"No, not really. I called at the Frankfurter Landesbank. Naturally, banking business is confidential; no one wanted to talk to an American muckraker."

"They won't help you if they don't know you; in your case, they won't help if they *do* know you," said Ross. "Anyway, I've some information for you."

"More than I could get for myself, I hope."

"You could have gotten it if you'd known where to ask . . . if you could speak German."

"Well, I can't speak German. And God forbid I should have to learn."

Ross stepped on his brakes to avoid colliding with a bicycle that had swerved in front of the BMW. He cursed under his breath as he accelerated and passed the bicycle, swinging the car into a northbound street.

"The police here in Frankfurt," Ross said, "have been in possession of two unidentified bodies for about a week. Nothing particularly interesting in that, except these two had died rather oddly—from overdoses of sodium pentothal injected in their arms."

"Truth serum," said Bert.

"So-called. Anyway, because of the way they died—two middle-aged men dressed in business suits—the Hessen state authorities were called in, then the boys from Bonn. It turns out that the two deceased parties are known agents of the MfS."

"Ministerium . . ."

"Ministerium für Staats-Sicherheit—the East German KGB. Now, that caused more than a little excitement. What had been a routine investigation suddenly became super-routine. And when it became super-routine, they did something they should have done a week earlier: They began to trace the personal effects they had found on the two dead men. And guess what? A set of keys found on one of them turned out to be the keys to the Volkswagen van that carried the bomb that killed Hildebrandt."

"Conclusion?"

"Not necessarily that the MfS killed Hildebrandt," said Ross, shaking his head.

"No," Bert agreed. "The keys could have been planted. And who killed their two agents?"

"Exactly. Who did? And why?"

"Do you have any ideas?"

Ross shook his head. "I'm like you. I'm off my beat."

*   *   *

Ilse Hanke liked her job at the Frankfurter Hof. She worked in the accounting department just behind the cashiers' desks, where guests' charges arrived and were posted to their bills. She was nineteen years old, with friends who toiled behind store counters or carried trays of food and drinks to demanding diners in dark and smoky restaurants. In contrast, she sat in a bright, cool office and tapped the keys that operated a computer.

She was a bright girl of uncommon beauty, who was accustomed to being escorted to dinners and shows and such. Her life, after work, had become a whirl of skiing weekends, Rhine cruises, flights to Majorca and the Costa del Sol—always in the company of admiring, affluent men who liked to be seen with her. They always picked up the check. She would not, though, let them buy her gifts of clothes or jewelry, and certainly she would not let them pay any part of the rent for her flat; that would change the nature of her relationships in an unacceptable way. She was at some expense, therefore, always to dress well and to keep up appearances, with her hair done right and her face tastefully adorned, and to greet her escorts at the door of a fashionably furnished flat, where she could offer them a drink of good schnapps before they went out. The cost of maintaining this life-style strained her modest paycheck.

On rare occasions, she was offered money for informatioin about hotel guests. This was verboten, but if her cash flow were low, she would be tempted, and she would accept. She had access to information from the guest records of the hotel. Who occupied room so-and-so? How did he pay his bill? What charges did he incur? And sometimes, what calls did he place? The hotel's computerized telephone system recorded every call a guest placed. If the guest charged the call to his room, his bill would show what number he called and what charges he incurred. If guests charged calls to their own credit cards, the calls were not posted to the hotel bills, but the information about the calls remained in the computer's telephone log.

Today was a good day. Ilse had been offered a better-than-usual price for a bit of information from the telephone log. When the accounting-room supervisor was called out by a cashier to explain an item in a guest's bill, she called up on her screen telephone log for Room 876. Her contact wanted information about an American guest, a Herr Bert Stouffer, who had stayed two nights. The record glowed green on the screen: half-a-dozen calls to numbers in Frankfurt, one overseas call to New York City. She glanced through the door and saw that the supervisor was intently speaking to the guest at the cashier's desk. She quickly pressed two keys, and the high-speed printer by her console began to rick-rack-rick-rack, printing what she saw on the screen. The information rolled out on a bill form, and she tore it off and stuck it in her purse. Another key tap and the record of Herr Stouffer's calls disappeared off the screen.

While Ilse Hanke was copying the record of telephone calls made from his hotel room, Bert Stouffer was belted, uncomfortably and impatiently, to seat 11B on Pan Am Flight 89 to New York. He had taken along a paperback copy of *The Hunt for Red October*, and he had finished it half an hour ago. Now he had nothing to read. He had gulped down about as much as the flight attendants were willing to serve him. And by his calculation, they were still a good two hours out of Kennedy.

"Like to look at this?" asked the young woman in the window seat.

She offered him a copy of *People*. He didn't want to read about the foibles of the famous, really, but she was young and pretty and meant to be polite. So he accepted the magazine, murmured his thanks, and began to idly leaf through it, scornful of the trivial pap that filled the pages.

Then he saw her. He was sorry he had accepted the magazine. He might have known. There was her picture, with silly damned cutlines declaring she was the worst-dressed "celebrity" at some insipid California party. Megan Wilkinson. As beautiful as ever. Still deftly playing her signature role, exhibiting her own unique combination of fresh young innocence and ripe wisdom, the virgin strumpet.

23

She was an actress. In that she was different from most of the "personalities" covered by *People*. She really was an actress.

He had seen her for the first time at the Back Alley Theater in Washington, in an obscure and turgid play that appealed chiefly to a little clique of self-proclaimed sophisticates. The little troupe of young actors and actresses had played it broad, mocking its pretensions, and they had made the show entertaining.

Megan Wilkinson was then full-figured and twenty-two. Her face was burned into his memory—those strong, searching violet-blue eyes, the thin upper lip pursed against a full lower one, the immutable expression of sweet skepticism. Her long hair was golden-blond but her brows were dark. She radiated a personality that filled the stage. The words crackled as they bounced off her lips, each line spoken exactly as it had been written, perhaps, yet with a subtle cynicism that told the audience she understood her lines fully and retained her right not to believe them.

He had encountered her a few days later at Duke Zeibert's. It was ironic, perhaps, that they were brought together by Gabe Spector, the drama critic for Catlett's *Washington Register-Herald*. Stouffer had invited her to join them for lunch.

Over crab cakes at Duke's, she had accepted his invitation to dinner following her performance that night. When they left the restaurant they caught a cab for her apartment, where both of them had gotten out. She didn't protest when he dismissed the cab.

Gazing out the window of the 747, Bert remembered vividly every word they had spoken that memorable night, her every gesture, the intoxicating beauty of her youthful body. Even when she was stretched on her bed, naked and feline, waiting for him to undress, he could not believe she would actually let him lie with her. Before he had touched her, he was hopelessly in love with her.

It was a blighted affair. She pursued her career to theaters in Minneapolis, Pittsburgh, Indianapolis, St. Louis, Columbus, Louisville, Houston. He chased stories from New York to Washington to Boston to Silicon Valley. He gave her a key to his apartment in New York and told her to use it as her own. Often he came home to find she had been there and had gone, leaving him a note.

He learned about the drudgery and insecurity behind the glamour. She had studied and sacrificed to become an actress. She had given up security and stability to pursue the spotlight, ever elusive, like sunshine through the clouds.

Few caught the skyrocket to stardom. Like most performers, she jumped from part to part. The competent performances were taken for granted; but one bad performance could sink her career. She could not accept steady outside work, since she had to be ready to answer a casting call at any time. So she had taken menial jobs as a waitress, then as a dress-shop clerk; she had also worked as a hostess in a restaurant, and had modeled nude for artists and photographers. But stuffed in her worn suitcase was a masters degree in fine arts from the University of Pennsylvania.

Bert had come home one night to find her bags inside the door of his apartment and Megan in the shower. When he slipped through the bathroom door and announced his presence, she had burst out of the shower—naked, dripping, and ebullient.

"Guess what?" she laughed.

"What?" he asked, holding her in his arms and kissing her behind her left ear.

She spun away from him. "New York, New York! It's a wonderful town!" she sang.

"You mean—"

"I've got a part! I've got a part! Oh, my God, I've got a part!"

"Off Broadway?"

"Of course, off Broadway! But it's a part in the Big Town at last!"

She had danced through his apartment naked, her breasts bouncing provocatively.

He had joined in the mood, taking her in his arms and holding her tight. She had kissed him eagerly.

"Honey . . . honey, listen. There's something about this part. I'll have to be nude on stage for about five minutes. Do you mind?"

He remembered how he had grinned. "No . . ." he had said just a bit hesitantly. "No, not at all. You'll be the most adorable nude who ever appeared on any stage anywhere."

"I've got lines to speak in the nude," she had explained, still gushing. "I'm pleading with this villain to let me put my clothes on again. I mean . . . you see, I'm a young woman being interrogated by thought police in Czechoslovakia, and they've taken away my clothes as a psychological ploy. It's a *real* play, Bert—not *Oh, Calcutta.*"

"Sounds great," he said.

She kissed him again. "I want you to be proud of me," she whispered, suddenly tearful.

"I'm already proud of you," he had said.

The play had run four months. She had received good notices but not the raves that would launch her career into orbit. The summer afterward, she had appeared for a week in Connecticut at the Westport Country Playhouse in *The Effect of Gamma Rays on Man-in-the-Moon Marigolds*. This was followed by a two-week appearance at the Guthrie Theater in Minneapolis as Mary Magdalene in *Jesus Christ Superstar*, followed by a three-month tour of the Midwest as Petra in *A Little Night Music*. Back in the Big Apple, she again began the round of casting calls—living in his apartment.

She bought groceries and kept house. He was never there for lunch, rarely for dinner, but he sat at the table with her many mornings and enjoyed the eggs she scrambled with onions and peppers and sometimes cheese, with ham or bacon, toast and marmalade, and coffee so strong they made jokes about it. When he came back to the apartment at night—often late at night—she was usually sitting under a lamp in the living room, studying a script, sometimes watching television, usually wearing a thin, short night-gown. When she knew he was coming, she would prepare something for a late night snack: a bit of brie, a small pizza that could be heated in a few minutes, or ice cream with brandy. The arrangement was all very domestic—for him, deliciously domestic. He should have asked her to marry him. Maybe his tragedy was that he hadn't.

He hesitated too long at the brink of matrimony—until one day she met Thad Catlett.

The intrusion of Catlett had been a surprise. The ease with which the man captured Megan had been a shock. It shouldn't have been. If he had known two years ago what he knew of Catlett now, he would have recognized the *modus operandi* from the beginning. On the other hand, if Megan had known she wouldn't have cared.

"Whatever Cat-lett wants Cat-lett gets." It ran through his head with the little phrase of music from *Damn Yankees*. Not just Megan. Anything. Everything. Whatever he set his greedy eyes on.

Of course, as it turned out, Thad Catlett had done Bert Stouffer an enormous favor. All unknowing. By robbing him of Megan Wilkinson, Thad Catlett had freed Bert for another love. She would be waiting for him at Kennedy Airport, probably. If she wasn't, he would see her later, probably not at his apartment, probably not at her place, maybe at the Rye Town Hilton or the Hyatt Regency in Greenwich. Bert closed his eyes and smiled to himself.

He had promised Charles he would be objective about Thad Catlett. Well, he would; he was a professional. But it would be doubly difficult.

TWO

1985

At the end of 1984, Catlett Communications Enterprises, Incorporated had owned the *Pittsburgh Star*, the *Cleveland Post-Advertiser*, the *Buffalo Register*, the *Philadelphia Courier*, the *Washington Register-Herald*, the *New York Sentinel-American*, the *American Terrier*, and sixty-eight of the small suburban sheets that Thad called "neighborhoods." Thad had failed, so far, to strike a deal for a magazine. He had also been unable to buy a television station.

On Tuesday, February 5, 1985, he caught the Concorde from New York to London. Next morning, he met with Wilhelm Hildebrandt, president and chairman of Verlagsgruppe Wilhelm Hildebrandt. Their meeting was arranged discreetly in an office provided by the Bank of Scotland in its Piccadilly branch.

Verlagsgruppe Wilhelm Hildebrandt was a holding company, which owned controlling interest in twelve separate publishing corporations. It published *Freideutsche Zeitung*, one of the most powerful newspapers in the Federal Republic. Its *Wirstschaftstage*, a daily business paper was called Germany's *Wall Street Journal*. Only *Stern* exceeded the circulation of its newsmagazine *Zwar*. It published magazines on skiing, sailing, motoring, architecture, art, and music. It also owned a book publishing company, Wilhelm Hildebrandt Verlag, which published one hundred fifty book titles a year.

That wasn't all. VWH also owned a minority interest in *Le Droit*, a Paris newspaper, and in a score of other book and magazine publishing companies in France, the Netherlands, Belgium, Italy, and Great Britain.

Thad was thoroughly prepared for this meeting. He'd had a researcher for the *Sentinel-American* put together a fat file on Hildebrandt. It contained the basic facts about Verlagsgruppe Wilhelm Hildebrandt, complete with a number of personality sketches. *Stern* had run a twelve-page illustrated mini-biography of Hildebrandt in 1981. The translation, done for Thad by a professor at Columbia, was bound inside the front cover of the file.

Hildebrandt had served as a *Leutnant* on a U-boat from 1939 to 1945. In May 1945 his captain had scuttled the boat in the harbor at Kiel, leaving the demoralized crew members on their own without pay, transportation, or an *auf Wiedersehen*. Hildebrandt had walked from Kiel to Frankfurt, some three hundred miles. Because he was in naval uniform, the British and Americans were generally helpful to him, he had told an interviewer. They had given him food and let him pass.

Once home, he had worked for six months helping to clear rubble, shoveling it into a wheelbarrow and trudging half a mile to where it was dumped. "During that time I grew muscles," he had told the *Stern* reporter. Then he began selling used books, displaying a selection on a pushcart, selling them off the cart, and taking orders for others, which he would deliver the next day—each for a few pfennigs. "The books, they had belonged to people. They had to sell them to raise money, you see."

He became a partner in the used book store, then bought the store with borrowed money and began to sell new books, too. "The people who had sold their books to raise money for food now came back looking for their books. Their empty shelves were so ugly, a symbol to them of what they had lost. Sometimes they bought back their own books, sometimes others. Later, they could afford new books. I made a small profit on each transaction. It was a good business."

In 1954 he expanded into publishing, at first just printing new editions of old classics. "I published nothing copyrighted at first. Then—" He became one of Europe's most successful publishers.

Wilhelm Hildebrandt impressed Thad Catlett—a bemused, sophisticated European, with a detached intellectuality that seemed at odds with a wariness of eye. He spoke English with a mellifluous German accent, characteristically with his chin tipped down a little, looking up with a faintly mischievous smile. They sat in leather chairs at a leather-topped table, in a small dark room redolent with the aroma of cigar smoke.

"I would have been glad to come to Frankfurt," said Thad, "if it would have been more convenient for you."

Hildebrandt dismissed the apology with a quick gesture. "Actually, I was looking for an excuse to come to London. I like to attend the theater."

Thad nodded. "In any event, I'm pleased that you consented to meet with me."

"Consent? There was no question of consent. You are one of America's most successful publishers."

"Thank you. I am sure you understand why I asked for this meeting. I am looking for the means to expand into a new field. You are looking for a way to enter the publishing business in America. It may well be that—"

"It may well be," Hildebrandt spoke up.

"Television," said Thad.

"Ja, Ja."

31

"We are not merely publishers, Herr Hildebrandt. We are *disseminators of information*, merchants of information. We are in the business of collecting and distributing information."

"Ja," said Hildebrandt.

"The most powerful way of merchandising information in the world today is television. And it also happens to be the most profitable."

"Except in countries where it is a government monopoly," said Hildebrandt.

"Well, that isn't the case in the States," said Thad. "In America, you can buy television stations." His lips curled as if suppressing a gargoyle's inward grin. "That is," he added, "you can if you have the financing."

"And you are extended a bit thin," said the German. "The American business press says you have borrowed heavily."

"The writers don't know as much about my financial structure as they think they do," said Thad. "I'll be glad to give you a synopsis."

"If you wish," said Hildebrandt.

"I own seven newspapers," said Thad. "Four of them are daily tabloids, in Pittsburgh, Cleveland, Buffalo, and Philadelphia. The *New York Sentinel-American* is a tabloid-size newspaper but a more complete newspaper. The *American Terrier* is a weekly tabloid, sold in supermarkets. The *Washington Register-Herald* is a full-service daily newspaper. In addition, I publish sixty-eight neighborhood weeklies in various cities. They are shopping guides, sustained entirely by advertising and distributed free."

Thad paused to light a cigarette. Hildebrandt pulled a cigar from his vest pocket, clipped it with a silver clipper, and lit it with a big wooden match.

"The sixty-eight neighborhood weeklies make money," Thad went on. "They generate a constant, secure revenue. I can give you the figures. The four tabloids are also profitable, year after year. The *Terrier* costs little to produce, sells three and a half million copies a week, and is the most profitable property I own. The *Register-Herald* loses about a quarter of a million dollars a month. The

Sentinel-American loses slightly more than that. I expect to turn the *Sentinel-American* around. The *Register-Herald* will probably continue to lose money."

"But it is your window on Washington, your newspaper of influence."

"Well . . . all my newspapers are influential. But you're right. The *Register-Herald* gives me national influence."

"It is also the one with the heaviest debt, and it is the one not owned by Catlett Communications Enterprises, Incorporated," said Hildebrandt, drawing on his cigar.

"Exactly," said Thad. "The *Register-Herald* is owned by the Register-Herald Corporation. I own all the stock, but it is pledged to the Cooper Bank of New York. The original loan in 1972 was thirty million dollars. We have continued to borrow to modernize the plant and to meet the expenses of a strike. So the Register-Herald Corporation is still indebted to the bank for just a little less than twenty-eight million dollars."

Hildebrandt let a thin stream of white cigar smoke filter through his lips. "It loses a quarter of a million each month *in addition* to the interest on that loan?"

"No, the quarter-million includes the interest."

"With your rate of inflation, that principal becomes less and less significant. On the other hand, if interest rates in the United States continue to rise . . ."

"I own fifty percent of the stock in Catlett Communications," said Thad. "I am personally obligated on the Register-Herald Corporation note, so my interest in CCE is at hazard to that extent. My wife, however, owns the other fifty percent; and my agreement with the Cooper Bank specifically excludes her and anything she owns from being taken to satisfy the Register-Herald note—even though she is a member of the board of directors of CCE."

"And CCE is indebted? . . ."

"I paid eighteen million for the *Sentinel-American*. CCE borrowed twelve million. That was only two years ago. CCE owes the full amount. My wife's stock is not exempt from that."

"And your net operating profit for last year?" asked Hildebrandt.

"After taxes, interest, and depreciation, a little over twelve million dollars," said Thad.

"Against a total corporate indebtedness of your two corporations of about forty million."

"Yes. I could, of course, sell off something—the *Terrier*, for example. I—"

"I can understand your reluctance to do so," said Hildebrandt.

"I can still finance acquisitions in the print field," said Thad. "Though, of course"—he stopped to smile—"I was outbid on the purchase of *Manhattan Magazine*."

"As was I," said Hildebrandt.

"Your bid alerted me that you are interested in the United States," said Thad.

"The paperwork has not been completed, so I tell you this in confidence," said Hildebrandt. "I have just completed the purchase of Knoll & Company, together with its paperback imprint, Tuck Books."

"That makes you an American publisher," said Thad.

Hildebrandt drew smoke from his cigar and let it drift out as he spoke. "But you are interested in television," he said.

"Yes. But I can't raise enough money. A station in a good market will bring one hundred million dollars—if you can find one for sale. I can't raise that kind of money."

"Then what sort of proposition do you have in mind?"

Thad crushed his cigarette in an ashtray. "You cannot buy an American television station, nor can your corporations. It—"

"Yes, I know," Hildebrandt interrupted. "One must be an American citizen." He shrugged. "And in Europe, broadcasting is a governmental monopoly."

"To put the matter most succinctly," said Thad, "I qualify to own American television stations, but I don't have the money. You have the money, but you don't qualify."

"So you propose? . . ."

"That we explore ways in which we might restructure Catlett

Communications Enterprises, Incorporated so as to make an investment attractive to you. I am not willing to surrender control of the business I have built over the past twenty years. I am, however, entirely willing to share control, particularly of the broadcasting venture."

"You have a television station in mind?"

"I do. But I doubt we could complete our arrangements in time to buy it. But there will be other opportunities."

Hildebrandt pushed his chair back from the table, flexed his shoulders, and leaned back. "It is a great deal of money, Mr. Catlett. We will have to think in terms of a consortium. If, on the other hand, the proposition becomes sufficiently attractive, we could probably find investors."

"Let me add two more elements to it, Mr. Hildebrandt. First, I am known in publishing as a man who understands his market and gives the public what it wants. I am often accused of pandering to public appetites. One can't do quite the same thing on television, but I think I know how to make a station profitable. *More* profitable, I should say, because I don't propose to buy a station that is in difficulty."

"Not a salvage operation," agreed Hildebrandt.

Thad's TWA flight from London landed at Kennedy at 2:15. He kept an apartment in the city, on Park Avenue, and he taxied directly there, not to his office. He did not call home. Officially he was not back from London. He showered, then hurried to Grand Central to catch a commuter train for New Haven.

Megan's play, *Night Trails*, was opening that night. He arrived in New Haven in time to attend the theater, assure her he was there, and then go to dinner with Brandy Ingraham (Brandon Englemeyer), who would write a review for tomorrow's *Sentinel-American*.

"Did you interview her?" Thad asked after they were seated and a double Scotch had been delivered to the table.

"At length," said Englemeyer.

"What do you think?"

"She's a beautiful young woman, to start with. She's intelligent, clever, and ambitious."

"Were you able to get any impression of the play? I mean, are the people in it—"

"The playwright is unknown," said Englemeyer crisply. "The director, Bill Beebe, has had some success. Her leading man, Richard Larimer, has a name; but he's a hack. If she's any good at all, my review will say that she carried him."

"What I want to know is—"

"—whether she has enough talent to justify a campaign to make the young lady a star." He shrugged. "I would guess she has—unless she stumbles badly. Anyway, it will test the power of the press."

"Of the *Sentinel-American*, anyway," said Thad with a thin smile.

"Well, the *Times* won't fall in line behind the *Sentinel-American*, you can be sure of that," said Englemeyer. "But . . . I'll give it my best shot."

"Understand, Brandon, I don't want a good review if she's not any good." Thad hesitated, groping for the right words. "She and I . . . that is, we have a relationship. . . . If your review is too blatant, it could . . . uh . . . wind up in the gossip columns."

"I understand," said Englemeyer. "You want to protect my integrity."

Thad smiled ruefully. "So be subtle."

"If she's good, she's good," said Engelmeyer. "I won't have to be subtle about that."

It was the third time Thad had seen her on the stage. He had watched her twice in Off-Broadway shows. He was no critic, but he did not like *Night Trails*. He hoped his reviewer liked it better. After the curtain came down and she had finished with the backstage folderol with which he was so impatient, she came to the bar where he had said he would meet her, where he had drained two double

Scotches, where he had brushed off an approach by a young woman who'd had a bit part in the play and did not guess that this tall, handsome graying man was waiting for Megan Wilkinson.

They took a cab to the motel where the cast of *Night Trails* was staying. The director passed him in the lobby but did not speak, uncertain how F. Thad Catlett would react to being recognized in the company of a young actress he was taking to bed. After all, offending F. Thad Catlett was not the way to promote a career. The publisher and the starlet disappeared into the elevator and emerged shortly in a dreary room that stank of stale cigarette smoke and disinfectant that had been used to clean the bathroom.

She was quick to undress. Megan was proud of her body. She had displayed it on stage and to artists and photographers, and she enjoyed showing it to him.

He was forty-six years old; Megan was twenty-four. He was keenly conscious of the twenty-two-year difference. Her youth was a constant wonder to him. Every time he saw her taut, sleek young body, he marvelled at her love. For she loved him. Or said she did. Insisted she did. He sometimes wondered why.

For his part, he was accustomed to being a presence wherever he went. A face once conventionally handsome had gained distinction and character as cigarettes and whiskey had etched lines on the smooth young cheeks, softened the eyes, and drawn down the corners of the mouth. His visage, once pleasant but forgettable, now interesting and memorable, loomed cheerfully above the wreckage of a hundred bottles. He spoke distinctively, slowly, with careful modulation, as if trained as an actor. Actually, he had trained himself, long and painfully, to eliminate every trace of his West Texas accent.

Megan occasionally complained about his smoking and drinking, and scolded him for not getting enough exercise. He lived too much in offices and airplanes, she told him. "You're a walking syndrome, you know. What is it they call your time of life, lived the way you live it—the hurricane years?" She would pinch the flesh on his belly. "Look at that. . . . Now that's not *necessary*."

Tonight they went immediately to bed. He reminded her that he had been up since 3:00 A.M., New Haven time.

He was ambling naked into the bathroom, scratching his bottom, just as Megan awoke and caught sight of him in the cold white light of early morning.

"I'm not sure I'd have fallen in love with you if I'd seen this view first," she said, yawning.

He glanced over his shoulder and grinned, then pushed the bathroom door shut.

"You weren't much good last night," she said through the door.

"I wasn't up to it," he grumped.

She giggled. "Is that a pun?"

"Fact of life," he said. "Plus jet lag."

"Well, finish your pottying and brush your teeth, and let's have a quickie before we go down for coffee. I'm not getting it anywhere else anymore, you know."

When he opened the door, she was sitting on the edge of the bed brushing out her hair.

She turned and smiled provocatively.

He glanced at the bedside clock. "I have a lunch meeting with Morgenthau at the Harvard Club," he said. "I have to catch a train for New York in—"

"Morgenthau can wait long enough for you to have a quickie. Just tell him you were having a quickie with Megan Wilkinson. He'll understand."

Thad shrugged, then headed for the bed. Afterward, she kissed his ear. "See," she whispered. "There was time."

While he shaved with the razor and gel she had brought to New Haven in her bags, Megan watched him intently.

"Thad . . ."

"Umm?"

"Do you love me?"

He stopped shaving and glanced back at her. "Yes, Megan. I do."

"Well, I love you, too. So what are we going to do about it?"

He resumed shaving. "Keep on doing what we're doing."

Megan sighed. "If I love you, Thad, and you love me, then . . . I mean, if I get a part, I'll maybe have to go away. I mean, if *Night Trails* isn't some kind of success, I may not be able to make it in New York. I'll have to go God knows where, and then we won't see each other. Our arrangement is . . . well, it's so *uncertain*. It's not even defined. Remember, I gave up a man who wanted to marry me. Did I make a big mistake?"

He wiped his face with a towel. "If I didn't have that appointment, we could have a long talk."

She nodded. "I know. Some other time. But I want an answer. Are you thinking at all of getting divorced? How many times have I asked? Don't you think I'm entitled to an answer? I want to be your wife, Thad. If I can't be that, I'm willing to be . . . well, whatever. But I need to know."

"All right, Megan. We'll talk . . . later."

Brandy Ingraham's review in the *New York Sentinel-American*:

MEGAN WILKINSON STUNNING IN *NIGHT TRAILS*

Megan Wilkinson shone last night in the New Haven opening of *Night Trails*, a drama-cum-thriller about cyclists and truckers gathered in an all-night truck stop diner where murder is on the menu.

Before the play's New York debut next month, playwright Fred Dunne hopefully will work out some of the problems that plague the script. This is his first outing, but his work looked craftsmanlike enough for us to believe he will be able to smooth out the dialogue.

Richard Larimer, playing the male lead as Thug, a concupiscent cyclist, is adequate as usual. Adequacy is his stock in trade, and in this play his chief contribution is that he does not get in the way of the brilliant acting of Megan Wilkinson.

Miss Wilkinson is a pleasure. Playing Lynda, a confused girl in hot pants and halter who has come to the truck stop on the back of Thug's motorcycle, she manages to put together subtly just the right combination of the conflicting elements in the girl's character—hot little trick flattered to be invited to ride with Thug, yet frightened as she finds herself in a milieu seamier and more threatening than she had bargained for.

She comes on stage behind the swaggering Thug, mimicking his swagger and happy to show herself off. Little by little, as the first act develops, she transforms an adolescent bitch into an apprehensive, then terrified girl. The subtlety by which she achieves this shift is a tour de force.

Miss Wilkinson has paid her dues in the theater, playing bit parts and supporting roles, and last night she demonstrated her mastery of the craft of acting.

The *Post* ran a page-six story the next day, with an enticing photograph of Megan: "The *Sentinel-American* says her acting talents are extraordinary. Perhaps. Among the jet set, she is known to be a close friend of *Sentinel* publisher F. Thad Catlett, who flew back from Europe to attend the opening of her play."

The play opened in New York on March 19. The opening was preceded by a series of photo-stories in the *Sentinel-American*, describing the return of the cast to New York, the struggle of the director and playwright to repair the play, the enthusiasm of the cast—and every word and movement of the "star," Megan Wilkinson.

The *Times*:

Miss Wilkinson's acting is equal to the demands of the play, which does not demand much. If it has a long run, it will probably be because some people, tourists especially, will come to ogle Miss Wilkinson in her hot pants and skimpy halter. Her best achievement of the evening was managing to make her way through a somewhat athletic performance without the displacement or entire loss of that halter.

The *News*:

Megan Wilkinson is fortunate to have been supported by an experienced actor like Richard Larimer. Her forte is display, not acting. Backed by a competent cast, she manages to hold her own through two acts of a demanding script. Her histrionics, plus ample views of her flesh, probably assure a reasonably long run for a play that might without her last a few weeks at best.

The *Post*:

Wow! Megan Wilkinson is okay. Don't take Aunt Mabel, and don't take the kids, but if you're an adult who can handle hard dialogue, chilling suspense, and raw sex, go have a look at Megan. You'll remember her after you've forgotten the play.

The *Sentinel-American*:

The superb acting of Megan Wilkinson, gracing a play that has been distinctly improved since previewed in New Haven, restores one's faith in the value of careful training and an apprenticeship in regional theater. Acting is a craft like any other—the tricks one learns from experience distinguish the pro from the tyro. Megan Wilkinson has learned them all. She and Richard Larimer, another pro, continue the best tradition of American theater.

Newsweek:

Someone's courage is to be admired. The courage to bring an

ill-written, ill-directed, ill-acted charade to a Broadway stage. The courage of Megan Wilkinson, who is required to strut about the stage scantily clad, mouthing vapid lines. She does the best she can, but no actress could bring life to *Night Trails*. Particularly when she is required to share the stage with soap-opera ham Richard Larimer.

Postscript: Miss Wilkinson's performance has been lavishly praised by the *New York Sentinel-American*. It may be merely a coincidence that she has been seen about town with its owner and publisher, second-string press mogul F. Thad Catlett.

Thad and Anne Catlett sat at breakfast in their home in Greenwich, Connecticut, on a cold, windswept Sunday morning. Papers were strewn on the floor around the table in the breakfast nook. Thad was slumped over the table, unshaven, draped in a terry-cloth robe, fingering a cigarette, sipping coffee. Anne, in tennis whites—she had court time on an indoor court at eleven—was scrambling eggs. The boys were showering upstairs and would be down in a few minutes.

"I'm going to say one or two things, then I'm going to drop it. So put down those papers and listen for a minute."

Thad looked up.

"I had an affair with Bill Shannon. You know it. The boys know it. Some of our friends know it. I don't deny any part of what happened. It began as a dream and turned into a nightmare. That may give you the idea you're entitled to have an affair, too. So . . . what can I say? Just one thing, Thad. You were never humiliated in front of the whole world. We don't have a friend, even an acquaintance, who hasn't read somewhere about you and Megan Wilkinson."

"The only thing that made the Bill Shannon episode tolerable," he said, "was that, when it came to a confrontation, you didn't lie about it. And I won't lie about this."

"It's true, then?"

He nodded.

"I'm not surprised." She turned to her eggs, stirring them vigorously. "Do you love her? Do you want to marry her?"

"First question: yes, a little. Second question: no."

"What does she want?"

Thad could not suppress a wry little smile. "She wants her career. More than anything, she wants to be an actress."

Anne stopped stirring the eggs and stared at him, studying his face with intense curiosity. She pondered for a moment, then resumed stirring the eggs. "Did you ever make love to her in this house?" she asked quietly.

"No. Absolutely not."

"Is she the only one of my models you ever—?"

That was how he had met Megan. Anne was a talented photographer. She had published three books of her photographs and had exhibited in galleries in New York, Washington, and London. Her mother was a sculptor. Megan had posed nude, first for Anne's mother for sculptures, then for photographs by Anne. Thad had met her when he came home and found Anne and Megan working in the studio.

"Mom!"

"What, Thaddy?"

"Where's my red cashmere?"

"At the dry cleaner."

"Jeeze!"

She turned toward the hall and stairway, where another shout might come. None did. She began to spoon the eggs into a bowl.

Anne was a stunning woman whose beauty was widely acclaimed. They had been married twenty years, and she had put a little flesh on her statuesque frame. The new weight filled out her jawline, her breasts, her belly, her bottom. She played golf and tennis, and the extra flesh was taut, not loose like his. Her legs, under the short tennis skirt, were muscled. She wore her honey-blond hair cut just below her ears and turned under smoothly. Her eyes were blue, her cheeks full and flushed.

43

She changed the subject. "You want me to put my CCE stock into a deal you're making with Hildebrandt. I still don't understand it."

"That's because the deal is still tentative and nebulous." He put down the newspaper and crushed his cigarette. "All I'm asking you to do is meet with the lawyers and accountants and listen to their proposals. I want you to know exactly what's going on."

"My father will represent me," she said. "I thought maybe I should have my own lawyer."

"Fine," said Thad. "Maybe he can give me some advice on the deal, too. But I want you to come to the meetings; don't leave it in his hands."

She nodded. "When my grandfather told me he was leaving me his stock in CCE, he told me to watch out for deals you'd make. He said you were too ambitious, and you'd mortgage everything we own. And you have, too. I wonder sometimes what would happen to us if everything fell apart."

"You wouldn't be poor, Anne," he said. "Even if I couldn't salvage anything, you would still have your own securities account, your own savings account, your jewelry and Cadillac and personal possessions. And your half of our equity in this house—all free of any pledges I've made."

"Well, I don't want Thaddy and Richard to discover one day that their father has been too busy for them, too busy accumulating a fortune and, instead, has left them broke."

"Then you make the decision," said Thad. "If you and your father don't like the deal, we'll turn it down."

"Which will block you at the pass."

He drew a breath. "It might, yes. To secure Hildebrandt's backing, I'll have to totally restructure the ownership interest and debt of CCE. But if it works . . . we'll own some television stations."

"Marvelous," she said dryly.

Thaddy ambled in. He was nineteen now, lean, lithe, taller than his father. His blondish-brown hair tumbled down over his ears— though this morning he had made the concession of combing it—

and he was dressed in faded blue jeans and a black cashmere sweater. He held a brown manila envelope.

"Brought you a present," he said to his father, handing him the envelope.

Thad opened the unsealed envelope and withdrew an 8 x 10 print of one of the nudes Anne had taken of Megan Wilkinson two years ago.

"I made that for you in the darkroom," said Thaddy insouciantly. "Thought you might like to have it."

"Thank you," said Thad coldly. He stuffed the picture back in the envelope, tossed the envelope on the stack of newspapers, and returned to scanning the *Washington Post*.

"I own half this company," said Anne Catlett to Charles Lodge Johnson. "You work for me as much as you do for Thad, really. I mean, I don't want to put you in an impossible position, Charles."

"Don't worry about it, Anne," said Charles. "If my position threatens to become impossible, I'll neatly duck out of it."

She sat in the bright, sunlit living room of his apartment, scanning the new decor with approval. He'd had the floor stripped, bleached, and refinished. The handsome wood floor was covered by only a few small rugs. The ceiling was crossed by tracks supporting spotlight fixtures. The walls had floor-to-ceiling bookcases on two sides of the room. The remaining wall space made a gallery for prints and paintings. He had switched off an elaborate system of high-fidelity components when she knocked at the door.

"I have no right to burden you," she said.

"It's not a burden, Anne. We are friends. Thad is my friend. And so are you."

"You may be Thad's *only* friend," she said. "At least"—she paused and smiled wryly—"his only *male* friend."

"If you want to talk about . . . uh . . . personal problems, perhaps I shall duck."

"I'll put you at ease," Anne said. "I didn't come to talk about

Megan Wilkinson." She glanced at her watch. "Would you mind pouring me a drink, Charles? It's almost noon."

"I'm afraid I don't keep rye on hand," he said. "And I didn't anticipate your visit."

"Scotch will be fine. On the rocks."

He disappeared into the kitchen to pour her Scotch. "I'll break my rule and join you," he said. "I don't drink before noon, but I can't allow a lady to drink alone."

"You've done your apartment beautifully," she said.

"Charlotte called me a nester," he said. "I do insist on decent quarters."

"You've bought a new painting."

"I sold my car," he said. "No good to me in New York. So, there it hangs on the wall, a 1977 Jaguar."

"Fantastic!"

From the first day they met, Charles had been a charismatic man, more so to Anne than to Thad, though Thad had developed a respect for him and had come to rely on him more than he had intended. Charles was medium in height and weight, dominated by a great bald dome. His eyes were mobile and piercing, amused, then sober, then amused again. Characteristically, he pursed his thin lips as if the world did not quite meet his Brahmin standards. He was the product of generations of Boston lawyers, Congregational ministers, Harvard professors, prep school headmasters, and dollar-a-year public servants. He never mentioned his Pulitzer Prize—less from modesty than from breeding—but he could not resist the temptation to let new acquaintances know he was a medal-winning swimmer and tennis player, the holder of master's points at bridge and a chess master as well. Charles Lodge Johnson was not a humble man.

He returned from the kitchen with their drinks. "I didn't mean to foreclose any discussion of a personal matter, Anne—if that's what you've come to talk about."

"Have you met her?" Anne asked as she sipped the Scotch.

"Yes. He brought her to lunch one day."

"The ironic thing is that I introduced them," said Anne. "She was a struggling actress—still is, I suppose—and needed money. She had put her name with an agency. Mother saw her and was impressed with her. So I hired her as a model. Thad came home one afternoon when she was posing for me." Anne sighed. "Well . . . it's on my mind, but it's not what I came to talk about. What I want to know, Charles, is what you think of this deal Thad is cooking with the Germans?"

"That does place me in an awkward position," said Charles. "I've expressed myself to Thad. If he hasn't seen fit to . . . well, if he hasn't told you the substance of our discussion—"

"Charles," she interrupted. "I can hear the wheels going 'round in your head. I can read your mind. You're thinking, 'She's angry about the actress and considering—'"

"No. That's not what I'm thinking."

"And I'm not thinking of a divorce, either."

He nodded, sighing. "Well, as to the Hildebrandt proposal, I'm not sure Thad is entirely cognizant of the implications. He is dealing with a highly sophisticated man, broadly experienced, with something of a reputation in Europe for being a manipulator. Wilhelm Hildebrandt has been a publisher for a long time, a corporate raider in the restrained European style for quite a while, too."

"What are his politics?"

"It depends on whom you ask. I know Thad thinks he's a fellow conservative."

"A neo-Nazi?"

Charles shook his head. "Oh, no. I have no reason to think that."

Anne carried her glass to the window and looked down at the street. "When I met Thad," she said, "he already owned the *Pittsburgh Star.* He was twenty-five. He had already forced his partners out and turned the newspaper into a tabloid."

"It had been a mouthpiece for the coal and steel unions in western Pennsylvania, as I recall," said Charles. "And a family business. The Knox family, wasn't it? And he forced the Knox heir out."

"It began making money for the first time in twenty years," said Anne. "He's already established what was called his special brand of yellow journalism, with plenty of boobs and bums, as they said. He's done it six times since. The Catlett formula. Except for the *Register-Herald* in Washington, they're all pretty much alike."

"I flatter myself that it was my assignment to make the *Register-Herald* something different."

"Of course. That's why he hired you. He wanted a voice in Washington, and he wouldn't be taken seriously with a boobs-and-bums tabloid. Anyway . . . nobody can take his success away from him. His family in Texas backed him with a couple of hundred thousand in 1958—by mortgaging the ranch, as they tell it. My grandfather—"

"Henry Trumbull Baynes."

She smiled. "After I married Thad, Grandfather Baynes backed his acquisition of the Cleveland paper. Since then, Thad has financed everything at banks. He's worth ten times what the Catletts are in Texas, almost as much, I imagine, as my grandfather was worth when he died. He's shrewd, Charles. Thad is shrewd. But I can't help but worry whether he's venturing into waters too deep for him."

"I said as much to his face. He just smiled."

"I can block him," she said grimly. She returned to the couch and gulped down her Scotch, draining the glass. "He can't cut the deal if I won't sign the papers. What would you do?"

Charles shook his head. "At this point, dear lady, I duck."

Anne sighed. "Pour me another short one, Charles," she said. "I've got to catch the train back to Greenwich, and on Saturday the bar cars don't serve."

THREE

1985

"He had a favorite line . . . a line he always used," said Donald Redding. "The land is littered with the corpses of good newspapermen who heard that line just before the axe fell. He'd say, 'I'm still learning the business.' Then he'd go on. 'I don't plan any big changes. You people know how to run this newspaper. I'll just be sort of watching. I'll have some questions, that's all.' Eighteen weeks after I heard that line—pfft!"

Bert Stouffer sat with Redding in the gloom of an Irish bar on Third Avenue, anonymous in the shadows, trying to talk softly enough not to be overheard but loudly enough to be heard above the chorus of conversation, some of the voices raucous from too much alcohol.

"Where did he get the money to buy the paper?" Stouffer asked.

"He borrowed thirty million from the Cooper Bank here in New York. He was still operating out of Pittsburgh then. He moved to Connecticut . . . sold his house in Pittsburgh and moved to Connecticut. . . . Bought the *Register-Herald* and never lived in Washington. Says a hell of a lot about him, Bert, a hell of a lot."

"Why'd they sell?"

Redding snorted. "The paper was losing two or three million a year. The family wanted out, and they got out. There were other bids, but Catlett bid high. 'I'm still learning the business, fellows. I'm just learning the business.' I'll never forget that line. For a month I believed it. You know? For a month I believed it."

Bert picked up his mug of beer. "You've got to concede, Don, that he improved the paper."

"He pumped money into it . . . expanded the editorial staff . . . gave it a new look," sniffed Redding.

"Who was Natalie Loff?" asked Bert.

"Oh, Natalie. She was a pro. She died a year or so ago. Cancer. She was an old-time Cleveland news-hen. He hired her for the *Post-Advertiser*. She'd worked for the *Plain Dealer* . . . and the *Press*, too, I think. Did a column. He made her assistant editor at the *Post-Advertiser* and then the same at the *Register-Herald*. I figure she sucked him off, if you want the truth. Cleveland guys said she did. You ever see her? A good-looking, dark-eyed broad . . . brash, bitchy. That was Natalie. But she was a newspaper woman. If he ever did learn anything, likely he learned some of it from her."

"And Johnson?"

"Hell, you know Charles Lodge Johnson. That Harvard prick. That's why Catlett picked him up, I suppose. Part of the Harvard elite."

Bert let that line slip past without comment. So far as he was concerned, Ivy Leaguers *were* elite; Ivy League credentials were a guarantee of at least a certain level of competence. He knew Charles Lodge Johnson and considered him a rare bright spot on the otherwise dismal Catlett record.

"It's probably because of Johnson that the *Register-Herald* didn't start running a bikini-girl feature."

Redding chuckled, then struck off on another subject. "How long's he going to get away with shooting fingers at the archdiocese?"

"What percentage of the old *Register-Herald* staff did he get rid of?" Bert asked.

"Only maybe ten percent," said Redding. "Our union let it happen because he created so many new jobs."

Bert glanced around the dark bar. "Well, Don, I've inhaled my quota of stale cigarette smoke. Let me pay for the beers. I'm checking out of this joint."

At home, Bert stepped into the shower, washed the stench of tobacco smoke off his skin and out of his hair, then sat down at his typewriter. What he had written this afternoon was still there, and what he had learned from Donald Redding was not going to contribute a thing to his project.

Project. He knew what was wrong with the project. He had written two hundred pages that had gone directly from the typewriter into the trash can by his desk. His work product for the past ten days was exactly five pages. The truth was that he didn't have much. Worse, he had been unable to exclude his scorn from his writing, so what little he had written was unpublishable.

Catlett. Catlett had seen Megan naked. That had started everything. She had come home gaily laughing that evening, telling him she had been posing for a Mrs. Catlett in her home studio in Greenwich, Connecticut, and Mrs. Catlett's husband had come in—and guess who he was? "I mean, Bert, he's the *newspaper guy!* You know, the *Sentinel-American* and those other papers. You know who he is. And he stands there and makes small talk with his wife, staring at me. And then he comes over and introduces himself. And, Bert! I could see it. He had a hard-on!"

51

Within a week, Catlett had called her. He had told her he was interested in featuring her as the Page Four Girl in his *Sentinel-American*. She had agreed to be photographed for it, but her agent was less than enthusiastic about her appearing nude in the *Sentinel*. So she had backed out, and Catlett had asked her out to lunch. Two weeks later her picture had appeared, not as the Page Four Girl but as part of a personality profile, portraying her as a promising young actress. By then, she was already sleeping with Catlett.

And why not? He could promote her career, which meant more than anything else in the world to Megan. He also flew her to Florida for one glamorous weekend, to California for another, bought her clothes and a diamond-studded platinum watch. Bert conceded bitterly that a half-employed free-lance writer could hardly compete with that.

He tended to excuse Megan and blame Catlett. The son of a bitch knew he was cutting in on someone else's girl. Megan had told Catlett about their relationship; she said she had even told him Bert's name. Bert had made a point several months later, long after Megan had switched beds, to meet Catlett and to mention that they had a mutual friend. Unless Catlett was a better actor than Megan was an actress, he had wholly forgotten the name Bert Stouffer. Obviously it meant nothing to him, which made Bert even more furious.

For the last ten days, Bert had been working on a story about Catlett Communications Enterprises, Inc. and its founder, F. Thad Catlett. Stouffer was a specialist in business and economic news. The focus of his story, if ever he managed to get it written, was how Catlett got money and how he used it.

He had accumulated a thick file on Catlett. If he wrote a tightly reasoned analytical article, from the business and economic point of view, he would not be the first who did it. As far back as 1968, a profile in the *National Journalism Review* had reported:

F. (for Frankie) Thad Catlett is still the *enfant terrible* of newspaper publishing, even though he attained the ripe old age

52

of 31 only last year. He is a chain-smoking, Scotch-gulping, hard-driven, personable young man with an obvious ambition: to be one of this country's most powerful newspaper publishers.

No one can say he won't make it. He has turned three failing newspapers into moneymakers. His formula dismays—even disgusts—many veteran journalists, but no one can deny his success. The *Pittsburgh Star*, the *Cleveland Post-Advertiser*, and the *Buffalo Register* have been snatched from the jaws of bankruptcy and turned into prosperous, even influential newspapers, by application of the Catlett formula.

The Formula

How does he do it? He gives his readers the best sports coverage in their cities and the most sensational local news, with emphasis on scandal, crime, and human-interest stories. He also provides simplified local political news, right-wing national editorials, games, astrology, comics, advice columns—and a daily diet of short skirts, bikinis, and occasional bare breasts. All this is served up in a tabloid format, with oversized headlines, red ink as well as black, exciting pictures, and plenty of exclamation points.

Sedate journalists, putting out newspapers along "respectable" lines, have been compelled to take notice. Who is this rebel coming up from the bottom ranks of local circulation?

But the more curious question is, where does he get the money? Each of his newspapers is modestly profitable, but Thad Catlett always seemed to have access to credit his profits could not possibly justify. An interview with Mr. Catlett produced no hint as to how he does it. Interviewing others in his organization was equally unenlightening. Mr. Catlett is almost conspiratorial in concealing the sources of his financing.

The *National Journalism Review* published a sidebar of what it called typical Catlett headlines:

"STUDENT" HOODS SEIZE
UNIVERSITY OFFICES
UNWASHED PROTESTERS URINATE
FROM WINDOWS!

* * *

POT-DRUNK ROCKERS BURN FLAG!
"SURRENDER, AMERICA!" THEY SCREAM

* * *

100,000 MARCH TO SUPPORT PRESIDENT!
SHRIEKING ADOLESCENTS DRIVEN
FROM PARADE ROUTE

* * *

SENATOR TEDDY DRIVES OFF BRIDGE
AFTER BASH!
YOUNG GIRL DIES IN HIS CAR!

* * *

REDS ROUTED,
VIETS KILL 2,000 CONG!

* * *

3,000 TOPLESS SWIMSUITS SOLD FIRST DAY!

* * *

MOM, NAKED, FLEES
KNIFE-WIELDING HUBBY!

*   *   *

"INFALLIBLE, HELL!"
—PRIEST ON POPE'S BIRTH-CONTROL BAN

Five years later, after he had acquired the *Philadelphia Courier* and the *Washington Register-Herald*, the *Wall Street Journal* had said of Catlett:

> The combined circulation of his tabloids now approaches three quarters of a million. His editorial policies are firmly applied to each newspaper. When he writes an editorial, it is published in all his papers.
>
> Acquisition of the *Washington Register-Herald* makes him one of the nation's opinion leaders. He had already achieved that status as the publisher of a quartet of tabloids in major cities. As the new publisher of a Washington daily as well, he has gained new prestige. F. Thad Catlett has become a force to be reckoned with in American journalism.

Digging through his notes, Bert came across something intriguing. Richard Nixon's White House counsel, Kenneth Asher, had served eight months of a one-year sentence for his part in the Watergate cover-up. He had also been disbarred. Now he was working for Catlett. That was interesting. The Nixon connection was tenuous, because the Catlett papers had at first defended Nixon and then dismissed him as "a squalid little felon." Why Asher, though? It was a point worth pursuing.

Bert leaned back. He was weary, as a person becomes after spending ten days assembling something that never quite comes together.

The problem was motivation: He wanted revenge. It was

55

unworthy of his profession. A reporter should not decide what the story is until he gathers the facts. Then he should report them as straight as he can, without bias; he should never present selective facts as the whole truth. Angrily, Bert stuffed his research back into the bulging folder and shoved the folder into a drawer. He pulled the paper from the typewriter and grabbed up the other pages that had been spared from the trash. He wadded them up and slam-dunked them—ten days work into the can. There was a mouse loose somewhere in the Catlett operation, but he couldn't put a finger on it. At this stage of his career, he had come to trust his judgment, his instinct, his experience when the documentation was weak. He sensed something was not quite right, and he would find it if he turned over enough puzzle pieces. But today, he was too weary.

They flew Lufthansa to Frankfurt—Thad; Anne; her father, Bayard Justin; Thad's lawyer, Melvin Bragg; and Charles Lodge Johnson.

A crisply efficient representative of Verlagsgruppe Hildebrandt intercepted them as they emerged from the plane. He introduced himself as Friederich Hoffman, led them through a quick, private passport check, and hurried them out of the airport to a black Mercedes limousine. Their luggage, he assured them, would be picked up and would follow in another car. He took them to a landscaped park on the outskirts of the city, where they were installed in luxurious rooms in the Gasthof Verlagsgruppe Hildebrandt, an aluminum and glass cube-shaped building that served as the company's VIP center for business visitors. With curt German efficiency, Hoffman laid out the schedule: Herr Hildebrandt thought they would like to rest part of the day. He would join them for cocktails at five, followed by dinner. Then they would hold a short initial business session after dinner. If there was anything they wished during the day—perhaps a tour of the city or a tour of Verlagsgruppe Hildebrandt—Hoffman offered to arrange it.

Though Thad was weary from the flight, he could not sleep. Neither could Anne. They ate a quiet lunch in a small dining room. In the afternoon, they strolled about the grounds. The Gasthof, they noticed, adjoined a larger glass cube, bearing a sign, Verhandlungs-zentrum—conference center. Other buildings circled an artificial lake—apparently the executive offices of the conglomerate.

"Impressive."

Anne nodded. "If you like Teutonic modern."

Wilhelm Hildebrandt appeared promptly at five in the room to which Hoffman had shepherded them. It was a richly handsome room, paneled in dark wood, with a gleaming parquetry floor. The windows were covered with dark red draperies. The furniture was upholstered in black leather. Dozens of tiny clear bulbs glowed in crystal chandeliers, giving a warm, subdued light. It was, Anne whispered to Thad, as if the smoking room of a London gentlemen's club had been transported to Germany and installed in this determinedly modern building. An odd effect, she thought.

Hildebrandt was a gracious host, taking care to chat with each of his guests, omitting no one. His etiquette, however, was methodical, as he turned from guest to guest, spending precisely the same number of minutes with each one. Hoffman was there, obsequious, watching for Hildebrandt's signals. Two other Germans tried to chat with the Americans, but they spoke a faltering, stumbling English, and except for Johnson, none of the Americans spoke even a faltering German. Though they tried to talk with Thad and Anne, the Germans were embarrassed when they could not make themselves understood.

After the social agenda, Hoffman was dismissed. His function was strictly to attend to the social amenities for the English-speaking visitors. Now it was time for business, and he was no longer required. In the conference room, the inability of the two Germans to speak English ceased to be a problem. There were microphones and headsets on the tables, and a simultaneous interpreter sat behind a window in a small adjoining room. English was spoken most of the time, and the two listened attentively on their headphones. When they had something to say, the Americans could press the phones to their ears and hear the translation.

"The basic terms of an agreement have been negotiated," said Hildebrandt, opening the discussion. "Now we must settle the details. First, I will explain the broad terms discussed by Mr. Catlett and me by telephone.

"Verlagsgruppe Wilhelm Hildebrandt will purchase forty percent of the capital stock of Catlett Communications Enterprises, Incorporated. Mr. Catlett owns fifty percent, and Mrs. Catlett owns fifty percent. We should like to buy twenty percent from each. We understand that this stock is variously hypothecated to secure certain loans from American banks. We will purchase the stock subject to those prior rights held by the banks, but we want the money we pay for your stock used to pay off those banks. We should not like to find two American banks as our partners. You have a seven-man board of directors. We should like to have three of those seats."

"And what do you propose to pay for the stock?" asked Bayard Justin.

"That remains to be negotiated," said Hildebrandt. "I believe we can come to a fair price, agreeable to everyone."

"A key question," said Justin.

Hildebrandt nodded at Justin, his fixed smile turning up the corners of his mouth and lifting his cheeks. "Assuredly," he said. "Now, in addition, we should like to have a contract with Mr. Catlett, requiring that he continue to devote his full time and effort to Catlett Communications Enterprises. Should he leave the company for any reason, he will agree not to engage in any competitive business."

"A no-compete agreement," echoed Bragg.

Hildebrandt nodded. "We could have approached our prospective new enterprises in another manner. We could have elected to establish a wholly new corporate vehicle. This one, however, is an established American communications company, with an established reputation and an established CEO in Mr. Catlett. Those factors will be beneficial."

"This locks him to the business," said Bragg.

"I am locked into mine," said Wilhelm Hildebrandt.

"What I want to know," said Anne, "is where the company is going to get the money to buy television stations."

"A most interesting question," acknowledged Hildebrandt, smiling in her direction. "It will come from a variety of sources, through a variety of means—some of which, I may say, must remain confidential. We will, I think, first issue some preferred stock. Some of it will be purchased by Verlagsgruppe Wilhelm Hildebrandt. Some may be purchased by others."

"Herr Hildebrandt and I have agreed," said Thad, "that we will not raise the money until we identify the first station we want to take over. Then we will raise enough to make a serious offer."

"VWH," said Hildebrandt, using the acronym for his company name, "can raise temporary financing if we should find ourselves in a position where we wish to move fast."

"And we will go into further details tomorrow," said Bayard Justin, glancing at his watch.

Hildebrandt smiled in agreement. "I should think Wednesday, too," he said. "Perhaps Thursday as well."

On Thursday morning Hildebrandt persuaded Thad to take a walk with him—around the lake and under the trees of the little park. The trees were covered with juicy-green spring leaves, and many of them were flowering.

"I wanted to speak with you alone," he said. "We have an important matter to discuss."

Thad understood. "Our hidden partners," he said.

"You will forgive me. I have not mentioned them before. I have been at pains not to mention them."

"But they have been on our minds," said Thad.

"Of course," said Hildebrandt.

"Are you ready to tell me who they are?" asked Thad.

Hildebrandt continued walking, clasping his hands behind his back, speaking quietly. "You have not done business in Germany. You have not done business with Germans. Not until now. You will learn that much animosity remains. Angry emotions boil beneath the surface. You can still find anger and hatred in the States if you penetrate deeply enough. Here the emotions are closer to the surface. Our country may appear stable and prosperous, but there is an undercurrent of emotion—angry, bitter emotion. And there are agitators who know how to exploit it. Do you understand what I am saying, Thad? Revolution. Revolution, Thad."

"The communists?" Thad asked.

"Yes, yes. But we have radicals who believe the communists are soft—too soft to perpetrate the deeds by which *they* expect to terrify our society and overpower our government. We also have millions of socialists who would nationalize everything, environmentalists who would have us dismantle all industry and try to survive like medieval agriculturalists, peace advocates who live in constant hysteria over the possibility of nuclear war and would surrender anything to prevent it. Then, of course, we are afflicted with neo-Nazis of various stripes, including those who would like to restore the Third Reich. I sometimes wonder if there is any commitment at all to the democracy we profess to practice."

"You think West Germany is on the brink?" Thad asked, a trace of incredulity in his voice.

"Germany is on the brink," echoed Hildebrandt. "I consider myself a very fortunate man. I have had four decades of democracy, four decades of a free economy in which to live my life, attain my goals, build a major business. Any of these radical groups, left or right, would destroy that. They are all alike in this: They believe they can solve all problems if they can just get their hands on enough arbitrary power to impose their cramped little ideas on the rest of us."

"We have our own know-nothings who think they know every-thing," said Thad. "We don't have a single terrorist group as notorious as the Baader-Meinhof gang, but we have a whole array of fanatical fringe groups. Fortunately, they divert most of their energy into feuds with one another."

"That has been our salvation in Germany, too," said Hildebrandt. "But I greatly fear those people. My newspapers and news magazines campaign against all of them, constantly. That is why, if you look behind you, you will see that we are followed at a little distance by two men who are ostensibly gathering litter into a cart. In fact, they have two Uzi submachine guns in that cart, plus other weapons. I am a target, you see. There are many who would like to silence me. Killing me would not change the editorial policies of my newspapers, but they think it would."

"I've received a few threats myself," said Thad.

"It is part of the price we must pay. To go on, though . . . You and I, Thad, represent the class that has something to lose. My publications speak for that class. So do yours."

"In America, that is the majority," said Thad. "The great majority."

"But do they understand?" asked Hildebrandt. "People with some real or imagined cause for dissatisfaction are susceptible to propaganda. They become easily persuaded that things could be no worse. They may not join the radicals; they are too— too suburban. But they become indifferent and stand by while the radicals seize power. It once happened in this country, you may remember."

"Yes," said Thad. "The world will not easily forget."

"So," said Hildebrandt, "a great many people who think as we do are prepared to invest in the venture we are contemplating. They expect to make money, it is true. But they are equally interested in seeing a segment of the great American television broadcasting industry secure in the hands of a company that will use its power to preserve our values."

"But broadcasting is governed by rules," Thad protested mildly, "that are commercial, not ideological."

"I am talking," said Hildebrandt, "about the power to reach the masses—people who never read a newspaper, never watch a television newscast. I am not talking about those who cannot understand. I am talking about those too indifferent to trouble themselves. I am talking about the apathetic, the nonchalant, the unconcerned."

Thad grinned. "A newspaper can have no influence unless it's read. A television station can have no impact unless it's watched. Our first priority must always be to get the public's attention."

"Precisely. You know as well as I do that we change few opinions with our editorials. We can exert a powerful influence, though, by selectivity—by what we print, what we omit, and how we play the news. Television is even more manipulative. We can weave subtle messages into television broadcasts that the public supposes are nothing but entertainment."

Thad mumbled something that sounded like a question.

"I hope we will be able to feature, in prime time, the motion pictures I am making in my studios in Munich. Americans, I fear, see too many old war movies with Germans as the enemies . . . too many new thrillers with Germans again . . . how do you say it? . . . as the 'heavies.' Americans have become inclined to associate Germans with yesterday's Nazis and today's neo-Nazis. I would like Americans to see, through my pictures, the real Germany, the true Germany. I want them to see beautiful German girls and handsome German youths who are human, not monsters—just like young Americans—who do the same things and share the same dreams. I want to produce love stories, adventure stories . . . no political propaganda."

Thad nodded. But a glint in his eye seemed to question what he was hearing.

Hildebrandt detected the questioning look. "Ah!" he said. "I am not naive. Nor do I suppose you are. . . ."

"We do expect to make a profit," interrupted Thad, frowning.

"Yes. But that will not be inconsistent with our objectives. We can still use our facilities to help preserve and promote a society in which men like you and me can survive and prosper."

"I would like to know the names of your investors."

"Of course. When we have completed our work on the details of our arrangement and you have returned home and identified a good property for us, then we will raise the capital we need, and you will learn the name of each investor. I could give you names now, but"—he shrugged—"the list changes from week to week. You will know every name. We will probably have secret participants—but not secret from you."

Thad extended his hand, and Hildebrandt grasped it.

"I believe we have a deal, Herr Hildebrandt."

On Monday, June 3, 1985, Thad and Anne sat down at a long mahogany table in a conference room in the Wall Street offices of the Cooper Bank and began the two-hour process of affixing their signatures to a stack of documents—the legal paperwork that effected the corporate restructuring of Catlett Communications Enterprises, Inc.

At first, they were alone with their attorneys—Bayard Justin representing Anne and Melvin Bragg acting for Thad.

"My congratulations, Mel," said Rustin. "I didn't think they'd agree to the repurchase clause."

"Yes," agreed Thad. "I owe Mel that one. At first I was skeptical, but Mel convinced me that we shouldn't go through with the deal without it."

"Explain it to me again," said Anne.

Her father explained. "Mel pointed out that this is strictly a personal deal," he said. "Thad has placed his confidence essentially in one man: Wilhelm Hildebrandt. Yet none of us know much about the rest of the management of Verlagsgruppe Hildebrandt—let alone the investors who may be behind him. So the repurchase clause provides that in the event Hildebrandt dies or otherwise leaves the position of chief executive of VWH, then you and Thad have the right to repurchase your shares of CCE for the same price you are now selling them, plus ten percent per annum."

"Fat chance we could finance that," she said.

"Who knows, five years from now?" said Thad. "In five years, we could repurchase for one hundred fifty percent shares that could be worth five hundred percent."

"But as long as Wilhelm Hildebrandt continues as chief executive officer of VWH, his company will own the stock," said Bragg.

"All right," said Anne. "I'll sign this Pikes Peak of paper." She shrugged. "I guess I have the best kind of advice—my father and my husband. I have my reservations about this Kraut Hildebrandt, but if the two of you are satisfied, who am I to say no?"

"It's not without risk," her father said. "But what isn't that's worthwhile?"

"How many times have I heard that line?" she asked.

No one from Frankfurt came for the closing of the complex deal. It was handled by Hildebrandt's American lawyers who appeared with briefcases filled with signed documents and the authority to sign others. The banks were represented by their own officers and attorneys. The handshaking and pleasantries took as much time as the execution of the documents.

Verlagsgruppe Wilhelm Hildebrandt paid $52,000,000 for forty percent of the stock in Catlett Communications Enterprises, Inc. The two banks—Cooper Bank of New York and United Industrial Bank of Pittsburgh—were paid $41,000,000, retiring all the long-term debt of CCE. Of the $11,000,000 remaining, Thad and Anne set aside $8,000,000 to cover the capital-gains tax the transaction would incur. They paid legal fees and other fees and expenses of $580,000. Then they deposited half of what remained into a trust fund for their two sons.

"I feel poor," said Anne wryly, with a wan smile, as she contemplated the check representing the balance left from the sale of her CCE stock.

Her father laughed at her. "Unless those Germans are boobs, my dear, you own stock worth twenty-six million dollars. And you're just forty years old. I've practiced law all my life and am not worth a fifth of that. You married an entrepreneur, my child!"

Thad laughed. "I've been called worse."

After a celebratory luncheon at "21," Thad returned to the grimy environs of lower Eighth Avenue, where Catlett Communications Enterprises, Inc. had established its headquarters in an embattled fortress. Thad had rented the building cheap when he moved the company from Pittsburgh. Natalie Loff had sneered that anyone who established his corporate headquarters in such broken-down real estate must not have expected to succeed. Until she was too sick to work, though, she came to her spartan office every day.

Because she had a special instinct for it, Thad had put Natalie in charge of the *American Terrier*, his weekly supermarket tabloid, and she had made it the company's most profitable enterprise. They had been unable to purchase a supermarket weekly, so they started the *Terrier* from scratch. With a small budget, Natalie had turned the tabloid into a money machine within six months.

She had infused it with her own personality. In the office of her successor, its present editor, hung a framed copy of her first staff memo, dated March 20, 1975:

> *Every* weekly issue of this newspaper *will* contain a story on at least one of the following: Elvis Presley, Jacqueline Kennedy Onassis, Elizabeth Taylor, or Patricia Hearst. Each issue *will* contain at least one photograph of at least two of the above. Patricia Hearst should be shown preferably wearing handcuffs. Jacqueline Kennedy Onassis photos are to portray the subject in a positive and glamorous way.

Natalie's small group of writers—"hired from God knows where," Thad had commented—had produced a tabloid directed at what she cynically perceived as the typical woman supermarket shopper. Although other CCE tabloids regularly published pictures of pretty girls with breasts bare, the *Terrier* never did. Instead, it featured the celebrity photos Natalie had demanded and:

**HARLAN, TEXAS, WOMAN SEES, TALKS WITH
JFK!
SCIENTISTS CONFIRM SPACE VOYAGE**

* * *

**DOCS SHUN CANCER CURE!
TOO SIMPLE, TOO CHEAP, SAYS DISCOVERER**

* * *

**EAT, DRINK, BE MERRY
—AND LOSE *POUNDS!***

* * *

**WAX SAINT WEEPS REAL TEARS!
DOCTORS CANNOT EXPLAIN
YEARLY MIRACLE**

* * *

**WOMAN, DEAD THREE DAYS, SITS UP
IN CASKET!
SAW FACE OF GOD, SHE SAYS**

* * *

**MARTIN LUTHER KING NOT DEAD,
SAYS PSYCHIC!
LIVING, STUDYING IN INDIA,
IN FAMOUS SEER'S VISION**

One reason Thad had hurried back to the office after the signing was that his Los Angeles attorneys had scheduled a conference call for 3:00 P.M., New York time. Their purpose was to discuss a lawsuit filed in the California courts by a Mrs. Herbert George.

This woman had, for two years, written a column for the *American Terrier* under the name of Janine Brethed. She called herself "a psychic astrologer," and she had established her name by predicting in 1976 that Elvis Presley would die within two years. The *Terrier* had received more than a thousand letters accusing Thad Catlett and Janine Brethed of having contributed to his death. During the ten weeks after Presley died, circulation soared above one million.

As a psychic, Mrs. George had a feel for the outrageous. She predicted that Queen Elizabeth would abdicate after it was proved Princess Anne was her daughter, not by the Duke but by a stableboy. She predicted that Richard Nixon would again be elected President of the United States and that his Vice President would be Jacqueline Kennedy Onassis. She wrote of her conversations with John F. Kennedy, who she insisted was not dead but living on a planet in another solar system and studying psychic astrology in preparation for his triumphal return to earth.

One of Natalie's last decisions, before she went home to die, was to retire Mrs. George—one of the few events the seeress had not foreseen. She had raised her price for the column once too often; anyway, Natalie sensed that readers were becoming incredulous at the blatant sensationalism of her predictions. Janine Brethed was replaced by Violet Duclos, who was a composite of half a dozen staff writers. Even Thad occasionally amused himself by writing a few astrological predictions.

The indignant Mrs. George sued. Her complaints were as imaginative as her predictions. She had claimed that she had established for the *American Terrier* a reputation for scientific accuracy in psychic astrology, that her column was largely responsible for the success of the newspaper, that she had been preemptorily fired for revealing startling truths that the editors had tried to suppress, and that the newspaper was now damaging her reputation by publishing "fanciful and inaccurate predictions, not based on thorough pyschic research."

The Los Angeles telephone call was five minutes late. The assembled attorneys notified Thad that the lawsuit could be settled for fifty thousand dollars. He rejected the offer outright. It had been his policy from the days when he owned a single Pittsburgh newspaper to never settle a libel suit but to fight it down to the wire; and, though this was not a libel suit, he intended to apply the same tactics with the delirious Mrs. George. No, he would not authorize a settlement. Yes, the case could go to trial.

Thad had an appointment at 6:00 P.M., too, with Kenneth Asher. They met in a bar at the Harvard Club.

"The deed is done," said Thad. "Forty percent of the company is now Dutch." He raised his double Scotch and smiled nervously. "What did the man actually say?"

Asher sipped sparingly from a martini. "Well, as I told you, he didn't say anything much. To be altogether frank, Thad, the President isn't too pleased with me since I came to work for you."

Thad scowled. "To paraphrase my final editorial about him—piss on him."

Asher chuckled. "He's his own best friend."

"Did he know the name Hildebrandt?"

"Oh, definitely. *Freideutsche Zeitung* was one of the last European newspapers to—in his words—abandon him. For a long time, when the editorial hounds were baying in Europe, Hildebrandt editorialized that the President was probably a victim of professional Nixon-haters."

"No inside information? No insights?"

"No. I'd have given you a full report on anything like that before this morning."

"Oh, I didn't expect anything that would have discouraged me from signing the papers," said Thad. "I was just curious to know if he ever met Hildebrandt, if he had an impression."

"I couldn't draw him into a conversation about Hildebrandt. I couldn't tell him, of course, that CCE was entering into a partnership with VWH."

Thad nodded. He was satisfied that Kenneth Asher had not, indeed, had a productive conversation with his former boss. Asher was a changed man. Thad had known him during the Nixon years. He had been crisply competent, with a first-rate mind, but like so many who had worked in the Nixon White House, he had become arrogant. Like Haldeman and Ehrlichman, Asher seemed to have left his critical faculties elsewhere when he acquired an office in the West Wing and tended, in the way of young men, to out-Nixon Nixon.

Eight months in prison and disbarment—followed by a year's employment in a Cincinnati public-relations firm, a sop offered him for his loyalty—had restored his inner cynicism and afflicted him with outer humility—too much humility, Thad thought.

Asher was a sharp communications lawyer. He had come to the White House from the Federal Communications Commission, where he had served since his graduation from Harvard Law. Thad had hired him at first as a communications consultant. Asher helped to plan the venture into television, offering cogent political guidance and legal suggestions. Now he was a full-time executive of Catlett Communications, with the title "director, planning, television acquisitions." Thad had equipped Asher's office with a full library of communications law, so the erstwhile presidential counselor and jailbird was a lawyer again, in all but name.

"This is going to take some careful tightrope walking," Thad said. "We must complete our acquisitions without disclosing any more than absolutely necessary about the German connection. There are still people in this country who are fundamentally opposed to German influence in any aspect of American life. I need hardly tell you who they are."

"I understand," Asher nodded. He sipped again from his martini, savoring the Beefeater gin.

"I've accumulated a comprehensive file, Ken. I'll have it delivered to your office in the morning. It's confidential, of course. Keep it a couple of days. . . . Yes, and please keep it in a locked filing cabinet whenever you aren't actually using it. Also, I'd appreciate it if you don't take it home. It's the report of an investigation into any possible Nazi, neo-Nazi, or anti-Semitic connection that might taint Wilhelm Hildebrandt and his chief managers. This is extremely sensitive, you understand. Our German partners were hardly likely to volunteer any adverse information, so we had to run our own investigation. But it looks good. I don't think there's anything there."

"He was a naval officer."

"Yes, a submarine officer. But he was not a Nazi."

"You could hardly run a business of any size in Germany and not have ex-Nazis on your staff," Asher suggested.

"No doubt," said Thad. "I've had his senior staff investigated, the men of his generation. Nothing. As for his younger staff, they would have been children during the Hitler era."

"What about the secret investors?" asked Asher. "How are you going to investigate them?"

Thad shrugged. "Does General Motors know the personal histories of all its stockholders?"

Asher responded with a quizzical smile. "Okay. Are you having dinner here?"

Thad glanced toward the dining room and wrinkled his nose. "I think I'll stay in the apartment and put something from the freezer in the microwave. I can't face the long haul to Greenwich tonight."

At the apartment, Thad placed some telephone calls and read the contents of two fat files that had been handed to him at the office. He was stretched out on the couch, fitfully dozing, when Megan let herself in.

He did not rouse himself immediately. He knew her routine: She would make a beeline for the bathroom, clean off the last of her stage makeup, and then slip into the shower. Then she would head for the kitchen and put the Mexican TV dinners in the microwave. She was predictable. The routine lasted fifteen minutes, then she confronted him, wearing a blue T-shirt and white panties. He stirred drowsily, pulled himself up from the couch, and wandered into the kitchen to pour them drinks. She began ripping up a head of lettuce for a salad.

"It went okay tonight," she said. "Larimer showed up about half smashed, but that usually improves his performance."

"I've got something to show you," he said abruptly. He handed her a big manila envelope he had brought in from the living room. "That's the front page makeup for tomorrow's *Sentinel.*"

"My God!"

NUDE STATUE OF GLAMOROUS ACTRESS! MEGAN WILKINSON IN THE BUFF! EXCLUSIVE PHOTOS!

Under the headline, a photograph of a four-foot high bronze sculpture dominated the front page. It was a voluptuous image of Megan, sculpted by Emily Baynes Justin, Anne's mother.

"I suppose you know that sculpture stands in the lobby of the Oilmen's Club in Houston," he said. "The club paid my mother-in-law thirty thousand dollars for it. I hired a man in Houston to photograph it for me."

The statue showed her as lithe, heavy-breasted, and gloriously joyful in her nakedness. But without the caption and story, few people would have recognized it as Megan.

"Shouldn't you have asked me first?"

"A surprise," he said.

"Arny will like it, I suppose," she said uncertainly. Arny was her agent. "Any publicity is good publicity, he says."

"I'm running the pictures of the sculpture in the other papers, except the *Register-Herald.*"

71

"In the *Terrier?*"

"Sure, in the *Terrier*. Together with an 'exclusive interview' in which you tell what an agony it was to pose nude and how you wouldn't have done it if the sculptor hadn't been a woman. At every checkout station in every supermarket in the country."

"But, Thad . . . I haven't been interviewed."

"Don't be naive."

The indignation slowly faded from her face. "Arny is getting some nibbles," she said quietly. "I might even get a movie deal . . . when the play closes, that is."

"We've got to keep the play running," said Thad. "You need that credit; a long-running Broadway play that paid off its backers."

"I don't know how long it would run without what you're doing," she said. "Everybody's so grateful to you. Especially me. I'm really very grateful, Thad."

"Mayo Gwanchi," said Thad with a shrug. "That's Chinese for 'Never mind.'"

"All the publicity that's done me so much good has done you a lot of harm, I'm afraid."

"I can handle it."

"Oh, I know you can. It's just that I— Well, I guess I'd better change the subject. I've got to be out of here in the morning . . . early. I mean, like before breakfast. Arny has arranged for me to meet with a television guy in the morning, and he wants me to get dressed and made up at his office, by two fellows who'll come in to do it. You know?"

"Sure. You hurry out and keep that appointment. It could be important to you."

"I'm sorry. I always make breakfast. Coffee at least. But, you know, it's—"

"Yes, it is," he said, patting her reassuringly on her white panties. "It's important."

FOUR

Wilhelm Hildebrandt named two American lawyers to the board of directors of Catlett Communications Enterprises. For the third seat, he appointed Friederich Papen, a vice president of Verlagsgruppe Wilhelm Hildebrandt. None of these directors ever appeared in CCE's offices except for board meetings. Friederich Papen, however, demanded detailed reports, to be mailed to him in Frankfurt. He seemed to regard CCE as another subsidiary of VWH.

A corporate bureaucrat, Papen pressed Thad for what he called the CCE business plan for 1987. At the end of one particularly demanding transatlantic call, Thad snapped—"How the hell should I know what we'll be doing in 1987? I'm still trying to figure out what's going to happen in the fourth quarter of 1985."

On Wednesday, August 7, Thad flew to Frankfurt, accompanied by Charles Lodge Johnson and Kenneth Asher. By now, Asher had identified a broadcasting company that might be ripe for takeover, and they intended to make a presentation to the Germans.

They reviewed the file during the first hour of the flight then, lulled by the drone of the engines, they lapsed into the transatlantic routine of eat, drink, and doze. Charles had brought along a book to read—*Beautiful Swimmers* by William Warner. After dinner, Thad leaned back and chatted with Asher.

In his personal appearance, Kenneth Asher was what industry headhunters called an IBM type—always dressed in dark suits, white shirts and striped ties of conservative cut and color, hair always neatly trimmed, sideburns always at mid-ear—a model of the bright, sincere young man. A platoon of them, all look-alikes, had trooped to Capitol Hill to testify before the Senate committee, and some had gone to jail.

Having downed two martinis before dinner, which was washed down with wine and brandy after, Asher was more forthcoming than was his nature. The conversation turned to Watergate and what it had cost him. . . .

"We're not divorced, but Cynthia . . ." He shook his head. "I don't think we'll ever live together again. She stuck with me all the way, until . . . First there'd been the glamour, then the long struggle, with her cast as the loyal, supportive wife, and then it was all over." He shook his head again. "She saw me in handcuffs, Thad. She watched me led out of the city jail and thrust in the back of a van to be hauled to a prison. It may not have been the end of the world, but it was the end of the marriage."

"I'm the last guy in the world to offer marital advice," said Thad. "But if I were you, she'd either live with me or we'd have the divorce. You're back on the upgoing escalator. I'm already paying you more than Nixon did. You have a future again."

Asher nodded gravely. "I guess my years of being vulnerable have got to come to an end sometime."

They slept uneasily the rest of the trip and at eight in the morning arrived at the airport in Frankfurt.

As customary, the CCE group was driven to the VWH park and assigned comfortable rooms in the VWH gasthaus. Hoffman suggested that Herr Papen would like to join Thad for lunch, alone if possible. Thad had anticipated a confrontation with the demanding Friederich Papen; the earlier it was over, the better. He shrugged his agreement and said he would need to be awakened; he was going to take a nap until noon.

Over a light lunch in a sunny private dining room overlooking the lake, Papen interrogated him, asking prepared questions and scribbling the answers on the sheets where the questions were typed. Papen was a tall man, spare and solemn, with a glowing ruddy complexion; his hair and eyebrows were snow-white. His carriage, manner, and tone of voice reminded Thad of an English butler in a 1930's movie.

"I am most curious about what you call the neighborhoods," Papen said. "I believe you say the company publishes sixty-eight of them."

"Sixty-eight, that's right," Thad said as he lighted a cigarette. "Suburban newspapers. Nothing much in them—just publicity for the local businesses, sports scores from the local high schools, social notes from the neighborhood, obituaries—no hard news, everything positive. They're distributed free. All the revenue comes from advertising. Every one of them makes a nice little profit; cumulatively, they're one of our better money-makers."

"It has been written of you that you were shrewd to see the profit potential in these little newspapers."

"We print the regional editions of the *American Terrier* on their presses, too," said Thad.

"What is this name, *Terrier*, Mr. Catlett?" asked Papen. "A breed of dog, yes. But why call a newspaper this?"

Thad smiled. "It's image," he said. "A terrier grabs its prey and hangs on, chewing and shaking. The implications—"

"I see." Papen frowned over his notes, then returned to a subject Thad had anticipated. "It is odd, Mr. Catlett, that your company does not have projections, even for next year."

"I am aware, Herr Papen," Thad said firmly, "that many American corporations spend a great deal of time and money preparing business plans—which are, for the most part, just exercises in conjecture. One of the reasons my businesses are profitable is that I do not overstaff. My executives are kept busy publishing newspapers—and sometimes acquiring new ones. I will not allow them to spend two months out of every year in fruitless cerebration."

Papen smiled thinly. "You are also called by an interesting American word—a maverick. Do you plead guilty to that, Mr. Catlett? Are you a maverick?"

Thad crushed his cigarette and picked up his Scotch. "The word doesn't offend me," he said.

In the afternoon, he met in the conference room with half a dozen VWH executives—most of them wearing translation headphones— and answered their questions about the likely outcome of the 1986 congressional elections, then about the 1988 presidential election. They asked questions about the American economy; they were especially concerned about inflation. They wanted to know how the United States would react to another Arab oil embargo. Was it possible the United States would invade Saudi Arabia and seize the oil fields? Toward the end of the meeting, the questions turned frivolous. Did he know Fawn Hall?

Hoffman arrived to announce that Herr Catlett would want to rest before his five o'clock meeting with Herr Hildebrandt.

Thad had anticipated another cocktail hour, but Hoffman said Hildebrandt would like to meet at the pool and sauna. Was that acceptable? It was, of course, acceptable. At five, Hoffman came again to escort Thad to a gymnasium on the top floor and roof of the main office building. The gymnasium was abundantly equipped, and outside, on the roof, was a running track and a swimming pool under a glass dome.

Hoffman led the way to a locker room, where he supplied Thad with German-style swimming briefs—a red pouch in front connected by straps to a little triangle of red cloth that covered his anus but certainly not his nates. Thad walked out on the roof a little hesitantly to find that Wilhelm Hildebrandt was already in the pool studiously swimming laps, wearing exactly the same costume except in dark blue. Other executives jogged around the track, puffing and sweating. Thad entered the pool gingerly—he found the water chilling—and swam back and forth a few times. He lifted himself to the side, wheezing, and sat waiting for Hildebrandt to join him.

He did not count Hildebrandt's laps, but the German tycoon must have completed a dozen after Thad arrived, stroking easily, without the customary Hildebrandt smile. His body was lean, his arms and legs muscular.

"Ach!" Hildebrandt grunted as he climbed out of the pool. "To qualify for the *unterzeeboot dienst*, I was required to swim a kilometer. I don't zink I could do it any more."

Thad was surprised at the brief lapse into German and accented English.

Hildebrandt ran his hands over his sleek, thin hair, pushing the water back. "So," he said. "Will you swim some more? Or shall we go to the sauna?"

"I'm out of condition, I'm afraid," Thad said, indicating he would be pleased to escape the pool.

At the door to the sauna, Hildebrandt tossed his swim briefs on a table and grabbed a towel. Thad followed his example, and they entered the hot room and mounted one of the cedar shelves. Two men, sensing that the chief executive wanted private conversation, got up and left. The suffocating heat pressed in on Thad, who began to sweat. Hildebrandt wrapped his towel around his head to keep the salty sweat from dripping into his eyes. Thad laid his towel across his lap.

"My friend," grunted Hildebrandt, "I am going to ask you to do me several favors."

Thad dabbed at his face with his towel.

"We have, I think, the beginning of a productive partnership. I have fifty-two million dollars invested in it already, and I expect that I, together with the men you will meet tonight, will invest many times that amount eventually. You have suddenly become very valuable to us. Of course, we can protect our investment by insuring your life for many millions, but you are too valuable to cover with an

77

insurance policy. I am going to ask you, first, to do what you see me doing—take at least half an hour every day to run or swim or whatever amuses you; anything for exercise. I am sixty-six years old and have not had a heart attack. You are forty-eight and will have one within five years—almost certainly—if you don't modify your life-style. I am surprised that I must say this to you. We have a lot in common, you and I, in the way we drive ourselves; but the time you take for this purpose is time you could not spend better. Please Thad. Do me this favor."

Thad grimaced. "Others have told me the same."

"So? . . ."

"You're a persuasive man. Agreed."

"I have more to ask. I want the corporation to purchase for you a car with some armor, at least the minimal amount; and I want you to hire a driver who can be licensed to carry firearms. My reasons are obvious."

"Isn't that a bit dramatic?"

"It is not," said Hildebrandt. "We cannot escape the spotlight we shine on others. The spotlight attracts fanatics. We arouse their emotions. We could easily become the targets of these faceless fanatics. You have, I think you said, a bodyguard."

"Not exactly," said Thad. "Farrigan is a gofer, an errand boy, a handyman . . . a friend."

"Then replace him. Or train him. Have him licensed to carry a weapon. A few minor precautions, my friend."

"All right."

"These are legitimate business expenses. A security system for your home, too."

"Okay."

Hildebrandt flexed his shoulders. His body streamed redolent sweat. "Ahh . . ." he murmured.

Thad was now choking from the heat.

"The gentlemen you are going to meet tonight . . . Their identities are to be kept strictly secret. They are all honorable, respectable businessmen. But for various reasons—theirs and mine—I have promised them confidentiality. If you have any question about any of them, address it to me later."

They met for drinks in the same room where Thad's group had assembled seven months earlier. Hildebrandt introduced:

Hans Dietrich, chief executive officer of Nördlisch Industriengesellschaft (NIG), an industrial group specializing in light industry, a manufacturer of household appliances, motorcycles, and office machines. Dietrich was Hildebrandt's age, a rotund, ruddy man, the very caricature of an English country squire. He had served as a captain in a panzer battalion in France in 1944 and was wounded in the fighting around Caen.

Ernst Dietrich, Hans's son, a vice president of NIG. Ernst was known in Germany as a race-car driver. He drove Porsches on the grand prix circuit. He was a Teutonic specimen who would have appealed to the race purists of the Nazi era—tall and light complexioned, with pale blue eyes, chiseled features, and short-cropped hair, almost white.

Josef von Klauberg, heir to the Klauberg fortune earned by his grandfather and great-grandfather in shipbuilding. There had been no Klaubergwerke in Kiel since 1945, but the family had managed to salvage their fortune out of the German collapse. After the war, Josef's late father and now Josef himself had managed their capital so well that it was four times what it had been in 1939. Josef von Klauberg was a member of the board of directors of VWH, of NIG, and of several banks. He was a member of the Bundestag. His hair was white but his face was youthful. He was a man of medium height and build, well manicured, fashionably attired, shod in Gucci loafers. His wife was crippled—a stroke victim—and he kept a young woman in a flat in Bonn. He was articulate and affable, a politician with an easy, engaging manner.

Klaus Schulenberg was introduced by name, with no mention of his background. He was a bullnecked, black-jowled man, in his early forties, with great dark eyebrows and a gloomy presence. He spoke

79

little, perhaps because his English was limited, perhaps because he didn't like to reveal himself to strangers. He was an enigma.

Most of these men, Thad learned over dinner, had thoroughly studied the documents that had been supplied in advance for them to read. Their questions were incisive.

"This Duncan Broadcasting Company," said Hans Dietrich. "Is it not an odd choice, Mr. Catlett?"

"I'm going to let Ken Asher address your questions about Duncan," said Thad. "He identified it as a possible target for acquisition."

"Mr. Asher, then," said Dietrich. "Why Duncan—or DunCast, as I understand it is called? It does not seem to be very profitable."

Asher spoke in the flat, humorless manner that had marked his testimony before Senator Sam Erwin's Watergate committee. Glancing down occasionally at handwritten notes, he spoke directly at Dietrich, who had asked the question, in a monotone and without a flicker of expression.

"The most appealing attribute of DunCast, Herr Dietrich," he said, "is the simple fact that it may be the only broadcasting company within our range that is also within our grasp. In looking at possible targets for acquisition, I omitted companies that operate just one television station—except two that operate major metropolitan outlets. On the other end of the scale, I assumed we do not consider it within our economic range to make a takeover bid for one of the major networks. It should be possible to acquire a controlling interest in DunCast, if it can be acquired at all, for less than fifty million dollars."

"Although we have the documents before us," said Hildebrandt, "I think we would appreciate it, Mr. Asher, if you would summarize the facts about DunCast."

Asher turned toward Hildebrandt. "Duncan Broadcasting Company owns two independent television stations, WMOA in Miami and WPAR in Tampa-St. Petersburg. WMOA is a VHF station. WPAR is UHF. They broadcast a lot of reruns and old movies, some game shows, and some local news. WMOA broadcasts two

Spanish newscasts a day, one at noon and one at seven, and runs a Spanish movie after midnight. They compete with network stations and public stations. Their ratings are distinctly lower than any of the network stations in their areas but above the public stations. Both stations are profit-makers. The figures are before you."

"Earnings seem to fall year by year," said Papen. "What's the problem?"

"The problem is that Gibson Duncan, who founded the company and started the stations, has become senile and had to retire. Under the new management, DunCast has experienced a steady decline in earnings, beginning in 1981."

"Why?" asked Papen.

"I think we should call it response to the community," said Asher. "They sell almost no advertising with the Spanish-language movies. The Hispanic community in Miami demands Spanish-language broadcasting but doesn't watch it. Both stations carry a heavy dose of evangelism—meaning subliterate, lunatic-fringe Protestant preaching—on which they make very little money. What's more, WPAR allowed itself to be pressured into dropping reruns of *Lieutenant Lynda*—some church people objected to what they called 'lewd costuming' and 'suggestive dialogue.' The show was pulling higher ratings than anything else they broadcast."

"What is this *Lieutenant Lynda*?" asked the younger Dietrich.

Thad answered. "It's a crime show featuring a policewoman, Lieutenant Lynda Drake. It was a network show for three or four seasons, then went into syndication. The policewoman is what American television critics used to call a 'jiggly girl'—meaning that she wears no brassiere and does a lot of running and jumping. Also, they manage to show her in a bikini every show, sometimes in shorts and a halter. It is implied, but never shown, that she sleeps with one of her fellow detectives, a Lieutenant Dugan. Not exactly an intellectual show, but entertaining. If we acquire the two stations, we are going to broadcast reruns of *Lieutenant Lynda*, I can tell you that."

Ernest Dietrich frowned over the report, which had been

translated into German before it was sent to Frankfurt. He had not read it and was scanning it now. "The present management of Duncan Broadcasting Company will resist any attempt to wrest control from their hands?" he asked.

"Yes, they definitely will," said Asher. "We'll have to make a takeover bid, a hostile bid. But there are enough unhappy stockholders that—"

"How do you arrive at the cost figure you mentioned?"

"To take over, you need to own half a million shares," said Asher. "That is, if you want absolute control . . . if you want to own a majority of the shares. The last bid was $85 a share. The last sale was $87.50. If you bid $90—"

"You don't need a majority," Papen interrupted.

"We're talking about a small company, closely held," said Thad. "I'd like absolute control. So, we're talking about $45,000,000."

"You might have to offer $95 a share to get it," said Asher.

"Yes," agreed Thad. "And there will be expenses. Still, I think Ken is correct when he says we can acquire DunCast for under $50,000,000."

"A comment," said Charles. "You gentlemen understand that the two television stations in question are located in Florida. They are *regional* stations. Their broadcast signal does not reach Atlanta, much less Washington, New York, or Boston."

"My associate Mr. Johnson," said Thad with a smile, "doubts the value of anything that doesn't reach New York or Boston. There are people living in Miami, too, Charles. And they watch television and buy products they see advertised. The Tampa-St. Petersburg market, for that matter, is nothing to dismiss. Anyway, Florida is a good place to learn the business."

Wilhelm Hildebrandt flipped over the pages of the report. "I am interested in your proposal for financing the acquisition," he said.

Thad glanced around the table. Ernst Dietrich was hastily scanning again. So, too, was von Klauberg. "That was worked out by several people. Once again, I will let Mr. Asher summarize."

Asher began again. Thad liked the way he responded—precise, factual, straight out of a computer mind.

"Our proposal," recited Asher, scarcely glancing at his notes, "is that the board of directors of Catlett Communications, Incorporated authorize the issuance of fifty million dollars worth of corporate debentures. We would like the investors represented here to purchase those debentures. The corporation will use the money to acquire a controlling interest in DunCast. Once the takeover is complete, the investors will exchange their debentures for preferred stock in Duncan Broadcasting Company. The preferred stock will be entitled to a priority on dividends. That is to say, DunCast will pay no dividends to the holders of its common shares until dividends have been paid to the holders of preferred shares. Should DunCast fail to pay dividends at all for three consecutive years, CCE will be obliged to repurchase the preferred stock at the original purchase price."

"So," said Thad. "This gives CCE three years to make DunCast profitable. I might add, it also imposes severe pressure to make it profitable."

"We have considered the various elements of your proposal very carefully," replied Hildebrandt. Then he proceeded with his analysis. In the first place, he said, it did not fix the amount of dividends that must be paid on the preferred stock. This must be a guaranteed five percent, he said. "If DunCast proves wholly unprofitable for a year or two, the cost of these dividends to CCE would amount only to twenty percent of your after-tax profits for last year. After all, our investors cannot assume *all* the risk of this acquisition."

"All this is negotiable," Thad said blandly. He had expected the demand.

"Another matter must be discussed, and it must be clearly understood," Hildebrandt continued. "Each of the investors here tonight would be embarrassed, for their own reasons, if it were to become public knowledge that he owns an interest in an American television broadcasting company. Herr von Klauberg is a member of the Bundestag, for example. Herr Dietrich the younger is considering becoming a candidate for a seat. Their investment in American television stations could become a political issue. Also, there may be other investors—I mean, other than the gentlemen represented here tonight. I must ask of each gentleman here tonight"—his eyes settled on Charles Lodge Johnson for a moment, then on Kenneth Asher—"an absolute pledge of confidentiality. All of us are interested in the success of the enterprise we are undertaking, and all of us hope it will be the first of many; but its very existence could do some of us lasting damage. Is this understood?"

Thad had suspected that Hildebrandt put on his puckish little smile every morning, like a shirt, and wore it all day. The man was shrewd, cynical, aggressive, probably ruthless. Even his thoughtfulness was probably a tactic. He had not made himself a multimillionaire and the head of a multi-billion-dollar conglomerate by being soft-spoken, courtly, and accommodating. He was suddenly adamantine, and likely this was the real Wilhelm Hildebrandt.

Charles Lodge Johnson had never allowed himself to be intimidated, not by anyone, and if that was what Hildebrandt had intended by staring at him, he had only succeeded in stimulating Charles's curiosity. "Just how, Herr Hildebrandt, will the debentures and preferred shares stand on the books of the corporation?" he asked.

Hildebrandt nodded curtly at Charles. "The debentures will be purchased partly by Verlagsgruppe Wilhelm Hildebrandt," he said. "From what accounts we take the funds"—he shrugged—"we are not required to say. There are certain trusts, furthermore, in the Frankenthaler Handelsbank. The bank will purchase debentures as investments for those trusts."

"I see," said Charles. "And when CCE is required to file reports as to the sources of the funds, those reports will say they come from VWH and the Frankenthaler Handelsbank."

"That will satisfy American law," said Asher dryly.

"Yes . . . but not American curiosity."

Thad, Charles, and Asher arrived at Kennedy International late on Friday afternoon. Anne was in Pittsburgh. Thaddy and Richard were staying with friends in Greenwich. Megan was still playing in *Night Trails*. Thad was hungry, craved more than would come from the freezer and microwave in his apartment, and did not want to dine alone. He telephoned his father-in-law, Bayard Justin, to report what the Germans had agreed to; the call did not generate an invitation to dinner. So Thad settled for an offer from Charles to join him for dinner at the Gaslight Club.

Charles led the way to the dining room, where they ordered steaks and wine. The cuisine was not distinguished, but the steaks were satisfying, the wine palatable, and the waitresses provocative in their corselets.

"God . . ." breathed Thad after their wine was served. "I'm tired. I feel like there's no end to my commitments. I ought to be out in Connecticut tonight, spending the evening with my sons."

Charles turned his head as a voluptuous waitress walked by on her way to another table. Her corselet lifted her breasts, displaying a contrived cleavage. She wore net stockings attached to the bottom of the corselet with garter straps—with ten or twelve inches of bare leg exposed.

"Thaddy? . . ." Charles asked.

Thad shrugged. "Nothing has changed. My nineteen-year-old son is a homosexual."

"Anne says he shows a real talent for photography."

Thad sighed. "He's shown no talent for anything else."

"But you've had no more problems?"

Thad's chin jerked up. "The one we had was bad enough, wouldn't you say. His tennis instructor . . ."

"Psychiatry—"

"Jiggery-pokery," Thad interrupted. "I'd as soon rely on the judgment of a psychic astrologer. Anyway, Thaddy has settled down." He shook his head. "Christ, Charles . . . I'd give up a whole lot and stay at home and play father if I thought it would help. He doesn't respond to me."

"And Richard?"

Thad pulled a cigarette from his pack. "Richard will probably graduate valedictorian of his high school class. He does everything right. We have to wonder where the flaw is. He has to have one, doesn't he?"

"If you look hard enough. . . ." said Charles. "That's you, Thad. You look hard."

Thad shrugged.

"You remind me of a bit of doggerel verse," said Charles. "Written by W.S. Gilbert. Remember:

> 'Oh, I am a cook and a captain bold
> And the mate of the Nancy brig
> And a bo'sun tight, and a midshipmite
> And the crew of the captain's gig!'"

Thad chuckled. "I remember. He was all those, because he had eaten them all."

"Any resemblance to persons, living or dead, is coincidental," said Charles, saluting Thad with a glass of red Bordeaux.

Charles's sharp, glittering eyes roamed and stopped on the long legs and bulging backside of one of the corselet-clad waitresses who was bent over a table, explaining a check to a customer. Thad's eyes followed.

Charles was the first to speak. "I understand that your friend Megan has signed a contract to make a picture in Hollywood."

Thad reached for his Scotch—this one a double on the rocks. "Yes. She's all a-bubble. As soon as the play closes—which it will do in six weeks or so—she's off to Lotus Land."

"My congratulations—Pygmalion," said Charles with a faint, suggestive smile.

Thad sipped from his Scotch, then held the glass before his face, as if to cover his smile. "You give me too much credit, Charles. She's a brave little actress."

"Hmm . . . You'll be damned well rid of her when she goes to California," he volunteered.

"That's just a bit too personal, Charles."

Charles ignored the comment. "She told a friend of mine that she is in love with you, that you are in love with her, that sooner or later you will divorce Anne and marry her."

"Who in the world told you that?"

"The man who loves her and would *like* to marry her—Bert Stouffer. He's a journalist, a Pulitzer winner, a friend of mine."

Thad frowned and bit a corner of his lower lip. "She has mentioned him. I've met him, haven't I? Yes. Ruggedly handsome fellow. *He's* in love with Megan?"

Charles nodded. "Before you entered her life."

"Apparently he didn't mean much to her."

"Apparently."

There was a long, awkward silence.

"Will he follow her to California?" Thad asked.

"I don't know," said Charles. "He might."

There was another long silence. This time Charles broke it. "God knows who else she may have said it to—I mean, that you would divorce Anne and marry her. That's why I congratulated you when I learned she's leaving for California. A circumstantial case can be made that you have done something very cynical."

Thad drew a breath, rubbed his cheek, then spoke slowly, evenly. "Charles . . . when you raise children, you learn some elementary techniques that can be transferred into adult situations. The child, let us say, becomes fascinated with an expensive camera, which it wants for a toy. Instead of snatching the camera away and placing it out of the child's reach, you hand the child a gaudy red rubber ball.

87

The child takes up the ball and forgets the camera. You're happy. The child is happy. You—"

"That is precisely how I analyzed your campaign to make a star of Megan Wilkinson," said Charles. "Quite cynical. You are happy. The child is happy.. But I wonder if the two other interested parties will be happy. I mean Anne and Bert. I—"

"The conversation," said Thad emphatically, "has gone far enough."

On Tuesday, September 17, Catlett Communications Enterprises offered $92.50 a share for the common stock of Duncan Broadcasting Corporation, the offer contingent on its success in purchasing 500,000 shares by November 1, 1985.

The officers of DunCast distributed a letter to their stockholders, urging them not to accept the CCE offer. It was a strident letter, charging that the offer was less than the stock's true value and that CCE was an unconscionable corporate raider bent on turning WMOA and WPAR into the broadcast equivalents of tabloid newspapers.

DunCast, meanwhile, cast about for a white knight. By October, it seemed to have found one and advised its stockholders that Piedmont Broadcasting would shortly offer $93.50 a share for their stock. The Piedmont proposition turned out to be an offer to exchange one share of DunCast for two shares of Piedmont, which was then selling at $32.50, plus a Piedmont warrant for $28.50.

Telegrams from Frankfurt urged Thad to raise the CCE offer to $95.00. Thad held firm. By October 29, he was able to announce that stockholders holding 501,345 shares had accepted the CCE offer. CCE bought controlling interest in DunCast for $46,374,412.

Thad and his officers moved quickly and efficiently to assume control of DunCast. Their German partners remained completely invisible.

Thad discovered that the officers of DunCast had provided

themselves with golden parachutes. In case of dismissal, DunCast's president and three vice presidents had granted themselves contracts guaranteeing annual payments equal to one hundred fifty percent of their annual salary for five years. This news brought swift action; Thad fired all four of them and notified them that he would not honor their contracts.

They sued.

In its new capacity as a CCE subsidiary, DunCast filed counter charges that the golden-parachute contracts constituted an unethical raid on the company's treasury by men who had held a fiduciary relationship to the company.

"Why bother?" Asher asked Thad when the subject came up. "What will it cost? Three million? What will it cost to defend the suit?"

"Some people get my back up," said Thad crossly. "First they made stupid mistakes that depleted the company's profits. They slashed the stockholders' dividends in half, then to a quarter. They knew the company was ripe for takeover, so they used their position as officers and directors to stick the company with unconscionable contracts. They arrange to leave the company with an exorbitant severance bonus after screwing everyone else. I won't let them get away with it! I don't care how much it costs!"

"A lot of companies provide golden parachutes." Asher shrugged.

"Well, these characters will have to fight every step of the way to rip another nickel out of DunCast. They may get it. They may win. But they'll know they've been in a fight for it. At least this will be a signal to anybody else who may try to protect its incompetent officers against a takeover by CCE. They'll understand CCE fights back. So don't talk to me about compromise. I won't settle. I will *not* settle."

In Miami, WMOA dropped its Spanish-language late movie and its noontime Spanish-language newscast. It continued to broadcast thirty minutes of news in Spanish, with the focus on happenings in the Hispanic community, from six o'clock to six-thirty and again from eleven-thirty to midnight. The Hispanic community protested.

Jesus Rodriguez, an attorney retained by the protesters, confronted Thad in a Miami Beach hotel suite. "You have an obligation to serve the community," he said. "This is required by the Federal Communications Commission."

"I am broadcasting sixty minutes of Spanish-language news a day," said Thad. "This is exactly what you got before I took over— except I'm giving it to you at better hours. Nobody was watching the noon news in Spanish. I can show you the ratings. As for the movie, that's not public service. That's strictly entertainment. You get me sponsors, and I will run your movies. I will not run them at a loss. Let's put the matter another way. If your community watches Spanish-language shows, sponsors will buy advertising on Spanish-language shows. Then I'll broadcast Spanish-language shows. I'll make a profit. You'll have your shows. Everybody will be happy. No?"

"No," said Rodriguez. "You are obligated to serve the interests of a minority community."

"Not by broadcasting movies that nobody watches," said Thad.

"The FCC requires—"

"Fine. Take your complaint to the FCC. In the meantime, if you can help us find Spanish-language shows that people will watch, that sponsors will pay for, let me know. But don't ask me to broadcast junk as a civic duty."

Two weeks later WMOA introduced a mid-evening show called *Bikini Naderia.* It was a game show, taped usually at a beach, sometimes at a swimming pool. Shapely girls and muscular boys, suitably bronzed, won prizes by answering questions drawn from a revolving wheel. All the girls wore bikinis, and the word spread that the briefer a girl's bikini, the more likely she was to appear on camera.

For the sake of the Hispanic activists, the FCC, and any other champions of minority rights, the show was conducted in Spanish.

But the ratings indicated that the viewing audience wasn't confined to Spanish-speaking neighborhoods.

The *Miami Herald* reviewer wrote:

> Some people thought it would be impossible for F. Thad Catlett to turn a television station into a tabloid, cast in the image of his newspapers. They guessed wrong. He is off and running. Soon, it appears, we are to have a tabloid television station in our city. Are we going to like that? I can't promise that we won't. It would be foolish to deny that his bikini show is fresh and fun and attractive to a lot of people. What next, Mr. Catlett?

Bert Stouffer shook his head when Jesus Rodriguez offered him a cigar. The gray-haired but sharp-eyed Cuban-emigré lawyer sat behind his desk, framed in a large window overlooking Biscayne Bay. But his attention was focused for the moment on the cigar he had lifted from the box, drawing into its broad tip the flame from a butane lighter.

Then he looked up and spoke. "The distressing thing, Mr. Stouffer, is that the community no longer has the slightest influence over the operation of this local television station."

Bert was not sure whether Rodriguez meant the narrow Hispanic community or the wider Miami community. Probably the Hispanic community, Bert thought.

Rodriguez continued. "We could wish we had a better case. The station under its former owners, I would have to admit, was badly managed. Still, one had a sense that one could go to the management of Duncan Broadcasting and—" He shrugged. "The station is managed from New York now. We have no impact."

"Has there been a change in editorial policy?" Bert asked.

Rodriguez smiled. "Oh, yes. Under the old management, WMOA hardly had an editorial policy that you could detect. The news might be slanted in one direction one day, another the next. The probable

91

truth, Mr. Stouffer, is that they were too inept to be consistent. Now . . . well, the editorial policy at least is consistent."

"Conservative," Bert said, as if he knew the answer.

"The station now supports President Reagan. It supports causes like American intervention in Nicaragua. This does not displease the Cuban community, I must admit. No, it is not the Cuban community that is unhappy with the new editorial policies of WMOA. There have been more complaints from the black community. One of its leaders has objected to the 'happy news' approach the station now takes to local news—I mean, stories about cheerleading contests, eighty-year-old ladies who jog a mile every morning, the biggest fish caught in surrounding rivers and bays, and, of course and above all, the latest styles in skimpy swim and sportswear. The Christian community is unhappy because WMOA charges television preachers the same price that every other sponsor pays. When the Reverend Jimmy-John wants air time, he has to pay the same scale as the sponsors of *Lieutenant Lynda*."

Bert gazed reflectively upon the blue waters of the bay. "Had you ever heard my name before today, Mr. Rodriguez?"

Rodriguez pursed his lips around his cigar. "I cannot say your name is a household word in Miami," he said as he pulled out the cigar and savored the smoke. "But I read the *Wall Street Journal*, and when you told me your name, it was familiar to me."

"I write about the world of business," said Bert. "Ten months ago we understood Catlett was overextended. Now he has come up with fifty million dollars—enough money to buy controlling interest in Duncan Broadcasting out from under its management. It was a typical Catlett operation. Bang! He takes over! Bang! He sweeps everybody out! He turns the company upside down, all the while protesting modestly that all he's doing is learning the business. Fifty million dollars. Have you any idea where Catlett laid his hands on fifty million dollars?"

"I would be one of the last persons Mr. Catlett would take into his confidence."

"I know, I know, but . . . Tell me, have you ever heard of the Frankenthaler Handelsbank?"

Rodriguez shook his head, puzzled.

"Do you follow my thought at all?"

"I'm afraid I do not, Mr. Stouffer."

"A part of the money Catlett used to buy the DunCast stock came from the Frankenthaler Handelsbank, which bought CCE debentures with trust funds. A part of it came from a Frankfurt bank. Part came from Verlagsgruppe Wilhelm Hildebrandt, the German publishers. And they used the money to buy two Florida television stations. Doesn't that seem odd to you?"

"I am trying to follow your line of thought," said Rodriguez.

"Is it possible," Bert asked, "that the funds came from Latin America? Is it possible they were passed through German banks and a German corporation to conceal their true source?"

Rodriguez shrugged helplessly. "I have no way to know."

"Hmmm . . . But is it possible that someone from Latin America has a fifty-million-dollar interest in a television voice in south Florida?"

"You are speculating, are you not, Mr. Stouffer? Do you have any information that suggests someone in . . . where? Nicaragua? Argentina? Chile? . . . expects to use these stations as a voice? Isn't this what you call a shot in the dark?"

Bert smiled ruefully. "I have to admit that. But the fifty million dollars came from *somewhere*, from *someone*. I intend to find out who."

FIVE

The *New York Post*, page six, January 9, 1986:

At "21," tête-à-tête for lunch—Hollywood body Mcgan Wilkinson and newspaper-TV mogul F. Thad Catlett. Joined shortly by Charles Lodge Johnson, Pulitzer-laureate VP to Catlett. Is CCE about to produce movies, too?

No. Apparently it was a parting of the ways for Megan and Thad—fond, fond friends. Megan's movie commitments, it seems, have priority over her romantic commitments.

She was staying at the Carlyle Hotel. Bert Stouffer telephoned her after reading the item in the *Post*. "Come on over," she said. He arrived at six. She met him in the lobby and they drifted toward the bar.

Megan got right to the point. "You have every right to hate me."

"No," said Bert. "I could never hate you. It turned out as I expected. I thought it would end this way. But, Megan, I don't blame you."

She touched her eye with a fingertip, flicking away a tear. "You are a good man."

"You are a beautiful woman . . . and a talented actress."

She glanced around, meeting the glances, quickly averted, of people at the bar. In her tight skirt and sable jacket, she was dressed to attract the attention she seemed to resent. "Jesus . . ." she breathed. The tender moment evaporated.

"I am told," said Bert, "your performance in *Night Trails* was superb. They say the play would have closed in two weeks except for you."

"You never saw it?"

Bert shook his head. "Sorry. I . . . well, I couldn't . . ."

The tender moment returned, gossamerlike. "Yes," Megan said simply, softly. Then she spoke in her normal voice. "I'm sorry, too. I would have liked to have your judgment. I always valued it, you know."

"What's the picture going to be called? *Adam McAdam?*"

Megan's back stiffened, and her eyes hardened. "It's a piece of shit, Bert."

Bert smiled. "Yes, I hear the producers are counting on you to turn their cowchip into gold. They expect to net six or seven million on this piece of shit. At least, it should increase your asking price on the glamour market."

Megan glanced miserably at him. "They've made me a piece of meat," she said.

"Business is business," said Bert, "be it a movie performance, a novel, or a jar of peanut butter."

"They are more interested in my breasts than my performance," she said sadly.

"No," retorted Bert. "What I'm hearing from California is that you have raised a B-grade exploitation picture several steps toward cinematic art."

"It's not *that* bad," she pouted. "B-grade . . . It was never that bad."

Bert smiled tolerantly.

"I'm gonna be a goddamned *star* Bert," Megan said fiercely. "They're already staring at me. They're not sure who I am . . . where they've seen me . . . whether I'm somebody special. But next year, when I come back here, they'll *know* who I am."

"It's what you always wanted," he said quietly.

She lowered her eyes. "Yes."

He put his hand on hers. "You know I love you, Megan."

"I know," she said. She looked tenderly into his face. "I'm so sorry."

"Sorry!" Bert blurted. "Sorry?"

She nodded. "I'm still in love with Thad."

"Jesus, Megan . . ."

"I can't help it, Bert. I'm going to live in Los Angeles . . . and I won't see him . . . and maybe I'll get over him."

"I could . . ."

"*No.* You couldn't help. I mean, not now. . . . The way I feel . . . well, there's just not going to be anybody else . . . not now."

He stiffened, biting his lip bitterly. "Catlett isn't worth it, Megan. Catlett is—"

"Never mind what you think he is, Bert. And please don't unload any more emotional baggage on me. Leave me alone. Let me work it out my way."

"Okay, Megan," he said. "Okay. I hear you."

Wilhelm Hildebrandt asked Thad to come to Frankfurt in February for a review. When Thad arrived, the VWH park was under a foot of snow, and the bare trees were draped in white. Even so, Hildebrandt plunged into the heated rooftop pool for his daily swim, followed by half an hour in the sauna. Again he asked Thad to join him. Thad relaxed in the warm water, watching the vapors rise in the crisp air as Hildebrandt swam his laps. Afterward, they sweated together in the sauna.

"Our associates are well pleased with the acquisition of Duncan Broadcasting," said Hildebrandt as they dripped in the dry heat.

"But they are eager that you identify other television stations. They want to expand."

"There are more than eight hundred commercial television stations in the United States," said Thad. "Most are highly profitable. Few come on the market every year. Kenneth Asher has his antennae up. He has found two possibilities, which I have rejected—one because it was too expensive, the other because the market was too small. We're watching and waiting until the right one comes along."

"This Asher. You trust him? He was a Nixon man."

"He went to jail for his loyalty to Nixon. He has now transferred his loyalty to me."

Hildebrandt nodded approvingly. "Ah. Good. But can you tonight assure our associates that we will acquire additional stations in the immediate future?"

"I believe so. Can they assure me of the capital a major acquisition may require?"

Hildebrandt slapped Thad on the shoulder. Sweat splashed from the light slap. "My friend, we have only begun our enterprise."

"We will take a closer look at two more stations: one in North Carolina, one in Dayton, Ohio," said Thad. "They would cost another fifty million dollars."

"Four stations. In our first year, four television stations. That would be good."

"One hundred million dollars," said Thad. "Plus the money you paid for your forty percent of my company. We're talking about a hundred fifty million. Already people are asking where the money is coming from."

"Tell me," said Hildebrandt. "We own two stations in Florida, which cost us approximately forty-six million five hundred thousand dollars, plus expenses. They were losing money. Already they are doing better. If we sold them right now, Thad, what could we get?"

Thad shrugged. "Sixty million maybe."

Hildebrandt smiled slyly. "So. We don't owe nothing. Hmm?

Excuse my English. We don't owe *anything*, in effect, because our property is worth more than we paid for it. Hmm?"

"But we haven't sold the first two stations," said Thad. "And the source of the capital—"

"We are not spending money," Hildebrandt interrupted. "We have invested in assets that have gained in value. But, let us change the subject. . . . My friends are anxious that we should enter the New York market. What can you report to them on that?"

"A station in the New York metropolitan area, if one were for sale, might cost a quarter of a billion dollars," said Thad.

"Is there one for sale?"

"Is that kind of money available?"

"It is possible," said Hildebrandt.

Thad closed his eyes, shutting off contact. Hildebrandt might think he was affected by the heat. What Thad really wanted was a moment to absorb and analyze what he had just heard. A quarter of a billion. Did he really want to go that far with them? The more money they poured into the venture, the smaller his share would shrink. He might awaken one day to find himself a very junior partner.

In the gasthaus a hundred meters from the executive office building where Thad sat with Hildebrandt in the sauna, Sepp Krueger followed Hanna Frank along the corridor, past the closed doors of the guest rooms. She was dressed as a maid and was wheeling a cart of towels, bedclothes, bathroom supplies, and cleaning materials. He carried a hand radio transceiver. Hanna stopped. She pulled a key from her apron pocket—a master key that would open any door in the gasthaus.

Sepp pressed the transmit button on his radio. "*Wir sind bei das Zimmer*," he said quietly.

"*Sie sind noch hier*," replied a curt voice from the transceiver.

He gestured at Hanna, and she unlocked the door. They slipped into the room, pulling the cart in with them.

99

Their job was elementary enough. Yet it had to be conducted with extreme delicacy. They were to search through the American's baggage and photograph all his papers, leaving nothing out of place, nothing that would arouse his suspicions.

Hanna was painstakingly efficient. She retrieved a camera from under the pile of towels on the cart, a small tripod from under the folded sheets, and affixed the camera quickly to the top of the tripod. She needed no lights. She set up the camera so that she could photograph documents on the windowsill, using the pale winter sunlight. While she was adjusting the camera, Sepp delved through the American's two bags, ever so neatly. One was an attaché case bulging with papers.

Hanna was practiced at the clandestine art of removing documents, photographing them, and returning them in precisely the order in which they had been found. She had been given no instructions as to what documents might be important. All Herr Papen had told her was to photograph everything. She preferred more precise instructions, though Herr Papen always demanded everything. All right. If time was short, she would simply photograph what came out of the briefcase in consecutive order. It would not be her fault if she missed something important. Herr Hildebrandt always told her exactly what he hoped she would find, and she could scan through the papers before she began to photograph them. Then she could be sure to get the most important papers in the available time.

While she worked at copying the contents of the attaché case, Sepp picked through the American's clothes and toiletries. Everything the American carried reeked of cigarette smoke, and he was so addicted to Scotch whiskey that he carried a bottle of it in his traveling bag.

Sepp found this kind of work distasteful, but Hanna enjoyed it. The secret intrusion gave her a sense of power over the American. She knew a great deal about him and he didn't even know she existed. She was an attractive woman, thirty years old, blond, a skier and mountain climber with a taut athletic body. She was an experienced intelligence agent, trained by the Bundesnachtrichten-dienst, which she had left when Herr Hildebrandt offered to double her salary. Sepp, in contrast, was merely a strong-arm, gun-packing bodyguard.

When Hanna completed the covert photocopying, she had an evening's work ahead of her. No one else would be entrusted with this film. In a cellar laboratory, she would develop the film and make a copy of each of the documents from the American's briefcase. She would deliver the prints and the film to the secure room just down the corridor from Herr Hildebrandt's private office, where she would carefully add them to the accumulating file on this man Catlett and his American company. It was an interesting file. She—

"*Sie anziehen,*" said the harsh voice on the transceiver.

Damn! Herr Hildebrandt and the American had left the sauna and showers and were dressing. Damn Papen for an idiot! He should have sent her to the room earlier. She began to work faster. In five minutes, she could—

"*Anschauen,*" said Sepp. He handed her a photograph, a black-and-white print of a young blond woman, quite nude.

Hanna put it on the windowsill and copied it, too.

In the photo laboratory, Hanna Frank removed the lab apron she had worn while working with the Catlett film. She checked the door to be certain it was locked. Then she shot the deadbolt that secured the room against anyone, even a security guard with a master key. Outside the door a red flag appeared, warning that the lab was being used as a darkroom. She laid out the stack of prints, just out of the dryer, on the table beside the copy camera stand. The table was equipped with small clips that held documents in place under bright lights while they were photographed on microfilm. She rolled the copy camera aside and moved into its place a tripod-mounted video camera.

One print after another, she copied them all on videotape, including the nude picture the American apparently carried for sentimental reasons. When she was finished, she took from a drawer the tool that opened the videotape cartridge. She was experienced; she performed each task with practiced hands. She copied the prints on the end of the tape, past the point where an industrial film made for VWH ended; then it was a simple matter—if you knew how—to snip a meter or two of tape off and reattach the remainder to the reel.

When the tape cartridge was closed again, Hanna stripped off her sweater and blouse. She wrapped the videotape around her body, securing it with bits of sticky tape. In the years she had been copying documents for her own file, the guards had never inspected her purse when she left the building. She was, after all, in a sense their superior. But in case it should happen, they would not find her bit of tape. At home she would splice it on the end of a movie, then run it on her videotape player to make sure she had clear copies. Later she would detach it and install it in one of the cartridges she would carry to Switzerland on her next ski trip. In her deposit box in a Zurich bank, she had almost twenty full cartridges of videotape, all carefully indexed.

Thad had never seen Charles's apartment. He was unaware that Charles had a roommate. The sophisticated and discreet Charles had seen no reason to discuss this aspect of his personal life with anyone, certainly not with Catlett.

At age thirty-two, Kathy Welling wanted to write a novel. This was no casual ambition, it was a consuming one. She wanted to write not just a novel but a great novel, a distinctive novel, a contribution to the permanent literary record of urban America in the twentieth century. She was also confident, if only she had the time, that she could do it.

Charles had given her the time.

They had met at a cocktail party. He was introduced to her as a Pulitzer-winning journalist, and she immediately launched into a discussion of her novel. Would he read a few pages, she begged. He protested that he never reviewed anyone's writing. She made a startling, straightforward offer: She would accompany him to his apartment and exchange sex for a critique of a couple of chapters of her novel. The temptation overcame his ingrained nobility; as courtly as possible under the circumstances, he accepted her offer. He even liked what she had written. He encouraged her to plug away at it. She complained impatiently that she couldn't find the time. After six or seven more visits, they struck a new bargain. She quit her job and moved in with him, bringing her typewriter and reams of typescript. She cooked the few meals he ate at home, slept with him and worked on her novel. The arrangement remained straight-forward.

He arrived home at seven on one of the nights Thad was in Frankfurt. She was hunched over her typewriter, which was set up in the living room. She glanced up as he closed and locked the door, gesturing that she was deeply engrossed in her work. He bypassed her, wandered into the kitchen, and poured himself a splash of brandy.

Suddenly she called to him. "Okay. I got it. You can talk now."

"How very nice," he responded, with a touch of sarcasm.

He returned to the living room, set down his snifter, and pulled off his jacket. "What a day," he muttered.

Kathy switched off her electric typewriter, yanked out the sheet, glanced at it briefly and, with no great enthusiasm, added it to a pile of sheets in the upside-down lid of a typing-paper box. She was clad in nothing but a brassiere and white panties—her usual working attire in the apartment. The thermostat and his heating bills crept up together. She was petite, no more than five feet two, with unruly dark hair hanging wildly around her ears as if she had not combed it, myopic brown eyes behind round steel-rimmed glasses, and a lush figure, her round little belly protruding playfully over the waist-band of her panties and her soft, bouncy breasts filling her bra to capacity.

"Want to see what I've written today?" she asked.

He agreed. She fetched the box of typed sheets.

"How many pages today?" he asked.

"Just three," she said reproachfully. "And I don't really like the third page."

He read her three pages. "Same problem," he said. "Baroque overwriting."

"Say you."

He shrugged. "Say I."

She shrugged. "You want it?"

"I should like it, yes."

"Well, go take a shower. You're too sweaty."

When he had showered, he emerged, dropped the towel around his waist, and sank down on the couch. She slithered down beside him. Fifteen minutes later he arose, depleted but exhilarated.

He sipped another brandy while she dressed, and then they barged out on the snowy street. A bitter wind whipped crystals of ice into their faces. To escape the torment, they hurried up the block to Tommy's Neopolitan Restaurant.

They were seated at a small round table with a red and white checkered tablecloth, a candle in a Chianti bottle, and a basket of breadsticks. Their waiter slammed a tray of olives, tomatoes, and celery, with slices of white cheese, on the table and asked if they wanted wine. Charles indicated that he did—the usual, the best Chianti in the house.

"Charles Lodge Johnson."

Charles turned. Across the small room, seated alone, was Bert Stouffer.

"Bert! Nice to see you. Are you alone?"

"Expecting a friend."

"Would you care to share some wine with us while you wait?"

"Love to," said Stouffer with a show of affability.

He made his way to them, drawing up a chair from an empty table. Charles introduced him to Kathy. He was, Charles told her, an investigative reporter who had won the Pulitzer Prize for his exposure of insider trading abuses by attorneys in prominent New York law firms.

Kathy was properly impressed. Bert Stouffer was a few years younger than Charles, and his strong, square-jawed face, marked with the faint scars of some old injuries, fascinated her. His blue eyes were almost hypnotic, even though one lid drooped a little, so that one eye was wider than the other. She saw in him a sober intensity. Maybe he was humorless; she couldn't tell yet.

Bert was impressed, or at least mildly intrigued, with Kathy. She was dressed in a long, loose black skirt and a black cardigan sweater over red leotards. She wore no underclothes beneath the leotard, and under the unbuttoned sweater her breasts swelled alluringly. She had tied her dark hair back, revealing the two gold loops she wore in her pierced ears.

"Kathy is writing a novel," said Charles.

"Oh?" said Bert. "Is it about Charles? If you write a novel about him, I want to read it."

Charles started to protest, then thought better of it and remained silent.

Bert wouldn't let go. "Maybe," he added dryly, "you could offer some kind of explanation as to why Charles abandoned journalism and signed on with F. Thad Catlett."

"That's simple enough," said Charles pleasantly. "My divorce from Charlotte left me in poverty. It was also time to leave Boston, where I was regarded as a failure."

"You were never a failure," said Bert. "You were a damned fine newspaperman."

"And the paper was losing circulation and money," Charles continued. "If I had not left, I should have been fired shortly."

"The trouble was, you were too good. Your work was—"

"—of the highest quality," Charles interrupted. "We had the most accurate and comprehensive coverage of New England politics. It was greatly appreciated by the few people who read it. The great American public wants its news processed and packaged in easy-to-digest capsules, spiced with a generous serving of sex, scandal, and sports."

"Lotteries, comics, astrology, and advice to the lovelorn," added Bert.

"Yes," said Charles. "The condiments have become more important than the main dish."

105

"So you joined Catlett," Bert concluded.

"People *read* the Catlett papers," chimed in Kathy. "What value is good reporting if nobody reads it?"

"You're right about the Catlett tabloids," snorted Bert. "No one ever accused them of good reporting."

"Except for the *Washington Register-Herald*," said Charles. "That's the only Catlett newspaper over which I ever had direct control. So, of course"—he shrugged—"it loses money."

Bert abruptly changed the subject. "Tell me, have you met Wilhelm Hildebrandt?"

"I have."

"I understand there are other secret investors?"

"I have met representatives of the investor group."

"Can you give me their names? Not for attribution."

"No, Bert, I cannot."

"Does it bother you, Charles, that a group of secret investors own two American television stations? Does it bother you that a German publisher has a hook in CCE?"

"No," said Charles. "I have seen no malign influence. If I ever should, then I will be concerned."

"Would you tell me?"

Charles considered the question, then said, "That would depend on the nature of the malign influence."

Anne placed an urgent telephone call to Thad in Frankfurt. His father had suffered a stroke. She had arranged for Thad to change planes at Kennedy International and fly on to Texas at once. She would meet him at the airport with the ticket and a suitcase packed with clean clothes. He mumbled something about his tight schedule, but she cut him off, saying, "It just might be your last time, Thad."

Thad had almost forgotten the dust and bleakness and flatness of west Texas, but the memory came rushing back as he returned to the remote house and the people who had never left it. He came home a stranger in an alien land. The house was infested with lanky young men and gawky young girls—nieces and nephews and cousins, some of whom he had never seen before.

Dick Catlett was alert, propped up in bed. He insisted it was unhealthy for a man to sleep in a closed room, no matter what the weather, so the open windows chilled the air. He was wrapped in wool blankets laden with the red dust that blew in on the wind. The hours he spent with his father were miserable for Thad.

"You've done all right, Frankie," his father said. "I s'pose, come right down to it, you could buy the whole damn fam'ly, ranch and all, and just write a check to pay for it."

He had always been "Frankie" at home, though the outside world had known him as Thad since he left west Texas in 1946. His mother and grandfather had installed him in Culver Military Academy; it was supposed to be his launching into the Texas gentry. There was nothing resentful in his father's words, just a statement of facts as he saw them.

Thad's sister Mary came to see him. She clutched a soft Bible in her hand, as if it were part of her wardrobe. The glint in her eyes suggested that she might have brought it to ward off the miasma of evil that surrounded her brother, whom she had heard denounced from the pulpit as a heathen pornographer. She was an ample woman, with a face once handsome but showing hard mileage. A fixed smile appeared to be painted on her face with red lipstick. Her visit was short. She offered to pray with him before she left; he acknowledged the need but declined salvation for the moment.

Thad and his mother watched for a chance to spend an hour alone, and they found it in the kitchen after dinner, while his brother, his sister-in-law, and their sons and daughters settled around the big television set in the living room to watch *Dallas*.

"Shameful, ain't it?" she asked in a hushed but raspy voice. "I mean, this household." She was the same: hard, dry, perceptive. "I didn't even suggest to Anne that she come, too. I don't think she was offended."

107

"I can arrange something different for you, something better," he said. "I mean, a better place to live. It looks like Billy and his family have taken over the house."

"Never mind," she said. "We took this place over from your granddad. I've become accustomed to it."

"Let me buy you a place close to us in Connecticut."

She shook her head. "Not while your father is alive. It would take a team of horses to pull him away from here."

"Would you leave it if he should die?"

"If he goes before me, yes."

"But meanwhile, you'll stay."

"I've become accustomed to him, too," she said wanly.

Thad cast his eyes on a quick tour of the kitchen. It was the only room in the house that gave him any sense of being at home. He had spent his early childhood here, crawling around on the linoleum floor, playing with the pots and pans, tugging at her apron, while she cooked. In his memory, it seemed as if she were always cooking, not just meals but jars of fruits and vegetables she "put up" every year. There was running water now, but there had been a pitcher pump in the sink then, and the drain pipe from the sink had simply run through the wall and discharged into the sandy soil of a flower bed.

"Remember the day you shot the rattlesnake in the backyard?" he asked.

"Good Lord . . ." she sighed. "You were seven. You were playing in your sand pile. . . . I looked out, and there was mister rattler, four feet long, wriggling right toward my baby!"

Thad smiled at the memory. "I don't remember being scared. A bad snake had come after me, but Mommy had taken care of it. Mommy wouldn't let anything hurt me."

"You know what day that was?" she asked.

"I do now," he said. "June 6, 1944. D Day. You called me in the house, and the radio was blaring the news. You explained to me what was happening."

"You understood it, too," she said. "That's why your granddad

108

and I wouldn't let you stay home and go to that awful district school. You might have turned out like your brother and sister."

"They're the salt of the earth," he said with a wry smile.

He detected an amused, but knowing, twinkle in her eye.

Back in New York, Thad summoned the security consultant he had hired in January. Louis Pittocco sat across the desk from him, smoking a large, expensive, fragrant cigar, watching Thad skim over the typewritten report Pittocco had brought with him.

"Ummm. Hmmm . . ." Thad mumbled as he read. "So my suspicions were well-founded."

"Unless you failed to follow instructions," said Pittocco.

"I did exactly what you said, Lou. Every paper was a clean Xerox of the original. I broke open a new ream of paper and loaded it in the machine. The girl who did the copying wore rubber gloves. She assembled and stapled the papers with rubber gloves. When I returned to New York, I handed my wife a locked attaché case, because I had to fly on to Texas. You had the combination, which I'd changed just before my departure. If there are any fingerprints but mine on those papers, then somebody entered my room in Frankfurt and looked through the papers."

"Every sheet has the same fingerprints," said Pittocco. "Every single one. A few have your prints, and a few have someone else's prints. . . ."

"Right," Thad interrupted. "At one meeting, I had to let one of the Germans look over a document. He hadn't brought his own copy."

"There are one hundred twenty-seven sheets with no fingerprints but this one strange set," said Pittocco. "Somebody picked up every single sheet. My guess is that somebody made copies. Also, the photograph you sent me—the nude. That's Megan Wilkinson, isn't it? Two sets of prints on that. One set matches the prints on the sheets of paper. So, somebody rifled through your suitcase, too."

"Son of a *bitch*!"

"How'd you like to foul the culprit up?" Pittocco asked.

"Yes?"

"Put a set of papers in an envelope. We can brush that paper in advance with a powder that will come off on the fingers of anybody who touches those sheets. When that person wets the powder—like to wash his hands—his fingers are going to turn bright orange. And they're going to stay that way till the skin wears off."

"I'll think about it," said Thad. "Problem is, if we do that, they'll know I know."

Pittocco smiled. His long thin jaw was black under the skin with whiskers, which created a dark shadow within two hours after he shaved. "You have the makings of a detective, Mr. Catlett," he said.

"Maybe," Thad grunted. "But not the inclination for it. What about the man?"

"I know a man I think will suit you," said Pittocco. "Retired lieutenant-detective, NYPD. Fifty-five. Knows his way around town. Licensed to carry a gun. He's a widower, and his kids are grown, so he's willing to put in a lot of hours for the right money. He gives off a good appearance. Dresses well. Speaks well. He's no pug-ugly. With him around, it wouldn't be obvious that you have a bodyguard."

"All right. Send him in to see me."

Kenneth Asher had been working under severe pressure. Though Thad made no point of it, Asher knew Catlett received almost daily inquiries from Frankfurt, Munich, Dusseldorf, and Berlin, asking when CCE would be ready to buy more television stations. Specifically, what was CCE doing about WGMH-TV, Greensboro, and WDHA-TV, Dayton? These acquisitions were not opposed by the station owners and managers, particularly after Asher was authorized to assure the principals that they would be retained in their jobs. So with a minimum of haggling, Catlett Communications Enterprises purchased WGMH-TV, Greensboro for $22,500,000 and WDAH-TV, Dayton for $34,275,000. Both were independent UHF stations.

At the suggestion of Wilhelm Hildebrandt and the approval of the German investors, Catlett Communications Enterprises formed two subsidiaries, Catlett Newspapers, Inc. and Catlett Broadcast Services, Inc., to own the newspapers and the broadcast stations. CCE became a management-services and holding company.

Catlett Broadcast Services, which could not call itself CBS and so listed itself on the board as CATSERV, issued preferred stock to raise the capital to buy WGMH-TV and WDHA-TV. The preferred stock was purchased—1.5% by F. Thad Catlett, 1.5% by Anne Catlett, .2% by Bayard Justin, .1% by Charles Lodge Johnson, .15% by Kenneth Asher, .2% by Melvin Bragg, 1.5% by Wilhelm Hildebrandt, 1.5% by Gertrud Hildebrandt, 15% by Verlagsgruppe Wilhelm Hildebrandt, and 78.05% by a trust fund administered by Frankenthaler Handelsbank and other German banks.

Thad decided to use the Dayton station, WDHA, for an experiment in scrambled late-night broadcasting. Through advertisements in the Dayton newspapers and circulars in the mail, he offered Dayton-area residents a subscription to special post-midnight programs on WDHA. Since the station had always gone off the air at midnight, the offer did not interfere with the regular programming. Subscribers rented a descrambler box, which they attached to their television sets. Many also rented special UHF antennas directed toward the station. At midnight, the station went on scrambled broadcasting and offered adult programming—R-rated movies, plus an adult game show based on the *Bikini Naderia* on WMOA in Miami. Shortly, telltale antennas, pointing toward the WDHA transmitting towers, appeared on homes in Xenia, Springfield, Lebanon, Urbana, Troy, and across the Indiana line in Richmond. The subscription programming included commercials, and dozens of area businesses chose late-night WDHA programming for their advertising.

The experiment was so successful that CATSERV introduced it in Greensboro, too.

Condemnation rose like thunder from country pulpits. It was the best advertising the late-night programming could have had. As a study on the MacNeil-Lehrer Report showed, many of the WGMH-pointed antennas in North Carolina were camouflaged in trees or interlaced with the VHF antennas that stood on rooftops all over the area. An elder of a Baptist church, vocal on MacNeil-Lehrer in deploring the late-night scrambled broadcasting of WGMH, was shown to have an antenna mounted under his eaves on the Greensboro side of his house.

All four Catlett stations—the two DunCast stations in Florida and the two CATSERV stations in Ohio and North Carolina—began to broadcast the *Janine* series produced in Germany by a subsidiary of VWH. Janine was a Parisian who travelled to the beaches of the world—especially those in towns like St. Tropez, where she could go topless—and ventured into a variety of erotic adventures. The series was available in six languages and in three versions—uninhibited, somewhat inhibited, and inhibited. The inhibited version was suitable for European and American network broadcasting. The somewhat inhibited was suitable for scrambled late-night broadcasting. The uninhibited version was suitable only for viewing in adult theaters and nightclubs. Viewers who had chanced to see Janine in adult theaters tuned in on her late-night adventures on WDHA and WGMH and were disappointed—but not so disappointed that they failed to tune in again.

WDHA and WGMH also broadcast "nudie" movies from the sixties—innocent color flicks in which bosomy girls went topless in all kinds of improbable situations.

Movies like *Last Tango in Paris* and *I Am Curious Yellow* were unavailable for late-night scrambled broadcasting. Their proprietors apparently were holding them back for something better.

WDHA and WGMH had been profitable local UHF stations. Under CATSERV control, their profits began to jump.

The United States District Court dismissed the suit brought by the

DunCast executives to enforce their golden-parachute contracts. The *Wall Street Journal*:

> The decision sent a shudder through executive suites in a hundred corporations. Coming on top of federal legislation imposing heavy tax burdens on golden parachutes, the judge's decision seemed to foretell the demise of a favorite device used by executives of takeover targets.
>
> Catlett Communications had moved for summary judgment on the grounds that corporate executives who commit their companies to golden-parachute contracts have breached their fiduciary duty to their company, and the contracts are therefore void.
>
> CCE president F. Thad Catlett refused to consider any settlement. "They almost broke Duncan Broadcasting, so they're out," he said. "You perform badly in an executive position, you belong on the sidewalk."
>
> One of the ousted executives, who now sells insurance for an Ocala agency, complained that Catlett had turned WPAR profitable by turning it into a "Playboy of the Air." "We could have made money that way, too," he said.

Anne was eating lunch alone in her kitchen in Greenwich. She had taken half an hour away from her work in the darkroom, where she was preparing black-and-white prints for a London gallery showing of her photographs. When the telephone rang, her reaction was impatience.

"Is Mr. Catlett there, please?"

"No. At this time of day, he is usually in his office."

The voice on the line was that of a woman, oddly thin and wavering. "Yes, I know. He's not there? I thought—"

"He's in Washington, actually. I can take a message."

"Is this Mrs. Catlett? You don't know me, but my name is Kathy Welling. I'm a friend of Charles. Charles Johnson. Charles collapsed on the street a few minutes ago. Someone called me, but I can't find out anything. I don't even know what hospital he's been taken to. I'm afraid he . . . needs help."

"Give me your number. I'll see what I can find out."

Anne called the office. The receptionist confirmed that Charles had, indeed, collapsed on the sidewalk as he was hailing a cab. No, she didn't know what hospital he'd been taken to. No, she didn't know how to find out.

"Well, I'm catching the first train from Greenwich. I suggest you make yourself an archive of information before I get there."

An hour later, she walked into Grand Central. The cavernous station reverberated with the usual crowd noises, as thousands of hurrying people surged through the station, their paths merging and crisscrossing. She paused to assess the congestion, then decided she would go through the Grand Hyatt and ask the doorman to get her a cab. No, better she call the office first. She headed toward a bank of telephones.

"Mrs. Catlett?"

The man speaking to her had warm brown eyes and an appealing face. He was dressed in clothes of conservative cut and color.

"Yes, I'm Mrs. Catlett."

"My name is Frank Dittoe. Has Mr. Catlett mentioned my name?"

Her eyes reflected a faint light of recognition. "Yes . . . as a matter of fact."

"I have a car waiting outside. Mr. Johnson has been taken to Lehman Hospital."

"Can you show me any identification?"

Amiably, the man reached inside his jacket and retrieved a small case. He showed her the identification of a retired New York City police detective, together with the small gold shield he was still allowed to carry.

Dittoe had double-parked a company car on Vanderbilt Avenue. When they reached the hospital and encountered bureaucratic officiousness, he applied just the right amount of pressure, with just the right amount of persuasion. Shortly, they were ushered into the

114

coronary unit on the second floor, where Charles was lying on a bed in an intensive-care unit, attached to wires and tubes, looking weak and pale.

"Preliminarily, we're calling it myocardial infarction," said a young white-coated doctor with a yarmulke pinned to his dark curly hair.

"Is his life in any danger?" Anne asked.

"It is right now," said the doctor. "With every hour the danger recedes. The gravest danger has passed; he might not have arrived at the hospital alive. But he did, and if he makes it through the next twelve hours, my prognostication will be optimistic."

"I don't suppose I can speak to him."

"I wish you would . . . briefly. He wants us to notify someone, but we can't quite make out the name."

With a nurse hovering nearby, Anne stood beside Charles.

"Charles . . . How're you feeling?"

His eyes rose toward her but seemed not to focus. "Who? . . . Anne? . . ."

"Yes, it's Anne, Charles. Thad's in Washington."

"Oh . . . yes . . ."

"Charles. Is there someone you want me to call?"

"Kathy . . ." he mumbled faintly.

"Kathy . . . Who? Where?"

"Home."

"Boston?"

"Here."

She did not press him.

"I'll find Kathy. You just take it easy, and I'll see you tomorrow."

She left her home number, to be called in the event anything happened. Then Anne began the paperwork for the hospital, identifying Charles's employer and his insurance carrier. But she became exasperated, snatched the admitting form from the clerk, and scrawled across it: "Account guaranteed, Mrs. F. Thad Catlett—reference, the Cooper Bank."

Dittoe was waiting in the maroon Ford, which he had double-parked on the street behind the hospital. He was perplexed when Anne asked about Kathy. She was trying to piece together what Charles had told her. "He said, 'Home.' But not Boston. Could he have meant his apartment? Let's drive over there. It's not far."

She pushed the button, and someone buzzed her in. Kathy met her at the door—by Anne's first impression, a short, plump, unkempt young woman, barefoot and obviously at home. This startled Anne. Inside the apartment, she found a man in a gray tweed jacket sitting on the living room couch.

"I'm Anne Catlett. You must be the woman who telephoned me. I located Charles at Lehman Emergency Hospital. I'm sorry, he's had a heart attack. He asked for you."

The blood drained from Kathy's face. "Is he? . . . Will he? . . ." She never completed the question.

"It's too soon. . . . He was able to talk. He gave me your name. . . . I figured you were the one who called me."

"Will they let me see him?"

"He's sedated. . . . I don't know."

Kathy drifted over to her typewriter, stroked it like a living pet, and dropped into her chair. She stared at the floor, her eyes afloat. "Charles . . ." The name slipped involuntarily from her lips.

Anne drew a deep breath. "He never mentioned you to me," she said hesitantly. "I guess I don't know exactly. . ."

"I live with him," said Kathy. "He's a kind man, a generous man, a—a decent man. Uh . . . this is Bert Stouffer. He's a friend of Charles."

The man stood and extended his hand. "Mrs. Catlett. I heard on the radio that Charles had collapsed. I rushed here to see if Kathy needed help."

Anne turned toward Frank Dittoe, who had entered the apartment behind her. "This is Frank Dittoe. Kathy, Mr. Stouffer. He works for my husband." She frowned. "You know, Frank, perhaps you should take Kathy to the hospital. She might need someone to run interference past the front desk."

Dittoe nodded. "Sure," he said. "You get your shoes on, miss, and I'll drive you to Lehman. Uh . . . I can drop you back at Grand Central first, Mrs. Catlett."

"I'll grab a cab," she said. "You go ahead with Kathy—and bring her home afterward, if you don't mind."

"I'll share that cab, if *you* don't mind," said Bert Stouffer.

When they vacated the cab at Grand Central, she knew who he was—a free-lance journalist. He had been frank enough to tell her that he had a journalistic curiosity in the arrangements between CCE and VWH. "I wouldn't want to enjoy your company on false pretenses." At the curb on Lexington Avenue, he tried to pay for the taxi, but she firmly thrust a twenty-dollar bill into the driver's money tray.

"Then maybe you'll let me buy you a drink," Bert offered.

Anne sighed. "Why not? The day's already shot. May as well squander another thirty minutes."

They stepped into the human swirl in the cavernous station and pushed into the flow leading to the Pan Am Building. They rode the escalator up to Charlie Brown's Restaurant and Bar. The last of the luncheon crowd was filtering out, and they were able to find a table in the bar.

Bert appraised her openly. She was forty. He didn't have to guess, he knew; he had researched the Catletts. If her husband still had to put a front on to conceal his rough country background, this lady surely had no such problem. She was the daughter of Bayard Justin, the Wall Street lawyer, and Emily Baynes Justin, the sculptor; the granddaughter of Henry Trumbull Baynes, whose Pittsburgh wealth had rated only one rank lower than the Carnegies, Mellons, and—

"I drink rye, Mr. Stouffer. What are you having?"

"Oh. A martini on the rocks, with an olive."

She was cool and composed, not likely to be ruffled. She had the self-confidence of a woman of breeding who has never had to worry about money. He liked the way she was dressed: wine-colored stone-

117

washed denim jeans, a silk blouse, and a sweater, not well coordinated and carelessly thrown on in her haste, yet every item expensive in the subdued way that whispered quality and taste.

"I've asked Charles a tough question, Mrs. Catlett," he said. "I would have asked your husband, but he's not an easy man to reach. Does it trouble you that forty percent of your family business is now owned by strangers, including strangers who, I hear, have not even been identified to you?"

"Why should I be troubled?" she asked. "My husband's business judgment has proved faultless over the years. I also had independent counsel."

He found it curious the way her eyes fastened on his. She had hardly blinked since they sat down. She offered herself for judgment, holding back nothing—either because she was totally confident in what that judgment had to be, or . . . or because she welcomed a positive appraisal and wanted to see what would result from it. He was not sure he wanted to explore the implications of that second possibility.

The waitress delivered their drinks. Anne Catlett stared for a moment into her glass of rye on the rocks, then tipped it and drank half of it. So. She *was* an interesting woman.

"Responsibility . . ." she said as she put down her glass. "When I was a child, I thought it was a bad word. I heard it often enough." She sighed. "Right now my responsibility is to go back out to Greenwich and see to it that my two sons have dinner—and hear their mother's nightly disquisition on responsibility."

"No time for—"

She had anticipated his question. "No. No time for a second drink. I'm sorry. Uh . . ." She glanced at her watch. "About ten tonight, I'll probably drop into a bar in Cos Cob. Called Tumbledown. It's on the Post Road, exit four off the turnpike. You couldn't miss it. *I'll* buy the drinks."

118

SIX

The Catlett house was located in Back Country Greenwich, as the locals called it, in perhaps the richest stretch of suburbia in the world. It was part of a beautiful land of gentle townships that antedated the American Revolution—Mystic, Old Lyme, Lebanon, Preston, Ledyard, Baltic, names that conjured up quaint and cherished images.

The house rose out of a hilltop, then slumped back into it. The flagstone terrace overlooked a verdant, sloping blanket of lawn stretching in every direction, with a fringe of trees—mostly birch, some dogwood and flowering crabapple—a pond stocked with trout, and a waterfall that murmured restfully through New England summer nights.

Greenwich proper—what locals called The Avenue—was three miles away. The shoreline of Long Island Sound was four miles. Little of Greenwich was visible from the house, just treetops and church steeples. The roaring Northeast Corridor—Interstate 95 and

119

the four-track railroad—was out of sight, beyond hearing and out of mind. One of the neighbors, Anne explained, referred to Back Country as "splendid isolation," meaning isolation, not just from the New York whirl, but from commuterdom itself.

"It will be pleasant when the weather is warmer," said Anne. "But for the moment, I suggest we have our drinks inside."

Bert followed her through the wide French doors into the living room. The interior, as he expected, was rich, a tasteful blending of oak, stone, and glass. He noticed that the place was protected by an intricate system of sensors, alarm horns, and television cameras. He had detected the security the moment he entered the driveway. Although the drive to the house had appeared to be open before him, he was suddenly confronted with a barrier that rose up and blocked the road after his car had passed the stone pillars. He had found himself staring into tree-mounted television cameras and speaking to a disembodied voice.

"Martini?" she asked. She was already at the bar in the living room. It was apparent that Scotch and rye were important elements in the Catletts' lives. The ice machine popped cubes noisily into a glass, and she began to mix his martini.

She wore gray flannel slacks, a light blue silk blouse, a green blazer, and gray shoes with high heels. A pair of small gold loops dangled from her ears. Her blond hair was cut to require little attention, swept back and rounded under her ears but above her shoulders. A wisp was free and fell across her forehead. She was slender, her face bright and full. She had made a graceful transition from girl to woman, and her comfort with middle age was apparent.

"That was the terrace and the view," she said. "But I can't believe you are terribly interested in real estate. You don't impress me as a man who would write for *House Beautiful.*"

The rationale for his visit was that he planned to write a profile of Thad Catlett. That is what they had talked about in the bar at Tumbledown the other night. He had found it difficult to believe this woman spent any time in singles bars, but the bartender had called her Mrs. Catlett and had pushed successive ryes at her without waiting for her to order them. Yes, he intended to write a profile of her husband, the press baron, lord of the tabloids. Sure he was. And he was here to see how the man lived.

"Anyway, you might like to look around," she said. "There are one or two interesting things in the house."

She showed him her husband's den, a spacious room overlooking a glass-enclosed swimming pool and conservatory. One wall of the room was covered with mementoes, autographed photos and framed editorials.

One editorial Bert vividly remembered. October 27, 1976:

WE ENDORSE—

We don't. We wish we could. When the American people go to the polls on Tuesday to elect a President for the next four years, their choice is between—

—A squalid little hack politician who has lived off the taxpayers for the past twenty-five years and cannot point to a single accomplishment to justify his pension. Nixon's creature. The author of Nixon's pardon. Along with Nixon himself, Gerald Ford bears responsibility for the successful—and never let us doubt it *was* successful—Watergate coverup.

—A redneck born-again peanut farmer who has run a brilliantly cynical campaign and will probably be elected President of the United States because the old political adage is undoubtedly true: "You can't beat somebody with nobody."

Ford is nobody. Carter is somebody. Deficient though he is, he's somebody. Perhaps we'll be better off with him than with four years vacancy in the White House. Perhaps. These newspapers endorse Ronald Reagan. He's not on the ballot now, but he will be in 1980. We'll wait. American democracy may then offer us a choice.

"He has always had a sharp tongue in his typewriter, hasn't he?" Bert asked as he stood before the framed editorial and read it once

121

more with as much amusement as he had found in it almost ten years ago.

"Word processor," Anne corrected. "He writes most of his editorials here." She nodded toward a desktop computer. "On the word processor. He has the same machine in his apartment in the city. When he finishes an editorial, it goes out on the telephone line, transmitted by this computer, or the one in the apartment, to each of his newspapers. He used to write the lead editorial every day. Not so many now."

Bert walked along the wall, glancing at half a dozen of the editorials Catlett had chosen to frame.

"I like this one," she said. She tapped the glass displaying an editorial dated July 3, 1982:

> On the eve of the celebration of the advent of American liberty, we mourn the Equal Rights Amendment. It would have been, in our judgment, a gesture, since almost everything American women thought they would gain from it they have gained already or will gain through means less drastic than an amendment to the Constitution of the United States.
>
> Even so, it would have been a positive gesture, and there are no valid arguments against it.
>
> The squalid coalition of know-nothings that has assembled to defeat Equal Rights is a shameful little cabal. It is frightening to see how unpleasant, small-minded fanatics can work their way on timid legislatures. We see once again a vivid demonstration of why state legislatures cannot be depended on for an honest exercise of government power.

Anne watched him, bemused, as he read the editorial. "You see?" she said triumphantly. "He's no right-wing ideologue. My husband is a statesman. . . . I need another drink. You?"

Bert followed her back to the living room, where she mixed him a second martini and poured another heavy shot of rye over ice.

"I understand," he said to her, "that you are an accomplished woman. I'm sorry I haven't seen an exhibit of your work, but—"

"I'll give you one of my books," she offered. "I might even autograph it."

"I didn't know you'd published."

"Complete with reviews . . . When I was pregnant with Thaddy. That was in '65 and '66. . . . I made a complete photographic record of my pregnancy, then of Thaddy's birth, then of the baby and how Thad and I responded to him. . . . Good reviews . . . In 1983, I did another book. . . . Focused on my mother—I mean, about her work as a sculptor. Her hands working with clay. The evolution of an idea into a form. That one got good reviews, too."

"Megan Wilkinson," he said softly.

"What?"

"She modeled for your mother. And for you, too. She was a friend of mine"—he paused—"a rather close friend."

Anne shoved his fresh martini across the bar. "How close?" she asked brusquely.

"I was in love with her. I guess I still am."

"Let's stop playing games. We both know the Megan Wilkinson story."

He nodded.

"How cute," she said. "Is that why you're here? Do you have some kind of idea that—"

"No."

She shrugged. "Come on. I'll show you my darkroom. I still have a portfolio of Megan. I'll give you some if you want them."

Toward the rear of the house she had a well-equipped studio and a darkroom-laboratory. He sat down on a leather-covered couch in the studio while she fumbled in a cabinet. She returned with several portfolios bulging with prints.

He had never seen Megan more beautiful. In Anne Catlett's photographs, she was not just a nude woman in erotic poses—as she had appeared on stage—but the epitome of exquisite form. He was moved.

"What can I say?" he asked quietly.

"Would you like to keep them?" she asked as she closed the portfolio.

123

He draw a deep breath. "No . . . Thank you."

She frowned over the bow she tied in the string on the portfolio. Then, impulsively, she turned to him and rested her hand on his.

What was intended as a kindly gesture, a gentle touching of the flesh between two people who shared the same pain, became a tender moment. He bent toward her, and she moved to receive his kiss. The moment, like a whiff of delicate perfume, evaporated quickly. She lifted her hand to his cheek.

"I'm afraid this is a bad idea," he murmured.

"I know it is," Anne agreed.

Wilhelm Hildebrandt suggested to Thad that an April meeting would be desirable. "I regret asking you to do all the traveling," he said. "But there are only two or three in your party. We would be ten maybe. I have some new people for you to meet."

Thad stopped by Charles's apartment on Sunday afternoon, April 15, before catching the evening flight for Frankfurt. Charles was thin and pallid, but his recovery was normal. He still hadn't informed Thad of the existence of Kathy, who stayed in the bedroom.

Since Charles was too ill to travel, Thad took Kenneth Asher to Frankfurt. The schedule was now routine: met at the airport by Friederich Hoffman, installed in the VWH gasthaus, an afternoon to rest, a summons for Thad to join Hildebrandt in the pool and sauna. The only variation was that the swim was scheduled an hour earlier than usual, at four instead of five o'clock.

"I have arranged," said Hildebrandt in the sauna, "for you to meet several prospective new partners. They are different people from our original group. You may find them less to your taste."

"I want to insulate our personal deal, yours and mine, from any possibility of anyone else's gaining control," cautioned Thad. "And CCE . . . I can't concede control of CCE to anyone. But we can create new corporations and adjust the stock so that new partners own their appropriate shares of new assets, without taking control of the old assets."

"It will provide something for the lawyers to do," said Hildebrandt.

"And I am sure you and I will come to a mutually satisfactory agreement," said Thad.

"I am sure of it. Let me explain, then, that our meeting tonight will be very different from anything we have done before. Our new investors . . . well, just let me say, they are different, the meeting will be different, and you will find it, I think, interesting."

"Well, I've never been bored," said Thad as he smeared the sweat off his face with a damp towel.

"Our new partners will be interested in Runkle," said Hildebrandt. "Wasn't it Kenneth Asher who found this opportunity for us?"

"I have many people exploring opportunities," said Thad. "But I'm willing to credit Ken with this one."

"It sounds like a most interesting idea."

"It is," said Thad. "But it won't be an easy acquisition. Runkle Broadcasting is a widely held stock. Our takeover bid will have to abide by federal regulations. Also, it's an Ohio corporation, and the Ohio legislature has passed legislation to protect Ohio corporations from takeover bids. They could tie us up and cause delay."

"What's the bottom line?" asked the German.

"I'd guess a hundred fifty million," said Thad.

Although Thad and Asher arrived at the cocktail party on time—having observed that events scheduled by Wilhelm Hildebrandt invariably began on the stroke of the announced hour—the three new investors were already present, in a tight knot around Hildebrandt, engaged in intent, quiet conversation. Thanks to the advance alert, Thad was not altogether surprised that they were Japanese—three small men in dark blue suits, smiling, bowing, conversing with elaborate politeness.

Hildebrandt introduced them. "Mr. Kengo Yoshioka, Mr. Susumu Uchida, and Mr. Juzu Morinaga. Mr. Thad Catlett and Mr. Kenneth Asher. I am sure you gentlemen will find much to talk about."

The three Japanese bowed.

"I am honored," said one, bowing separately to Thad and Ken, repeating their names. "Mr. Catlett, Mr. Asher."

Thad had not yet fixed the names in his mind, much less identified them correctly with the right faces, so he addressed them jointly as "gentlemen." "The pleasure is ours," he said.

"So Mr. Catlett . . ." the same Japanese began, then stopped abruptly. He looked past Thad. "Ah!" he said with a broad smile. "Young ladies!"

Hildebrandt lifted his chin slightly and gave Thad a look of amused cynicism. Friederich Hoffman led into the room a group of eight attractive young women, all wearing silk cocktail gowns so similar that Thad wondered whether the company had dressed them. Nervously circling the women like a collie herding a flock of sheep, Hoffman guided them across the parquetry floor. He tried to introduce them but stumbled over everyone's names. If the scene had been set to music, it would have made excellent comic opera.

One of the young women did not wait to be introduced. She touched Thad's arm and said, "Mr. Catlett? I am Hanna Frank. I work for Mr. Hildebrandt. Would you join me at the bar?"

Thad looked toward Hildebrandt for some hint of instruction. But the German's attention was on the Japanese men as they paired off with the young women. Failing to catch Hildebrandt's eye, Thad allowed himself to be steered toward the bar.

"What's your position with the company, if I may ask?" Thad inquired conversationally.

"I am in book publishing," she said. "I hope to make a trip to New York soon, since we have a book publishing subsidiary there now, you know."

Her English had a slight, sensual German flavor. She was striking: blond, with a solid, busty figure; the image, he thought, of a Teutonic maiden. Her iridescent green dress was cut to emphasize her cleavage. He wondered idly whether the dress came from her own closet or the corporate wardrobe room.

She asked the bartender for Scotch and instructed him to pour another for Mr. Catlett. She nodded at the laughing group from which they had separated. "When I learned you were here this evening, I decided I would spend the evening with you, not with—uh, that is, if you don't mind."

Thad chuckled tolerantly.

The delighted Japanese chattered away in accented English, and their new girl friends frowned and laughed, understanding no more than half of it. The Japanese were not in the least hesitant about stroking their girls' legs and hips and even more sensitive places as they stood and talked. They had no doubt why these young women were here.

"They all really do work for VWH," said Hanna Frank, sensing Thad's unspoken question.

The girls slithered into their places at dinner beside the men they had been paired with. The Japanese were fully occupied with wine, women, and food, so no business conversation was possible. Hanna Frank talked with Thad about her favorite American authors: Sinclair Lewis, John Dos Passos, Ernest Hemingway, F. Scott Fitzgerald, James Thurber. He had to acknowledge that she was better read than he was.

Hoffman staged a show after dinner. The language difficulty was no impediment. He had employed five girls to perform a striptease, after which they assembled naked and proceeded to prance provocatively among the guests.

"You will forgive me," one of the Japanese said to Thad. "My name is Kengo Yoshioka." He bowed, though sitting. "I have looked forward to meeting you, Mr. Catlett."

"Well, I'm pleased to meet you," said Thad.

"We shall talk tomorrow very nicely, hmm?"

"Yes . . . tomorrow."

The Japanese bowed again and returned his attention to the nude dancers.

Thad looked at him for a moment, trying to fix in his mind something that would distinguish him from the others tomorrow. Yoshioka was of an indeterminate age. His black hair was graying at the fringes. It was cut bristly short on the sides. Thad wondered if he were not perhaps as old as Hildebrandt and, therefore, maybe a World War II pilot who had bombed Pearl Harbor. He seemed relaxed enough. His right arm encircled the waist of the plumpish girl he had chosen, and his left hand cupped her right breast.

"You are the most handsome man here," Hanna said to Thad. "Has anyone ever told you that you resemble the late Richard Burton?"

He responded with a bemused grin.

"Seriously. You're not a twin, of course, but I mean . . . you are tall, your face is shaped the same. You— There is a resemblance."

"He liked Scotch as well as I do," Thad acknowledged.

"What else did he like?" she asked mischievously. "Perhaps we will find out."

Thad drew in his lower lip and considered the proposal for a brief moment. Then he nodded. "Why not?"

In the conference room next morning, Kengo Yoshioka proved to be the most senior member of the Japanese delegation, though it was not entirely clear how he had attained this status. He was the chief executive officer, as it was explained, of more than one corporation. His companies exported millions of television sets to the United States each year—and more than a million to the rest of the world— under the famous name Videosonics. Other companies under his control exported electronic components that made almost every-one's computer partly Japanese.

Susumu Uchida was a top executive—though perhaps not the CEO; their titles were difficult to understand—of Chikuma Motors Company, which exported hundreds of thousands of Nagakos to the United States every year.

Juzu Morinaga was an independent business consultant, an anonymous expert but uncommonly shrewd in appraising business assets.

These were the Big Three who had participated in last night's revelry. But they were attended by five male secretaries and assistants. German and Japanese interpreters worked behind the glass.

"Mr. Yoshioka and Mr. Uchida represent Japanese interests who may be prepared to help finance our attempt to purchase a controlling interest in Runkle," said Hildebrandt. "Mr. Morinaga is their adviser."

Yoshioka spoke. "Mr. Catlett . . . the economic health of Japan is utterly dependent on export. We must export our goods. It is distressing that many Americans wish to impose heavy burdens on our trade. There is increasing talk in Congress of import duties and quotas. President Reagan has repeatedly declared his commitment to the principle of free trade. Yet he imposed a crippling tariff on semiconductors. The powerful AFL-CIO demands trade restrictions and it controls the Democratic Party. . . ."

Kenneth Asher could not restrain himself and laughed aloud.

Yoshioka bowed at him and continued, unperturbed. "We view with alarm the prospect that the 1988 presidential election in the United States might result in a protectionist administration. We hope it will be possible, most confidentially and most ethically, to exert an influence over the American electorate in this regard."

"We believe we understand the temperament of the American people," spoke up Uchida. "We understand that any effort by us to influence opinion would be most negatively received. For that reason, our meeting, any investment we make—indeed everything about our business relationship—must be strictly secret. Do you agree?"

"Furthermore," said Morinaga, "I believe your government would resist acquisition of American broadcasting stations by foreign corporations. Is it not so?"

"It is so," said Thad.

"It is very difficult to use a television station to editorialize," interjected Asher. "The extent to which you can do it is very limited."

"We are aware of the limitations," said Kengo Yoshioka. "We are, even so, willing to consider, in conjunction with our German friends, backing your effort to acquire the three television stations now owned by Runkle Broadcasting. Many details must be worked out. As you would say, the *t*'s must be crossed and the *i*'s dotted. We can discuss the details. Nothing can be accomplished in America without attorneys, so we have brought our attorneys. Is it not so?"

Ernst Dietrich touched the flame of his lighter to the tip of a short, thin cigar. He nodded at Papen. Papen pressed a button on the VCR's infrared controller, and a picture appeared on the screen.

"Herr Catlett," grunted Dietrich.

The video camera had not been well-positioned, though placed perhaps as conveniently as possible in the circumstances, well back within a heating duct high on the wall. The wide-angle lens, used to capture as much of the room as possible, distorted everything. The picture was in black and white, with a black stripe across the bottom giving the date and time.

The camera had been activated by the opening of the door. Hanna came in first, then Catlett. Their voices sounded hollow because of the placement of the hidden microphone. They wasted no time on formalities. She undressed. He undressed. Within less than a minute, she was on her back on the bed, and Catlett was astride her. As he concentrated on his exertion, she looked up into the camera and stuck out her tongue.

"*So ein Kerl*," muttered Dietrich. What a fellow.

There was no conversation on the tape. Catlett turned over and went to sleep. Hanna got up and headed for the bathroom.

Papen pressed the rewind button, then inserted another cartridge into the VCR.

Asher appeared on the screen with the girl named Trude. They were more lively, laughing, joking, finding drunken amusement in her thick-tongued effort to speak English. They disappeared into the bathroom for a long time, out of range of both camera and microphone. When they emerged, they were stark naked. She plumped up the pillows for him, and he made himself comfortable while she began the anticipated rituals. Afterward, they lay happily together, murmuring quietly.

Papen switched off the VCR. "*Nichts mehr*," he said. Nothing.

"*Schade*," mumbled Dietrich. Too bad.

On previous visits, Thad had not seen Wilhelm Hildebrandt's private office; he realized this as he was ushered into the inner sanctum and directed to an oversized black leather couch. This was a room, he speculated, that Hildebrandt shared only with people he trusted. A meter-long model of a World War II U-boat was displayed in a glass case. On the walls hung framed photographs of Hildebrandt in the uniform of a naval officer. In one picture, he stood on the bridge of a U-boat, strikingly handsome in white cap, turtleneck sweater, and uniform jacket with full insignia. The man had no reason to be ashamed of his war service, Thad supposed; it must have been difficult for him to keep silent, as the loser on the wrong side, about those important years of his life.

Hildebrandt did not use a desk; he sat behind a long table. His guests settled on the couch and on two matching chairs. The room had that London-club atmosphere that Hildebrandt seemed to favor: parquetry floors, Oriental rugs, paneled walls, warm light.

The elder Dietrich and Josef von Klauberg had appeared for the first time for this intimate meeting. They had not attended the dinner last night nor the meeting with the Japanese this morning. Hildebrandt had passed the word, too, that he did not want to see Asher.

"We must express our concern. . . ." said Hildebrandt. "We are reluctant to do so, but—"

"We must say what we must say," said von Klauberg.

"Of course," said Thad. "What is it you must say?"

"We are concerned about *this*," said Hildebrandt, rising abruptly and striding around his table to hand Thad a clipping mounted under a sheet of clear acetate. "Your editorial."

131

Thad recognized it; he had written it.

AND AGAIN, MR. PRESIDENT,
IF YOU PLEASE

We applaud the bombing of Libya, as most Americans do. A forceful reaction to the insane murderer Qaddafi is the only way to deal with him. We hope this will be just the first in a continuing series of raids, until the murderous regime of Qaddafi and his squalid little gang of cutthroats are outside, and Libya is freed.

Americans are grateful to Mrs. Thatcher, who conducted herself as an ally. We condemn the cowardice of the French president, also of the other European "statesmen," who trade with Libya and value their francs and marks more than the lives of the victims of Qaddafi's terrorism.

"My own company does no significant business with Libya," said Hans Dietrich. "If Europe were to be deprived of Libyan oil, however, it would cause severe economic dislocation in this country. My company would not be spared. I must express to you my concern over this editorial."

"I must concur," said von Klauberg stiffly. He started to say something else, but Thad cut him off.

"I will tolerate," he said grimly, "no interference with the editorial policies of my newspapers. In fact, I decline to discuss the subject." He rose from the couch. "So, if that is all, gentlemen . . ."

"We have not interfered, and we do not now interfere, Thad," said Hildebrandt firmly. "I cannot believe, however, you really mean to deny us the right to express our concerns. Anyone who writes a letter to the editor may express his disagreement with your editorials. Are you saying we are not allowed the privilege that you grant to a common reader?"

Thad paused at the door. "When you call a private meeting for the purpose, it is more than an expression of concern. I interpret it as pressure. And I won't tolerate it."

He left the room.

"Do you think they understood that the SEC procedures and the Ohio lawsuits we expect Runkle to file may tie up the acquisition until it is too late to influence the 1988 election?" Asher asked Thad.

They were once again high over the Atlantic on a 747 bound for New York.

"We told them plainly enough," said Thad.

"They liked your promise that your newspapers will continue to support free trade."

"God, don't tell Charles I promised them that," said Thad. "The idea of a newspaper promising to take an editorial stand for any other reason than an objective evaluation of the facts offends his sense of ethics. I consider myself ethical, too, but—"

"Situation ethics," said Asher dryly. "I went to jail because of mine."

"Yes, but I'm not committing a crime," said Thad. "There are no laws governing editorials."

"The only part of the deal that troubles me is the goddamned secrecy," said Asher. "I got burned on that once."

"That was for perjury, my friend. If you're ever subpoenaed to testify about anything involving my business, just tell the truth. I've never asked anyone to lie for me. Never will."

"Sorry."

Thad changed the subject. "What I have in mind is this," he said. "You and Mel work on it. The bid for Runkle stock will be made by Catlett Broadcast Services. The bid will be funded by lines of credit on several banks—chiefly American banks. The lines of credit will be backed by the assets of CCE, ostensibly. Actually, you know, we're good for two hundred million in a pinch. But there will be escrow accounts in the banks that issue the lines of credit. Those accounts will be backed by United States government bonds, various state bonds, corporate bonds from blue-chip corporations, and so forth. All negotiable. All that security will be the property of Videosonic, Chikuma, NIG, and VWH. They're going to back us to ninety percent. The bankers will keep that confidential."

"There's a risk," said Asher. "Are the SEC and FCC going to know about this?"

"What the SEC is going to know is the truth," said Thad. "And the truth will be that the deal is secure, that the Runkle stockholders who sell to us will get their money in cash, and that there is no water in the deal. What the FCC will know is that the Runkle broadcasting licenses are moving into the hands of an American corporation."

"So how are the Germans and Japanese secured after the takeover is accomplished?" asked Asher.

"We'll form a holding company to hold the Runkle stock," said Thad. "Catlett Broadcasting Services will keep ten percent, and the rest will be deposited with the banks to secure the loans made against the lines of credit. That will free the securities the Japanese and Germans deposited—except a small amount the banks will want to hold as a reserve. The interest on the loans will have first claim on Runkle dividends. Second claim will be a fund to retire the loans."

"Where are our so-called investors getting any profit out of this?" Asher asked.

"They're not investing money, actually," said Thad. "They're just depositing assets to secure the loans. They'll continue to collect the interest on the bonds they've deposited. They'll recover most of their bonds when the stock is deposited to replace them. What they're taking is a risk, and they've read the risk; they think we'll increase Runkle profit fifty percent in the first year, so it's really no risk at all. In return, they're getting the editorial support they want. And down the line, we'll have to hand over an equity interest in Runkle. We'll set aside some stock for them. We'll let them buy it cheap."

"Christ," muttered Asher. "You've got it all figured out, haven't you?"

Thad smiled. "I estimate it will take about twenty-four pounds of documents. There's a job for you for the next six months."

Asher nodded thoughtfully. "Say . . . would you back me if I tried to get myself readmitted to the bar?"

"Sure," said Thad. "Of course. But why do you want to be readmitted to the practice of law? You want a title? I can't make a disbarred lawyer general counsel, but how about something like vice president for strategic planning?"

Asher smiled nervously. "I'd appreciate that, Thad."

"You've earned it," said Thad. He signaled the flight attendant and told her to bring another Scotch for him, another martini for Asher.

"Speaking of strategic planning, what's your decision on cable? What did you think of Gottschalk's memorandum?"

"I didn't agree with it," said Thad. "The trouble with cable, as I see it, is that it's a franchise operation, meaning that you've got to get franchises out of local politicians. That's likely to take the crossing of some palms with silver. You're also at the mercy of every community kook who thinks he should have a voice in programming and management."

"Plus the fact that it costs a bundle to start a cable system, plus the fact that they've been by no means uniformly successful," added Asher. "And to that I'd add the fact that there is going to be competition from video tape recorders and disc players, whose prices are bound to come down sharply."

"Yes," said Thad. "As a matter of fact, I've been thinking of running a little fifteen-minute segment on our stations, telling people they are welcome to tape our programming for their own home use and giving them some tips on hooking up their machines. Instead of issuing dire warnings against taping, welcome them to do it."

"You may as well. They're going to do it anyway."

"I haven't heard Gottschalk's arguments in support of his report and recommendation," said Thad, "but I'm not sanguine about trying to go into the cable business."

"On the other hand," said Asher, "cable may be our only possible entry into the New York market."

"You know what I'd rather do?" Thad said. "I'd rather sit on Long Island or over in Jersey or up in Connecticut and send a signal back into New York. UHF stations. We can scramble at night, which will be the key to getting people to put up the necessary antennas. Gottschalk doesn't think people will put up directional UHF antennas, just to pick up one station. My attitude is, they will if that's what they have to do to see something they want to see. Anyway, UHF antennas are cheap and easy to install."

"You can put up UHF antennas in apartment windows," said Asher. "But what about the people on the wrong side of the building? UHF antennas have got to point at the station."

"That's why I say two stations," said Thad. "Two or three. Coming at the city from all directions."

"You'll still have people who can't pick up a distant UHF signal," said Asher. "It'll be blocked by buildings."

"So we lose some," said Thad. "Can we get the licenses?"

Asher nodded. "The competition for UHF channels is waning. But don't forget your community-service obligation."

"Easy enough," said Thad. "Before we go to our late-night scrambled broadcasting, we'll give the local folks community news, public-service stuff. The profit from these stations will come from our scrambled, prime-time shows . . . the adult entertainment. During the day, we can provide service-oriented, local broadcasting for the communities surrounding New York."

"Who's going to fund this one?"

"We are. I talked it over with Hildebrandt. I think we can fund this one ourselves—I mean, CCE and VWH, without the other Germans and certainly without the Japanese. Hildebrandt agrees. I'm going to let Gottschalk work on this one. He knows how to establish UHF stations. You work on the Runkle acquisition. That's the big one."

Four successive publishers had turned down Kathy's novel.

Charles came home one afternoon to find her squatting in the middle of the floor, slowly ripping up the thousand pages of typescript. The floor was covered with the litter of the rejected novel. This time she had received only a rejection slip, not even a form letter.

"Take a shower, and we'll do a round in bed," she said. "At least I do that pretty well."

Charles sat down heavily on the sofa. He was slimmer since his heart attack. And grayer. His physicians had assured him that the damage was not crippling and that he retained an almost normal life expectancy. Yet only gradually had he recovered his wit and optimism, and he hadn't recovered either in full measure. In two months, he had aged ten years.

"Kathy, I—"

"Please, Charles. No words of consolation, no Charles Lodge Johnson philosophy. Shit. I have to face it. I am not a writer."

"I won't bore you," he said wearily, "with tales of people who papered their walls with rejection slips and then—"

"Then wrote a million-dollar best-seller," she interrupted. "No, don't bore me with your stories."

"All right," he said. "Suppose it's true. Suppose you are no writer. You—"

"You never really thought I was," she interrupted.

He shook his head. "I think you have a—a certain facility for it. But I also think you make all the mistakes every would-be novelist makes. Worse, you insist on them."

She flung a handful of paper away from her. "What do I do now, Charles?" she asked tearfully.

"I believe you are doing precisely the right thing," he said. "It should be torn up. Now, if you have the courage, you will regard it as a learning experience, and you will start over, maybe, to write something readable and publishable."

Kathy, on her hands and knees, began to scoop the torn-up paper into a pile. "I've been living with you on the pretense that you were supporting a novelist engaged in literary works . . . in the noble process of creation. What pretense can I use now, Charles? Maybe it's time for me to get out."

"We don't live together on condition that you publish a novel, Kathy," said Charles soberly.

She stopped gathering paper and looked up into his face. "On what condition, then?" she asked with gentle bluntness.

"So far as I am concerned," he said, "you live here because I care for you. And, hopefully, because you care for me."

A tear squeezed down Kathy's cheek. "I do," she said.

"Fine. So that settles that. Shall we walk up to Tommy's and have a nice Italian dinner?"

"It's really stupid. I don't know why I do it."

"Anne—"

They sat over dinner in Le Shack, an exquisite small French restaurant in Cos Cob, about three miles from her home. Bert had come by train for the tête-à-tête. She had picked him up at the station, and before the last train left for Grand Central, she would drive him back and linger on the platform with him until the train arrived. She had vetoed his choice of wine, and they were sharing a bottle of vintage Bordeaux with a savory platter of beef, artichoke hearts, and mushrooms in a mysteriously spiced wine sauce.

"Why should I burden you," she asked, "with stories of my personal life? It must bore you half to death."

"Not at all," he said.

"You're Jewish, aren't you?" she asked.

"It depends on who you ask. The Nazis would have sent me up the chimney. My mother had me circumcised, and my father had me baptized." He chuckled quietly. "I refused to be bar mitzvahed *or* confirmed, thereby offending both families. My parents are still alive. I'm not exactly their favorite son. Frankly said, I have too much education to swallow either of their religions. I guess I'm an atheist."

She shrugged. "I understand. Thad and I don't make a point of it, but I suppose we're really atheists, too."

"Even though," said Bert, continuing his line of thought, "my father is a devout Presbyterian—"

Anne giggled softly. "I never heard of anyone being a devout Presbyterian."

"Even so, the mother of my child refused to marry me because she and her family consider me a Jew," said Bert. "So there's a hidden chapter from *my* personal life."

"You? . . . A child?"

"She graduates from high school this year. I see her two or three times a year."

"Bert, I'm sorry."

He shrugged, then smiled, examining his wine glass intently. "Personal lives," he said. "How was it Thoreau said it? 'The mass of men lead lives of quiet desperation.'"

Anne added, "And 'What is called resignation is confirmed desperation.'"

"So you have two sons. One thinks he wants to study for the priesthood . . . this son of two atheists. And the other is? . . ."

"Homosexual," she said. "He just dropped out of school—the State University of New York at Purchase—and is living with . . . How shall I say it? Is living with other young men of his own kind, in an apartment in Westchester. And, you know something? I'm not so upset about him. His grandmother is an artist. I'd like to think I am, too . . . through my photography. And so is Thaddy. He's working on a book of photographs. He has a publisher interested. He works in my darkroom occasionally. I've seen his pictures. They're going to shock the world, but I think he'll be recognized as a sensitive, expressive artist."

Bert turned his attention to his meal for a moment. Then he said, "Anne, you know I'm trying to figure out how Catlett Communications can finance all the things your husband is committing it to. You and I . . . well, it's an odd situation. You and I . . . did . . . what we did. And I hope we will again. My God, I don't want to abuse our—our feelings for each other. If you don't want to talk about business at all, just say so. I—"

"The subject seems to have more emotional impact for you than it does for me," she said. "Ask me anything you wish. If I don't want to answer, I won't." She smiled impishly. "I don't even promise I won't lie to you."

Bert drew a small notepad from his jacket pocket. "I'm sorry," he said. "The notebook looks a little dramatic, I suppose, but I want to be accurate about these figures. Catlett Broadcast Services—CATSERV—is offering sixteen dollars and twenty-five cents for Runkle common. Your husband always insists on absolute control, reducing everybody else to minority status, so I figure he's got to have one hundred sixty-five million dollars available. And this amount he seems to have obtained from four banks in the States and our old friend the Frankenthaler Handelsbank. Ostensibly, that's all backed by pledging the total assets of CCE—stations, newspapers, and the typewriters on the secretaries' desks. Are you mortgaging the sum total to buy three midwestern television stations?"

"It's all in the various documents that have been made public," said Anne.

"The interest on the loans is going to run over twenty-five million," Bert protested.

"A tax-deductible business expense," she said. "Besides, the gross earnings from the three stations last year exceeded thirty million."

"And I suppose once CCE has control, it will put out an issue of preferred stock in Runkle," said Stouffer.

"The transaction is economically sound," said Anne.

Bert put down his notebook and pencil. He glanced around the restaurant for a moment, then returned his eyes to Anne. She was dispassionately fielding his questions, at least as well as Charles Lodge Johnson could have done. The distance between herself and her husband could not possibly be as great as she had indicated. He even began to wonder whether Thad Catlett, in fact, was fully aware that she was sitting here in Le Shack in Cos Cob, eating dinner with Bert Stouffer.

Bert rejected the thought. Catlett certainly did not know that she had tumbled with him on the couch in her studio a month ago.

"CCE brought suit in federal court to circumvent the Ohio state law on takeover bids," said Stouffer. "How in the world did your lawyers get that judge to rule so quickly?"

"Simply by pointing out that the whole purpose of the Ohio law was to delay a tender offer and give a target corporation time to organize resistance. Our counsel pointed out that if the court did not rule quickly, the whole purpose of the suit would be frustrated. When Runkle tried to sell the crown jewels, the judge saw the point immediately. He enjoined that tactic, then heard the case and ruled. The Sixth Circuit has refused to stay the order, so the bid is ongoing."

"Stay? When did you hear that the stay has been denied?"

"This afternoon," she said.

Bert shook his head. "You're ahead of me."

"I should hope so. It's my business. That is, it's mine as much as it is Thad's."

"When Runkle management learned of the tender offer, they tried to sell off two of the stations—to make the company less attractive to CCE and discourage the effort to buy its stock."

She nodded. "That's what's called trying to sell the crown jewels. It would have been a cheap little trick. It would have left the Runkle stockholders with only one station."

"And a cash-rich corporation," said Bert.

"No. They'd have taken stock or debentures from the purchasers," said Anne. "The tactic was bad for the stockholders but good for the managers. Clearly, they were only concerned about preserving their jobs, not protecting the stockholders. If it had worked, Thad would probably have withdrawn the tender offer, and the managers would have been left with their jobs."

"The word is that Catlett is going to acquire Runkle," said Stouffer. "They've tried to get Turner to give them a better offer, but he's not going to."

"So I hear."

"That puts your husband in the mainline of broadcasting. What'll he have now, seven stations?"

"Ten, if the FCC approves the application for the three New York-area UHF outlets."

"But the Runkle stations are mainline stations—VHF, two of them network affiliated. I don't suppose he'll scramble those at eleven o'clock."

"I haven't heard him say, but I suppose he won't."

"He's built himself quite an empire in twenty-five years. I understand he's bought a corporate jet."

"You might be surprised to learn something, Bert. He visits every one of his newspapers and stations at least once a month. He keeps a personal hand in everything. Can you imagine how much time he was spending at La Guardia Airport? The jet is stationed at Westchester Airport, ten minutes from our home. It's not a perk; it's a necessity."

"Freedom of the press *does* pay," mused Bert, "—if you're an owner."

She dismissed the subject by focusing her attention on her plate, loading her fork with beef and artichoke heart. She gulped down the food and sipped some wine.

Bert stuffed his small notebook back into his inside jacket pocket. "The food here is excellent," he said.

"They are Belgian. I mean, the people who run the restaurant. I come here often, often alone. Thanks for keeping me company."

He glanced at his watch. "My pleasure," he said.

"You don't need to be at the railroad station for an hour and a half," she said. "I . . . uh . . . I'd invite you to the house, except that my good Catholic son Richard is there, wide awake and reproving."

"Where does he think you are?"

"At the country club. Maybe after dinner we could go for a drive. We might find someplace where we can pull off the road and . . ."

"Like a couple of high school kids," said Bert.

Her face was flushed. He could almost look through her eyes into the image in her mind. She would be pure pleasure, performing what she was envisioning, what had brought the color to her cheeks. But— My God, why?

SEVEN

Colin Fleming crushed his cigarette in the great overflowing ashtray on his desk, grabbed his hat and briefcase, and stalked out of his office, locking the door behind him. On his way out, he barked terse instructions to his secretary, then thrust his head into the office where Stan Ross hunched over an ancient manual typewriter, pecking out a story.

"Out for a while, Stan," he announced. "A short meeting, then lunch. Won't be back until mid-afternoon."

Stan Ross glanced up from his story and grunted an acknowledgment. Colin could be mysterious. He was off to a meeting, but he didn't say with whom. He was going to lunch afterward, but he didn't say where. So be it. Stan couldn't demand to be told. Colin was the bureau chief, and Stan, though second-in-command in the Frankfurt office of Reuters, was decidedly his junior. Colin had fifteen years on Stan, a pronounced sense of hierarchy, and a practiced instinct for status protection. One way to safeguard his status, Stan understood, was to withhold information from his subordinates.

Fleming sensed the unspoken musings behind Stan's grunt. For Fleming was an old hand. He'd been a subaltern in the army and knew how subalterns thought. He assumed Stan resented him a bit. But Fleming didn't care. Stan was a sharp young reporter, an American who knew his verbs and adjectives. Fleming would probably recommend him to be the next bureau chief. In fact, Fleming was secretly willing to hasten Stan's advancement by taking early retirement.

He might even retire this year if London didn't show the proper appreciation for the story he was working on. It was a bombshell he should be ready to explode in a few weeks. Just a few more weeks.

He stopped first at the bank—Frankfurter Landesbank—and made a withdrawal from the bureau's discretionary expense fund. Two thousand marks. He would have to explain that. He would gamble two thousand marks to find out whether this new source was gold or garbage. If he struck the mother lode, it would be worth two thousand *pounds*.

From the bank, he hurried to Prinz Friederich Strasse and into the pension grandly called Prinz Friederich Hotel. He climbed the stairs to the first floor, searched for the correct room, and knocked. The transaction was completed very quickly, very furtively, very nervously; he was out of the room in less than a minute. He scrambled down the stairs and stepped out on the street.

Colin Fleming looked at his watch. His timing was . . . Suddenly, his body seemed to explode. The pain was agonizing. Then it faded. So did the light.

From a window high in the room Colin Fleming had just left, Hanna Frank watched in horror. She had wanted to be sure he was a safe distance from the hotel before she followed. He had paused to check the time. And the man she was now staring at had shot him twice in the back. A young fellow, wearing a turtleneck sweater, carrying a brown paper bag—with the death pistol inside. He snatched up the Englishman's briefcase and walked rapidly but calmly away, leaving the brown paper bag on the street. He carried the briefcase with him, taking the documents she had just sold to the Englishman!

She had to risk returning to her flat. Her passport was there, as well as her bankbook and her key to the deposit box. She scooped these up frantically and grabbed a small, empty suitcase on her way out. She took no clothes, no toiletries. She fled the building through the service door at the rear. On the street, she stopped a taxi. The driver dropped her at the bank. She withdrew every mark she had, then opened her deposit box and packed her tapes in the suitcase. She quickly tabulated her capital: the Englishman's two thousand marks and another seven thousand three hundred from her bank account. She found a cab outside the bank; trembling with fright, she studied the driver to see if he resembled the sinister young man in the turtleneck sweater. Satisfied, she asked him to drive her to the railroad station.

Within half an hour after the death of Colin Fleming, Hanna Frank had escaped the city. Two days later Friederich Papen reported to the police that an employee of VWH was missing. He did not disclose what she had been doing for VWH, and the police added her name to a routine missing-persons list. Attractive young women, after all, often walked away from their jobs without notice.

The Federal Communications Commission issued licenses for three new UHF television stations in the New York metropolitan area. CCE put the stations—WYRK-NJ, WYRK-CT, and WYRK-LI—on the air by summer. The plan worked exactly as Thad had foreseen. The towns welcomed the stations; local merchants began immediately to buy the cheap television advertising. With one camera crew per station, the stations operated cheaply yet provided coverage of local events. WYRK-NJ even broadcast a few Little League baseball games and promised to broadcast high school football games in the fall. Otherwise, the programming was dominated by reruns, movies, and occasional concerts and documentaries purchased from public stations.

Eleven o'clock at night was the witching hour when the three stations changed personalities and switched to scrambled broadcasting, which continued until five the next morning.

The scrambled programs were the same as those tested and marketed in Miami and Dayton. They consisted heavily of English-dubbed specially edited movies from Hildebrandt's motion-picture studios in Germany.

The plots followed the same basic formula: attractive, well-scrubbed European men and women lived in fashionable upper middle-class homes, drove late-model cars, and spent their vacations in the Alps or along the Mediterranean. In the course of their adventures, they invariably managed to appear on the screen in various stages of undress throughout the film. Most of the movies were comedies; typically, a couple of guys stole a girl's bikini top, or maybe the bottom, too. She would chase after them, topless or nude, across beach, into car, down highway; a nude chase scene with laughs.

In the dramas, the villains were often radicals of the left, out to destroy the happy times of the middle class. In the end, the bad guys would be frustrated by the courage and cleverness of the young capitalists. The cast always seemed to have trouble keeping on their clothes. In a touch of sado-masochism, the heroine might be stripped and tied to a chair in a Red hideout. Invariably, the heavies would lose their pants during the chase and rescue scenes. Often, a busty proletarian girl, baring her breasts as a gesture of political defiance, would fall in love with one of the handsome middle-class heroes—and with his way of life and political philosophy. Then she would abandon radicalism for the good life, as they faded into the sunset.

CCE established a television studio on the Upper West Side, in an old warehouse; in this low-rent location, the company began to produce much of the broadcast fare for WMOA-TV, WDHA-TV, WYRK-NJ, WYRK-CT, and WYRK-LI.

146

An amateur striptease contest was taped in the studio, an hour-long, once-a-week program. Almost anyone with an acceptable figure, man or woman, could compete for a thousand-dollar prize and the right to return the following week as one of the featured strippers who opened and closed the show. All strippers were expected to remove all their clothes, although the tapes were edited for the Dayton station, where the contest ended a bit prematurely. The producer's only real problems were two: excluding prostitutes, addicts, and assorted oddballs; and achieving some kind of ethnic mix so that the show was not given over entirely to blacks and Hispanics. To solve the latter problem, he was compelled to hire some contestants, picking them up from cheap model agencies.

Oddly, *The Strip* was treated with a degree of seriousness in some newspapers and magazines. The *Times*:

> What's different, and curious, is that most of the strippers look like real young men and women, instead of like the painted, overcoiffed plastic female creatures that have come lately to dominate the pictorial features of *Playboy*. WYRK-NJ's strippers are not all young, not all slender, not all bosomy. What is more, we were surprised to see that some of them look genuinely embarrassed to find themselves standing stark naked in the front of a studio audience and the cold eye of the camera. Half the contestants are male, and some of them look as if they might faint before the time comes to scurry off camera and grab up something to cover themselves. Take a close look at the boy who brings in the box from the deli, or at the girl who checks you out at Finast. You may have seen him or her naked Tuesday night.

Naturally, articles like this boosted the show's ratings. One Tuesday night at midnight, Gollier Ratings found that eleven percent of New York families in the television audience were watching *The Strip*. For a scrambled UHF station, it was a coup.

Though this late-night broadcasting was scrambled and available only to paying subscribers, the programs were interrupted four

147

times an hour for two-minute commercial breaks. At first the only advertiser was the *Sentinel-American*. But within a few weeks, *The Strip* was fully sponsored—by an automobile agency, a chain of appliance stores, and a beer distributor.

Bill Gottschalk made a deal with an overextended Atlantic City casino operator to tape shows in the casino nightclub. The shows featured comics who relied on sex and scatology for their humor—which provoked raucous laughter—and a chorus line of six topless dancers. The *Live from Atlantic City* show—which wasn't live—drew a six percent rating on Wednesday nights. When Gottschalk preceded the show with fifteen minutes of instruction on the rules and odds of casino gambling games, the rating jumped to nine percent.

Bert accepted a martini from Kathy. It was a Sunday afternoon. The window air conditioners in Charles's apartment were losing the battle against the simmering summer heat that radiated from the asphalt streets below, and the granite and sandstone buildings surrounding.

Charles, in violation of his usual decorum, wore a knit golf shirt. Each time he saw Charles Lodge Johnson, Bert found the man thinner, grayer, more harried-looking. His great bald dome was pale, as if it had not been exposed to the summer sun. The girl was also a mystery to Stouffer. Like the shorts, she did not fit Charles's style. His wife, Bert remembered, had been a lofty blond: angular, cool, elegant. Kathy's contours pressed loosely against a white tank top and black shorts.

"Did you know Colin Fleming?" Bert asked Charles.

Charles shook his head. "I've talked to people who did. They don't think he was killed by a jealous husband."

"I didn't know him, either," said Bert.

"I understand he had something to do with breaking the Profumo case," said Charles. "But that's history."

Bert pointed at a book lying on the coffee table. "I see you have a copy of *Lifestyles*."

"I bought it," explained Kathy. "Curiosity got the best of me."

"May I?" Bert asked. He wished he hadn't mentioned it; having called attention to it, he was obliged to pick it up and look at it. The truth was, he had been given a copy, but he did not want Charles to know that. "I've heard a lot about it," said Bert.

"You know, of course, who Frank Teltac is," said Kathy.

He knew, all right. Frank Teltac was Frankie Thad Catlett, Jr. The book was a fat quality-bound paperback. It was a study, mostly in photographs, with poetic captions, of the lives of young homosexual men. They were portrayed in all the elements of their lives: working, studying, playing, cooking, cleaning, listening to music, watching television, going out together, staying in together, sleeping together, and—more artistically than graphically—engaged in carnal activities. Thaddy appeared in a score of the pictures, including sexual poses.

Bert had never seen Thaddy but had formed a mental image from his mother's remarks; he was surprised, therefore, when he first saw a picture of him. The boy was tall as his father—well over six feet— and lanky, with an intimation of the physical. He had a prominent Adam's apple, a long, bony solemn face, and dark straight hair that stood high above his forehead and toppled carelessly to his brows.

In one full-page picture, Thaddy sat naked in an artistic pose on a sheepskin rug. Beside him was another naked youth flexing his muscles. Anne had identified him as Alan, one of Thaddy's roommates in the White Plains apartment. The two youths appeared tautly self-conscious, with silly expressions.

Another half-dozen photographs featured a stocky, big-muscled, bullnecked, block-jowled eighteen-year-old boy; first in a pair of gym shorts, heaving a steel shot; then in a jock strap, grinning awkwardly; and finally without the jock strap, subdued and embarrassed, but visibly proud of his body.

Bert happened to know this sequence had stirred a bitter controversy. Although the boy had signed a release, his parents were humiliated and threatened to sue. Anne had shown Bert these pictures a month before the book was published.

149

The book had been widely reviewed. The comments covered a broad range:

—"In *Lifestyle* the pornographer attains a new level of arrogance."

—"Honest, if nothing else, it contributes to our understanding of the eccentric lives of these young men."

—"Warm, caring, sensitive—in every way an artistically successful portrayal of a way of life chosen by millions."

Thaddy had been paid an advance of only two thousand dollars for his book, but advance sales had moved the publisher to do a second printing even before publication date, and now it was in its third printing.

"I hardly need ask what your boss thinks of this," Bert said to Charles.

"Actually, he's rather proud of his son," said Charles. "He could wish the subject matter were otherwise, but the boy's talent as an artist has achieved enviable recognition."

"And Mrs. Catlett?" Bert asked. He knew the answer, but he wanted to hear what Charles would say.

"Anne has a highly developed aesthetic sense," said Charles. "The boy could not have done the book without her cooperation."

"I met her, you know," said Bert. "When you were in the hospital. Would you mind hearing a question about her?"

Charles shrugged.

"How closely is she in touch with the business? How much time does she devote to it?"

"She is erratic," said Charles. "Sometimes she's closely in touch. At other times she seems to ignore it. She is less interested in the day-to-day operations than in corporate matters, particularly acquisitions." Charles turned down the corners of his mouth and shook his head. "She owns as much of the company as Thad does, you know."

"Does he confide in her?"

Charles sighed. "You are skating on thin ice; those are personal questions that I am not going to answer. I think he does—but erratically. Copies of corporate documents are sent to her for her approval." Charles smiled. "Her packages of documents are sometimes referred to as 'the queen's boxes.'"

The Federal Communications Commission hearing dragged on into Friday afternoon. Thad was not called as a witness until after three o'clock. It was not a regulatory hearing, but rather a public hearing to consider whether certain judicial decisions should alter existing FCC regulations. Thad had been invited to testify about the impact of his company's apparent triumph over the Runkle tactic to invoke Ohio state law as a defense against acquisition.

"You will understand, honorable ladies and gentlemen, that I am advised by counsel not to testify about pending litigation. I hope it will be possible to answer your questions without so doing."

One commissioner, noting Kenneth Asher at Thad's side, inquired dryly, "May I assume, Mr. Catlett, that Mr. Asher is not your counsel?" The question was pointed, in the shape of a needle.

Thad ignored this attempt to embarrass them. "No," he said, "Mr. Asher is my vice president for strategic planning. Mr. Bragg is my counsel."

"Continue your statement, Mr. Catlett," said the chairman wearily.

"Mr. Chairman, I believe the decision of the Sixth Circuit Court of Appeals, if it stands, is a positive development in communications law. Acquisition of licensed broadcasting stations by companies such as mine, tending to concentrate those licenses in the hands of fewer and fewer corporations, is a matter of proper concern for this commission. The public interest is best served by a variety of broadcasters—provided that they are financially sound and otherwise competent. But whether a given acquisition is in the public interest should be a matter for this commission to decide, applying laws passed by Congress. It should not be a matter for the fifty state legislatures to meddle in."

All day the hearing room had been quiet. Now the television cameramen, in their assigned positions, began to adjust their cameras to capture the testimony of F. Thad Catlett. He was accustomed to being in the eye of a public storm, but his dramatic acquisition of television stations, along with his controversial adult programming, had made him a lightning rod. In the corridor outside the hearing room, when he ducked out for a cigarette, a woman reporter had tried to question him about his son's book.

Back in the hearing room, the needle-wielding commissioner inquired sweetly, "What about state and local control over the broadcasting of pornography, Mr. Catlett?"

"I have no opinion on that," Thad responded curtly. "I have never broadcast pornography and don't intend to."

"If that is your answer, then it raises another question," said the commissioner. "Would you enlighten the commission. What is your definition of pornography?"

"I'm going to rule that line of questioning out of order," snorted the chairman. "Particularly at this hour on a Friday afternoon."

Ten minutes later, in the corridor outside, Kenneth Asher congratulated Thad on an effective presentation. "Of course you'll never be rid of the militant right," he said. "They're going to hound you about what they call pornography."

"It's curious," said Thad with a rueful smile. "I've been a conservative all my life. My newspapers have always supported the conservative cause. Yet I'm a heretic to some of these people. I'm not doctrinally pure." He shook his head. "Well, to hell with them. You going back to New York with me? There should be a car waiting outside. The plane is at National."

"No thanks. I'm spending the weekend in Washington. My wife has agreed to let me stay in her apartment, believe it or not. But you might want to offer the congresswoman over there a ride to the airport."

"Who?"

"Congresswoman Jennie Paget," said Asher, nodding toward a dark-haired woman who was engaged in earnest discussion with a commission lawyer. "She represents the Thirty-seventh District of

New York. She's probably going home to Scarsdale for the weekend. She's a power on the House Committee on Interstate and Foreign Commerce. Not a bad person to know."

"Introduce me," Thad asked.

Asher walked over to the woman. "Excuse me, Mrs. Paget," he said. "Kenneth Asher of Catlett Communications. If you're going to National, Mr. Catlett has a car picking him up. Cabs may be scarce."

The congresswoman turned toward Asher and smiled distractedly, uncertain whether he were brashly interrupting her or offering a legitimate kindness. Her quick, automatic smile changed to an easy, curious frown as she began to recognize Asher.

"Kenneth Asher, Mrs. Paget," he said again. "I'm with Catlett Communications Enterprises. I represent Mr. Catlett over there. His car and driver are picking him up to take him to National Airport. If you need transportation . . ."

She glanced at Thad. "Oh, yes. Of course. I heard his testimony," she said. "Yes, I have a plane to catch. Thank you for the offer."

She nodded at the FCC attorney in a manner that suggested dismissal more than farewell. Then she stooped to pick up her attaché case.

Thad watched the encounter between Asher and the congresswoman. After retrieving her case, she strode briskly toward him, allowing a smile to develop and extending her hand as she approached.

"Mr. Catlett. Jennie Paget. Thanks for the offer. Catching a cab out there right now could be a bitch."

Thad returned the smile. "It's a pleasure to meet you. I've seen your name in the papers often."

"In *your* newspapers," she replied with good humor. "And I still believe in a free press."

Thad reached for her attaché case, but she waved him off and started toward the elevators. He grinned at Asher and hurried after her.

Jennie Paget. He seemed to recall that she was a Democrat. Even on television, where he remembered seeing her once taking part in a panel discussion, she came off as she did now: spirited but brusque, her speech direct and clipped. She was not taller than five feet four, and her energetic little body was taut—probably the product of disciplined exercise. Her dark hair was carelessly coiffed, medium length, as if it had been hastily combed once this morning and, thereafter, tousled by the wind and perhaps by an impatient hand run through it. She had touched her lips with lipstick this morning but wore no other discernible makeup. Her eyes were beautiful; tiny flecks of brown and green floated in pools of blue. Otherwise, she could not be described as beautiful—unless it was hidden behind her look of crisp, assertive efficiency.

When she settled in the back seat of the car and crossed her legs, he saw they were shapely and strong.

"This city gets oppressive in the summer," she said, "like the inside of a boiler." A tiny bead of perspiration appeared just beneath her lower lip, but she ignored it. "I don't think I will ever get accustomed to it."

"Do you mind if I light a cigarette?" he asked, reaching for a pack.

"To tell you the truth, I'd appreciate it if you didn't. Not in the closed car, please."

He withdrew his hand from the cigarette pack.

She gazed out the window, with frequent, furtive side glances at him.

He was aware of her secret appraisal. All his life women had caressed him with their eyes, and he had come to expect it. At age forty-nine, he peered out at the world from beneath overhanging brows. His rugged face, though unchiseled, was a pleasing tangle of deep lines. Though he did not often smile, the lift of his brows and the merry glint in his eyes betrayed an active sense of humor.

"Are you taking the shuttle?" she asked.

"The company jet," he said.

"A capitalist."

"A pirate," he said. "Corporate raider. Business buccaneer."

154

"I'm not trying to abolish capitalism. I'm not opposed to the free enterprise system. I'm not one of *those* Democrats."

"In that event, can I offer you a ride to New York? We'll be landing in Westchester. I live ten minutes from the airport. My driver can drop me off and take you wherever you want to go."

She contemplated the invitation for a moment. "Members of Congress should be careful about riding around the country in corporate jets; but it's too damned hot and I'm too damned tired to worry about it."

They spent as much time on the taxiways at National as it would take flying to Westchester Airport. But the interior of the plane was cool. The pilots laid out a tray of hors d'oeuvres, and the bar was stocked with an assortment of liquors, wines, and soft drinks. Jennie Paget shared Thad's taste for Scotch. He poured stiff drinks, and they munched on the hors d'oeuvres.

"Frankly, Mr. Catlett, I'm glad you don't have a newspaper in my district. I suspect I'd be a target."

"I'm glad, too, Mrs. Paget," he said. "It would be painful to oppose so charming a liberal."

"Like hell," she laughed.

He lifted his brows. "If we are going to be so candid, can we drop the Mr. Catlett? It's Thad. . . ."

"Jennie." She glanced out at the airliners taxiing ahead of them. "I like your life-style, Thad."

"It's hard to keep up with the life-styles in Congress, but I try."

"Some of us oppose all the perks and pay raises."

"What's this? Your second term?"

"Third," she said. "I'm one of the Young Turks in Congress. I think your newspapers call us Turkeys. I was just thirty when I arrived in Washington. They put me on the Agriculture Committee."

"Another Scotch?" he asked, noting that she had drunk her first one as quickly as he had his.

"Thank you," she said. "It helps to wash down the week's frustrations."

Thad's curiosity wasn't satisfied. "What are you, thirty-six? Third term in Congress. Since you are *Mrs.* Paget, I suppose there is a *Mr.* Paget."

"Have you ever heard of the law firm Davis, Polk & Wardwell?" she asked. "My husband is a partner at Davis, Polk."

"I write editorials against lawyers, too," he said, his eyes reflecting bemusement.

"And lawyers sue newspapers," she retorted in the same spirit. Then: "You've looked at me for the last hour," she said. "What do you think? Would I be content to sit home in Scarsdale and have babies?"

"No, and I won't add the comment that maybe you'd be better off. I can see you wouldn't."

"Thank you for excluding yourself from ninety-two percent of the population," she said, lifting her glass and taking a big swallow of the Scotch.

They were distracted and looked out the window as the Falcon jet swung around into the runway. They remained silent as it settled on the runway, then surged forward and rose swiftly into the air.

Thad took a long hard look at the congresswoman. Then he blurted out, "God, I can't see you, Jennie, puttering around the kitchen, running a household. If there's one thing you're not, it's domestic."

"And you don't object?"

"No. Absolutely not."

"Christ!" She reached across the little fold-down table that separated them and closed her hand over his. "Thad, you're either a liar or a real man."

He turned his hand over and squeezed hers. "Count me among your admirers, Jennie Paget," he said.

While Thad was enroute home from Washington, Anne received

the dire call from Texas that his father had died. She packed bags for them both and intercepted Thad as he deplaned. The Falcon was hastily refueled, and they flew off for Midland. They spent a painful three days in west Texas. In oppressive heat and dust, they endured the protracted rituals of death.

When the ordeal was over, Thad convinced his mother she should return with him to New York. The prospect of a jet flight, more than her real wish to leave the ranch, intrigued her. Alma Catlett, at seventy-two, took her first airplane ride.

Assured a lucrative return on *Lifestyles* and recognized as a sensitive photographer of the male form, Thaddy opened Frank Teltac Studio in a loft on the Upper East Side and began to attract clients from the theater. Late in July, he and Alan moved from White Plains to the studio, where they lived in the same space where they worked. Alan developed film, made prints, scheduled appointments, and became Thaddy's business manager.

In August, Anne flew to London for an exhibition of her photographs at a Soho Square gallery. Her mother's book, *Emily Baynes Justin, American Sculptor*, had just been published in England. Anne included in her show additional pictures of her mother; some contrasted her mother's gnarled, wrinkled clay-encrusted hands with the sleek young body of her model. The *Times* called the show "an exquisite display of the artistic power of the thoughtful and perceptive camera worker."

Anne's two sons and her mother-in-law, having never traveled outside the United States, decided to accompany her on the trip. Alma Catlett was childlike in her fascination with everything she saw. While Anne and Thaddy stayed close to the galleries, Richard and his grandmother visited the many tourist attractions. She chronicled the odyssey with Polaroid pictures, which she spread all over the hotel suite.

Anne had also arranged for a smaller second-floor gallery to display a collection of Thaddy's male nudes. Of his work, the *Times* said: "Although realistic to the ultimate degree, the photographs are not obscene. It is a striking exhibit, one well worth a visit." His pictures were for sale, as hers were not, and he sold almost all his photographs, for fifty pounds apiece. Exultantly, he told his mother that he wanted to live in London. As soon as he could make the arrangements, he said, he was going to move there. Meanwhile, he met with two London publishers who were interested in publishing an English edition of *Lifestyles*.

While his family was taking London by storm, Thad moved his corporate headquarters to a floor of the Pan Am Building. The old downtown building remained headquarters for his newspaper publishing enterprises, but his broadcasting enterprises, together with the corporate management, moved uptown. "For the first time in twenty-eight years," the *Times* commented, "F. Thad Catlett will sit in an office removed from the clatter of a newsroom."

He had rushed the move so that Wilhelm Hildebrandt, paying his first visit to CCE, might be received in more impressive new offices, rather than the cramped, littered downtown offices. Thad summoned his station managers, assistant managers, and news managers to New York for a weekend meeting with Hildebrandt and himself.

The new headquarters contained a large conference room, where the managers assembled. A beaming Hildebrandt spoke to them. "I came here for a business meeting. I did not come to confer on editorial policies for the CCE television stations. Although I am Thad's junior partner in some of his enterprises, the editorial policies of our broadcast stations and our newspapers are matters for his discretion."

Thad sat at the head of the table, sucking on a cigarette and scanning the notes he would use when he rose to speak. Hildebrandt had suppressed his own domineering nature and had gone out of his way to be deferential. Yet Thad couldn't help being jarred by the word *our—our* stations, *our* newspapers. It was true that Verlagsgruppe Wilhelm Hildebrandt owned forty percent of Catlett Communications Enterprises, but Thad had not yet reconciled himself to thinking of CCE as anything less than his property—his and Anne's.

Hildebrandt resumed, meticulously reading his speech from a small notebook. "But if I may be excused for being presumptuous, I would like to suggest some broad guidelines that your European partners hope will be considered.

"First and foremost, we believe that we who are in the business of disseminating information to the public have a responsibility to support liberty and democracy on both sides of the Atlantic. We hope that our news policies will always reflect a positive view of how free people live and what they achieve, in dramatic contrast to the way of life imposed on the populations of the so-called socialist countries. We, your European associates, believe in responsible capitalism."

The station managers, from Miami, Tampa, Greensboro, Dayton, and the three New York area stations, applauded timidly. Hildebrandt continued for another twenty minutes, charming them with humorous little asides and a self-deprecating reference to his wartime service in a German U-boat. He left them surprised and a bit flattered that this distinguished German executive had prepared a speech for them.

Then Thad spoke. . . .

"Bob and Len and Dick know how we solved a little problem in Dayton. I want all of you to know how we did it. I need hardly tell you that the whole broadcast industry faces a serious challenge from certain vocal religious sects, not only that we broadcast hour after hour of their programming but that we do it on the basis of what they call 'the Christian discount.' We had that problem in Dayton. Our predecessor management had been unable to resist the pressures, I guess. Anyway, we were overloaded with that programming. Now, the Christian fundamentalists may be wild with

159

enthusiasm, but that audience is small, and once the evangelist is off the air, they don't stay with you. Televangelism was costing us money.

"I flew out to Dayton three weeks ago, and we sat down with the members of the Dayton Ministerial Association. We offered the ministers two hours every Sunday morning, free. We will broadcast from their churches on a rotating basis, on a schedule that they set up. A rabbi asked if we could do something for his people, so we gave the Jewish congregations a Saturday hour. They are not going to want to broadcast services apparently, but some films and lectures on Jewish history and culture. The new religious programming began last Sunday. As of that day, we cancelled all the televangelists—I mean, all of them. We are meeting our community obligation in a more effective way, by broadcasting the services of mainline churches."

Thad paused and smiled faintly. "I need hardly tell you, the Bible-bangers are shrieking their heads off. You have anything to add, Bob?"

The station manager flashed a triumphant grin. "They threatened to sue us. They threatened to boycott any business that advertises with us. We've simply told them to talk to the Ministerial Association. They can get on the schedule with the other denominations. One of them, who calls himself Brother Simon Lackwater, protested that the Ministerial Association is nothing but a front for secular humanism, that it is infiltrated with communists."

Thad lit a cigarette while the Dayton man talked. Then Thad resumed.

"All of you," he said, "have received a written policy statement about the coverage of demonstrations. I mean that as a directive. With the rare exception—which you in your discretion may make—our cameras and microphones are not available to demonstrators interrupting public events or blocking public streets. If in the judgment of our reporter on the scene, the demonstrators have any kind of rational point, he is to invite them to designate a spokesperson, and that spokesperson may come to our studios and tape a statement. No screaming. No mob scenes."

Thad fingered through the policy statement and stopped at the third page. "Let me read a few sentences. 'Our stations will air varying points of view, *including opinions with which management does not agree.* Opinions may not, however, be screamed at our microphones, and opinions expressed with excessive profanity will not be broadcast. From time to time, our stations will broadcast invitations to people with points of view they wish to express on the air. They should be instructed to contact our stations and ask for interviews. Their statements should be brief and, if possible, should accompany our newscasts. Reasonable requests will be met.'

"It is our intention to increase, not diminish, public access to our broadcast facilities. But let me emphasize. . . . I do not want our microphones and cameras constantly pointed at unwashed hooligans who are not even articulate enough to explain what they are protesting."

On Saturday evening, he invited Hildebrandt and his managers to dinner at The Four Seasons. Then he met alone with Hildebrandt in his apartment until it was time to drive to the airport.

"We are doing well," Hildebrandt said. "I am pleased. We may not agree on everything, but what two strong-minded businessmen would? Please don't be antagonized by what you are likely to hear from some of our investor-partners. Some of them are impatient. They don't understand why the Runkle acquisition has not been completed. Also, I think some of them expected the DunCast stations would double their revenues in six months. Anything less . . ." He shrugged.

"We have had the DunCast stations ten months," said Thad. "Revenues are up sixteen percent. That means their value as assets has increased more than twice that. It's not bad."

"I serve as a buffer between you and one or two of our partners," said Hildebrandt. "You should be aware . . . your strong statement that you would make your own editorial policies was the source of some angry comment. But don't let it concern you. I stand between you and those people."

The following Friday, Thad placed a telephone call to Congresswoman Jennie Paget in Washington. He was closeted with Asher and his secretary, who was taking some notes, when the call was completed.

"Jennie . . . listen. The Falcon will be at Washington National this afternoon and has to deadhead back. It will be coming back empty. I thought you might like to ride to Westchester in comfort."

"Thad Catlett, you are my favorite Republican," she laughed.

"There's plenty of Scotch on board."

"I just had an encounter with the Speaker that will require a dose of Scotch. How can I thank you?"

"I'll tell you how. My family's in England. Your husband's in San Francisco. . . ."

"How in the world did you know that?"

"I'm in the news business. We have our sources. But I'm working up to an invitation. I find myself alone at dinner time, and it occurred to me that you might be alone, too. Would you? . . ."

"I would like that. Where?"

"Why not some place in the city? I'll have my car drive you in from Westchester."

"With a post stop for a change of clothes," she said.

"Fine. I'll arrange an eight o'clock reservation. The Falcon will be at National by four. I'll wait here at the office until you arrive."

He thought he detected a hint of excitement and expectancy in her voice. He smiled inwardly. He hoped he was right.

"Trish," he turned to his secretary. "Tell the pilots to have the Falcon at Washington National by four o'clock. They're to bring Congresswoman Paget back to Westchester. Then have Frank pick her up and drive her in here."

162

The secretary departed to make the arrangements. Thad smiled slyly at Asher.

"Well," said Asher. "This appears to be lobbying beyond the call of duty."

"You suggested I get acquainted with her. She could have some influence on any attempt in Congress to block our acquisitions."

"How did you know her husband is in San Francisco?"

"Lou Pittocco. He checks out the man's schedule from time to time . . . strictly on the casual."

"And the Falcon to Washington to pick her up," Asher chuckled.

"Lobbying has its expenses," said Thad dryly, returning his attention to the papers before him.

He took Jennie to dinner at La Grenouille that night. As he drove her home to Scarsdale, he asked if she would keep him company at dinner again Sunday evening.

He picked her up late Sunday afternoon and drove her to an inn near West Cornwall, Connecticut. They walked along the tumbling stream by the inn before they entered.

"Oh, God," she sighed after the waiter had left two double Scotches on their table. "This place is lovely. You've brought me to a romantic spot, Thad. I find that a little disconcerting."

"Why?"

"Well, we had dinner in New York in a very public way. Tonight we're away, alone; nobody knows where we are. It's a different kind of meeting, Thad. And I agreed to it."

"It's exploratory," he said.

She was wearing a gray cashmere dress with a strand of pearls around her neck. She fingered the pearls. "I'm almost afraid to ask what you think we're exploring," she said.

"Possibilities," he said.

She nodded. "Ummm . . ." She looked directly into his eyes. "I don't know, Thad. I can't think of anything to say. This isn't your usual political situation."

"What if I asked you to go to bed with me tonight?"

She shook her head. "I won't. I won't."

163

"Do you want to?"

"Damn you! I wish I could say hell, no. Even so, I won't."

"I want to, too," he said. "But like you, I'm not sure it's a good idea."

"Maybe you shouldn't ask me to dinner again."

"I'm not listening to you, Jennie," he said. He slipped his hand over hers.

"I suppose I can always say no."

"Yes. But . . . let's not think about the complications." He squeezed her hand gently. "Right now, let's just enjoy the evening."

A few minutes later, she left the table to go to the women's room. As he watched her walking through the inn, making her circuitous way around tables and displays of old New England farm implements, he rubbed his chin hard with his fist. That beauty he had looked for and had not seen at first . . . It was there. He saw it now. God, but she was appealing!

EIGHT

She had brought her own bottle of rye, and she had emptied it down to the middle of the label. ("Take out your pen and mark the bottle if you want to write about how much I drink.") Then she was sick. ("Honest to God. I'm not a big drinker. See what this has done to me.") She slipped into a deep sleep on his couch. He did not want to leave her alone, so he sat at his typewriter and worked while she slept. The murmur of the electric typewriter the ringing of the telephone, had not wakened her. Then . . .

"Oh, Bert, Jesus Christ! I've made a fool of myself. I don't eat breakfast, and I didn't have lunch, and—"

"It's okay, Anne. It's okay. Forget it. You are looking at a fellow victim. I might even have been a success in life . . . had it not been for my love affair with the martini."

She rubbed her eyes and sat up. "Strange . . . I feel okay now. Nap . . . Jesus, Bert! What the hell time is it?"

"Not yet five."

165

She sighed loudly. "Well . . . God bless Alma. She's my mother-in-law. Lives with us now. She's going to buy a house in Greenwich; but as of five o'clock tonight, she lives with us. She can fix Richard's dinner."

"When's he leaving?" Bert asked.

"Next week. Harvard. He's a freshman at Harvard. The apple of his father's eye—straight as an arrow, button-down shirts, enrolled at Harvard."

"Richard's entering the priesthood, isn't he? I didn't know Harvard had a divinity school."

"Father MacDuffy told Richard a year or two at Harvard—even four years and a degree—would do him no harm. Richard, I'm afraid, is a bit pliable. His father wanted him to enroll, his priest placed an imprimatur on the idea, and so Richard is going to Harvard. I'll tell you something, Bert. I wish he had Thaddy's backbone. I hate my older son's life-style. Thad is alternately outraged and embarrassed. But Thaddy had the goddamned courage to live the way he wants to live, to go against Thad and me and society, if necessary."

Bert left his typewriter—where his writing had begun to bore him—and wandered to the window. He gazed down on the heavy traffic, which gave off waves of heat and fumes and noise. "You tell me too much about yourself and your family," he protested. "As a journalist, I want to collect all the facts I can gather about the Catlett family, but I don't feel right about using anything I hear from you."

"Bull . . ." she dismissed his moralizing. "Anyway, I've got to have something to eat."

"You won't get home in time for dinner," he said. "How would you like to try a little neighborhood Hungarian place a couple of blocks over?"

"At seven o'clock?" she asked. "What can you do for me at five o'clock?"

"Microwave a wiener or two," he said. "Thirty-second supper. I've got buns. May even have some mustard, too."

"Sounds marvelous," she said.

She ate two hotdogs but drank a beer with them, which did not impress him as a positive development for the evening. As she wolfed her food, she addressed the next subject on her mind. She wanted to go to bed with him. She began to undress while still munching the last bite. Then she stretched out, naked, curling and smiling coyly just as Megan had done.

Anne was the least inhibited woman Bert had ever known. She exhausted both of them. This was the first time they were under no time pressure, no apprehension of interruption. She laughed when finally he rolled away from her and complained he was finished for the day.

She blew a noisy sigh, letting her lips flutter. "Lord, I could get really stupid about you."

Bert pulled her into his arms and pressed her face to his shoulder. "I'm the one who's doing something stupid," he said. "Anne, you . . . I think you should know . . . I have to tell you. . . . I'm really suspicious that your husband and Wilhelm Hildebrandt are—"

"It's all legal and moral," she quickly responded. "I've been watching closely. My father is watching."

Bert persisted. "Even if it's legal and moral, isn't it possible that it's a bad game? Bad for the public interest. Bad for the national interest. Bad . . ."

"What?" she asked, raising her head. "What's so bad?"

"What are they up to? What do they have in mind? Truthfully," he asked.

"Making money," she said.

He shook his head. "There's more, something more. They're empire building. They want power. Power. Some men will do for power what they'd never do for money."

"So Thad's an ambitious man. Since God's job is taken, he'll settle for being an emperor."

"But who will be the emperor?" Bert asked. "Will it be Catlett or

167

Hildebrandt? The Germans aren't pouring hundreds of millions of dollars into American television broadcasting just to make Thad Catlett the king of television."

"What do you expect to find, Bert? The German investors will make loads of money—more than Thad and I get out of it. They're loaded with investment capital. They're looking for someplace to put it to work. Where are they going to go? Africa? The great American boob tube is a far better risk than King Solomon's mines."

"Maybe . . . But it's my job to ask questions."

She pulled back from him. "And I'll answer them, Bert . . . if I can. Any questions at all."

"If you're not willing to give us your name . . ."

"I will give you my name once I know you are interested."

". . . and the name of the company from which you say you took these documents."

She glanced nervously out the window. She could see the Wall, grim and menacing. She could see past it into East Berlin; her eyes were drawn to the television tower that stood like an obscene finger over everything in that dreary half of the city.

"If I tell you . . ." She stopped short, shaking her head stubbornly.

The man was at the end of his patience. "I must know who you are and how you got access to the documents before I can evaluate them. If we decide not to use your materials, we will hold your name absolutely confidential, as I have promised repeatedly. If we decide to use your materials, then we will have to reach an agreement. Most likely, your identity will be obvious, anyhow, from the materials you say you have. You had access. Now you are no longer there. We can put the pieces of the puzzle together." He shrugged. "If you don't trust us, we cannot deal with you. The decision is yours, Fräulein."

The woman was full of doubt and fear. Not knowing the news business, she was uncertain whom to go to. Could she trust this stranger to protect her anonymity? She knew vaguely that above this man were superiors, any one of whom could overrule him after she had exposed herself to a widening circle. For days, she had hung immobilized, but she was driven by desperation.

She heaved a sigh of resignation. "My name is Hanna Frank," she said, biting her lip. "I worked for Verlagsgruppe Wilhelm Hildebrandt."

The man's eyebrows rose. *"Hildebrandt?"*

"Yes, Herr Prager. My documents contain confidential information about VWH and companies that do business with it. Also, I have information about individual businessmen."

Viktor Prager went to the door and latched it. He picked up his telephone and gave instructions to hold his calls. He had been a journalist all his life, and he sensed this young woman was about to lay in his lap the coup that had always eluded him. He ran his hand across his close-cut, bristly gray hair and began to pack his pipe.

"You can trust me, Fräulein Frank," he said. "And I can speak for our organization. We will grant you confidentiality; I mean, we will protect your identity. So now, tell me what you have and how you got it."

"To begin with, Herr Prager, I was employed by the BND for three years. . . . I was trained by them. . . . Then Herr Hildebrandt offered me a position with his company, doing much the same work I did for the BND. There were also some assignments. I don't think the government of the Federal Republic would have asked."

Prager was scribbling notes. "Commercial espionage?" he asked.

"I don't think I would dignify it with that term," she said. "As you may know, VWH maintains a gasthaus on the grounds of its corporate complex outside Frankfurt. Six of the rooms are equipped with hidden television cameras that can make videotapes of the guests. All the rooms are also equipped with hidden microphones—very sophisticated ones, I can tell you, that no one would ever find."

"The telephones?"

"They were tapped by highly sophisticated equipment. Many businessmen routinely carry in their briefcases devices that can detect a tap on the line. The wires pass through sensor coils that pick up and amplify the slight electromagnetic radiation generated by active telephone lines."

"You *have* some of these videotapes?"

"No. I didn't have access to those. One of my functions was to enter the rooms while the guests were attending meetings. I would photograph the documents they carried in their briefcases. I photographed tens of thousands of documents over a four-year period. I—" She allowed herself a slight smirk. "In four years, I encountered one locked briefcase I could not open."

"You've brought some of these copies?"

"I have brought *all* of these copies. I developed the film myself and made the prints, in the VWH laboratory. I used the video camera in the laboratory to copy all the prints. I have those tapes . . . cartridges, each one with thousands of images. A few of the images are photos; the gentlemen's wives and mistresses probably."

"Do you have *any* idea what those thousands of documents are?" asked Prager, his original enthusiasm diminishing. He laid down his pen, stopped taking notes, and puffed his pipe.

"Documents that VWH thinks worth copying," she said. "Documents that give them an unethical advantage over the businessmen they deal with. The copies are kept in locked files in a room very near Herr Hildebrandt's office. I can help you to understand some of them. In some instances, I knew what was going on."

"You had access to other—"

"I was employed also as a hostess, Herr Prager. That would be the euphemistic word. Sometimes I slept with the company's business guests. The cameras videotaped the sexual activity. I am a star of Herr Hildebrandt's secret films. I cannot show you any of my performances. As I said, I had no access to them."

"Give me a name," said Prager. "Who did you sleep with?"

Hanna didn't hesitate. "Herr Catlett, the American newspaper publisher. He is the last man I was assigned to."

"F. Thad Catlett?"

She nodded. "The American."

"You have documents of his?"

"Yes. They are reports to him about various American broadcast companies and the difficulties in trying to acquire them. One of the documents is a report about the American presidential election in 1988. It contains derogatory information about some of the likely candidates. The Catlett newspapers will probably accuse one Republican of embezzlement. They have evidence that he, as they put it, 'skims' money off the gifts sent by the pious to a religious fund. I don't understand all the American terms fully."

"What did Catlett talk about in bed?"

"About my English. About my German accent. He talked about how hard it had been for him to get rid of his Texas accent. He was sent away from home as a child, to a private school where his strange accent was ridiculed. He struggled to rid himself of it. He gave me some examples of how he used to pronounce certain English words."

"But he did make love with you?"

"Oh, yes."

"And it was taped?"

She nodded affirmatively.

Prager drew on his pipe and blew white smoke up in a pencil-thin stream. He studied the dissipating wisp of smoke intently. "Why did you leave VWH, Fräulein?"

Hanna stiffened her back. "You are aware that Herr Colin Fleming, the English journalist, the Reuters man in Frankfurt, was murdered."

"Yes. I knew Colin. He was my friend."

"Well . . . He was shot as he left my hotel. We had met secretly in a hotel room. I gave him some documents . . . prints off videotape. Two minutes later, on the street beneath the window where I witnessed the whole thing, he was shot. The man who killed him took his briefcase with my prints in it."

"You *saw* the murder of Colin Fleming? Have you talked to the police?"

She shook her head. "I have nothing to add to what they know. Except . . . Of course, they don't know about the briefcase."

"You think he was killed because he had those documents in his possession?"

"How could they have known he had these documents? If they had known that, then they would have known I was in the hotel room, then they would have come after me." She shook her head. "I've thought and thought about it. I think it must have been a coincidence that they shot him right after he met me. Otherwise, I would be dead, too. But . . ."

"But whoever killed him got the copies you had just given him."

"Sold him," she corrected.

"And where have you been since?"

"Zurich. Rotterdam. Now Berlin."

"Hiding?"

"Yes."

"Just what do you expect to be paid for this set of tape cartridges, Fräulein?"

"I want a job," she said. "I want protection. Until those documents have been made public and the Fleming murder has been solved, my life is in danger. I—"

"Do you actually think Wilhelm Hildebrandt would order your death?"

"Probably not," she said. "I really can't think he would . . . that anyone in VWH would. But—but the company *did* copy other people's papers, tape their telephone conversations, provide girls to entertain them and then videotape what they did."

"And someone killed Colin Fleming."

"And got the documents I had sold him."

"So someone involved in all this is capable of murder."

Prager reflected on his last statement for several moments before he spoke. "All right, Fräulein Frank," he said briskly. "I cannot make the decision this afternoon. In fact, I can't make it by myself at all. I shall have to discuss the matter with my superiors. Obviously, we will have to see some examples of what you say you have, before we can make any substantial commitment. Can you return tomorrow?"

"Tomorrow morning?"

"Say at ten. Bring one or two cartridges. Can we play them on an ordinary VCR?"

"Yes. I will bring a cartridge."

Seven hours later, Hanna Frank stepped into the alley behind a big, busy cafeteria just around a corner from the Kurfurstendamm. She wore the demeaning gray uniform the management required of women who cleaned tables and carried trays of dirty dishes from the huge dining room to the bustling, steamy kitchen. They scraped leftovers from the dishes into cans; when the garbage level approached the top, the can had to be lugged out to the alley and dumped into the portable bin that would be picked up during the night. She had scraped leftovers into a can that was full and had been told gruffly to take the can out.

The traffic noise from the Kurfurstendamm reached the alley, as did flickers of the street lights reflected off the windows of nearby buildings. The can was huge and heavy. The strain of lifting it hurt her arms and shoulders. She hated this work, but it had been the best she could get without producing a resume. She had gone through her money alarmingly fast, living in Zurich and Rotterdam on a tourist visa, where she had been denied the right to work. Here in Berlin she had rented a room; the job paid her weekly rent. The drudgery and the desperation had driven her to take the risk of going to Prager.

She dragged the can toward the bin. She would have to lift it to dump the garbage. If it was too heavy, she would have to lighten it by pulling out the garbage with her hands and flinging it in the bin by the handfuls.

Her mental grousing over the distasteful task was interrupted by a voice from behind.

"Hanna."

She swung around. *"You!"*

"Of course. Sooner or later."

"Please . . . You don't have to—"

"But I do. I'm sorry, Hanna."

He fired only once. The nine-millimeter slug struck her sternum, and the impact threw her back like a loose-jointed marionette. Bone exploded inward and burst her heart. Her brain functioned just long enough for her to realize, with horror, that she had been murdered.

Although the lawsuits were neither dismissed nor settled, CATSERV made its offer for the stock of Runkle Broadcasting. A block of offices in the Pan Am Building was set aside as a command center. Because Runkle was widely held (there were tens of thousands of stockholders, no one of whom owned more than three percent of the stock), the offer had to be communicated by mail and advertising to as many as possible of the stockholders.

Runkle management fought back with an urgent mailing to its entire list of stockholders. The notice, in large block lettering, declared, in part:

A MESSAGE TO OUR STOCKHOLDERS

Our company is the latest to fall under attack by corporate raider F. (for Frankie) Thad Catlett. For many years Mr. Catlett has been in the business of buying up newspapers and turning them into what the newspaper industry calls "boobs and bums" tabloids. Lately he has applied the same techniques in the broadcast field. He acquires stations, turns them into "boobs and bums" television stations, and reaps short-term profits at the expense of their stockholders. The long-range survival of these stations depends on community tolerance, FCC tolerance, and audience tolerance—any one of which may be abruptly withdrawn.

Mr. Catlett is offering $16.25 a share for your stock. That is not a fair price. Your stock is worth more. Your board of directors and officers believe your shares are worth a minimum of $19.00 a share. Your company is not sick. Your investment is secure. Why sell your stock for less than it is worth?

Two days later, CATSERV ran a reply in the *Wall Street Journal* and a dozen other metropolitan newspapers across the land:

A MESSAGE TO RUNKLE STOCKHOLDERS

Runkle management says $16.25 is not a fair price for a share of Runkle common. The directors and officers of Runkle Broadcasting say the stock is worth $19.00 a share. How many shares are they buying at $19.00? How many are they buying at $16.25? Who is paying $19.00? Who, besides CATSERV, is offering $16.25?

Check the stock listing in your newspapers. Yesterday, the best bid for Runkle common was 15½. It was offered at 15⅝. The highest bid for Runkle common in the past 12 months was 15⅞. Who offers $19.00? We would like to know. We have already bought some Runkle common, and if we can get $19.00 for it, we might sell.

Your management is lying. You can't get $19.00. Except from CATSERV, you can't get $16.25.

The tender offer was limited. If by December 31, 1986, CATSERV had not received acceptances representing a controlling interest, the offer would be withdrawn. Acceptances began to trickle in. Then the trickle swelled. No flood developed, however. The issue remained in doubt.

Thad's mother, Alma Catlett, was in paradise.

When she returned from London, she found letters from Billy and Mary, demanding when, if ever, she was coming home. She was not, she replied. She wanted her share of her husband's estate, as it had been willed to her; but Billy could have the ranch. Thad would deed over to Billy the interest left to him, and she expected a modest income as her share of what the ranch earned. When she died, the ranch and all would belong to Billy. Mary, she wrote bitterly, lacked

175

the sense to own and manage anything; any property she owned would likely be deeded to the first "Christian confidence man" who got to her, and she, Alma, would not abet that. With Thad's help, she would purchase a comfortable house in Greenwich, and she had no expectation ever to return to Nance County, Texas. Ship her things, she wrote. And "y'all come for a visit as soon as I have a house."

She bought a noisy, smoky used diesel Mercedes, and shortly she became a familiar, if colorful, figure in Greenwich; the dear old Texas lady who guided her banging car into a parking place and strode down the walk in western boots, tight blue jeans, and a checked shirt to the liquor store, where she threw back her head and laughed out loud over her discovery that in Connecticut she could buy bourbon in two-liter bottles. Greenwich loved her. Policemen trotted across the street to explain to her that she could not park in a crosswalk, and they chatted with her in the middle of the street, telling her where to go to find whatever it was she was looking for.

She became a beach crawler, too, going almost every summer day to the Greenwich beach in her black maillot swimsuit, sunglasses, and huge floppy straw hat. She carried a beach chair and towels and newspapers and usually a book. No one ever saw her wet more than the bottoms of her feet in the salt water, which she preferred to keep at a respectful distance. She became widely quoted by people who swore they overheard her make memorable remarks to her grandsons: "I never thought I'd see the day when I'd go out in the afternoon sun and lay down in the sand and get myself sunburnt of a purpose." Amused whispers also spread that her thermos was filled with iced bourbon, not iced tea.

"Seein' those kids playin' in the sand," she remarked to Richard one afternoon early in September, when they had returned from London, "makes me think of the day when your dad was playin' in his sandbox and a big ol' rattler came a-slitherin' across the yard toward him. Your dad ever tell you? I shot that snake with a thirty-thirty."

Richard stared across the Sound, at Long Island. He was not wearing sunglasses and squinted into the glare. At nineteen he still looked thirteen: thin, pimpled, self-conscious.

176

"Your great-grandfather used to say that thinkin' all the time is unhealthy."

Richard sighed. "Sorry."

"I know you got a smile down deep inside you somewhere. I've seen it sneak out sometimes. Somethin' wrong, son?"

He shook his head.

"Don't bullshit me, Richard. I know damn well you got somethin' on your mind, somethin' you haven't told your mom or dad, somethin' you haven't told your priest friends."

The boy stiffened. "Everybody always thinks Thaddy probably does . . . you know, does things to me. Well, he doesn't. He never did. He never even suggested it. And that's the truth."

"But you're a-thinkin' he almost might as well, considerin' what everybody believes, huh?"

Richard raised his head and glanced sharply at her.

Each began forming his thoughts. Alma spoke first.

"Lord knows, your late grandfather—you were named after him—had his shortcomings. But he was a good man. Steady. Hard worker. A kind man . . . decent. No intellectual. Fact is, he was thickheaded. Provincial. He was happy to live on a ranch down the road from a li'l ol' country town. He was curious about what went on in other places but never curious enough to want to go see fer himself. Nance County was as good a spot as he ever wanted to be."

Richard nodded acknowledgment. "I remember him," he said.

"Well, I took your dad . . . his son . . . away from him. Or maybe 'twas the other way around. Maybe I took the father away from your dad. I sent your dad off to school when he was just a li'l boy. And I made certain he was never at home again. Wanted to get him away from Nance County, you know, away from the dry dirt. I wanted him to be somethin' bigger. Guess I got my wish. He's a big man today . . . a real big man. But I wouldn't be surprised if he lost somethin' along the way. He lost his father. He never saw a man workin' at bein' a father. He never learned how to be a father."

"He's all right," said Richard. "I've got no complaints."

"Not complainin' about nothin'?"

Richard shook his head.

177

"Well maybe you oughta," she snapped.

The boy remained silent, his eyes focused on something distant. Then he spoke softly, hesitantly. "They don't accept my vocation. . . . I mean, my call to the service of God. . . . They don't understand that."

"I don't either," she confessed.

"No one who hasn't heard the call can understand it."

"I got only one thing to say about it, Richard. I won't try to influence you. But I will say this: A lot of people in this world rely on crutches to get 'em through life. There are all kinds of crutches. Some folks find their crutch in a bottle. Some find it in powders and pills and palliatives. Some lay down once a week on a psychiatrist's couch. And some folks find their crutch in the scriptures. If you honestly believe you got a draft notice from God, you got to respond, I guess. Ain't no higher authority. But if it's a crutch you're lookin' for, you may lose it one day. Then you'd find yourself a cripple, without a crutch. Might fall flat on your ass. Somehow, I don't think God would like that. Can't help believin' the True God wants you to have strong legs, to walk tall. . . ."

Richard remained grave, staring across the water at the Long Island shore in the haze. "The True God," he said softly, "wants me to follow in His footsteps."

"Yes," said the grandmother. "But don't lean too hard on Him, Richard. Walk on your own two feet."

They could have disappeared into the populace and no one would have noticed them. Still, they found it necessary to be conspiratorial, to hide their tryst from any possibility of discovery. They were, after all, public figures.

She was a congresswoman, a candidate for reelection in November. Her Republican opponent was an attractive older man—attractive, articulate, aggressive, with simplistic solutions to complex problems. Her solutions were more complicated and, therefore, more difficult to reduce to campaign slogans. The

Republican candidate was pounding hard on her "ivory tower theories." Her reelection was not certain.

She was accompanied by a media magnate who had been called variously Muckrakers, Inc., the Garbage Collector, empire builder, corporate raider, robber baron, pornographer, anti-Christ—and many other names, more commonly found scrawled on back-alley walls.

It was a foggy September Friday night when they slipped out of Washington, crossed the Woodrow Wilson Bridge, and drove south on I-95 toward Richmond. At Fredericksburg, he pulled off the highway and parked at a Sheraton Inn. He registered as Mr. and Mrs. Frank Catlett and presented an American Express card with the name F. T. Catlett. He listed a Boston address because their Avis car had Massachusetts plates. He felt foolish, but Jennie was nervous. She seemed to take some comfort from the deception.

In their room she began to unpack, showing him what she had brought: a sheer black peignoir, black satin high-heeled slippers, two quarts of Glenlivet, and a single silver cup from which to drink it. Impatiently, he seized her and kissed her, then began exploring her body with his hands, unfastening, unbuttoning, unzipping.

"We've waited so long," she whispered.

"No longer," he grunted.

They sank to the floor, never reaching the bed.

After a brief but passionate encounter, they showered together, soaping and rinsing each other and becoming more familiar with one another's bodies. It was, for each of them, an ingenuous exploration. She ran her hands over his wet, soapy flesh as though she had never touched a man before, and he handled her intimate parts with the curiosity of a schoolboy first touching a girl. He was surprised at how new the experience seemed. He had all but forgotten how delectable it could be. He had all but forgotten those early sensations.

At a table apart in the dining room, by candlelight, they sat with their knees touching, their hands together under the table. She stared at his face, and tears dampened her eyes.

179

"I didn't want this to happen," she said. "I really didn't intend for this to happen."

"I know...."

"I don't think you do. The incredible truth, Thad, is that I've fallen in love with you. At my age ... with my experience ... I've fallen silly in love."

He looked directly into her eyes. "Only once in my life have I told a woman I loved her. Now I'm saying it a second time. I'm forty-nine years old, and I've fallen in love. I never expected to be saying this. It isn't at all what I originally had in mind. But I have to confess, Jennie, I feel like a lovesick school kid."

"I think I know what you had in mind. You thought it would be useful to have a friend on the Committee on Interstate and Foreign Commerce."

He reached for her hands. Another emotion welled up that he hadn't felt for a long time. Suddenly, strangely, his eyes were afloat, and a salty tear spilled down his cheek.

They shared a moment of tender silence, more eloquent than words. Then Thad spoke again. "I love you, Jennie. You said you didn't want it to happen. It was the last thing in the world *I* had in mind. But it's also the best thing that could have happened."

The wire story was distributed by Reuters North European service, but not a single American newspaper published it. It rattled off the Reuters printer in the offices of Catlett Communications Enterprises. But the story was lost in a blizzard of news that swirled up from the printers of AP, UPI, Reuters, PR Newswire, and the other wire services subscribed to by CCE.

Bert Stouffer did not monitor the wire-service traffic, so he would have missed it. But it arrived at his apartment by mail, with an attached note on a memo sheet from Sally Wood at the *Times*. "Know you are looking at the machinations of the Hildebrandt organization. Is this of any interest?"

Berlin, 25/09/86:14.40—The body of a woman found shot to death in the alley behind a cafeteria in the central district of West Berlin has been identified as Hanna Frank, 30, an employee of Verlagsgruppe Wilhelm Hildebrandt.

Frank formerly was employed by the Bundesnachrichtendienst (BND), security service of the Federal Republic.

She was shot to death on the night of September 23 in an alleyway behind a cafeteria where she was employed as a busperson. She was killed by a single shot from a 9 mm pistol.

Earlier, she had been reported missing by an officer of VWH after she failed to appear for work several days in succession and telephone calls to her apartment were not answered.

The spokesperson for VWH declined to speculate as to the motive for the murder. The BND similarly refused to comment, saying only that Frank left the agency voluntarily four years ago.

Bert telephoned Charles Lodge Johnson and persuaded his secretary to put him on the line.

"There you have it, Charles," Bert said. "She worked for BND, then for VWH, and now she's been murdered."

"Hundreds of people work for VWH in Frankfurt," said Charles nonchalantly.

"How many of them have an intelligence-agency background and get themselves mysteriously murdered? Want me to send you a copy of the story?"

"I have a quick source for it here," said Charles. "Thanks, Bert. I'll read the whole story."

Charles hung up the phone, swung around, and pressed the button to activate his NEXIS terminal. The little red box had a screen and keyboard; its internal electronics included an autodialer, which put it in contact with a computer center in Dayton, Ohio. Charles pecked out a command that gave him access to an electronic library of wire-service stories, then typed a command that told the computer to look for the name Hanna Frank. In a moment he had the story on the screen. He pressed another key, and the story rattled off a printer located in the secretarial pool. A minute later, when he was back on the telephone on a different matter, a secretary came in and deposited the printout on his desk.

Charles stuffed the printout in his pocket and barged off to keep a luncheon appointment with Kenneth Asher. Over their table at the Press Box, Charles handed the paper to Asher.

"I don't recall meeting the young woman in Frankfurt," he said. "Does the name mean anything to you?"

"*Christ, yes!* We've got to get Thad on the phone!"

Thad returned from Washington late in the afternoon. At the office he detected an aura of urgency. Both Charles Lodge Johnson and Kenneth Asher wanted to see him immediately. He summoned both of them to his office, anticipating that they wanted to talk about the same thing. They did. They handed him the Reuters story.

"Pretty damn obvious," he snorted. He rose from his desk and stood with one foot on the windowsill. He could see La Guardia Airport from his window, could see all the way to Greenwich, in fact, on a clear day. "If she came to VWH from this"—he grabbed up the printout and looked for the word—"Bundesnachtrichtendienst, then she was no common hostess. Funny damned thing, though. Our conversation was innocuous. Maybe they were setting me up for—"

"What odds would you give me," asked Charles, "that you are the star of a dirty little film?"

"Christ!" exploded Asher. "Then they filmed me, too!"

"They could hardly be so crude . . . so naive . . . to think they could get much mileage out of films like that," said Thad.

"We don't *know*, of course, that we *were* filmed."

Thad frowned over the Reuters story, drawing in his lower lip and gnawing on it thoughtfully. "An intelligence agent," he muttered.

"Hired away from this BND.... Or maybe she wasn't hired away.... Maybe she still worked for them."

"I doubt," said Charles, "that the government of the Federal Republic would assign a young woman to grant you sexual favors."

"Don't be quaint, Charles," said Asher. "That's how the diplomatic game is played today."

"I haven't told you this," said Thad, "but there's something more. They searched my bags ... my briefcase ... probably photocopied everything I was carrying. Some of the memos had nothing to do with their business. We don't have to speculate about that. I *know* they did it."

"What are they up to, do you think?" asked Charles.

"Simple enough," said Asher. "To get control. I'd guess they want control—control over the television stations, control over the newspapers, too, if possible. Hildebrandt has a voracious appetite. And I get the impression some of his associates are not accustomed to working in subtle ways."

"But what do they want?" pressed Charles. "Financial control? Editorial control?"

"Politics. Power," said Thad grimly. "The struggle for power is intense. People will go to greater lengths for power than for money."

"You think maybe they've got their hooks into somebody?" asked Asher. "I'll bet they've got films of many visitors."

"I would guess that they make pictures of everybody who stays in that gasthaus," agreed Thad. "Just routine blackmail in case they should need to use a little unfriendly persuasion. Think of all the people who've stayed there ... who've been lured between the sheets.... Lord, they must have the world's most exclusive porno library ... a veritable *Who's Who* in bed."

"Well, what are we going to do about it?" demanded Charles, half defiantly, half anxiously.

"Well, we're certainly going to play the game a good deal more cautiously," said Thad.

"May I suggest a strategy?" asked Asher. "Don't let them know we're wise to them. Then start feeding them *disinformation*."

"Yes," Thad interjected. "I'm for it. But if we start playing their little game, we'll play for keeps." He was pleased with his decision. "That's right, we'll keep them on the hook. We'll wait for the right time . . . when we can win an important victory by letting them sneak into my briefcase and copy something that will screw them good."

"What about this yacht cruise?" Charles asked.

"We'll go, of course," said Thad. "Sorry, Ken, but Hildebrandt was rather specific. He just invited Charles and me. Said Charles needs the sun and sea air."

Asher shrugged. "I couldn't leave here now, anyway," he said. "Not with the Runkle fight in full fury. You should tell our Kraut friends that we may need another transfusion of cash. . . . I think we're going to make it. As of today, we have acceptances from 37.2% of the Runkle stockholders."

"I am confident," said Charles, "that your security specialist, Mr. Pittocco, can equip our luggage with devices that will tell us if we've been the victims of—"

"I wouldn't do that," said Asher. "If they are at all sophisticated, they'll detect your devices. Then they'll know you're suspicious."

Thad smiled slyly at Charles. "What are you going to do if they offer you some late-night entertainment . . . bedtime with Beatrice?"

Charles raised his chin and pinched back his smile. "I should probably decline on the grounds that my weak heart could not stand it."

"Think of it as a duty to the company, Charles," said Thad. "After all, it might look suspicious if you declined."

"Considered in that light, I shall perhaps rethink the question," said Charles dryly.

NINE

Mistral was a sleek, gleaming eighty-foot motor yacht, designed originally for an oil-endowed Kuwaiti sheik. A change of governments at home had brought a change in his fortunes, compelling him to forsake the *Mistral*. No other playboy had the wherewithal, given the decline in oil loot, to pay the upkeep; so the yacht had been purchased in 1982 by a French-Italian consortium, which chartered it as a floating conference center. Among its advantages was that it could slip into select Mediterranean or Atlantic ports at night and pick up passengers who preferred that their presence at certain meetings not become a matter of public attention.

Thad and Charles boarded *Mistral* at St. Tropez, where it was backed up to the quay, the largest yacht in the harbor and a magnet for the eyes and cameras of scores of tourists. They wondered aloud who owned this sea palace and who might be aboard. Many names were circulating on the quay and in the waterfront cafes where

185

people sat under awnings, sipping aperitifs and wine: Frank Sinatra. Prince. Madonna. Michael Jackson. Bob Hope. What's-his-name, the King of Saudi Arabia. When the black Mercedes that had brought Thad and Charles from the airport at Nice pulled up, crewmen hurried down from the deck to take their luggage. A crowd pressed close. "Who the hell's that?" "Shut up, he's a Mafia guy."

Wilhelm Hildebrandt sat inside the glass-enclosed lounge, looking comfortable in a dark blue shirt and white duck pants. He wore sunglasses against the glare off the water.

"Welcome aboard," he said as he rose to shake hands. "This was Mr. Yoshioka's idea. I hope you like it."

When Thad and Charles were alone later in Thad's teak-paneled cabin, Charles observed, "Somehow, this adds an odd, new dimension to our relationship with our partners."

Thad pressed a finger to his lips. He pointed around the cabin, gesturing that microphones might be hidden anywhere.

Annoyed, Charles thrust his mouth two inches from Thad's ear. "Conspiratorial," he whispered. "Secrecy."

Returning to the lounge, dressed casually for yachting, they found that Friederich Papen, Ernst Dietrich, and Klaus Schulenberg were aboard—Schulenberg newly arrived and still wearing a double-breasted suit.

"I fear," said Hildebrandt as Thad and Charles ordered drinks at the bar, "that we are not going to have the best of weather for our seaborne meeting." He squinted apprehensively at gray clouds forming over the Mediterranean and the coastline to the west. "That looks like a storm."

"You should know," said Thad. "You're the sailor."

"Unfortunately," laughed Hildebrandt, "*Mistral* cannot submerge. I hope no one is subject to *mal de mer*."

"Are we expecting Mr. Yoshioka?" Thad asked.

"Later," said Hildebrandt. "Also others. Some of our associates did not want to make a public appearance on the quay in St. Tropez."

As they sipped their drinks and chatted casually about the sea and the weather, avoiding any business conversation, they heard a disturbance on the quay behind *Mistral.* Thad stood and stared to see what was hapening. The cause of the commotion was a group of tall, leggy girls, looking like a chorus line, leaving two vans and trooping up the gangplank to the deck. Herded by Friederich Hoffman, they hurried toward the bow and disappeared out of sight through a door forward of the bridge. Hoffman reappeared alone at the gangplank, saluted Hildebrandt stiffly, and departed the yacht.

"I was hoping to see Hanna Frank among them," said Thad innocently.

"You don't know what happened to her?" asked Papen.

Thad shook his head and touched his lips to his Scotch.

"I'm afraid the young lady is dead," said Papen. "Uh . . . it's worse than that. She was murdered. She disappeared about three months ago, then two weeks ago she was found dead in Berlin . . . shot . . . murdered . . . in an alley."

"My God," said Thad. "That's terrible."

"The authorities questioned us, because she had worked for us. But we could tell them nothing . . . why she moved to Berlin without notice . . . why she was killed . . . it's all a mystery. The crime remains unsolved."

"Horrible," muttered Schulenberg.

As the crew loosed the mooring lines and *Mistral* eased slowly away from the quay, the wind freshened, and a brisk, light rain swept the decks. By the time they had passed beyond the mole and out of the harbor, the seas had risen and the yacht rolled in the gray-green waters. Visibility diminished and the gloom, like a closing eyelid, shut out the town and the harbor. But the big yacht, driven by its throbbing diesel engines, moved authoritatively out into the Mediterranean. Through the skylight in the lounge, the businessmen could see the radar antenna rotating silently on a mast just behind the bridge. They could see the officers of the ship, behind glass swept by wipers, peering intently. One officer was hunched over the radar screen, pressing his face to its hood.

Shrieking and giggling, the ten girls scrambled along the rain-swept deck and rushed into the lounge. Inside, they shook the rainwater out of their hair, cast off a variety of windbreakers and sweatshirts, and assembled, puffing and laughing, wearing nothing but skintight, scanty bikini bottoms.

One of the girls approached Thad at the table where he was seated with Hildebrandt. "May I join you, gentlemen?" she asked in French-accented English. Hildebrandt gave her a curt, affirmative nod, and she slithered into a canvas-bottom deck chair beside Thad. "My name is Leonie," she said. "Is that Scotch you are drinking? May I have some?"

It seemed impossible that this trifle of a girl—pretty, animated, bright-faced, with pendulous little breasts hanging loose and bouncing as she squirmed in her chair—could be another Hanna Frank; but he would be careful with her. He noticed that another girl, a blond with huge white breasts, had attached herself to Charles, who was conspicuously fascinated with her.

Hildebrandt ordered a Scotch for Leonie and a fresh one for Thad. Before the drinks arrived, a crewman appeared with a message. Hildebrandt read it and dismissed the man.

"The weather has delayed the other participants in our meeting," he announced. "Our first business session must be delayed until morning. With your consent, Thad, we will begin early. In the meantime—" He grinned. "Perhaps you won't be bored."

Dinner would be served at eight. Thad took Leonie to his cabin for an appetizer, then settled on the bed for an hour's nap with her in his arms.

Whether or not she was a spy, he knew one thing about her: She was French. She eschewed deodorant and underarm shaving; this gave her an earthy, faintly acrid odor he identified with French women. When they left the cabin, she trembled slightly from the outside chill. He tossed her one of his cashmere sweaters, and they returned to the lounge. With her bare hips and exposed long legs below his black sweater, he thought she was sexier than the topless girls.

The roll and pitch of the yacht caused about half the passengers to feel queasy. Only Thad, Charles, Hildebrandt, Dietrich, and four of the girls sat down for dinner. Although the men were dressed in casual clothes and the girls, except Leonie, were bare-breasted, the dinner was served by candlelight on white linen, with heavy silver engraved with tangled Arabic characters. From soup to coffee, with champagne and Bordeaux, the meal was superb.

After dinner, Hildebrandt called for a backgammon board. He, Charles, Dietrich and Charles's big-breasted girl played. Thad and Leonie and the other two girls sat apart. The wallowing of the yacht became more pronounced, until glasses had to be removed from the tables. Hard gusts of wind lashed the windows with rain and spray.

"Perhaps we should submerge, Herr Hildebrandt," Charles suggested.

"God forbid!" said Dietrich.

Thad watched with amusement as Charles proved to be a formidable master of backgammon. Hildebrandt apparently took some pride in his own game, but he was overpowered by Charles. After a while, Charles rose from the table, stretching, and announced he was going to retire. He did not take his girl to his cabin.

The girl made her way to the bar and asked for brandy. While it was being poured, she found her sweatshirt and got into it. Thad was startled at the sweatshirt. It was lettered DUKE UNIVERSITY. He stepped up beside her. She glanced at him, lit a cigarette, and told him bluntly, "I can answer your questions before you ask them. The answers are yes, just lucky, I guess, and Barbara. The final answer is no." She smiled mischievously, "No, Leonie would not be upset if you switch."

In his cabin, she removed the sweatshirt and bikini bottom and stretched out on his bed.

He handed her a note: "Room bugged?"

"I don't think so," she whispered close to his face. "Not that I know."

He handed her a pair of his pants and a windbreaker. He pulled on his pants and a golf shirt, then led her out onto the deck. The yacht was still climbing six-foot waves, plunging its bow into them, but the rain had stopped, the wind had dissipated, and they could stand at the rail and talk.

"The last girl they provided for me was murdered not long afterward," he told her urgently. "Did anybody mention that?"

"Mr. Catlett," said Barbara. "I love France. I love the Riviera. I can't make a living in France any way except this way. Nobody asked me to write up a report on what you say. Nobody gave me a set of questions to ask you. In fact, who could have guessed you'd walk up to me and ask me to take Leonie's place? I don't know what this yachting party is about. I don't think I want to know. And if somebody got murdered, I particularly don't want to know about that. If it was because she was with you, I'd like to beg off."

"It wasn't because of that. Do you know the other girls?"

She shrugged. "I've seen some of them around."

This one was smart enough to lie. Maybe Leonie wasn't, but this one was. But as she had said, who could have guessed that he would walk up to her and ask her to take the French girl's place in his cabin?

"What are they paying you?" he asked.

"Five thousand francs," she said.

"I'll add another five thousand."

"For what?"

"Listen to what you hear, from all the other girls. I'll be in touch after we're off this floating—"

"Whorehouse?"

"It's more than that. . . . Much more. But listen; be careful. I'm not asking you to spy. Just be alert and hear what's to be heard."

"Who am I going to be with? Not with you?"

"Tonight, yes," he said. "Tomorrow . . . We'll see."

She clutched the rail and stared into the dreadful black darkness of the tossing sea. "A girl got murdered, huh?"

Thad slapped her on the bottom. "Make it ten thousand francs," he said. "And if you get murdered, I'll double it."

*   *   *

190

Thad woke at dawn, conscious that the steady heartbeat of the diesels had stopped. He peered out the porthole. The *Mistral* was stopped, gently wallowing in a peaceful swell. A wet mist hung in wisps over the sea, but through breaks he could see a shoreline in the far distance. Then out of the mist a smaller boat approached the yacht—a forty-two-foot cabin cruiser by his expert estimate. The cabin cruiser maneuvered alongside. Bumpers were tossed out by both yachts as they rubbed against each other, rising and falling with the waves. A man on the smaller boat tossed up lines.

Thad recognized Kengo Yoshioka as he bobbed into sight, reaching out for a helping hand from the deck of the smaller boat to the deck of *Mistral*. After Yoshioka, two more Oriental men emerged from the cabin and were helped aboard the yacht. Finally, a young European came out and, disdaining the hands extended to help him, made a quick jump from the smaller to the larger deck. All four new passengers were dressed in business suits. They passed from Thad's sight, leaving crewmen to hand up their luggage.

The rendezvous at sea had taken no more than three minutes. Then the cabin cruiser pulled away from *Mistral* and churned toward the shoreline.

Breakfast was served on the open rear deck at eight. A buffet table was set up, with heaps of eggs, bacon, ham, and potatoes, platters of fish, trays of fruit, pitchers of juice, pots of tea, coffee, and milk, and bottles of champagne. The three Orientals showed up in their business suits; all the other men, including the European, appeared on deck in pants and sweaters. The girls made a brief appearance in their scanties, then scurried back for jackets and sweaters against the crisp morning wind.

"Allow me to introduce Christian Thyssen," said Wilhelm Hildebrandt to Thad.

Thyssen was the young man Thad had seen leap briskly between yachts. He was a robust, solid young man, maybe thirty years of age, with pale blue eyes, hair cut bristly short, and pink apple cheeks. "Herr Catlett," he said in a clipped tone.

191

Thad shook his hand. Thyssen turned abruptly and, with a gesture, summoned the two new Orientals.

"Herr Catlett, I would like to present Dr. Kim Doo Chung and Herr Park Il-Sung. They are from Korea."

Dr. Kim seized Thad's hand. "We have met, Mr. Catlett," he said in perfect English. "I live in Washington. We met two or three years ago at a reception following a concert at the Kennedy Center. It was most brief. I doubt that you would remember. I met your lovely wife on that occasion. I hope she is well."

"Yes. Thank you."

"Our Korean friends may wish to invest in our enterprises," said Hildebrandt.

Thad nodded noncommittally. That explained the Koreans. So who was Thyssen?

Hildebrandt introduced the Koreans to Dietrich and Schulenberg. Thad noticed Hildebrandt did not seem to think it necessary to introduce them to Charles.

Thyssen stayed close to Thad. When Hildebrandt was out of earshot, he said, "Are you familiar with the name Dr. Kim Doo Chung? He is a promising and powerful man in Korea, with close ties to the government . . . an entrepreneur who has achieved great success. His business, it might be said, is the Americanization of Korea. Dr. Kim has built many American-style office buildings, hotels, and commercial centers in Korea."

"He said he lives in Washington."

"He commutes between Washington and Seoul. You might call him the unofficial voice of the Korean government in Washington. He's not a diplomat, not official. . . . You understand, I am sure."

"I know the government of South Korea has an unofficial presence in Washington," said Thad.

"Yes. Dr. Kim," said Thyssen.

"I see."

Barbara edged up to Thad as Thyssen hurried away to rejoin his two Koreans. She had slept with Thad last night. Her black hair flew around her face in the wind, and she tossed it back. "Well?" she asked. "Who? . . ."

"Thyssen," he whispered.

A business meeting was called after breakfast. The girls were dismissed and the men settled around tables in the lounge. Wilhelm Hildebrandt presided. "Since Mr. Thyssen has brought our Korean friends," he said, "perhaps he would like to explain their interest in our operations."

Christian Thyssen nodded at the two Koreans. "Dr. Kim will speak for himself," he said.

Dr. Kim Doo Chung rose. He was, Thad observed, a self-contained man, with the thin, chiseled features and high cheekbones that typically distinguished Koreans from Chinese. His hair was gray at the temples, and it looked as if it had been styled in a fashionable Washington parlor. His dark blue suit was skillfully tailored, in an American fashion that set it apart from the bulkier suits worn by the Germans before they changed. His black Gucci loafers gleamed.

"Have you heard this story?" he began. "Some months ago a delegation from North Korea came to Seoul. As you know, there has been little contact between north and south for many years, and these North Koreans had never been in South Korea before. As they were driven through the streets, they could not contain their amazement over the tall buildings, the new construction, the din of prosperity. They saw the traffic congestion—thousands of automobiles packed in the streets. 'Ah,' said the chief of their delegation to the chief of ours. 'We know what you have done. You have brought every automobile in South Korea into Seoul, hoping we will believe all these are owned here.' Our man laughed and said, 'So. You have caught us in our deception. It was easy to bring all these automobiles into Seoul. What was difficult was to bring in all those skyscrapers.'"

Everyone laughed appreciatively.

"You see," said Dr. Kim, "my people live in a nation under siege.

193

Only the presence of the United States Army deters the armies of the North from overrunning us and stealing what we have built. We need the American military backstop, and we need to expand economic relations. We are an enclave of capitalism, an island of free enterprise, on the communist frontier. We present a dramatic contrast to the communist regime of Kim Il Sung, who has turned his country into a massive concentration camp.

"Yet," Dr. Kim went on, "our government is constantly condemned by liberal elements in the United States. Your enemies are our enemies; we stand as a bulwark against the spread of communism. Yet we are constantly attacked by Congress. Our recovery from the devastation of the Japanese occupation is one of the world's great success stories. Yet we are constantly criticized by the news media. It is true that occasionally we must take emergency measures against communist demonstrations and other treasonous activities. We must preserve order in our country. At the first sign of incipient anarchy, the North Korean Army will once again cross our borders. So let me address a question to you: Can we be confident the United Nations will again send armies to our defense?"

He paused to smile at his own rhetoric.

"We wish to make friends," he said. "Herr Thyssen has suggested that it may be possible for us to invest in a modest way in your media enterprises. We seek the friendship of leaders in the field of American opinion."

"Dr. Kim can guide a substantial amount of money into our projects," said Thyssen.

"And . . . uh . . . what is your role, Mr. Thyssen," Thad asked.

"I represent myself, Mr. Catlett," said Thyssen. "I arranged for Dr. Kim and Mr. Park to meet with this group, simply as a favor to all concerned."

"You should understand, Thad," said Hildebrandt, "that Christian Thyssen is himself a source of a part of our funds. He is the heir to a considerable fortune, and he has been persuasive enough to convince a number of other wealthy people to invest in our enterprises."

"I regret that we have not met before now, Mr. Thyssen," said Thad.

"As I do," said Thyssen.

"Very well," said Hildebrandt firmly. "We are here to review what we have achieved so far and to consider new opportunities. I believe Thad and Charles have a report for us."

Thad shoved a small stack of papers into the middle of the table, for distribution. "You have been sent periodic reports," he said. "This summary will give you an update on what has happened since your last report. I want to review the most important developments. First, when Charles and I left New York, our last word from Kenneth Asher was that we have received written acceptances from shareholders holding 37.2% of the stock in Runkle Broadcasting Company. We should have the majority of the shares before December. With Runkle, we will acquire three fine midwestern television stations—Columbus, Cincinnati, and Louisville."

"That is good," said Dietrich.

"I hope all of you realize," Thad went on, "that, in view of the fact Runkle management went to court to stop us, this has been achieved in an extraordinarily short time. I must tell you that I am rather proud of my staff. They have done an excellent job. Now—"

He went on to review the several aspects of each television operation they had acquired since the consortium was formed. He spoke for most of an hour, noting that Christian Thyssen and the second Korean, Park Il-Sung, scribbled extensive notes. Thad usually smoked as a nervous release, and the smoke curled around his face until his upper forehead disappeared in the haze.

Thad concluded his discourse triumphantly, punctuating it with a puff of smoke. Papen had a few questions, as he always did. No one else asked any.

"Good, good," said Hildebrandt, again taking charge. "Now, Thad, I believe you have a suggestion for another acquisition."

Thad glanced at Charles. "I think it may be possible to acquire Conroy," he said. "I mean Conroy Publishing. You all know the name, I'm sure. Conroy Press publishes sixty or more hardcover

195

trade titles a year—and somehow manages to lose two million dollars a year in the process. But the company also has the ConPac imprint: paperbacks, on which it makes a handsome profit. Besides that, the company publishes a wide variety of technical and trade publications, under various imprints, all of which are profitable. Conroy is highly visible in the American publishing industry."

"When some prominent person wishes to publish his memoirs," Charles added, "very often he approaches Conroy."

"And you say this company is for sale?" Papen asked.

"The founders were Mason Conway and William Royal," said Thad. "Royal is dead. Conway is sixty-eight and retirement-minded. Most of the stock is owned by members of the two families, the rest by employees of the company. The younger Conways and Royals have other interests. The company has been essentially without firm leadership for two years. Buying it won't require a takeover fight. We could simply go to Mason Conway and make him an offer. If he accepts, a majority would fall in line."

"Is anyone else bidding?" asked Dietrich.

"I thought Rupert Murdoch might," said Thad. "But apparently he isn't going to. Other than that . . . No."

"How much would you bid?" asked Papen, his pencil poised to write down the number.

"Unlike many publishers," said Thad, "Conroy prints and binds most of its own books—which, incidentally, means we can very readily create new imprints if we wish. The company owns a formidable plant. I think it will take one hundred twenty million dollars to buy it."

"I should like," said Christian Thyssen, speaking quietly but incisively, "to suggest we pursue that proposition. I should like also to suggest we defer the decision until we have discussed at least one further idea. Do you object to that course of procedure, Herr Catlett?"

Thad was surprised at how Thyssen seemed to have taken control of the meeting, but he shook his head. "Not at all. I don't object at all."

"Thank you," said Thyssen. "I know Dr. Kim has some suggestions and I myself would like to share some ideas that could be beneficial . . . ideas that will involve raising considerable additional capital."

"I am very much interested," said Dr. Kim, "in the possibility of acquiring a major motion picture studio. Nothing else this group could acquire would have so much impact on American opinion, particularly among the young. But there is a more practical reason for acquiring motion picture facilities. If we wish to produce pictures for broadcast on the CATSERV television stations, we cannot rely on the Hildebrandt studios. There is a limit to how many German films Americans are willing to watch. I suggest we should also begin to make videos of all kinds. There will be a great profit in this, as well as the opportunity to convey our message in a most effective way."

"No doubt," said Thad. "But what major studio do you have in mind?"

"We have reason to believe," said Dr. Kim, "that we might be able to acquire Lion Pictures—if we use the right tactics."

"It would take a three-hundred-million-dollar investment," said Thad. "Probably more. We would never recover it."

"But think of what we could achieve!" cried Dr. Kim, rubbing his hands together, startling everyone by his outburst. "Movies! Videos! The most effective way of communicating."

Thad shrugged. "I am willing to explore the idea," he said. "But I warn you. There will be emotional bidding for Lion."

"I can assure you of a substantial infusion of investment capital," said Dr. Kim meaningfully.

Hildebrandt suggested a two-hour break at eleven-thirty, out of consideration for those who had traveled far and were functioning on different time zones. He summoned the girls to the lounge, and they came immediately, clad only in their bikini bottoms. The bartender also appeared and began to open champagne.

Thad and Charles stepped out on the rear deck and huddled at the rail.

Charles, indicating the Koreans in the lounge, snorted. "Sure, they're harassed by certain elements of American opinion. Some people do object, strenuously, to their suppression of dissent."

"Believe me, there is far more suppression of dissent in North Korea," said Thad. "Yet all I read in the liberal press is about suppression in South Korea. Our South Korean friends don't make me uncomfortable. I'll judge them by the color of their money, not their place of origin."

"If they invest money, they'll expect to exert an influence. I know the name Dr. Kim Doo Chung. His status is a mystery. He spends most of his time in Washington, and it is unclear whether he represents his business interests or the Korean government's political interests. He's a shadowy figure. I'd be wary of establishing a relationship with him."

"And who is Thyssen?" said Thad.

"There is German money in Korea," said Charles. "But let me make some inquiries after we get home. If you wish, I'll investigate to find out exactly who Christian Thyssen may be. He's no errand boy. Did you see how much some of them defer to him?"

"Very curious."

Leonie nudged up to Thad, who abruptly dropped the conversation. Charles felt moved to return to the lounge and seek out the girl who had spent the night with him. Thad led Leonie to the bar. Thyssen was sitting at a table, talking earnestly with Barbara. From time to time, he glanced uneasily out the window. Another storm was developing, judging from the cast of the sky, and the green water began to spit and spew white foam.

As they nibbled at lunch, the rain swept in again, and *Mistral* resumed its rolling. Christian Thyssen was one of those who abandoned his lunch. The storm gained power, the seas heaved menacingly, and the captain abandoned his course, turning the bow of *Mistral* into the wind. Shortly, its sharp bow was slicing into rolling seas, and green water sloshed across the foredeck and down the side decks. The girls were afraid to venture on deck and return to their cabins.

Hildebrandt spoke urgently into the telephone. "I am assured there is no danger," he told everyone when he laid the instrument down. "The captain tells me she has ridden out far more powerful storms than this. Besides, he is assured by the weather watch that the storm should abate in an hour or so."

They could not resume their meeting. Since the men's cabins were accessible from the rear lounge, some went below with their girl friends in tow. Barbara sat down with Thad.

She mentioned Thyssen. "I am invited to spend a week in his Alpine chalet," she said.

"Did you accept?"

"Tentatively."

"I'll arrange a way for us to keep in contact after we're ashore," he said.

"It will be easier for me to call you. I'll always know where to find you."

"What's your name?"

"It's really Barbara. Barbara Shirer."

The storm abated in mid-afternoon, and by five the sun shone in long streaks through breaks in the gray clouds. The seas were slower to diminish, and *Mistral*, back on course, wallowed in eight-foot swells.

Thyssen returned to the lounge, bestowed a thin little smile on everyone, and sat down again at the long table. The two Koreans did not return, perhaps because they remained nauseous, perhaps because they were occupied with their female companions. Hildebrandt himself looked a bit uncertain of his stomach and began to sip mineral water.

The girls were instructed to go to their quarters and to return at eight. The men pulled up chairs around the table, absent Schulenberg and the Koreans.

"Acquisitions," said Hildebrandt, setting the tone of the session. "Further acquisitions. We have two propositions before us."

"Speaking for my father," said Dietrich, "and also for Herr von Klauberg, who authorized me also to speak for him, I can say that our chief interest right now is in expanding the Catlett media empire"—he smiled disingenuously—"as some Americans call it."

Thad started to respond, thought better of it, and coughed to smother the remark he was about to make.

Dietrich continued firmly. "We have only begun to achieve our purpose. The stations so far acquired give us, at least potentially, a significant voice in America. We understand the limits under which you have to operate. We understand the necessity for our message to be a subtle one. But we must amplify our voice. Our only concern now is that more be done."

"More?" asked Charles. "I am not sure I understand."

Yoshioka bowed stiffly toward Charles. "My associates and I," he said, "are not dissatisfied with the way Mr. Catlett uses his resources. We have been most pleased with his editorials about free trade and the undesirability of imposing restraints on imports. I believe President Reagan has been influenced by these editorials."

"At least he knows he has strong support," said Thad.

"Herr Catlett's association with our group has made him a far more wealthy and powerful man," observed Papen.

"I suppose no one has any objection to that," said Hildebrandt.

"His strength is our strength," said Yoshioka.

"With your consent," said Thyssen, with an air suggesting he had no intention of waiting for anyone's consent, "I would like to place before us the acquisition *I* have in mind. I have made certain observations and inquiries. I believe it may be possible to acquire control of States Broadcasting."

"*States?* You mean? . . ."

Thyssen turned to Thad and answered his unasked question with an emphatic, affirmative nod.

Thad shook his head negatively. "What do they have . . . uh . . . fifteen stations?"

"Fourteen," said Thyssen. "And the company feeds programming to twenty more."

"That makes it a network," said Thad. "And that will raise all kinds of regulatory problems. We have an American expression that expresses my reaction: 'It's a can of worms.'"

Thyssen smiled condescendingly. "Forgive me, Mr. Catlett.

Uh . . . Thad. May I? Thank you. Actually, States is not a network. I have obtained a little legal advice. It is not a network, as that term is used in federal communications law. Although States outright owns fourteen television stations and feeds programming to twenty or so others, it is not a network. Why? Because its affiliated stations—even the ones it owns—are not required to broadcast the network programming in their market areas. They are at liberty to reject the States feed and instead broadcast, say, reruns of *I Love Lucy* or *Beverly Hillbillies*. Under American law, that makes a legal difference."

"I stand corrected," said Thad. "I hadn't looked into the question. But even so. *Fourteen* television stations? The amount of money we would need is far beyond anything we have talked about before. Have you done any research into that question? What would it cost to buy States?"

"Half a billion dollars," said Thyssen insouciantly. "Maybe six hundred million."

"I question that," said Thad. "Fourteen stations—"

"The company is losing money," said Thyssen. "Many of its stockholders are not happy."

"States," said Charles, "calls itself the 'family network.' It's the chief broadcast resource for the so-called Christian right. It offers the most dull, most dreary, most boring programming this side of Moscow. Its management is not quite sure whether reruns of *Lassie* are entirely acceptable for 'Christian family viewing.'"

"For which reason the company may be getting rewards in heaven but not on earth," said Thyssen. "In Biblical terms, the stations have low ratings, which have begat low advertising, which has begat low income. In other words, States is losing money."

Smiling at Thyssen's allegory, Charles offered, "Maybe I can provide some background. States was founded by the late William Laird Collins, who was a true pioneer in television. He owned four stations in Michigan, Indiana, and Wisconsin, and he formed States by merging Collins Broadcasting with three other small companies. I believe the company was originally called Midwestern States

Broadcasting Company. When William L. Collins died, his stock went into a family trust. The dominant trustee is Lucas Collins, who happens to be a dedicated born-again. He has allied States with a gaggle of evangelists, and they preach a hard line."

"If you try to take away their television network," said Thad, "they'll declare holy war."

"The managers may put their religious credo ahead of profits," said Thyssen. "The stockholders do not."

"There is no limit to what the televangelists will do," warned Thad again. "They can stir up the hornets. They've got political sting. They can beat us."

"We have our own means of fighting," said Thyssen grimly.

"Ah, but we may not have to think in such terms," interjected Hildebrandt. "Is it your judgment, Thad, Charles, that we might acquire these stations if we can raise the money?"

Thad's face clouded. "It would be a hard fight. It would take on new dimensions, beyond anything we have faced so far." He frowned, then shrugged. "But with enough money, you can do almost anything."

"Let us analyze," said Thyssen. "Let us reason. Do you disagree, Herr Hildebrandt?"

Hildebrandt shook his head. "I am apprehensive," he said. "But I cannot disagree."

"Time is of the essence," said Thyssen. "We must move decisively."

"But not recklessly," said Hildebrandt.

At eight, dinner was served, again an artfully prepared and served meal, but again one appreciated by less than all of the voyagers. Dr. Kim Doo Chung appeared for dinner, but the plates set for Park Il-Sung, Klaus Schulenberg and Friederich Papen remained empty. Only one of the girls, Schulenberg's, showed up.

Christian Thyssen was struggling with *mal de mer*, but he nibbled manfully at his food, determined not to show his weakness. Charles

Lodge Johnson was at the top of his form, untroubled by seasickness and anticipating with relish the backgammon game he had arranged with Hildebrandt and Thyssen for later in the evening.

Mistral pitched and rolled, and the crew took care not to pour glasses or cups full. Candle flames swayed.

Thyssen lifted his glass in toast. "To our cause!" he said.

"Which is?" Thad asked.

Hildebrandt rushed in to interrupt Thyssen. "The dissemination of our message," he said.

"May I be so bold," Charles interrupted, "as to ask that someone define our message more specifically?"

Thyssen turned to Thad. "Do you wish me to do this?"

Charles flushed. The implication was obvious that, as Thad Catlett's employee, he was not a person of real consequence in this meeting, not a person who could ask a question and expect an answer.

"It might be," said Thad, "a useful exercise."

Christian Thyssen stared at his hands, on which he wore two big gold rings, then began to speak. He seemed to expend a painful effort in choosing his words. "I believe our interests have been defined," he said. "On the other hand, there can be no harm in restating them. Some of them are specific, such as Herr Yoshioka's interest in guiding American opinion away from destructive trade barriers. Our new Korean friends have their interests in preserving the special relationship between the United States and Korea, and counteracting the intemperate criticisms from certain people. We in Germany are concerned with more general problems. We are deeply troubled by the continuing advance of state socialism. We are troubled by the peace-at-any price sentiment. We fear *we* might be the price that the pacifists would pay. We view with dismay the new isolationism in America, which today is represented by the Democratic Party. Some of its leaders are no longer willing to assert U.S. leadership in world affairs. And nothing is more destabilizing in international affairs than for a superpower to lose its way in the world. We are alarmed by the rise of a movement like the Green

Party in Germany. We are anxious to preserve our values." He paused and smiled apologetically. "A simple statement has turned into a speech. I am sorry. Many of us feel strongly about these things."

By his second night aboard *Mistral*, Thad had become accustomed to the constant rumble of the big diesels and even found the sound soothing. He was deep in sleep at three A.M. when an intrusive sound penetrated his consciousness. He opened his eyes and tried to identify the sound he thought he had heard. Then he heard it again—a rapping on his door. He dragged himself out of bed and shuffled to the door.

"Who is it?"

"Barbara."

He opened the door, and she pushed her way inside. She was still almost naked, wearing only the bikini bottom that had been the girls' required costume. She brushed past him into the center of his small but luxuriously furnished cabin. He had left a light burning in the head, which filled the cabin with an eerie half light. But there was enough light to see that the young woman's face was wet with tears.

"Barbara . . . What in the world? . . ."

"I've been dismissed," she said. "He's had enough of me."

"Thyssen?"

She stiffened. "You asked me to attach myself to him."

"Yes . . . But . . ."

"He's tired of me now. He told me to go back to the girls' cabins . . . up in the bow . . . where the crew sleeps."

"I don't understand . . . . Did you learn anything about him?"

She smiled bitterly. "Oh yes, Mr. Catlett," she said. "Look."

Barbara turned her back to him and pulled the bikini bottom down, baring her bottom. Thad gasped. The soft flesh of her nates was crisscrossed with welts. She winced as she pulled the bikini up again.

"Herr Christian Thyssen is a sadist," she said. She glanced over her back and sighed. "You see what he did. Oh, with much precision. No marks that will show outside my bikini. Those are *cuts*! Then he made me suck him off. And then he gave me two thousand marks and told me to go away."

"You could have refused," said Thad. "You should have refused."

She shook her head. "Not with him. Mr. Thyssen does not like being told no." She touched the stretched fabric of her bikini. "That *hurts*, Mr. Catlett."

"I'm sorry, Barbara. I promised you ten thousand francs. Make it ten thousand dollars."

"I wouldn't do it for the money again," she said. "I don't want to *see* that—that bastard again. I learned something about him, all right, Mr. Catlett. Thyssen is a *nut*! He's crazy!!"

"If he asks to see you again," said Thad, "let me know. I'll look out for you."

"Mr. Catlett," said Dr. Kim over breakfast the next morning, "I hope it will be possible to acquire Lion. If it is not, let us discuss the possibility of making a movie together. I can see the possibility of making a great profit, while at the same time educating Americans about the difficulties my country faces."

"Message films seldom make money," said Thad.

"I understand. Let us meet in Washington to talk of it more."

"As of this morning," said Thad, "I seem to have authority to bid for Conroy and a mandate to plunge headlong into a fight for States. I suspect I'm going to be quite busy for a while."

"When you come to Washington—and you *must* come to Washington from time to time, as every businessman does," Dr. Kim persisted, "please make a point of being my guest."

"I will do that," promised Thad.

The men who had come aboard from the cabin cruiser left *Mistral* the same way. Thad and Hildebrandt stood alone at the stern, watching *Mistral*'s screws churn up a boiling white froth as the cruiser roared away toward the French shoreline.

"You see an element of the encumbrances I carry," said Hildebrandt.

"I do indeed," said Thad.

"Isn't there an American expression—'Youth must be served'?" asked Hildebrandt. "His generation—I mean Thyssen's—has seen nothing. They know nothing. All they have ever experienced is success. They cannot understand caution."

"I have heavy feet," said Thad. "I am prepared to drag them if necessary."

Hildebrandt nodded. "But not on your efforts to acquire States Broadcasting. That requires light feet."

TEN

Bert raised his wine glass and peered at the rich red light from the candle shining through the vintage Chianti. "Congratulations to you, Kathy," he said. "I understand you sold your novel."

Kathy grinned with ingenuous enthusiasm. "Yes. It's not even finished."

"An achievement," said Bert, tipping his glass.

Kathy accepted his toast and sipped the wine. He had been curious about this singular relationship since the first time he saw her in Charles's apartment. Charles was a lofty, high-domed Bostonian, studiously reserved, whose incisive, clipped speech and disciplined intellect marked him as a member of the Bostonian aristocracy. She was an earthy young woman, with the open, guileless appeal of a tramp dog wagging its tail. Tonight, when Indian summer had raised the temperature to eighty-nine degrees, she had come to the Italian restaurant in a long black skirt and a black halter, more suitable to the arty crowd than the Harvard set.

"It is quite simple, actually," said Charles, raising his brows and staring down his cheeks. "Once she decided she was not going to write the Great American Novel and dropped her New Jersey-baroque style of English prose, she allowed her perceptiveness to emerge. She also discovered that writing a fine novel is not the work of a lifetime; it can be done in a few months, if one has the talent."

"Good for you, Kathy," said Bert. "I've always wanted to write a novel, but I never had the courage."

Charles sniffed. "Next you'll tell us you'll write one—just as soon as you can find the time."

"If I had the time *and* the talent," said Bert airily, "I might write a short novel."

"In that case," said Charles, with mock gallantry, "you are welcome. Our door is open to novelists, would-be novelists, and other lost souls."

Kathy laughed gaily.

But Charles became sober. "I've got a question for you, Bert. Have you ever heard of a German named Christian Thyssen?"

Bert reflected a few moments, then slowly shook his head. "Fritz Thyssen was an industrialist who contributed a great deal of money to the Nazi Party during its rise to power," he said.

"I've checked that possibility already," said Charles. "Christian Thyssen is not of that family."

"Why do you ask?"

Charles drew a deep breath. "Off the record, Bert," he said. "Last week Thad and I attended a meeting of some of the European investors. This young man appeared . . . out of nowhere. He's new to us . . . a take-charge type . . . no more than thirty years old. I'm curious. Thad's curious."

"Do you want me to make a few discreet inquiries?"

"Could you? We'd rather keep out of it. We wouldn't want the wrong people to find out we're behind the inquiries."

"Sounds ominous."

"No, just cautious."

Bert said no more, but he thought it odd that Charles Lodge Johnson, perhaps with Thad Catlett's knowledge, was asking him, Bert Stouffer, to inquire into the background of one of their investors. He would cooperate.

Sitting alone in his apartment, Thad watched the televised debate between Jennie Paget and her Republican opponent, Gordon Baker. He had never before seen her functioning as a politician. He saw a side of her personality he had not observed, and he was startled by her command of facts and her understanding of issues. Baker apparently had not confronted her before and tended to condescend to her at first. He walked into a flurry of political jabs that left him staggering. Stunned, he came back, swinging aggressively. But she ducked and dodged until she caught him with his guard down.

Baker lashed back. "Would you be willing, Mrs. Paget, to submit to a urine test to demonstrate, as I have done, that you do not use illicit narcotics?"

"You are asking me to urinate in a bottle, Mr. Baker? Do I have to let you witness it? Otherwise, how can you be sure I didn't substitute a sample one of my secretaries smuggled to me? And, supposing you and I can provide certified urine for the test, Mr. Baker, what will that prove? Does it prove anything more than that we laid off heroin and cocaine temporarily? What evidence do we have from your highly publicized urinalysis that you didn't get high on the Fourth of July? Or quaff three martinis in rapid succession Friday night at the—"

"*Mrs. Paget!* I did not quaff three martinis anywhere Friday night!"

"I will accept your word, Mr. Baker. But you cannot prove it by urinalysis."

*   *   *

She had a key to Thad's apartment, and two hours after the debate, she let herself in. He was asleep, and she woke him.

"I need Scotch," she said.

Thad opened one eye and looked up at her. Then he opened the other eye and looked at his bedside clock. "It's still a few minutes before midnight. I guess we can reopen the bar," he announced. Then he asked casually, "Where's Martin?"

"Off in the wilds of Minnesota, trying to convince a federal judge that black is white, day is night, or up is down. I don't know. Frankly, my love, I don't care."

Thad got up and pulled on a pair of pants. "I watched the debate, Jennie," he said. "You were great. I mean it. I didn't realize how good you are."

"Unfortunately, most of the voters weren't watching. They'll probably judge him by his mellifluous voice or blow-dry hairdo," she sighed. "Seriously, most new members of the House look and sound like TV anchormen."

Thad shrugged. "Anyway, you racked his ass."

She poured herself a stiff drink—and one for him. "What would I do if I were defeated?" she asked. "What would we do if I weren't in Congress?"

"The same thing we'll do if I go broke," he said.

"You can't be serious," she said.

"I'm not serious," he agreed. "You'll be reelected, and I'll make another million dollars."

Jennie swallowed half her Scotch in one gulp. "Somebody want to give me a urine test?" she asked mischievously.

"You made him look like a fool on that exchange," said Thad.

"It wasn't too hard. He *is* a fool," said Jennie. "A maturely handsome fool with an authoritative voice. It isn't *what* he says; it's *how* he says it that's winning votes."

"You'll win, Jennie."

"I have to. Christ, I don't know what I'll do if I don't."

"You'll be the sixth-ranking Democrat on the Interstate and

210

Foreign Commerce Committee. That should entitle you to an important subcommittee chairmanship." He grinned. "Why do you think I've been courting you?"

Jennie dropped her skirt and kicked it aside. "One advantage of Ronald Reagan's Republican resurgence," she said, "is that it kept knocking off the senior Democrats on my committee."

Thad pulled her close to him. "I'm in love with an important woman," he said. He pulled up her blouse and unhooked her brassiere. "Someday I may have to testify before you, Madame Chairperson."

She shook her head quickly. "God forbid," she said.

He pushed her back so he could admire her breasts.

"Would you believe," she asked, "that someone in this campaign asked me for my *measurements*? I was half flattered, half furious."

"It's none of their business," he objected with mock severity. "I want exclusive rights to your measurements."

She allowed an appreciative smile that slowly faded into a solemn thin line. "Don't you ever testify before a committee that I chair," she blurted. "We've got to avoid it some way. . . . I would have to withdraw. I would have to explain that we . . . uh . . . have a personal relationship."

She turned away from him and stalked to the window. "If you and I could . . . If we could both get divorces and make all this legal, I'd give up the sixth rank on the committee." She turned around and smiled bitterly. "It would cost me my seat in Congress. It would cost you half your corporation." She shrugged. "I think we had better make love."

Afterward, as they lay together, taking small sips from a shared glass of Glenlivet, she asked him about States Broadcasting.

"There are whispers in the wind that you are going to beard the born-agains in their dens. I hear you have more money in the collection plate than they do. What is it? A billion dollars, Thad?"

"Not a billion," he said. "Half a billion."

"Can you raise it?"

"Maybe. You know, I've essentially kept CCE safe since we sold forty percent to Hildebrandt and company. I mean, CCE has been mine—and Anne's. I've kept control of my newspapers. But this time . . . For the first time, I'm risking loss of control of the business I've built over the past thirty years."

"But why? . . . Why would you do that?"

"Jennie . . . Think about it. If we acquire States Broadcasting— fourteen television stations, *fourteen!*—we'll have one of the most powerful media conglomerates in the *world!*"

"You already must be overextended. How can a company so deeply in debt raise half-a-billion dollars?"

"There's no mystery or magic to it," he said. "We're going to issue preferred stock in Catlett Communications Enterprises. The pre-ferred, of course, will have a first claim on earnings. That is, the holders of the preferred stock get their dividends, no matter what. But the dividends are only 3.5%. We can meet that easily enough. It's less than a million and a half a month. On the other hand, we've agreed to redeem the preferred within three years after issue. If we fail to redeem it, it is automatically converted into the right to buy fifty percent of the common stock in CCE—half of Anne's and half of mine. I can't redeem it in part. I have to redeem all or nothing."

"Anne has agreed to this?"

"Not yet."

"You could lose everything you've built."

"My investors can grant extensions," he said. "They want returns on their investment, not control of CCE."

"Are you easing out of the driver's seat, Thad?"

"Oh no. Not yet. I've got hotshot lawyers working on everything. No, I'm not giving up control. But I'm risking it; I won't kid you about that."

*   *   *

Thad wanted Conroy Publishing Company. He wanted to be a book publisher; he always had. It was unfortunate that the opportunity to purchase Conroy had come up at the same time he was trying to buy Lion Pictures and States Broadcasting. But the Conroy acquisition was his personal project, and he pursued it personally.

Thad called on Mason Conway on May 3, in the Conroy Publishing Company offices on Third Avenue.

Conway, though sixty-eight, looked younger. His eyes were clear, his face weathered but unwrinkled, his hair rich, without a taint of gray. He smoked a thin cigar as they talked. His office was lined with shelves, on which were displayed many of his publishing triumphs—best-sellers, histories, biographies, memoirs of statesmen, stars, and pundits. Some had won Pulitzer Prizes, others National Book Awards.

"Why not speak frankly?" he said to Thad. "My people would be appalled if I sold the company to you."

"What people?"

"Oh, my editors. The people I depend on. You can't operate without good editors. And they can walk out on you and start their own imprints, you know. I think you'd lose many of my people. And they could take the top writers with them."

"Because they wouldn't want to work for Thad Catlett."

"Well . . . I said I'd speak frankly. Your reputation does not appeal to the kind of people who work here."

"Do their attitudes govern you?" Thad asked.

"No, not necessarily. I feel some loyalty to them. They may influence me, but they don't control me."

"I will pay $52.25 a share for enough stock to give me control."

"I can get $54.25."

Thad shook his head. "I don't think so. But I'll go $53.00. Top."

Conway leaned back, puffed on his cigar, and contemplated Thad for a long, lingering moment. "You're talking cash?"

"Nothing but," said Thad.

213

"I've come to think of myself as a millionaire. But I've never had the cash in hand. . . . Always in the bank," said Conway. "This would give me my million in spending money. And my son and daughter, too."

"And your favorite nieces and nephews," said Thad. "Set for life."

"What about my editors?"

"I don't expect to make any major changes," said Thad. "I'll be learning the business."

CCE issued preferred stock in the amount of $135,000,000. None of the purchasers bore names like Hildebrandt, Dietrich, Thyssen, Schulenberg, Yoshioka, or Kim Doo Chung. Entered on the stock certificates were the names of investment services, banks, trusts, and estates. It would be, as the *Wall Street Journal* pointed out, extremely difficult to identify the owners of CCE Preferred, 1986. The terms, however, were made public through the SEC filing, and it was pointed out in the business press that F. Thad Catlett had put at risk his undiluted ownership and control of Catlett Communications Enterprises. The article went on:

An odd development, most observers thought, since tight personal control, asking no one else's by-your-leave, has become a personal trademark of F. Thad Catlett. On the other hand, acquisition of Conroy makes him overnight a formidable force in book publishing in the United States. He may have considered that worth the risk.

A bit more difficult to understand is his bid to buy a lion's share of Lion Pictures. If he acquires control of this major motion picture studio for less than $400 million, it will surprise the film industry. If he manages to do so, he will have acquired $550 million in new debt this year. Even if he can sell preferred stock at the extremely favorable dividend commitment he arranged for the issue that financed the Conroy acquisition, his interest costs will exceed $19 million a year. Since Lion has barely broken even each of the past three years, acquisition will impose a severe financial burden on CCE.

"No goddamn wonder the network's on a downhill racer," said Thad to Kenneth Asher.

They were sitting before a huge television set in Thad's office in the Pan Am Building. For five hours they had been watching tapes of prime-time broadcasting taken off the States Broadcasting network. They examined the programs for two nights only—Wednesday and Thursday. They had eased the boredom with a heavy dose of liquor—Scotch for Thad, a martini for Asher. Even Thad's secretary, Trish, who ordinarily did not drink in the office, had retreated to the refrigerator and bar and mixed her second Rob Roy.

"They couldn't possibly be making more than nickels and dimes with this kind of advertising," said Thad. "Japanese knives that can cut bricks or tomatoes equally well and stay sharp for a century. Albums of 1950's music. Multipurpose tools for the home handyman. 'Talking Bibles.' Automobile wax. None of it available in stores." He shook his head. "No automobile commercials. No breakfast foods. And, of course, no beer commercials. Not even Preparation H."

"Not as bad as the program content," said Trish. She was a thirty-five-year-old Brooklynite with a pronounced accent. "Adolescent drivel."

"Nothing worth watching is acceptable to the Christian right," said Asher.

"That's why the stock can be picked up for peanut shells," said Thad. "Those fourteen stations are just waiting to be plucked like plums."

"Not so easy," said Asher. "The evangelicals can stir up a political storm."

"I have a raincoat," said Thad.

"It will take more than a raincoat to ward off the inquisitors. They'll cut off your balls," said Asher.

"Let me worry about the family jewelry," said Thad. "You put the financing together. You and Mel and whoever else you need. I'll handle the public relations."

Thad retained the firm of Gibson, Dunne & Crutcher in Los Angeles to represent CCE and make an offer of $13.00 a share for the stock in Lion Pictures. Within five days there were bids of $13.25, then of $13.50, then of $15.50. Pepsi-Cola bid. Cap Cities bid. A Canadian-Dutch-Belgian consortium was formed to bid.

On October 29, Thad notified Hildebrandt, by cable, that he would not raise the CCE bid above $15.00:

HIGHER BID WOULD RAISE LION COST TO US ABOVE $350 MILLION. THIS WOULD MAKE HEAVY LOSSES INEVITABLE. CURRENT BID ALREADY TOO MUCH. NEW BIDDERS ENTERING CONTEST. AM WITHDRAWING.

Within hours, he received a cable from Christian Thyssen in Berlin:

DO NOT WITHDRAW FROM LION BIDDING. WE ARE PREPARED TO BACK YOU TO $400 MILLION, MORE IF NECESSARY.

Thad answered:

NOT INTERESTED IN LOSING PROPOSITION. FUR-THER BIDDING BAD BUSINESS JUDGMENT.

Thyssen telephoned.

"I understand your point of view. Please understand that to us owning a major American picture studio is worth taking a loss."

Thad stood at the window of his office, looking out toward Long Island Sound. He had a foot on the windowsill, a cigarette in his left hand, the telephone in his right. He watched a light rain form, gradually obscuring the view.

"I cannot drag my company into a continuing loss," he said. "Lion is marginally profitable in the hands of the people who run it now. I could hardly see a break-even if we could have picked it up for three hundred million. Four hundred million? . . . We'd be buying a constant drain."

"Do this for me, then," said Thyssen. "Bid it as high as four hundred million. I guarantee that within thirty days after you buy it, a new group will purchase it from you. We will lend you the money to back up your bid, as you know. Within thirty days, we will take the stock off your hands for all that you paid, plus your costs."

Thad puffed out his cheeks and blew a loud breath. "Look, I don't mean to imply that I don't trust your word, but I can't put my company into debt for hundreds of millions of dollars on a verbal assurance, given over the telephone, that you will form a group and buy the stock."

"If I say I will do it, I will do it!"

"What if you're killed in an airplane crash day after tomorrow?" Thad asked coolly.

"You are bypassing an important opportunity."

"Paying an exorbitant price for a marginally profitable motion picture company is no opportunity."

"It is to me. I am willing to invest the money."

"Well, I am not."

Thyssen remained silent for a long, significant moment; then he responded in a voice that spoke contained anger. "Very well. The opportunity is lost." He hung up.

On election night, Thad sat alone in his apartment, watching the

217

returns on television. He focused intently on the local returns from Westchester County, where the last poll had shown the Republican Gordon Baker within a percentage point of the incumbent Democrat Jennie Paget. In the early returns, Baker pulled ahead. During the middle of the evening, Jennie drew even with him. About midnight, with ninety-eight percent of the votes reported, she led by 1,112 votes. Baker appeared before the cameras and conceded to "a gallant lady." At her headquarters, Jennie was surrounded by cheering, screaming campaign workers and could hardly make her statement. Ebullient, she called her husband Martin up to the microphone and kissed him on the cheek.

Not long afterward, she called Thad. He congratulated her. She remained elated but exhausted. He could detect it in her voice. She was emotionally depleted. He said he wished he could be with her.

The following Saturday night, Thad and Anne encountered Congresswoman Jennie Paget and her husband Martin at a dinner dance held at the Greenwich Country Club to raise money to provide Christmas meals for needy families. Tickets were five hundred dollars per couple, and the Pagets' tickets had been donated by one of Martin Paget's corporate clients.

"I'm not sure whether you've met my wife," said Martin Paget.

"Indeed I have," said Thad. "I would know her anyway from her television appearances."

Paget was bald, peering like an owl through rimless spectacles, a man of conspicuous self-satisfaction. He looked to be forty-five or forty-six—to Jennie's thirty-six. Thad had met him twice; Davis, Polk & Wardwell were New York counsel for Lion.

"But I've not met either Mr. or Mrs. Paget," said Anne.

"Then allow me, Mrs. Catlett," said Jennie. "I'm Jennie. And this is Martin. Both of us have met Thad, and we're now pleased to meet you."

Thad was going through anguish. Anne, exquisitely draped in rustling rose-colored silk, would have made any man proud to be her husband. Poised, self-assured, striking, she was recognized by half the assembled people as the wife and partner of the notorious F. Thad Catlett. The diminutive Jennie, in contrast, was plain. Dressed in a simple black-and-white gown with bold cleavage, she looked up into Anne's eyes, then into Thad's. In the quick meeting of her eyes with Thad's, she expressed her ingenuous love. He tried to return the same message, wholly unsure that he could convey it without words. But no words were possible. After a moment, someone intruded, eager to speak to Thad, then the knot of couples around them expanded. Once Thad tried to touch Jennie's hand but could not reach it.

The Catletts, as patrons of the ball, were shortly ushered to one of the special patrons' tables, while the Pagets joined the president of Martin's client corporation at the company table. Thad and Jennie could not see each other. Nor could they find an opportunity, though they tried, to dance together.

On Thursday, November 20, Anne telephoned Bert from Grand Central Station, saying she had just come down from the CCE offices in the Pan Am Building and had not had lunch. Would he like to join her somewhere? she asked. He suggested an Irish pub on Third Avenue; half an hour later, they met there.

She ordered a double rye; when it arrived, she told the waitress to bring her another one. Between bland conversation, she drained both glasses. Then she pulled from her purse a sheet torn from a wire-service printer.

"I can't believe what we've gotten into," she sighed. "If I ever write a book about my life, the title will be, *Just One Damned Thing After Another.*"

"I couldn't believe he did it," said Bert. "There had been rumors, but I couldn't believe it would happen."

"Look at this," she whispered huskily, handing him the sheet.

Bert was astonished. Anne's voice had broken, and her eyes were flooding with tears. He stared at the AP story:

> Rep. Robert McCluskey, D-Okla., announced today that the House Committee on Interstate and Foreign Commerce will open hearings in January on the possible impact of an

219

acquisition of States Broadcasting Company by media mogul F. Thad Catlett. "Of particular concern," said the committee chairman, "is the fact that the Catlett interests are unwilling to disclose the sources of their funding."

In a related development, Senator Eugene Borman, R-Miss., announced he was introducing a bill to block Catlett's acquisition of States. "It is not in the public interest," he said, "for a chain of fourteen television stations to fall into the hands of a man whom many believe to be an atheist and a pornographer."

Asked if he himself believes that F. Thad Catlett is an atheist and pornographer, Senator Borman replied, "Well, I do wonder just what sort of man he is. His son, we are given to understand, is what they call a 'gay.'"

"That's rotten," Bert muttered. "Rotten."

"It's the truth, of course," she said in a thin voice. "But we didn't need to see it on the AP wire."

"Gene Borman's a *bastard*."

Anne clenched her teeth. "He may have bitten off more than he can swallow," she said evenly. "He has just declared war on F. Thad Catlett, and my husband knows how to fight back. His philosophy is, 'Don't let the jackals get you down, or they'll gang up on you and tear you apart.' My husband believes in making it so painful for the first jackal that the others will back off."

"Gene Borman is an unguided missile, with warheads likely to strike anywhere," said Bert. "He launches his missiles from behind the embattlements of the United States Senate. He has full congressional immunity. In contrast, Thad will be held accountable for anything he does. It won't be a fair fight, Anne."

"Thad has tangled with bigger bastards than Borman," she said. "A district attorney in Pittsburgh. State legislators in Ohio. A labor leader. A federal judge. Thad destroyed them. He did it with a deadly attack in his newspapers. And let me tell you something. Every one of them had it coming."

"It's still wrong, Anne, for newspapers to conduct personal vendettas."

"How much do you want to bet Thad will find something on this Senator Borman and make him wish he'd never heard the name Thad Catlett? What do you want to bet he's going to hate the day he publicly called my son gay?"

"Anne . . ."

"What do you want to bet we'll *destroy* that son of a bitch?"

Thad sat down in the elegant private dining room of Dr. Kim Doo Chung's Washington residence. The small dining room—on the second floor and apart from the grander rooms below—was furnished in Oriental style. Thad recognized the paintings, with men in strange black hats and women in billowing ceremonial dresses, as Korean. The room was lighted only by the flames of small oil lamps. A dozen lamps basked the room in flickering light, warm and enchanting. A scent had been added to the oil, and a light fragrance hung in the air. There were no windows. The walls were covered with hangings—delicately painted scenes in soft pastels.

"I hope my servants do not offend," said Kim.

"Of course not," Thad replied.

They were being served by two almost identical Oriental girls, so much alike they must have been twins. Thad judged they were no more than thirteen or fourteen years old. With silent, attentive skill, they served wine and food; a Western meal, French cooking.

They never left the room. A more mature young woman brought in trays and placed them on stands from which the girls served. When not serving, the twins stood behind Thad and Kim, watching, ready to move instantly to refill a glass or to retrieve a slipped napkin.

Dr. Kim Doo Chung was everything that impressed Thad as a typical middle-aged Korean: short and compact, narrow-eyed, more muscular and rugged than the Chinese or Japanese. He wore a gray silk jacket and black silk pants, with bright red embroidered slippers.

221

"Yes, we have achieved more economic than political progress," he said. "I think, however, our priorities have been correct. Economic progress can become the foundation for social progress. I fail to see how an impoverished nation can achieve democracy. Forty years after the establishment of our nation, in spite of a long and destructive war, we in the South have achieved a standard of living that is the envy of the North. Marxists everywhere hate us. For we stand as dramatic evidence of the bankruptcy of Communism."

"I understand you agreed with me," said Thad, "when I stopped bidding for Lion."

"Yes, you were right," said Kim. "I am just a minor partner, but I live in this country." He shrugged deprecatingly. "I have many good friends—in business, in the Congress, in the Administration. I know America better than any of those Germans, better even than Yoshioka."

"Lion is not profitable," said Thad. "What we could have done with it could not possibly justify committing half a billion dollars to an unsound investment. I don't mind losing money if it serves a good purpose. I still lose money on the *Register-Herald* here in Washington and on the *Sentinel-American* in New York. But they strengthen my overall operations. Lion could never have justified the enormous cost."

"I agree," said Kim. "Still, I wonder if we should not consider investing in some motion pictures—without the necessity of owning the studio, without the huge overhead."

"Specifically?"

Kim smiled. "I do not refer to martial arts films," he said. "They are childish. They could have no impact on public opinion. But I believe there is both a national need and a market for patriotic films—pictures that feature a strong American hero who confronts Red terrorists and shoots them down. America needs to be reminded of the eternal struggle between force and freedom."

"We could establish a new macho hero," Thad acknowledged.

"Yes. You produce the movies. I will back the investment. It will be our secret. We need not notify our German friends."

"I think we are obliged to consult with them," said Thad firmly.

Kim's plastic smile widened. "Of course. You will, I hope, forgive me if I am naive about Western business practices."

"When I see any naiveté, I will forgive it," said Thad.

Kim's smile never wavered. "I am extremely interested in this movie. We can achieve two purposes: bolster patriotism in the United States and earn a worthwhile profit."

"I am already on record," Thad reminded him, "that message movies bomb."

"Ours need not," said Kim. "All we need is a good script."

Thad chuckled. "I hope you aren't too optimistic," he said.

"You will do me a great favor if you will consider this project," said Kim. "Now, if I may, let me do a favor for you."

Thad lifted an eyebrow quizzically.

Kim leaned forward confidentially. "Am I mistaken in supposing, my friend Thad, that you would like to . . . what is the word? . . . retaliate . . . against the senator from Mississippi?"

"You are not mistaken," said Thad tersely.

Kim's smile disappeared. "I can provide you with some information about Senator Borman," he said. "All I ask in return is that you do not disclose its source. Also, if you should require it, I can tell you some interesting things about Representative McCluskey."

"I'll accept the Borman information," said Thad. "I hold no brief against McCluskey."

Thad insisted that both his sons be home for Christmas. That meant accepting Thaddy's apartment mate as a house guest for the weekend, since Thaddy would not let Alan spend Christmas alone. When the two boys arrived, carrying one bag between them, Thaddy made it plain that Alan would not sleep alone in a guest room.

Richard surprised everyone. He had invited a girl, named Betty, to join him. She would spend Christmas with her own family but would arrive at the Catlett estate on December 28 and stay until the New Year.

Alan, though he still did darkroom work and other chores for Thaddy, was a dancer and had at last won a role. He was lithe and slender. His face was pallid and somber. His role required him to shave his head, so he faithfully shaved it every morning though the show was in recess for the Christmas weekend. He was pleasant, respectful, and courteous. Except for his relationship with their son and the temporary Yul Brynner look, Thad and Anne found it difficult to find anything objectionable about him.

"Alan and I have come to a decision," Thaddy said the afternoon before Christmas. "We're going to move to London . . . as soon as Alan's show closes, which it will early next month. We've talked to people over there. We think we can do better with both our careers in London."

Thad and Anne were sitting with Thaddy and Alan, reviewing a score of black-and-white prints spread out over a table and the floor. These were pictures of dancers and would be part of Thaddy's new book.

"Senator Cornpone running you out of the country?" Thad asked quietly.

"No one of importance to me," said Thaddy, "has the least interest in anything he might say. If anyone is driving me away from New York, it would be you. Whatever I do in New York, I am identified as your son. I would like an identity of my own. This is not intended as a reflection on you. I am certainly not ashamed of you. On the contrary, I'm proud of you and mother."

Their son had never said that before, and both Thad and Anne were moved.

"I just think a little distance between us will be good for everyone concerned," Thaddy concluded.

On Christmas afternoon, Thad was called to the telephone. His private line in the den had been ringing, and Alan had picked up the phone. He was unaware that this line was never answered by anyone except the master of the house. Thad thanked him and ducked into the den to take the call.

"Thad? I hope I'm not interrupting anything."

"Jennie? Of course not. It's great to hear from you."

"I have only a minute. The house is full of people. But I just couldn't let this day go by without calling you."

"That was thoughtful, Jennie. It brightens my day."

"I love you with all my heart. Merry Christmas, Thad."

"Merry Christmas to you, Jennie. I love you, too."

In another part of the house, with less secrecy, Anne sat down and dialed Bert. He told her he was leaving for Virginia the next day. He was driving down in a rented car piled with presents for his daughter.

Richard's friend Betty showed up on Sunday the twenty-eighth. She was blond, busty, and broad-hipped, a short but solid young woman. She brought a bag of cashmere sweaters and blue jeans, no dress, no skirt. Richard began to wear blue jeans and sweaters to dinner so Betty would not be the only person at the table in casual clothes. When Anne suggested to Richard that she take Betty to a shop on the Avenue and buy her a dress for their New Year's Eve party, Richard said no, they must not embarrass Betty. The girl would hardly have been embarrassed, Anne concluded. So far as Betty was concerned, she and Richard were the only ones correctly dressed. So far as Anne was concerned, Betty was a prepped little brat. But she was the first girl who had ever let Richard sleep with her, and poor Richard was stricken.

"Did you hear what she said to me?" Thad asked Anne after a small dinner party on Monday night.

"I didn't even notice you talking to her," Anne said.

"In front of the Parkers, who were standing there about to leave, she volunteered brightly that her father says our balance sheet must be 'something to see.'"

"What did you say to her?"

"I said yes, we were thinking of framing it and hanging it on the living room wall."

In their bedroom, they undressed. Anne went to the bathroom, then inside her closet, and she came out wearing a provocative white lace bed jacket. She left it open. He was sitting on the bed, and she stood for a moment in the light of a floor lamp, letting him look at her.

Responding to the unspoken invitation, he stripped down and rose to embrace her. Their bodies pressed together, and they kissed. Then she stepped back.

His belly bulged, and the flesh at his armpits was flabby. But he was still tall and erect, with a rugged dignity. When he was dressed, his clothes hid the slackness of his flesh. It was not hidden now. He sensed her appraisal. "I'm tired," he said.

"Maybe I don't excite you anymore," she said.

"Of course you do."

"But you're tired. So let's wait until tomorrow night. It'll be your last night home for a week or more."

"Right," he said. "Tomorrow. Maybe in the morning."

On Tuesday, December 30, Thad made a quick trip into Manhattan. He went straight to the office to sign some urgent papers and to review some year-end reports. At noon he caught a train back to Greenwich and arrived at the station at one. Anne met the train; Thaddy and Alan were waiting with her in the car. She drove east two exits on the turnpike and turned off at Old Greenwich. Thad's mother Alma had bought a house not far from the beach, and this was her day to assemble her family around her table for the midday meal, which she persisted in calling dinner.

The house was creaky and cramped, but it suited the old lady just fine. She had furnished it to her taste, and she was comfortable in it. She met them at the door in blue jeans and a woolen shirt.

"Richard?" she asked when the four of them had come in.

Anne shook her head; Richard and Betty had not accompanied them.

"Oh? I see," said Alma. "Richard will make a crackerjack

preacher," she assured Anne, "though I can't see how he's going to make much of a living."

Out of the corner of her eye, Anne could see Thad showing Thaddy and Alan the .30-.30 rifle his mother had mounted above her mantel. Anne assumed he was telling them how their grandmother had shot a rattlesnake on D Day.

"He doesn't *have* to make a living," Anne explained to her mother-in-law. "Neither does Thaddy. We've set aside a substantial trust fund for them."

"But he's gonna study classical *Greek?*"

Anne smiled. "And Latin. And he'll teach classical languages at a Catholic university." She shrugged. "Nothing's permanent. If Betty were permanent, she wouldn't sit still for that. So I know Betty's not permanent. . . . And I doubt his choice of career is."

"Remind me to send that Professor Harrington a box of candy, anyway," said Alma Catlett.

She had set up a buffet. They picked and nibbled. And they drank Scotch and bourbon; those were the only choices. She was awkward about Alan but not hostile. ("They only do it in private, I s'pose.") They enjoyed a leisurely afternoon, reminded Alma she was expected at the New Year's Eve party by nine, and drove home a little before four.

"Hey," said Richard when they reached the house. "The phone's been ringing off the hook. One of the calls is from Germany. Here's the call-back number."

Thad strode into his office and returned the call.

"Anne . . ." He stood in the doorway, pale, then started to slump and grabbed at the door for support. For a horrified instant, she thought he was suffering a heart attack.

"Thad? What!—"

"Wilhelm Hildebrandt is dead."

"Oh, Thad! No!"

"Oh, my God! . . . He was murdered."

ELEVEN

Thad had called an urgent meeting in the conference room at corporate headquarters. He stood solemnly at the head of the table. Seated on the two sides were Anne and her father Bayard Justin, Charles Lodge Johnson, Kenneth Asher, Melvin Bragg, and Willard James, an accountant from Deloite, Haskins & Sells. Thad had asked the accountants for a report. On this morning, January 12, 1987, the report was ready. All of them had read it, and the accountant was prepared to respond to questions.

Waving the report accusingly under their collective noses, Thad declared, "This confirms my judgment. The company has borrowed heavily to fund its expansion into the broadcast industry and to acquire Conroy. I mean, this debt figure"—he slapped the report with the flat of his hand—"is terrifying."

"More than four hundred million dollars," said Bayard Justin, nodding his agreement. "And if you succeed in acquiring States, you will be in debt for more than a *billion*. And that *is* frightening, Thad."

Thad hesitated, his lips pursed. "Yes. . . . But look at the assets. We paid $135,000,000 for Conroy. Conroy is worth every dime of it. We paid $46,374,00 for DunCast. Those two stations are worth at least $60,000,000. We paid $56,775,000 for the Greensboro and Dayton stations. Those are worth $59,000,000. It cost us $40,000,000 to set up the three WYRK stations. We've been offered $55,000,000 for them. Runkle . . . well, we went a little heavy on that. . . ."

Thad paused another moment to reflect, then again slapped the report. "All right. Counting the preferred stock as debt, we have borrowed $413,000,000. For that money, our auditors tell us we have acquired assets that are now worth $459,000,000. We've bid rather carefully, and some of our properties have already appreciated in a very short time, partly because we manage them well, partly because the market perceives our policies and techniques will increase revenues. On the books, our acquisitions net out at $460,000,000."

"Assuming you could sell them," said James.

"Right," agreed Thad. "Now . . . the newspapers, what we owned before our new investors came along, are now valued at $141,000,000."

"And your point is?" asked Justin.

"My point is that because of the death of Wilhelm Hildebrandt, we are entitled to repurchase the forty percent of CCE stock that we sold to VWH. You remember, you yourself put that in the contract—a right to repurchase in the event of Hildebrandt's resignation, retirement, or death. We can buy back our stock for the $52,000,000 they paid for it, plus ten percent per year. VWH has owned the stock for eighteen months, so we can repurchase for about $60,000,000. The company's net worth is about $187,000,000, and we can buy forty percent of it for about $60,000,000. Apart from recovering total ownership and absolute control of our company, it's a great deal financially."

"It will take a hell of a loan," said Bayard Justin.

"Anne has agreed to it," said Thad.

*   *   *

Bert Stouffer's flight from Frankfurt arrived at Kennedy Airport at 3:20 P.M. He was handed a note by one of the flight attendants, just before he left the plane: Mrs. F. Thad Catlett was waiting for him inside the terminal.

She'd had a couple of drinks while she waited; that was a bit obvious. But she urged him to stop by a bar in the Pan Am terminal for a drink . . . "before we have to face the traffic."

Seated at a small round table in the dimly lighted bar, she fumbled in her huge purse and extracted two folded newspapers. "Look at those," she said. "What'd I tell you?"

Bert looked first at the *Washington Register-Herald* edition for Wednesday, January 7. The story she wanted him to see was spread across the front page.

"MY GODDAM BASE! MESS WITH IT AT YOUR PERIL!"—SEN. BORMAN

Senator Eugene Borman, R-Miss., threatened a legislative vendetta against members of the Senate Armed Services Committee last October when several senators dared to suggest that Hork Field, a Mississippi air base that has been condemned as useless by the Defense Department, might be closed at an annual savings of almost one hundred million dollars.

"You mess with my air base, and I'll tangle up every goddamn bill you have the slightest interest in!" yelled the hard-drinking Mississippian at the closed session of the committee. Senators, who asked not to be quoted by name for fear of Borman's vengeance, described him as hysterical and probably intoxicated during the session.

"Monument to Waste"

Hork Field, established in 1943 as a training base for Army pilots, should have been declared surplus after World War II, according to a presidential commission created to identify and condemn waste in government. Its chairman, industrialist J. Peter Grace, called the Mississippi base "a monument to waste."

Seventeen times since 1948, Hork Field has been identified as a wasteful, pork-barrel operation. In the interim, it has cost American taxpayers at least $3,000,000,000 (that's three billion dollars) to keep open.

Bert laid the paper aside, then reviewed the story on the front page of the next day's edition of the *New York Sentinel-American*. This one was accompanied by pictures.

GRASS GROWS ON RUNWAYS OF SENATOR'S PET AIR BASE!

Mississippi Senator's Billion-Dollar Boondoggle

A chance taxpayer who should happen to stray onto Mississippi's Hork air base would find grass growing in the cracks in the runways, with a few superannuated planes parked here and there. These are training planes for the Mississippi National Guard, a force of more than two thousand airmen and airwomen, who are kept around to defend the local cotton fields from enemy invasion. They assemble at the base occasionally for training that will be useful only if World War II should be refought. Another three thousand civilians are kept on the payroll doing nothing much that anyone can see.

From this high ground, the story descended into a low-level attack upon Senator Borman, not only for squandering the taxpayer's money, but for siphoning money off from military projects that are really needed.

"War, huh?" grunted Bert, handing back the two newspapers.

232

She stuffed the newspapers into her purse. "That's just the beginning," she said. Then moving to the next subject on her mind, she asked, "Did you find out anything?"

Bert shook his head. "Not much. My impression is that the government of the Federal Republic is somehow embarrassed by the shooting of Wilhelm Hildebrandt and is covering up something. But that's just a gut feeling, no facts that I can pin down."

"You won't believe what I did this morning," she said, changing subjects again.

"What?"

"Signed a note for sixty million dollars. Under the terms of our agreement with Hildebrandt, we were entitled to repurchase the stock Verlagsgruppe Wilhelm Hildebrandt bought in 1985, if anything should happen that would remove Hildebrandt as chief executive officer of VWH. We're exercising that option. We met this morning, finalized the decision, and signed the papers."

"I wish you hadn't told me," said Bert grimly.

"Why?"

"I can't write into a news story anything I hear from you. It would be a breach of ethics."

"I suppose I've just told you something Thad wouldn't want to make public," she agreed thoughtfully.

"How will you react if I begin publishing a series on the relationship between Catlett Communications Enterprises and Verlagsgruppe Wilhelm Hildebrandt? How will you feel if I publish something highly embarrassing to your husband? What if it's something that damages the business?"

"Just what do you think you're going to find, Bert?" she asked. "Do you think Thad has done something improper?"

Her hand was on the table, more than halfway across toward him, as if she were encouraging him to touch it. He laid his hand on hers. "Your husband is an aggressive, some say ruthless, businessman. He is limitlessly ambitious. In the last two years, he has financed major acquisitions. Exactly how much money he has used and where he got it are secrets."

"A little over four hundred million," she said, not without a lift of pride and defiance in her voice.

"How? The assets of CCE couldn't have secured that much credit."

"It's really rather simple. A consortium of businessmen, Germans mostly, have backed Thad."

"I'd like to know why. Granted that some Germans have surplus capital. Granted that America is the safest place to invest their surplus. But television? Why would they sink their money in CCE for the acquisition of television stations? For profit? Surely you're not going to tell me the Germans were merely looking for the best return on their money?"

"Each of the broadcast properties acquired by CCE in the past two years has appreciated substantially in value," she said slowly and emphatically.

Bert breathed a sigh of resignation. "Okay. One more question. Then I'll drop it. Do you know the names of the people who have invested? The Germans, I mean. Or whoever they are. Can you identify them?"

Anne shook her head. "Thad knows," she said tersely.

Bert raised his hand to summon their waitress. Their drinks had not arrived and he had decided not to waste any more time in this place. He had intended to cancel their order, but the girl came with the drinks, so he accepted them and paid her.

"Bert?"

"Hmm?"

"Is there any reason why you have to go back to your apartment tonight?"

He shrugged. "I suppose not."

"Damn house is quiet at night now that the boys are both gone. And the traffic on the Van Wyck is going to be murderous. Why can't we just find us a nice motel around the airport somewhere?"

He felt uneasy about it, but he agreed.

*   *   *

They had enjoyed the Sheraton Inn at Fredericksburg, so in January they returned there. Thad, producing Charles Lodge Johnson's American Express card, checked into the inn with Jennie. They registered as Mr. and Mrs. C. L. Johnson, New York City. They left Washington on Friday evening in swirling snow, and by the time they reached Fredericksburg, the roads were icy and dangerous, with four inches of snow on the ground.

The apprehension that attended their first weekend here was long past, and they could spend this weekend comfortably, leisurely napping together in their room, watching a film on cable television, and enjoying long, relaxed meals in the restaurant. They had become a devoted couple, their relationship cozy, their romantic interludes mellow.

"I wish you didn't get so much media attention," she said to him as he sat on the edge of the bed fingering a cigarette, breathing nicotine, and watching the eleven o'clock news.

"Me, too," he grunted as he watched himself appear briefly on the screen in his familiar role of media mogul.

"I mean, it makes you so—so public. There you are staring sternly at everyone who has his television set turned on to ABC World News. Someone is bound to recognize you here. I'm no national figure, but I've also had some national visibility. Someone around here is apt to figure out that we're not exactly Mr. and Mrs. C. L. Johnson."

"I know, I know," muttered Thad. "It's hard to remain anonymous when your face keeps appearing on the television screen. It's gotten worse since I became a movie producer. My news value used to be limited to the financial pages. Now I'm in the gossip columns."

"It's your deal with Dino Bronte that's attracted the spotlight," said Jennie.

"It was a coup, signing up that Sicilian egomaniac," snorted Thad. "We're going to make the rottenest picture ever seen and the most profit ever made."

"Who's doing the script?" she asked.

"I don't even know. Some hack hired by the director. We signed up Lucien Feinberg, and Feinberg brought along his writer."

"This is how you make a record profit?" she asked with a skeptical smile. "You may lose your investment."

Thad shook his head. "Jennie . . . honey, I don't have a *nickel* of my own money in it. I'm just fronting for one of my investors."

"Which one?"

He hesitated. "Confidentially? It has to stay in this room. The financing was advanced by a Korean billionaire. Dr. Kim Doo Chung."

"*Kim Doo Chung* is one of your investors? Thad!"

"He wants to make a new Rambo out of Dino Bronte. Feinberg has come up with a name for him, 'The Electrocutioner.' This character is going to fight Communists. Kim wants the American people to see what a bunch of nasties the Communists are."

"Kim Doo Chung is a shady character, Thad," said Jennie.

"Rumors are whispered about every billionaire," said Thad, "by people who wish his money were theirs. The man has been honest and honorable in all his dealings with me."

"I don't know, Thad," said Jennie. "I think Kim is too far over the line. I don't mean to meddle in your business, but—"

"I have the relationship under control," said Thad.

Jennie shook her head apprehensively. "I must be unsophisticated," she said. "I swear I don't understand this diverse empire of yours and its strange financial underpinnings. Forgive my suspicions . . . but are they *using* you, Thad?"

"When our relationship began, I owned seven general newspapers and sixty-eight neighborhoods," he said. "Now I control ten television stations and Conroy Publishing. If that's being used, I hope they continue to use me."

"I have an uneasy sense that the only thing about you that I'm totally excluded from is this mysterious partnership of yours. Tell me something. Does your wife know all about your secret partners?"

"She owns half interest in my enterprises. I don't hide anything from her," he said. He turned away from the television set. "You and

I have talked about this in the past. Your duties as a congresswoman some day may clash with my business interests. All you need to know from me is that I'm not doing anything illegal. For the rest, we both will be better off if you get your information about CCE from public sources . . . for the protection of both of us."

"I spoke to McCluskey," she said soberly. "I asked him why he thought it necessary to hold hearings about CCE and States. He's serious about it, Thad. Very serious. He thinks the merger of CATSERV and States could discourage competition and become a detriment to the public interest. I can't go any further with him. I can't discourage him."

"Jennie, for God's sake! I didn't ask you to do anything like that. And I don't want you to!"

Jennie lowered her eyes. "I couldn't bear to see you hurt."

"Well . . . I can assure you that I've done nothing wrong, nothing illegal, nothing I need to be ashamed of. The truth can't hurt me, so I'm not afraid of the truth."

"I love you," she whispered. "And that's the truth!"

"And I love you. But don't try to protect me on Capitol Hill. Or *you* might get hurt."

"First I get a midnight telephone call from Frankfurt," complained Charles. "Now you ask me to meet you in—"

"Charles!" Bert interrupted. "You can call this meeting conspiratorial if you want to. You asked me to get some information for you. I have some. This is where and how I choose to give it to you."

Charles glanced around the small Mulberry Street restaurant Bert had chosen for their noontime tryst. Though Bert sometimes made a game of knowing nothing about food and wine, he had chosen—not inadvertently, Charles was sure—an excellent place, a minor landmark of Little Italy.

"I asked you, as I recall, to find out what you could about one Christian Thyssen," said Charles. "May I hope you have learned something? I must confess to you that I have not."

"It wasn't easy," said Bert. "Your Mr. Thyssen covers his tracks very, very thoroughly."

"Need he?"

Bert shrugged. "I'll let you judge. But I want you to understand that I've gone an extra mile to get this information, my friend. I hope it generates a new forthrightness between you and me."

"I have always been forthright with you, Bert," said Charles with a mock-innocent smile.

"No, you haven't. I expect you'll convey this information to your friend, Thad Catlett. Maybe he won't hold me in quite so much contempt in the future."

Charles sighed. "I hope the information is worth the prologue," he said dryly.

"All right," said Bert. With his fingernail, he traced a thin line on the white tablecloth. "When I was in Frankfurt, I asked a few people about Christian Thyssen." He shook his head. "No one had heard the name. Or maybe they just elected not to tell me. That pissed me, Charles, to tell you the truth. If the man is rich and powerful enough to be one of Thad Catlett's German investors, he should be well enough known to be recognized."

"Or maybe he uses a pseudonym with us," said Charles.

"Maybe. But he didn't. I chased him down."

"But it wasn't easy, as you say."

"You had better appreciate this. I called in an IOU. I have a contact in Tel Aviv. Used to be high in Mossad . . . Israeli intelligence. Mossad keeps a silent watch on shadowy Germans."

"Is Thyssen a neo-Nazi?" Charles asked, raising his brows.

Bert stopped talking as their waiter approached with a basket of garlic bread, a platter of fried zucchini, and their wine.

"Have you ever heard of an organization called Bund für das Neues Deutschtum . . . BND?" Bert resumed.

Charles shook his head but leaned forward as a signal that he wanted to hear about it.

Bert spoke in a low voice. "How do you define Nazi?" he asked. "Or neo-Nazi? One thing the BND is not is anti-Semitic. As our Mossad contact points out, there aren't enough Jews left in

Germany to fuel the old anti-Semitic sentiments. In fact, the new generation of Nazi types tend to fear—even secretly admire—the Israelis. No, Mossad does not regard the Bund für das Neues Deutschtum as anti-Semitic. But it *is* anti-democratic."

"Are you saying that Christian Thyssen is a member of this organization?"

"Yes. But you should be even more interested in who founded it. It was founded in 1968 by none other than Wilhelm Hildebrandt. He was the leader. His murder was probably a political assassination. The mantle may now have fallen on Thyssen."

"But what is it, Bert? What is this—this BND? It's not a political party . . . not one that I ever heard of."

"No. . . . And it's not a terrorist organization or underground operation. It's simply an organization of wealthy Germans—and a few Austrians—who despise the memory of Hitler but look back with a certain fondness on Kaiser Wilhelm."

Charles couldn't suppress a laugh. "Oh, surely!"

"Mossad infiltrated to make sure that BND is not a resurgent Nazi cabal. In the view of its members, democracy has always weakened Germany, while monarchy and militarism have always brought strength, prosperity, and glory. They loathe socialism by whatever name. They loathe the Greens. They want to see Germany reunited, and by reunification they want another Anschluss first, the restoration of the German nation, East and West, then the merging of Germany and Austria."

"All of which makes quite plausible the theory that Wilhelm Hildebrandt was murdered by agents of the East German regime," said Charles.

"It's possible," said Bert. "It's also possible that he had opponents in West Germany who wanted to stop him."

"But you are suggesting, I assume, that Thad's . . . uh . . . relationship with these wealthy German investors is, in reality, a relationship with this BND."

"Do you know whether Catlett has ever heard of BND?" asked Bert.

"I can tell you truthfully. He has never mentioned it to me. I can also tell you he has never betrayed any sympathy, not the slightest, for its anti-democratic views."

"If I were you, Charles—certainly if I were Thad Catlett—I would pursue this damned thing. It'd be embarrassing if you were to discover that you're in business with BND. And it would be devastating if it later turned out that the BND membership included a character like Dr. Joseph Mengele."

Charles's face betrayed that he was aghast.

"It's possible," said Bert. "Mengele had close ties to some wealthy Germans."

Charles nodded. "Yes. We must pursue it. I—I'm grateful to you, Bert. I know Thad will be."

Bert looked at his menu. "Now it's my turn to ask a favor. How good are you at keeping a secret, Charles?"

Charles smiled thinly. "Very good. I was once a journalist, you know."

"I helped you," said Bert. "Now I need your help . . . with a personal problem."

Charles gestured obligingly. "If I can . . ." he said.

"It will involve a conflict of loyalties," said Bert. "I must have your word that you won't tell Catlett what I am about to say."

"Sorry," interrupted Charles. "After all, I *am* on the man's payroll. I really can't withhold information from him."

"It's *not* business information," Bert said. "It's personal. There may be a business implication, but it's a personal matter. I can't tell you anything about it, Charles, unless I have your word you won't tell Catlett. It's important to me."

Charles rubbed his palms together contemplatively and thought about it for a moment. "As I said, Bert, I used to be a journalist. My most highly developed sense is curiosity. I have always had a compelling need to know even those things that I had to pretend I did not know. . . . Very well. You have my word."

Bert laid down his menu. "This has to do with Catlett's wife, Anne. She says you are her friend. Well, here it is: She and I are romantically involved. . . . We're having an affair. It's been going on for about six months."

Shocked, Charles pushed back his chair as if he meant to get up and leave the restaurant. His face reddened. "Bert! For God's sake!" he exclaimed angrily.

"It creates a difficult professional problem for me," said Bert.

"Professional problem! What profession are you practicing when you are in bed with Anne Catlett?"

Bert could not suppress a wry smile.

"And what have you learned from her?" Charles demanded as he suddenly realized the implications of Bert's confession.

"More than I want. That's the problem. Whether you believe it or not, I have tried to discourage her from betraying any confidences to me. That's my problem. Ethically, I should refuse to see her."

"Morally, you should stop seeing her."

Bert sighed his acknowledgment. He picked up his menu again and lowered his eyes, diverting his gaze to the listings. "That's not so easy," he said quietly.

Charles turned his head aside and lowered his chin, stroking it thoughtfully. "Are you trying to tell me you're in love with each other?"

"We haven't reached that point."

Charles looked fiercely into Bert's face. "She's a splendid woman," he said. "She's also a lonely woman. Thad has . . . well, he has indulged in affairs over the years—though his biggest affair has always been with his ambition. He—"

"I have had a belly full of Thad Catlett, to tell you the truth," said Bert bitterly. "He's an amoral manipulator of other people's lives. Including mine."

Charles's eyes widened, startled. "What has he ever done to you?"

"He took Megan Wilkinson from me."

The startled expression hadn't faded from Charles's face. "He didn't know that, Bert. I promise you, he didn't know that."

"Would it have made any difference? I loved that woman."

Charles abruptly became Charles Lodge Johnson—lofty, curt, precise. "If you loved *her*, you loved an ambitious young woman who was not worthy of you, Bert."

241

"Then Catlett moved in, used her, and then got rid of her in a way only he could have. Leaving me—"

"Have you told Anne this?"

"No."

"I shouldn't wonder," said Charles dryly.

"Well, thanks for nothing," snapped Bert. "I should have expected a reaction like this. No doubt you assume I seduced Anne to get information out of her. Now you think I am sleeping with her to get revenge on Catlett for robbing me of Megan. If you think that—"

"Thad will think it," said Charles.

"Does he care? I mean, about her?"

"Yes, I'm sure he does, in his way."

"She cares about him, too. She's proud of him. But he doesn't satisfy her, either emotionally or physically. I'm not sure he ever did, from what she tells me. She's lonely, and she's lovely."

Charles glanced around the restaurant, which was becoming noisier as it filled with a lunchtime crowd. "I fail to understand," he said, "why you have elected to tell me all this."

"You may know something I should know," said Bert. "I mean . . . Has she ever done something like this before? Do you know?"

"Not to my knowledge," said Charles. "Neither she nor Thad have ever specifically mentioned any such thing in my presence."

"I want to put you on notice, as a friend. I'm going to do my best to figure out what's going on between Catlett and this group of Germans," said Bert. "I can't help wondering how much he knows himself. I've tried to make her understand my position and my problem. I *really* have discouraged her, Charles. I'm not using her."

"And when Thad finds out, you think he'll believe that?"

"That's much less important to me than that *she* might believe it. And that you might."

"Are you looking to me for advice?"

"Yes."

"Quit seeing her. At least until you've published whatever it is you are going to write. Then . . . well, after that, it becomes a problem for all of us."

"The information has come to me from a source you may not much care for," said Charles to Thad, "but I have no doubt whatever of its reliability. Bert Stouffer is a careful, responsible journalist."

"I know who he is," said Thad.

They were in Thad's office. Big flakes of snow hung suspended in the updraft outside the windows, moving slowly up and down and laterally. Charles watched them distractedly.

"Bert is not on our side exactly, you know. He is determined to write—"

"I know," Thad said.

"Probably I should not have asked him to—"

"If you hadn't, we might not have found out. I'm tempted to give him another name to check out."

"Schulenberg?"

Thad shook his head. "Hanna Frank."

Charles turned away from the snowflakes. "Don't forget, Bert is an independent journalist, and he is determined to—"

"I know what he's trying to do," said Thad. He leaned back in his chair and clasped his hands behind his head. "I'd rather have him doing it than somebody else. As you said, he's a careful journalist. He's a pro. With ethics. I wish he were the only one on our backs."

"Do you know him personally?"

"Oh, indirectly. He and Megan had a thing going. She told me about him."

Charles nodded with inward understanding. "You don't really want him to check out Hanna Frank?"

Thad shook his head. "No. I don't think he'd engage in any reckless speculation, but I don't think we should tempt him that far. This would give him two murders to work on, and maybe connect. His enthusiasm might overcome his professionalism."

243

"I trust you are not going to confront our partners with what we've learned. . . . When you meet with them next week, I mean."

"No. This is supposed to be a reorganization meeting to replace Hildebrandt. If they choose to tell me about BND, I'll listen and feign surprise. It's their hand; I'll let them play it."

"If they choose to tell you, BND might be a little less ominous."

Thad nodded. "We'll wait and see how they play the hand. He glanced at his telephone, where three lines were lighted, one ringing. "Looks like I'm much in demand," he said wearily. "Can you believe it? The old man is weary. This is my year to turn fifty, and I'm beginning to feel it."

"You need a vacation," suggested Charles as he started for the door. "Shall I tell Trish you're ready to start returning calls?"

In a moment Trish came in with a pile of telephone notes. She tapped one of the pink notes with her finger. "Lucien Feinberg," she said. "Either drunk or hysterical."

"All right. Get him on the line."

Feinberg was the director engaged for the Dino Bronte film, *The Electrocutioner*. He was in Los Angeles. Trish reached him immediately.

"Listen, Thad Catlett," he said with a hoarse, dramatic voice. "I gotta have a reading. Just who the hell do I answer to? You or that Korean bastard? Which? Who? What?"

"Be specific, Lucien. What are you talking about?"

"Your Korean buddy, Kim, calls me every couple of days. Wants this in the film. Wants that in the film. And yesterday he sent a local Korean—you know, Lop Cock Too or some shit—to deliver me a case of Stolichnaya, with Dr. Kim's compliments, offer me a nice girl if I'd like my ashes hauled, and by the way, have I made all the script changes Dr. Kim wants? I mean, look, I know how to work with the suckers who put out the money for this shit, but I thought you were calling the shots."

"I am calling the shots. I'll speak to Kim."

"Please do that. The way those guys talked . . . I mean, Jesus man, I don't want to wake up some morning with a dead racehorse in my bed."

"I'll speak to Kim. Meanwhile, you speak to nobody. You understand me?"

"What about the changes?"

"Make your own judgment. If they don't screw up the picture, why not make our Korean friend happy? But from now on, all changes come through me. We'll get together in a couple of weeks and go over the script. Don't tell Dino anything about this. You haven't, I hope."

"No, man."

"Well, don't. Let's keep this between you and me. And it may be, Lucien, that we'll have to sweeten your coffee a little bit. Keep quiet. Keep calm. And keep in touch."

"You got it."

Thad flew to Washington. He wanted to see Jennie before he took off for Europe. But first he would call on Dr. Kim. He arrived at Kim's mansion on Massachusetts Avenue N.W., in the middle of the morning, just in time to see a limousine pull out of the garage and speed east, its back-seat occupant ducking down when he spotted Thad approaching the front door. Kim received him in a sunny little yellow and white office decorated with Oriental hangings and figurines.

"I know it isn't the Oriental way, but I find it necessary to speak bluntly," Thad told him. "You risked publicizing our relationship by calling Feinberg. I had supposed the confidentiality of your role is just as important to you as it is to me."

Kim smiled unctuously. "You must forgive me, Thad. I let my enthusiasm for our motion picture affect my judgment."

"Let our Hollywood associates do their work," said Thad forcefully. "When they are finished, we will review it. Then we can consider changes."

"The message must not be lost," said Kim.

"But it can't be too obvious, or it will backfire. Frankly, our Hollywood production team is more competent than we are. They know what will make a picture a success."

"But their motives may not be the same as ours."

"Our motive is to make an effective film," said Thad. "To be effective, it must be professional. That means we must rely on professionals who know how to make motion pictures. If the critics call our picture propaganda and the audiences feel they've been brainwashed instead of entertained, the project will be a failure."

"A point well taken," said Kim. "I will do as you suggest. But I will insist, sooner or later, that the film meet all of the specifications of our agreement."

The February meeting of the group Friederich Papen chose to call The Consortium was held in a chalet high in the snow-covered Bavarian Alps. The chalet was large, private, and surrounded by armed guards. Once again, Thad arrived on time, only to find that several members were late. They would appear in time for dinner, Papen promised; in the meantime, would Thad care to ski?

Thad preferred to remain inside, lounging on a leather couch in front of a great window that afforded a spectacular view of the mountains. Kengo Yoshioka emerged from his room carrying two pairs of Nikon binoculars. With these he could identify the skiers on the nearest slope—Ernst Dietrich, Klaus Schulenberg, and Christian Thyssen, with three attractive young women.

"It is easy, is it not," said Yoshioka quietly, "to see in them their Viking forebears? Dietrich and Thyssen are the perfect Nordic specimens the Third Reich so much prized. But Schulenberg . . . well, he has the coloring and facial structure of Hitler himself."

Thad lowered the binoculars and gazed into Yoshioka's solemn face. He wondered whether Yoshioka, too, had learned of the BND and was troubled by the knowledge. Why else would he speak in such terms?

"It is just an observation," murmured Yoshioka.

Thad feigned insouciance. "We know the importance of eternal vigilance," he commented carefully.

"Yes. . . . But it may be wrong of us to focus our vigilance always on the same people."

"Do you have anything specific in mind, Mr. Yoshioka?"

An inscrutable smile crept across Yoshioka's face. But Thad had learned that a Japanese smile often meant something solemn was about to be said. Yoshioka chose his words carefully. "I have a sense—do you share it?—that our departed friend Hildebrandt was a restraining influence on our surviving associates and that we may be about to hear some . . . how shall we say? . . . less moderate expressions of opinion."

"I share that apprehension," said Thad.

Yoshioka bowed. His bows from a sitting position amused Thad. Then Yoshioka lifted his binoculars to his eyes and began to study the slope and the skiers again.

Other members arrived during the afternoon. By the time The Consortium assembled around the fireplace at six, it was a complete group: Thad, Yoshioka, Uchida, Kim, Park, Thyssen, Papen, Schulenberg, von Klauberg, Dietrich senior, and Dietrich junior. Once again, someone had arranged girls for the evening. They were dressed in sweaters and ski pants, and most of them were ruddy-cheeked from exposure to the cold.

Thad noted gratefully that Barbara Shirer was not among them, though several other girls from the *Mistral* cruise, including Leonie, were present.

Over dinner, Dr. Kim Doo Chung began to talk about the film. "The concept is acceptable," he said. "The script, with some adjustment, is also acceptable. The actor, Dino Bronte, is a popular American star and will draw people to the theaters. I have some difficulty with the director and possibly with the film editor."

"Dr. Kim's agents have visited the set and tried to influence the director," Thad reported. He thought he had settled this problem with Kim, and he was in no mood for another exercise in Oriental courtesy.

"Mr. Lucien Feinberg," complained Kim, "is not dedicated to our point of view."

"Precisely how do you define our point of view, Dr. Kim?" asked Yoshioka.

"The hero of the film, *The Electrocutioner*," said Kim, "is to encounter vile crime on the part of Communists—"

"Rape, murder, blackmail, and general ugliness are not enough," snorted Thad. "He wants those Communists to be even more vile."

"The judgment is for *us* to make, Thad," said Kim. "We own the picture."

"No, you don't," said Thad quietly, with steel in his voice. "*I* own the picture. My company is indebted to you for the modest amount of money it is taking to produce it."

"Am I to understand your judgment will prevail over ours?"

"Absolutely," said Thad coldly. "One hundred percent."

"That may be unacceptable," said Kim darkly.

"Your investment in the project is five million dollars," said Thad. He reached into his pocket and withdrew a checkbook. He scribbled a check and tossed it across the table to Kim. "Here. I've returned your investment. You're out."

Kim pushed the check back across the table. "Whenever could partners in an enterprise buy each other out simply by repaying the original investment?" he asked. "We are entitled to our share of the profit. But let us not be emotional."

"If you don't keep your hands off *The Electrocutioner*, the entire investment will be lost down the drain."

"It is not supposed to be a work of art," said Kim.

"It damned well isn't going to win any Academy Awards, you may be sure. It's two things: entertainment for the subliterate and a piece of crude political propaganda. Feinberg is going to soften it. At my direction. And you're going to have to accept that. If we filmed the picture you are demanding, distributors wouldn't even book it into theaters."

Christian Thyssen intervened. "We can spend precious time debating this minor project or we can turn to more important issues. I will suggest, Dr. Kim, that you accept Herr Catlett's judgment and the judgments of the professionals he has hired. After all, if you know better than they do how to make a film, why didn't you fund it and shoot it yourself?"

Kim started to respond, but Thyssen's cold blue eyes stopped him. The Korean smiled wanly; it was an oval-shaped Jimmy Carter smile, like a bowl of yesterday's cornflakes. "Very well," he murmured.

"When the table is cleared and the personnel of the inn have left the room, there are several issues we must discuss," said Thyssen. "But we will defer until then."

The dinner was a full and hearty meal: roast beef, veal, potatoes, boiled vegetables, red wine. Most of the conversation was of Hildebrandt, how he had died, some reminiscences, acknowledgment that his courtly manners were but the moss on a character of granite. He would be missed, they agreed, by all of them. No one seemed to dispute that he had been murdered by Communist agents.

After the dishes were cleared and the men began lighting their tobacco, Thyssen once again assumed control of the meeting. He was the youngest member of the group, yet the Germans around the table raised no objection to his taking charge.

"We were a little surprised, quite frankly, that you repurchased your common stock in CCE," said Thyssen.

"That was the deal Hildebrandt made with me," said Thad.

"Does it represent a want of confidence in the remaining members of our consortium?" asked Papen.

"It represents an opportunity to make a substantial profit by taking advantage of a provision in the contract between my company and VWH," said Thad. "Do any of you think Wilhelm Hildebrandt would have failed to take advantage of any opportunity the contract offered him?"

"CCE is indebted to members of The Consortium to the extent of four hundred million dollars," said Thyssen. "Nothing about that is changed."

"Nothing about that is changed," Thad agreed.

"Actually it is," said Papen. "The assets acquired with that money are appreciating in value. Formerly, VWH owned forty percent of those assets. Now it owns nothing. *We* own nothing. Except CCE's debt obligations."

"Which will be paid," said Thad.

"Will we continue to be represented on your board of directors?" asked Papen.

"No."

"Then how do we have any control over you?" asked the younger Dietrich.

"You don't," said Thad. "You never did. With forty percent of the stock and a minority position on the board, you had no control. You had influence. Which you still have. Wilhelm Hildebrandt understood that."

"We are here to talk about investing hundreds of millions more," said Papen. "Exactly what is our relationship?"

"We might call ourselves partners," said Thad. "We work together. I have no control over you. You have none over me."

Thyssen's cold eyes glanced around the room. "I believe we have an understanding," he said.

"I believe we do," Papen agreed quickly.

Thyssen turned to Thad. "We should most like to hear about developments in the States Broadcasting acquisition."

"I think we'll be able to buy controlling interest," said Thad. "A majority of the stockholders are even more disgruntled than I thought. But we will be opposed in Washington. An effort will be made to stop us. I'm not concerned about the Federal Communications Commission. What we're doing does not violate law nor policy. What I am concerned about is that we will be under severe pressure to reveal the identities of all our investors—not just you gentlemen, but everyone who is providing the funds that you control. I have been subpoenaed to appear before the House Committee on Interstate and Foreign Commerce. I cannot lie to Congress. I cannot refuse to identify the members of this group."

"I think this need not be a matter of any great concern to us," said Thyssen. "You cannot testify to what you do not know. We will tell you how much money we will make available for the acquisition of States Broadcasting. You can testify to what I am about to tell you."

Thyssen paused to take a sheet of paper from his briefcase. "I will give you a copy of this," he said to Thad. "The total amount of capital we can make available to CATSERV for the purchase of States is $600,000,000. It would be foolish to pay more, do you not agree?"

"It would be foolish to pay that much," said Thad. "I would hope to get it for less."

Thyssen allowed a thin smile. "As the case may be. The following companies are prepared to purchase preferred stock in CATSERV to finance the acquisition: Verlagsgruppe Wilhelm Hildebrandt, $210,000,000. Nordlisch Industriengesellschaft, $190,000,000. Berliner Unternehmungsgesellschaft, $150,000,000. Videosonics Corporation, $30,000,000. And Chikuma Motors Company, $20,000,000."

"How am I to explain," Thad asked, "how VWH can purchase $210,000,000 worth of preferred stock in CATSERV? I'm not aware of the financial condition of the other companies, but I know VWH does not have access to that kind of money."

"Correct," said Thyssen. "Each of the German companies will sell debentures to raise the money. We have already begun the process. There will be many thousands of investors behind the funding. We will pay them a good rate of interest. We anticipate no difficulty in selling the debentures."

"Who is Berliner Unternehmungsgesellschaft?" asked Thad. "I'm not familiar with the name."

"That is *my* company," said Thyssen. "Americans find the acronym amusing. Berliner Unternehmungsgesellschaft is BUG."

"If you must mention my name during your hearings," said Joseph von Klauberg, "please say only that I have attended some of your meetings as an observer. Whether I am the source of any capital, you have no knowledge. That is the truth. You *don't* know."

"And I," said Dr. Kim, "have invested in *The Electrocutioner.* You do not know whether or not I am buying any of the debentures. This is also the truth. Again, you don't know."

"You don't need to know," said Thyssen. "Do you? I might tell you that these arrangementes were conceived by Wilhelm Hildebrandt and had been essentially put into effect before he was assassinated."

"It may well be," said Ernst Dietrich, "that those who killed him had learned of what he was doing and thought to prevent it by assassinating him."

"Who do you mean?" Thad asked.

"Your Christian fanatics," said Dietrich blandly. "Who else?"

The evening meeting broke up at eleven. The men had dined alone; now they were offered sex for dessert. Thyssen, Ernst Dietrich, and Schulenberg latched on to three of the girls. They wandered, arm in arm, into the cold crisp night where the staff had built a roaring fire that sent a geyser of orange sparks into the darkness. They settled on benches and stared into the fire, nuzzling, laughing, and sipping hot drinks. Their muted laughter seeped through the big window.

The elder Dietrich gently informed the girl assigned to him that he would sleep alone and suggested that she join the party around the fire. Thad dismissed Leonie, too, whispering that he might see her later. Noting this, Yoshioka sent his girl along with Leonie. The two Koreans and Uchida headed straight for their rooms, half dragging their girls after them.

Papen finished his drink and left Thad and Yoshioka alone. The Japanese magnate, indicating the departing Koreans, commented quietly, "For many generations we Japanese governed Korea as a colony. We regarded the Koreans as a subject people and deservedly so: crude in their manners, lax in their morals, and deficient in their understanding. I do not subscribe to the doctrine that one ethnic group is superior to another or that one has the right to colonize another. But . . . you see my point."

Thad responded with a noncommittal smile.

"The worst you have heard about Kim Doo Chung is probably true," Yoshioka continued. "He has made himself rich by methods that will not bear investigation. He pays bribes. He engages in blackmail. And if he himself has not been a party to murder, he is no more than one or two persons removed. He is Korean, after all."

Kim Doo Chung and Park Il-Sung appeared in the dining room during breakfast, dressed for departure in overcoats and hats. They apologized for their premature exodus, explaining that they had received an urgent summons back to Washington. Kim asked the others to advise him of the decisions they reached. He would welcome the opportunity to invest further in the enterprises the group was promoting, he said.

The remaining members of the group gathered around a table facing the big window and the view of the ski slopes. Except for Yoshioka, who had come down from his room in a blue suit, they wore bulky sweaters and ski pants. Ernst Dietrich had even brought a red and green knit ski cap with a ball on top, which he laid before him on the table.

"I would like your reaction this morning, Herr Catlett, to the proposition," said Christian Thyssen, "that the members of this group be allowed to appoint people to the staffs of publications we might acquire."

"Specifically?"

"We have heard it may be possible to purchase *Twentieth Century Review*. Have you heard that?"

"Yes," said Thad. "For a quarter of a million or less. Fusty old periodical. Its circulation couldn't exceed thirty thousand. It's an academic publication."

"Actually, Herr Catlett, its circulation is twenty-one thousand, mostly professors. Among its subscribers, however, are twelve United States senators and thirty members of the House. Eighteen magazines are mailed to the State Department. Your CIA has five subscriptions. The editorial departments of leading newspapers—including, incidentally, your *Register-Herald*—subscribe. What you call think tanks utilize it. It is rather influential in a subtle way."

"It's losing money and threatened with extinction," said Thad.

"Exactly," said Thyssen. "But suppose, Herr Catlett, you were to buy it, making some comment that you wish, as a public service, to keep the poor old *Twentieth Century Review* alive. It has a skeleton staff—just two paid editors and some volunteers who work in basement rooms in a building on the Columbia University campus. Contributors receive only token payments for articles. Their incentive is not money but prestige. And their articles are quite authoritative—factual, reasoned, persuasive. Most articles are written by recognized authorities—academics, statesmen, senators, cabinet members. . . . It is—"

"What do you expect to do with it, Herr Thyssen?"

"First, we would assure its subscribers that it will continue. Second, we would assure them and demonstrate to them that its character will not be changed. But then . . . I should hope we *can* change its character in subtle ways. The present editors invariably select for publication articles that represent a particular point of view. I would like to make the *Review* more, shall we say, catholic."

"How?"

"I would want you to appoint a new editor in chief. I have in mind a senior professor, a noted historian. His appointment will shock no one. But I know we can count on him to change the magazine's orientation. There are, after all, people equally authoritative and respectable who do not accept the viewpoint of the writers now favored by the *Twentieth Century Review*."

"Could you please be more specific?" asked Thad as he lit a cigarette.

"The *Review* is too liberal," interjected Papen. "It is worse than that. It is left wing. The writers published in it almost invariably oppose any firm action against Communist aggression. They are hysterical on the subject of nuclear weapons. They—"

"There are experienced senior scholars, diplomats, et cetera," said Thyssen, "who can elucidate the opposing point of view factually and authoritatively and persuasively. We should like to open the pages of the *Twentieth Century Review* to them. It must, of course, be done gradually and subtly, lest the journal lose its influence."

Thad shrugged in bewilderment. "The only element I don't understand is my role in it. Acquisition of the *Review* by CCE will immediately raise suspicions and invite criticism. Why don't you funnel the money in through some other channel—another organization you create for the purpose—and exert control directly through your chosen editor in chief?"

Thyssen shook his head. "To be frank, Herr Catlett, becoming the publisher of the *Twentieth Century Review* will increase your own respectability. Also, if you own it and employ the editors, there will be no mystery about who is behind the magazine. We would also like to see the magazine published monthly, and your participation would explain that. I want to emphasize, however, that we do not want you to exercise editorial control. We want you to hire the man we designate. He will select the articles."

"I control all my publications," said Thad.

"You will like the way our man edits this one," said Thyssen. "If any dispute arises, we can then arrange for you to sell the *Review*. In the meantime, your participation in this project will make it far easier for us to launch it, and we should appreciate your agreement. Think of it as simply a small element of a much bigger overall relationship between us."

Thad pursed his lips. "I'll consider it. But first, I'll want to know who your professor is."

TWELVE

Thad did not return directly to New York but flew to London for two days with Thaddy who, by now, was better known as Frank Teltac. His new book *Dancers* was out. It was selling well in the States, if not as well as *Lifestyle* had sold; but it had become a London sensation even before it was published. This had transformed Frank Teltac into a chic celebrity, in heavy demand as a portraitist and the only photographer before whom serious dancers and actors would pose nude.

"I've turned down *Playboy* and *Penthouse*," he said, a breathless excitement bubbling through an affected blasé pose. "I'm keeping a distinct artistic dignity in what I do."

Thad had taken Thaddy and Alan to dinner in a restaurant he favored—Wheeler's Sovereign, in Mayfair. They alternately sipped their before-dinner drinks and munched on olives and celery and bits of dark bread. Thad nursed a double Scotch. Thaddy and Alan were drinking white wine.

257

"Dad?"

"Uhmm?"

"I'm not sure you've heard anything I said."

Thad rubbed his cheeks hard with his right hand. "I have been listening. I promise you, I've heard everything you've said. I . . . uh . . . am a little tired. I'm sorry."

"What kind of life do you live?" demanded Thaddy with an irritated pout. "You—"

"Thaddy! How long has it been since I've said anything about the life you choose to live? *Chacun à son gout*, my boy."

The flush in Thaddy's face deepened. "I suppose," he snapped, "I should attribute this to the Scotch. . . ."

"Just tired," said Thad wearily. "Just a little tired."

British Overseas Airways radioed Kennedy urgently that its flight should be met by an ambulance. A loudspeaker announcement in the arrival area produced no response from anyone who was supposed to meet the ailing passenger. The passenger, who had been identified as F. Thad Catlett, multimillionaire American publisher, was carried off the 747 by medics and hustled into an emergency van. Since he was rational and seemed in no immediate danger of expiring, the paramedics agreed to deliver him to the hospital he specified: Greenwich Hospital, Greenwich, Connecticut.

It was not a heart attack.

The *Times* reported next morning on its front page below the fold:

F. Thad Catlett, one of America's most influential publishers and broadcasters, was taken by stretcher from a British Overseas Airways 747 at Kennedy at 3:40 P.M. yesterday and rushed to Greenwich Hospital in Greenwich, Conn.

Hospital spokesperson Katrina van der Meers said that Mr. Catlett was not suffering from a heart attack as originally feared, but collapsed from exhaustion aboard a British Overseas Airways flight from London. He is responding positively, she said, to treatment and is listed by the hospital as in "satisfactory" condition.

Mrs. Anne Catlett could not be reached immediately, but Mrs. Alma Catlett, the publisher's mother, arrived at the hospital within an hour after her son's admittance. She confirmed the hospital's diagnosis that her son is suffering from nervous exhaustion, not a heart attack.

Mr. Catlett's elder son, F. Thad Catlett, Jr., is in London, where he is a prominent portrait photographer. A second son, Richard Catlett, a student at Harvard, is reported to be on his way home to be with his father during his illness.

"Charles . . ."

Charles Lodge Johnson stood awkwardly beside the bed, uncertain what his deportment should be before his stricken superior. Charles's arms were wrapped around a bundle of newspapers and magazines.

"Charles. Sit down where I can talk to you at a more familiar level. I don't seem to hear so well. I can't decide whether people are talking in subdued tones, or I have lost part of my hearing, or they're giving me something that affects my auditory nerve."

"Consider yourself fortunate," said Charles. "The less you hear of most conversations, the more tranquil you will be."

"How long have I been here, Charles? The doctors and nurses are disinformation specialists. . . . It's wretched, being a patient. Everybody thinks they're entitled to lie to you."

"You've been here four days, Thad," said Charles.

"Oh . . . yes. Anne flew back from Pittsburgh. Richard came down from Boston. Tell me the truth, Charles, am I dying? Why is everyone rushing to the hospital? This . . . uh . . . gathering of the clan is unnerving."

Charles cleared his throat. "I have no information to the effect you are dying," he reported.

"Would you tell me?"

"Yes. I would."

The corners of Thad's mouth turned up in a faint smile. "You would, you bastard. I know you would. The only one who would, too."

"The world is like a soap opera," said Charles. "When you return, you will be astonished at how people are still engaged in the same silly routines that occupied them when you tuned out. You will be surprised at how little progress they have made. You could stay away six months and not miss a thing."

A look of alarm flashed over Thad's face. "No!" he declared.

"Oh . . . I'm sorry. I didn't mean you *would* be away six months."

"Six more days at the most," Thad muttered. "Can't let things fall apart."

"They won't, Thad."

"You, Charles. You more than anyone else. And Anne . . . Get her into the office. Yes . . . and Ken Asher. There's not much the three of you don't know. Get together."

Thad's eyes flooded with tears. He hyperventilated.

"Thad . . . It's all right. We will—"

"Charles . . . There is something you must do for me. You have to understand. You *can* understand. And you've got to be more loyal to me . . . more circumspect . . . than you have ever been before."

Charles placed his hand on Thad's. It was beyond his emotional capacity to clasp and squeeze it, but he patted it, uncomfortably restrained. "Sure. What is it?"

"You're too damned good for this world, Charles," said Thad.

"It's the only world in which I function," said Charles.

"In this world—" Thad lowered his voice, "I am going to ask you to do something for me. It has nothing to do with business. It is personal. It's a matter of trust."

"I have long felt that our friendship is personal trust," said Charles.

"I feel it is," said Thad. "That's why I can trust you to take care of a most personal and sensitive matter for me."

Charles raised his brows. "I'll do the best I can."

"Please, Charles . . . There is someone in agony . . . waiting for word from me."

Charles had anticipated the nature of the request. "Who? . . ." he started to ask.

"I love her, Charles."

Charles turned to the window and stared at the town of Greenwich, compact and tidy. "You love whom, Thad?"

"Jennie Paget."

Charles swung around. *"The congresswoman!!"*

Thad confirmed his exclamation with a helpless shrug. "It's not just—I mean, it's real, Charles. And if you think about it, you'll know why it's—why it's also impossible."

Slowly, Charles returned to the bed.

"Call her for me, Charles," Thad whispered. "Tell her I'm okay and thinking of her. And, Charles, arrange somehow to bring her here. I don't have to tell you how secret that must be."

Charles nodded gravely. "I shall see to it," he said.

Anne sat firmly in the thronelike leather chair behind Thad's desk. Facing her were Charles Lodge Johnson, Kenneth Asher, Melvin Bragg, and Trish Rubin, Thad's secretary.

"He is doing a bit better," she reported. "He's at home, with special nurses and his mother watching over him. The doctors say he suffered emotional and physical collapse. There is no point in my concealing from you what the doctors are not telling anyone outside the family, that Scotch whiskey and cigarettes contributed to his breakdown. It's going to be several weeks before he's back in this office, perhaps much longer.

"But, you are going to hear from him by telephone. Most of the time, he's entirely rational. But I should caution you that there may be times when . . . Well . . . Ken, perhaps you should tell everyone about the discussion yesterday afternoon."

261

Kenneth Asher, looking gray and tired himself, began slowly, awkwardly. "Well . . . as Mrs. Catlett said, he . . . uh . . . telephoned. . . . He wanted a report on the States acquisition. . . . I brought him up to date. I gave him the names of some major stockholders who have committed their stock to us. He wanted to know about the House hearings. I told him they've been postponed for a month. He seemed on top of everything. Then he began to talk about Wilhelm Hildebrandt. Hildebrandt said this. Hildebrandt would do that. It took me a minute or two. . . . Then I realized he believed Hildebrandt was still alive."

"Of course, this means you can't take orders from him," said Anne. "Clear everything with me. I mean everything that comes from him. I'll be available. I make a poor nurse, so I'll leave the nursing to others. I'll fill in for him, except that I won't travel as much. You'll find me here most of the day, every day. And most nights I'll sleep in his apartment here in town."

Anne suddenly halted; her emotions had seeped to the surface. "I—I'll have to rely on all of you," she said huskily, suppressing a sob. Then, regaining her composure, she declared, "There's simply too much going on; this company has too much at risk to be put on hold. That's what Thad repeats and repeats when he's in touch with reality. Everything has to go forward. Charles, run the newspapers for me. Ken and Mel, win the States battle for me. Charles and Mel, you've met the Germans. I haven't. You'll have to help me with them. I hardly know their names. And, Trish, where the hell's the ladies' room?"

Anne did not get away from the Pan Am Building offices until after seven-thirty. She had approved the next day's editorials for all the Catlett newspapers; she had ordered a new series of articles on Senator Eugene Borman; she had taken telephone calls from Christian Thyssen in Berlin, Hans Dietrich in Hamburg, Friederich Papen in Frankfurt, Kengo Yoshioka in Tokyo, and Dr. Kim Doo Chung in Washington. At the suggestion of Kenneth Asher, she had placed calls assuring four big States stockholders that her husband's temporary absence from the head of CCE affairs would not interfere with the company's commitment to acquire States. She had responded to an inquiry from the office of Representative Robert McCluskey, who wanted to know when Mr. Catlett would likely be able to testify before the House Committee on Interstate and Foreign Commerce. She had reviewed circulation figures from three of the newspapers. She had studied a memorandum from the advertising director of the *New York Sentinel-American*, explaining why advertising revenues were down (department store closings had cost several pages of advertising, and shops selling high-ticket items did not advertise in tabloids because of a perception that tabloids were read only by blue-collar families). Lastly, she had telephoned Thad in Greenwich, had found him rational but sleepy and distracted, and had reported to him briefly on what she had accomplished.

"Thank God you're here, Bert," she said when she stepped into Charlie Brown's and found him waiting at the bar. "Have you been waiting long?"

"Long enough to get two drinks ahead of you," he said.

She glanced around. The bar was crowded and smoky at this time of the evening. "Let's go to the apartment," she said.

"*His* apartment?"

"Yes. I can't face a train ride to Greenwich every evening and returning to Manhattan every morning."

Bert entered Thad Catlett's apartment with a troubled sense of intrusion. This was where Thad and Megan had lived and loved. Bert watched Anne open the bedroom closet and find women's lingerie, open the bathroom closet and find women's cosmetics. Anne seemed undisturbed by these things. She closed the closet and cabinet doors with the wry comment that the apartment was equipped for romance.

She poured Scotch for herself—Thad kept no rye there—and let

Bert mix his own martini. She removed her dress and pantyhose; in a half-slip and bra, she sat down on the couch and propped her feet on the coffee table.

"Charles briefed me for the first time this afternoon about this—this Bund für das Neues Deutschtum," she said. "He told me you were the source of the information."

"Yes. He asked me long ago to check out Christian Thyssen."

"From the way he spoke about you—nothing specific, just something in his voice—I suspect Charles knows about us," she said. "If he does, then Thad knows, since there is no other way Charles could have found out. But it makes no difference, as you can see."

"Anne—"

"Do you know anything more about the BND? Anything new? Anything I should know?"

"I'm flying to Germany again," he said. "I've got a lead. I may be on the scent of a big story . . . bigger than just the question of where Thad Catlett finds the money to buy all those television stations."

"Are you going to tell me what the lead is?"

"Let it wait until I get back, Anne. If it's a false lead, there's no point in your worrying about it."

"How long will you be gone?" she asked. "I was counting on your company at nights . . . to relieve the loneliness of this place."

"I hope to be back in four days," he said.

"Where in Germany are you going?"

"Berlin."

Viktor Prager received Bert Stouffer in his office, which overlooked the Berlin Wall. When they had shaken hands and Bert had settled in a solid wooden chair, Prager took another moment to pack and light his pipe. He spoke fluent English. He pointed out the Wall, the television tower, the ruins of the Reichstag building that still stood on the far side of the Wall. Stouffer asked a few questions about the Wall and the checkpoints. Then they turned to the reason for Bert's visit.

"I pursued the investigation for some considerable time," said

Prager. "At first I was skeptical of everything the young woman said. But after she was killed . . . obviously that gave credibility to her story. I learned other facts that bolstered her credibility. But as I slowly picked up more pieces to this puzzle, I was forced to conclude she had exaggerated. In any event, I was not able to piece together a rational explanation for the disparate facts. I had other, more pressing cases, so I dropped the matter. May I ask how you came to know of my inquiry into this?"

"Stanley Ross called me from Frankfurt," said Bert.

"Oh, yes. The young Reuters man."

"I visited Frankfurt in January," said Bert. "I wanted to know more about the death of Wilhelm Hildebrandt. Stan didn't mention you then. Somehow the connection came to his mind last week, and he telephoned me."

Prager sucked on his pipe and nodded. "The connection was? . . ."

"When you called him to inquire about Colin Fleming, you asked if Fleming had been working on a story about Hildebrandt."

"Yes. The young woman told me she had been employed by Verlagsgruppe Wilhelm Hildebrandt. She also said that she had met with Colin Fleming only minutes before his death. In fact, she said she was a witness to the shooting. She said she had given Colin some copies of documents she had taken from VWH."

"And when you talked with Stan Ross, you asked if Fleming had been working on any story that could have involved F. Thad Catlett."

"Yes. She mentioned F. Thad Catlett the day she was here."

"Can you tell me what she said about Catlett?"

Prager smiled. "She said that her duties at VWH occasionally included partying. She was expected to have sex with certain visitors to the company gasthaus. She said that she spent a night with Catlett . . . that their activities were secretly recorded on videotape. That tape was locked in the Hildebrandt archives, she said. Also, she told me she had photographed the contents of Catlett's briefcase during one of his visits. She offered me copies of those documents, which she said included scandalous revelations about possible 1988 presidential candidates."

"Let me see . . ." mused Bert. "Colin Fleming was murdered in May. Hanna Frank was shot in September. Wilhelm Hildebrandt was ambushed on December 30."

"I reopened my file when Hildebrandt was assassinated," said Prager. "So far . . ." He shrugged.

"It doesn't fit together?"

Prager shook his head. "Hanna Frank was lying when she told me she witnessed the murder of Colin Fleming. I reported her statement to the police in Frankfurt, and they obtained VWH records from their security office. At the time Colin was killed, the records showed that Hanna Frank was on the VWH premises. She told me she had a large number of videotapes, which she would bring me. When her room was searched, there were no tapes and no evidence to suggest she ever had any. When the Frankfurt police examined her flat, they found no VCR, no way she could have viewed videotapes on her own television set."

"But she told you she had slept with F. Thad Catlett," said Bert, counting off points on his fingers. "She told you she had photographed the documents in his briefcase. She told you the contents of some of them. You would not have paid her for any of that, I suppose, until she produced it. Part of what she said must have been the truth. Granted that she might have been a fraud, looking for money, but how would she have come up with the name Catlett, of all people, and how would she have guessed what he had in his briefcase?"

"Do you really think he had such a document in his briefcase?"

"I know he did," said Bert. "The man who accompanied him to Germany . . . when his briefcase was opened . . . has confirmed it. Is it possible, by the way, to obtain the fingerprints of the late Hanna Frank?"

"I can get you a copy of the police record."

"The Berlin investigation into her death?"

Prager turned down the corners of his mouth. "It remains an open case," he said, "but it is six months old now."

"Let me change the subject," said Bert. "Have you ever heard of an organization called Bund für das Neues Deutschtum?"

"Why do you ask that?"

"Shouldn't I have asked it?"

Prager sucked on his pipe. "Well . . ." he said, pondering his answer. "It's a somewhat shadowy organization. Quite legal, however. Nothing conspiratorial. It is an organization of German businessmen, most of them wealthy . . . men who are interested in reviving German patriotism. It's not a political party, though I think it might become one if it ever gains enough members. Surely you don't think it is in any way involved in these murders?"

"Is Christian Thyssen a leading member?"

Prager frowned. "Christian Thyssen is a wealthy and successful young businessman here in Berlin. He inherited a substantial fortune and has greatly increased it by shrewd investments. I should not be surprised if he is a member of the BND. But do you ask because you think there is some connection?"

"Hildebrandt and Catlett were partners in an effort to build an American communications empire—if that's not too dramatic. I understand Thyssen is a secret partner."

"That is consistent with his character and reputation," said Prager. "He also has influence with others who would invest their money in any enterprise of his."

"Would Thyssen consent to be interviewed?"

Prager shrugged. "You can inquire."

Herr Thyssen would have consented to an interview, according to his office, but unfortunately he was out of town. Bert flew to Frankfurt.

He accompanied Stan Ross to the *pension* grandly called Prinz Friederich Hotel. Stan spoke German to the old concierge. Yes, she surely did remember the day that the Englishman was shot on the street outside. Yes, she remembered the young woman who had checked in just before the shooting and departed shortly after. No, she was not aware that the Englishman had visited the young woman in her room. No, the young woman was not named Hanna Frank. The concierge offered to produce a register book and show the gentlemen that no Hanna Frank had been in the hotel that day. The police had already inquired.

"Show her the picture, Stan."

Ross showed the old woman a photograph of Hanna Frank. "Yes, that looks like the young woman, but she wasn't called Hanna Frank. See, here is the signature in the book. . . ."

Bert had stayed one night in Berlin; he stayed the next night in Frankfurt. Early in the morning, he taxied to the airport to board his return flight to New York. He checked his bag, picked up his boarding pass, and headed for the departure lounge.

All such places were alike in every major airport in the world—a human stockyard of pressing, pushing people funneling through assorted gates. The display on the board indicated his flight would depart twenty minutes late. He paused at a bookstall to browse, looking for an English-language book for in-flight reading. He found a paperback murder mystery by Elliot Roosevelt, featuring his famous mother as amateur detective. He sat down and immediately became absorbed in the novel.

"Herr Stouffer?"

He was startled. "Uh . . . yes."

"My name is Bruno Schmundt. This is my identification. I am an inspector with the state police."

Bert glanced at the identification card. The man's picture was affixed, and it looked authentic.

"I would appreciate a little informal chat with you," said Schmundt. "Nothing official. I won't delay you. We are mildly curious as to why you have opened a new investigation into the deaths of Colin Fleming and Hanna Frank. You were also here in January to inquire about the assassination of Wilhelm Hildebrandt. American journalists are justly famous for developing sources of information that official investigators have overlooked. We wonder if you have learned anything that we ought to know."

"I'll let you know the moment I do," said Bert. "I don't work outside the law."

"Hanna Frank told Herr Prager in Berlin that she witnessed the death of Colin Fleming. She told him she had passed some documents to Herr Fleming only minutes before. Do you believe she was killed because she was a witness to the murder? Do you believe she was killed because she gave documents to Herr Fleming?"

"It would seem likely, wouldn't it?" said Bert. "She wasn't robbed in Berlin. She wasn't raped. What could have been the motive for killing her?"

"What do you suppose was the motive?" asked Schmundt. "What do you suggest?"

"I don't know. I would like to know."

"She said she stole documents from her employer, Verlagsgruppe Wilhelm Hildebrandt. She said she passed some of those documents to Herr Fleming. We have no evidence of any of this except her word. VWH says she never stole anything. No one at Reuters ever heard Fleming mention her—or mention any woman who was providing him documents. She told Prager she had videotapes, but no one has been able to find any."

"Your point?" asked Bert.

Schmundt drew a deep breath. "We in Frankfurt honor the memory of Wilhelm Hildebrandt. We are honored to have the company he founded here. It employs many of our citizens, and it is a contributor to many public causes. We should not like to see its reputation damaged. *Unless* . . . unless, of course, there is hard evidence of wrongdoing at the company."

"Let me give you two facts you may want to pursue, Herr Schmundt," said Bert. "Within half an hour before his death, Colin Fleming withdrew two thousand marks from the Reuters discretionary fund. Also, the concierge at the *Prinz Friederich Hotel* recognizes a photograph of Hanna Frank as the young woman who checked into the hotel, using another name, within the half hour before Fleming was killed."

"Maybe he was killed for the money."

"Maybe he was," Bert said, "—by someone who saw him make the withdrawal at the bank, followed him, waited until he paid a short visit to a hotel room, then coolly murdered him on the street in view of a hundred witnesses, grabbed his briefcase but did not search his person, and calmly walked away."

"I urge you not to jump to conclusions," said Schmundt. "You will have our cooperation in any further inquiries you wish to make. Here is my card. Please call me whenever you wish. And"—he paused and licked his lips—"may I hope you will bring to our attention any further significant facts you discover?"

Walking through Kennedy Airport, Bert could not overlook the front page of the *American Terrier*, displayed on racks:

OL' GENE HIGH—OR HIJINKS?
MISSISSIPPI SENATOR FUMBLES, STUMBLES

The front page was given to a photograph of Senator Eugene Borman clinging to the door of a car and obviously falling to the ground. The caption under the picture read:

Senator Eugene Borman, R-Miss., laughs as he falls to his knees in the parking lot of an Alexandria, Virginia watering hole. The two girls cracking up in the background were not identified.

He spoke briefly on the telephone with Anne that evening. He agreed to come to her husband's apartment the following evening.

"My God, lady," he said to her after they had poured their drinks, "I thought maybe with you in charge, the vendetta against Senator Borman would at least get an intermission."

"You think I like him any better than Thad does? Here. . . ."

She thrust a copy of the *Washington Register-Herald* at him. It contained another story on the senator.

"NOT DRUNK"—BORMAN
"PARKING LOT SLIPPERY"

Senator Eugene Borman, the flamboyant Mississippi Republican who appeared unsteady on his feet in a front-page photograph in this week's *American Terrier*, today denied that he was drunk. He explained that the parking lot was slippery and he lost his footing.

A statement issued by the senator's office contended that the senator had dined at the Alexandria restaurant, that it had rained while he was inside, and that he had slipped on wet leaves as he walked from the restaurant to the parking lot.

The statement did not identify the two attractive girls who were seen with him in the picture. They were shown laughing uproariously as Senator Borman, arms flailing, took a pratfall.

This is not the first time the senator has appeared in public apparently intoxicated. Two witnesses observed Borman one afternoon last month staggering out of his office, his hat askew. He was about to attempt a precarious descent down the marble steps of a Capitol Hill office building in broad daylight.

While witnesses gaped incredulously, two of Borman's frail secretaries, teetering on high heels, half dragged and half led their distinguished boss out through the door and down the stairs. The senator's receptionist, Eileen Davenport, awaited him outside in an automobile. The stuffing of Borman into the car was a scene so memorable that the witnesses were able to describe it in detail a month later.

"Here's another one," Anne said, offering Bert a copy of the *New York Sentinel-American.*

SOBRIETY IN THE SENATE
—OR THE LACK OF IT

Intimates of Sen. Eugene Borman, R-Miss., admit he has a drinking problem. His Senate environment is conducive to indulgence. He is freed from the hourly necessity to work and produce—demands that discipline the habits of most men. Whenever he wishes, he can shut himself behind the thick oaken door of his office. His constituents and callers can be held off indefinitely with stories of high-level meetings that allegedly occupy his days.

He has also found the permissive attitude of his fellow senators hospitable to elbow bending. The Senate contains an occasional alcoholic whose identity is concealed with the cooperation of a tolerant press. When there is voting on the Senate floor, obliging senators to hang around for roll calls, bars are automatically opened in the ornate offices of senior senators who have acquired office space in the Capitol building. There, under tinkling cut-glass chandeliers, senators can find the stimulation that might be lacking in a dull debate.

This permissiveness has given Borman encouragement, if he needs any, in a pursuit he instinctively finds agreeable. Former employees say he starts drinking even before he arrives in his office, hung over from the night before. He keeps a bottle of bourbon, they say, in his office refrigerator. He has another in his desk drawer, another in a filing cabinet. His glass, though always within reach, is hidden from view in the recess of a small telephone table beside his desk. And he keeps his office uncommonly dark so that visitors can't focus on him too clearly.

By mid-afternoon, all pretenses are abandoned, and a staff aide is recruited as bartender. In the company of admiring companions, Borman whiles away the afternoon. The waiting room fills up with visitors who sometimes sit around for hours in vain. By late afternoon, Borman is likely to pass out on the red leather divan in his office. It is part of the staff's duties, while making excuses to visitors, to break out cold towels, black coffee, and hot soup in an attempt to revive him.

Bert couldn't suppress an occasional involuntary chuckle as he read.

"That's not all," said Anne. "We're using television, too. Our camera crews have taped a special on the senator's favorite boondoggle, Hork Field. It'll run on all our stations next week. We offered it to other stations, and seventeen independents have picked it up. Hey, I'll run it for you."

She loaded a cartridge into the VCR. The twenty-minute tape showed that grass did, indeed, grow in cracks in the concrete of the Hork runways. The aircraft sitting on the ramps were mostly World War II vintage trainers and transports. The base seemed to be centered around luxurious-looking officers' and enlisted clubs, which were also open to civilian employees.

Other scenes showed Air Force personnel living off the base—as all married personnel had to do—in ramshackle housing, some of it with substandard sanitary facilities, for which they paid excessive rents. The beneficiaries were the local landlords and merchants who, in interviews, expressed their gratitude for good ole Gene Borman. "I honestly don't know what would happen to this town if the base should ever be closed," said the operator of a tavern. The announcer commented, "If the town outside Hork Air Force Base were granted an emergency subsidy, it could maintain its present prosperity for ten million dollars a year. That would cost American taxpayers only ten percent of what it costs to keep this obsolete installation functioning."

"We offered this to the networks," Anne said as the VCR rewound the tape. "They turned it down. But CBS sent their own crew to look at the base. They ran a three-minute segment on the evening news, Monday night, showing a little of what we've got and reaching about the same conclusion, that Hork Airbase should be closed."

"Suppose the senator sends up the white flag," Bert suggested. "Suppose he withdraws his opposition to the CCE acquisition of States."

Anne was on her way to the kitchen to pour herself a second drink. "He helped to drive my son out of this country," she said. "So far as I'm concerned, my newspapers will be on his case for the rest of his political life."

Bert scowled at the newspapers scattered over the coffee table. She had called them "my newspapers." He wasn't sure how well he liked this side of Anne.

Alone in his office in the Greenwich house, Thad stared at his

273

computer terminal. He was anxious to activate it and communicate with his New York office, but he was uncertain what he would say. So he shuffled off and wandered aimlessly through the house, dressed in the adbare jeans he had not worn for years, with a shabby gray sweatshirt. He was not allowed to drink, and he had been encouraged to give up cigarettes. His doctors had decided he needed rest, even if they had to force it upon him. The only way to keep F. Thad Catlett out of action, they agreed, was to subdue him with chemicals. The nurses made certain he took the pills—four a day that did not sedate him but impeded his ability to focus.

Sometimes when Anne telephoned to report to him about developments in New York City, he understood and spoke authoritatively; other times he was uncertain as to who was who and what was what. Charles and Kenneth called on him. Afterward they consulted with Anne to decide whether to carry out his instructions. He ordered them to buy *Twentieth Century Review*. They were astonished at the idea, but they made an offer for the musty academic journal. He also told them to halt all further funding for *The Electrocutioner*, but with Anne's consent, they ignored the order.

The nurses limited his access to the telephone, but they let him call his son in London. Thaddy was out, so Thad spoke for thirty minutes with Alan. The young man reported that Thaddy was doing "marvelously well" in London and had applied for permanent residence status. Thad also telephoned Charles's apartment and reached Kathy. He told her that Charles was his best friend in the whole world.

The next day Charles arrived at the house, unannounced, with Jennie Paget. He curtly dismissed the morning nurse and closed the door behind them. Jennie stepped hesitantly into the office where Thad sat at his desk, staring vacantly through the window at the swimming pool.

"Oh my God!" Jennie cried, dropping to her knees on the floor beside his chair. "Thad! Thad! Do you *know* me?"

He clasped her in his arms. "Of course I know you," he whispered.

"Do you love me?"

"Never more," he murmured. "If things had been different, you could have been with me when I needed you. . . . But—"

Her lower lip quivered, but she responded fiercely, "I'll resign from Congress. I'll confront your wife and tell her. I—"

"Let's not make decisions when I'm like this. . . ." Then he turned to her pleadingly. "Jennie, what did Charles tell you about me?"

She squeezed his hand, her eyes brimming with tears. "That this is temporary," she whispered. "That you'll be all right."

"Trust Charles. I trust him. He'll make arrangements for us to see each other. Tell him to restrict the doctors. . . . I don't like what they're doing to me. They're keeping me drugged, Jennie. I know they mean well, but their good intentions could ruin me. Be sure to tell Charles. . . . Tell him. . . ."

She nodded. "I'll tell him," she whispered.

"Tell him I think I know who killed Hildebrandt."

"Who?"

"My mother. She always hated him. She shot him with her rifle."

Jennie's eyes filled with tears, and she dropped her head in his lap. He petted her. "Don't worry. It'll be all right," he said softly.

Delivery trucks appeared routinely at the house. Dr. Kim Doo Chung sent two cases of Chateau Lafite Rothschild and one hundred pounds of aged prime steaks. A dozen red roses were delivered twice a week, from Christian Thyssen. A congregation in Tennessee sent a crate containing fifty Bibles, with a suggestion that "one be placed on every table in every room in the Catlett mansion."

A card arrived in the mail, wishing Thad a speedy recovery, signed Ron and Nancy Reagan. Other remembrances came from senators and representatives, governors and mayors, publishers and editors, and hundreds of citizens whom he had never met. One of the nurses spent the morning separating all this from the hate mail that also flooded in. This was seen only by the nurses, who stuffed it in garbage bags and hauled it in the packer truck to the landfill twice a week.

275

"I see nothing to gain from it," Charles told Anne. "In fact, I'm highly suspicious."

They sat in Thad's office—now her temporary domain—late on Tuesday afternoon of the fourth week after Thad's collapse. Kenneth Asher was also present.

Charles continued. "In another month, Thad himself will be fit to travel. Then I can accompany him. In the meantime, I am—"

"It's curious that they specified Charles," said Asher. "Certainly, I have no desire to go to Frankfurt. I'd be content never to see the damned VWH gasthaus again, but I'm the one who could give them a detailed report on our progress with States. I'll be glad to brief you, Charles, but—"

"It's damned curious they didn't ask *me*," said Anne. "And to relieve you of any inhibitions you may have about discussing this subject, I want you to understand something. I know all about the sordid events in Germany. I know Thad slept with a girl provided by Hildebrandt last April. I know that girl—her name was Hanna Frank—was later murdered in Berlin. I know that VWH makes photocopies of every paper carried by people who stay in the guest house. Apparently, they copied the papers Thad was carrying. Probably they have copies of everything you brought in your baggage while you stayed there. They have more . . . much more. They have videotapes of everything you did in your rooms—of Thad's romp with Hanna Frank, of your bedroom antics. You are subject to blackmail if that makes you vulnerable."

The two men were aghast.

"Are you sure?" Asher blurted. "How do you know all this? Did Thad know? I mean, do you know something that Thad never knew?"

"I doubt Thad knew all of it," she said. "And as to how I know"— she glanced at Charles, whose face still registered his dismay—"I don't want to say right now. But I *do* know."

"All the more reason that I shouldn't go to Frankfurt," Charles finally said.

"I disagree," she replied. "They have asked for you for a reason.

They have something on their minds . . . something they want to tell you. We need to know what it is."

"They want to find out whether Thad is ever going to regain control of this company," said Asher simply.

Anne nodded in agreement. "Well, he *is*!" she said fiercely. "But even if he doesn't, they need to understand that this company will—" She stopped. Her voice had broken. Her cheeks burned, her eyes suddenly afloat. "This company is *not* turning soft. By God, we'll take on anyone who tangles with us . . . starting with that redneck Borman. We've been too easy on him! Let's crush him, gentlemen! Meanwhile, Charles, you go over there and play hard-nose. I mean it. Hard-nose!"

Charles Lodge Johnson arrived in Frankfurt on March 19. At past gatherings of The Consortium, Charles, as Thad's hired help, had the status of a lackey. But this time, he got the full red-carpet treatment. He was met at the airport by the late Wilhelm Hildebrandt's factotum, Friederich Hoffman.

"Mr. Catlett enjoys a swim and some time in the sauna when he arrives from New York," said Hoffman. "The pool and sauna are available to you if you want to use them."

"Thank you," said Charles. "But I think I would rather catch up on my sleep."

He was ushered to his room, where he stretched out on the bed and returned to his reading of Kathy's novel. He had read it half a dozen times until he had almost committed it to memory. But Kathy had begged him to read it again to give his opinion of the publisher's changes. She wanted to know whether he thought she was justified in her complaint that the editors had damaged the novel.

This was one novel he had hoped Thad would never read. Charles was a character in the story, and Thad loomed in the background like a dark, ominous storm ever threatening to break. Probably that was her impression of the man she had never met.

Kathy had changed his life—that is, Kathy and the heart attack.

277

He had slimmed down, and he enjoyed life differently. She had made him reassess his self-image as an Ivy League sophisticate. If he began to swell with self-importance, she punctured his balloon. She laughed at him; he laughed at her. His imposing bald dome, the lift of his chin, the devilish sparkle in his eyes still dominated his personality. But he had been tempered.

His telephone rang.

"Charles Johnson? This is Christian Thyssen. Ernst Dietrich and I are taking the helicopter this afternoon to fly Herr Yoshioka over the romantic part of the Rhine Valley . . . the deep part of the valley, the swift waters, the castles, the Lorelei. . . . It is only about twenty minutes from here in the helicopter, and we have more than two hours before the cocktail hour. We have one more seat available and thought you might like to fly with us."

"That's most considerate," said Charles. "It should be a delightful experience."

The black helicopter was noisy and vibrating; Ernst Dietrich at the controls seemed confident. He maneuvered the chopper skillfully, keeping in constant radio contact with air traffic control. He whisked over forested country north of Wiesbaden and reached the Rhine at Rudesheim, swinging around the great, stout female figure of the Niederwald Monument and dropping down for a closer view of the river and the castles, some intact, some in ruins, lining the promontories on both sides of the river. It was a spectacular view, and Yoshioka shot a whole roll of film in five minutes, then fumbled in his hurry to load another.

Dietrich circled the Lorelei ruin, then eased the helicopter down to a landing in a clearing on the outskirts of the village St. Goarshousen. A car that seemed to have been waiting for them rushed to the clearing. Charles wondered whether it might be the police, come to complain of an illegal landing; but the driver trotted toward the helicopter, grinning and calling in German. Soon they were crowded into the car and rolling a few hundred yards into the village, where they were deposited at a small wine tavern and escorted to a table on a stone terrace overlooking the river.

"Picturesque, isn't it?" asked Dietrich. "Once this was a monastery. The little tavern was the monks' winery. They sat at this spot four . . . five hundred years ago and drank their wine, as we are going to do. The wine is excellent, as you will see."

It was indeed, a flinty dry white wine, chilled in a small wooden tub of ice carried to their table. The green bottles were without labels. A white cheese on a board, with a basket of biscuits, was placed before them. The table was in the shade of an ancient oak. A gentle breeze stirred the white tablecloth.

"We are concerned, Charles, about the state of Thad's health," said Thyssen after a few minutes conversation devoted to the setting. "Can you give us any assurance?"

"An absolute assurance," said Charles. "He will recover fully. There was nothing wrong but simple exhaustion. He merely needs to rest. In a few weeks, he will be active again."

"The schedule has been disappointing. The last acquisition has gone much slower than we expected," said Thyssen. "We should have control of States Broadcasting by now."

"Not at all," said Charles. "All the acquisitions have gone amazingly fast. And this one is progressing well. Thad's absence has cost us no time whatever."

"Have you a report for us?"

"I had supposed it was for the entire group," said Charles, "but there is no reason why you gentlemen should not have a preview. The price offered for the States Broadcasting stock is eminently fair, and hundreds of the stockholders have accepted it. The management is attempting the usual tactics to discourage stockholders from selling to us. Absent government intervention, we will pick up a majority of the shares. The problem is, we may encounter government intervention."

"Senator Borman?"

"The unhappy fact is that Borman represents a large and vocal body of opinion in the United States. He has introduced a bill to prevent our acquiring States. Senator Warren Gallagher, chairman of the Subcommittee on Communications of the Commerce,

279

Science and Transportation Committee, has indicated he will hold early hearings and expedite the bill."

"They cannot pass it before the acquisition is complete," said Yoshioka.

"But they can compel us to disgorge," said Charles. "We've got to stop the bill."

"Politics," grunted Thyssen. "Politicians. They are . . . beneath contempt."

"The price of democracy," said Charles, raising his wine glass.

Thyssen ignored the comment. He exchanged glances with Ernst Dietrich. His face, handsome in a hard way, darkened. "Charles," he said heavily, "we are concerned about something. A report we have received. We hope you can clarify the matter."

Charles nodded. "I hope so, too," he said blandly.

"The report," said Thyssen, "comes from so far away as Tel Aviv. Do you know what I am talking about?"

Charles shook his head. "I have no idea," he said, taking a sip of wine.

"The report involves the name Bert Stouffer," said Thyssen. "Now do you know what I mean?"

Charles put down his glass. "Possibly . . ." he said. "But I do not play guessing games—not with anyone. Suppose you tell me what you have in mind."

"Bert Stouffer," said Thyssen grimly, "is a close personal friend of yours. He—"

"Omit the word *close*," Charles interrupted. "He is a personal friend of mine."

"You employed him to—"

"No," Charles interrupted again. "I have never employed him. The Catlett organization has never employed him. Not in any capacity."

Christian Thyssen was silent for a moment, obviously struggling to control an anger boiling deep inside him. "Charles," he said, "have you ever heard of an organization called Bund für das Neues Deutschtum?"

"Yes, I have heard of it."

"Do you know anyone who is a member?"

"It is my understanding that you are a member."

"You understand that because Bert Stouffer told you so," said Thyssen.

Charles nodded. "That is quite true. Bert Stouffer told me."

"Yes. And Stouffer got the information from a journalist in Tel Aviv, who in turn telephoned an agent of Mossad, who told the journalist that I am a member of the Bund für das Neues Deutschtum. And back the information came to Stouffer . . . then to you . . . and then, I suppose, to Thad."

"So?" asked Charles calmly. "Is it supposed to be a secret?"

"The BND is a private organization that does not disclose its membership," said Thyssen. "It was once infiltrated by an Israeli agent whose assignment was to learn whether we had established a neo-Nazi and anti-Semitic organization . . . *and he found out and reported we had not.*"

"That's how it was reported to me," said Charles. "And that is exactly what I told Thad."

"When this man Stouffer called Tel Aviv, he explained to his contact that he was inquiring for you. Indeed, it was your name more than Stouffer's that moved the man to contact Mossad. What I would like to know, Charles, is why you went to all this trouble? If you wanted to know if I was a member of BND, why didn't you simply ask me?"

"Routine inquiry about a new member of The Consortium," said Charles, reaching again for his wine glass. "We wanted to know who you are. Don't you take the trouble to learn who we are?"

"It is true, then, that Stouffer was acting for you?"

Charles shrugged. "He was doing me a favor. I did not hire him. I did not pay him."

"Who is paying him now?" demanded Thyssen. "He has been in Frankfurt and Berlin, asking questions about the murder of Wilhelm Hildebrandt, asking questions about the murder of Hanna Frank. Is he working for you now or just doing you another favor?"

"He is not working for me or making any inquiries at my behest. Neither is he working for Thad."

"It happens that I *am* a member of BND," said Thyssen. "So is Ernst Dietrich. So is Klaus Schulenberg. What would you like to know about our organization?"

"I would be interested in its purposes," said Charles.

Thyssen rose slowly from the table and gazed out over the fields and the Rhine Valley. He spoke as one who carried the double burden, albeit confidently, of leading the German race to a more glorious destiny and of shaping up that race's cowed, contemporary specimens for the journey. "For three generations, Charles, we Germans have been taught to be ashamed of our country. I was born eleven years after the war, and still I was taught in school that I shared the guilt brought on our country by Adolf Hitler. Our people's natural patriotism and pride has been made suspect. The Bund für das Neues Deutschtum is an organization of men like me— that is, businessmen with some resources—who want to restore our national honor. We are opposed by milksop pacifists, greedy socialists, juvenile environmentalists . . . and the timid. We are opposed also by Communists of all stripes, particularly by the East German regime. They suspect we want to reunify our country."

"That is why we must be careful," said Ernst Dietrich. "The Communists would rather kill us than let us revive German nationalism."

"This, of course, explains the murder of Wilhelm Hildebrandt," said Thyssen. "He was murdered by agents of HVA. You have heard of HVA, yes? . . . Hauptverwaltung Aufklarung—the external intelligence agency of the German Democratic Republic. And why did they assassinate Hildebrandt? As a warning to BND. We are becoming too strong."

"Do you think they killed Hanna Frank, too?" asked Charles.

"That is possible," said Thyssen. "We don't know."

"And Colin Fleming?"

"Again, it is possible. But we have no information."

"The money being raised to acquire American television stations is from the BND?" Charles asked.

Thyssen allowed a cold smile. "The BND is poor," he said. "But some of the money *does* come from members."

"And in return for this financial support you expect the stations—even the CCE newspapers—to support the general objective of the BND?"

"Uhh . . . In a sense, yes. Very subtly. This was thoroughly understood between Thad Catlett and Wilhelm Hildebrandt. CCE, we believe, is a conservative-oriented news organization, opposed to communism, realistic about Soviet intentions, and . . . It is a natural alliance."

"I see," said Charles.

"You seem skeptical."

"I do not believe Thad Catlett has made any commitment to *ally* himself with a political organization of any kind," said Charles.

Thyssen responded with another icy smile. "He retains his independence, of course."

"Totally," said Charles.

"Understood," said Thyssen. "Understood." He slumped back into his chair and refilled his glass with the white wine. "We believe Thad understands our purposes."

"Would you define them for me? . . . more concisely?"

"Allow me," interjected Kengo Yoshioka. "Mr. Johnson . . . I believe you will understand, when you are acquainted with all the facts, that the creation of so large a communications conglomerate, as we contemplate, will have incalculable advantages. Besides television stations, we will acquire a motion picture studio, then perhaps additional magazines and book publishers. The orientation of the communications industry remains socialistic and internationalist. We think it vital to balance that orientation."

"Balance? . . ." Charles mused.

"Balance, Mr. Johnson," said Yoshioka. "We do not wish to dominate, only to have as strong a voice as the opposing side."

"What about our Korean associate?" Charles asked. "Where does he stand? I suspect he may define *balance* somewhat differently than you do. How much weight does he have with this group?"

"There is an English expression, if I recall," said Ernst Dietrich, frowning. "*A loose cannon*, is it not? Dr. Kim is a loose cannon. It may become necessary to lash him down."

"I think that would be wise," said Charles.

"We take your point," said Thyssen. He glanced at his watch. "We haven't much more time. Enjoy another glass of the wine. We will take a few bottles with us. Meanwhile, I would like to raise another point with you."

Charles poured himself another glass of the wine.

"It occurs to us," said Thyssen, "that we have helped Thad to become an exceedingly wealthy man. Your own contribution to our enterprise has been considerable, but you remain only a salaried employee of Catlett Communications Enterprises. This troubled Wilhelm Hildebrandt. He was planning to correct it. *We* would like to correct it."

"The conversation may be heading in an unfortunate direction," said Charles.

"If you think I would suggest something so crude as buying your loyalty away from Thad, please give me more credit. What we have in mind will be proposed *to* Herr Catlett. We are thinking of creating a new position for you, a sort of liaison position between us and Thad, affording us more frequent and more complete contact than these occasional meetings afford. This position would pay a generous salary and would involve what I believe American businessmen call an equity position. That is, you would own a share of our joint business. You would be a millionaire from the beginning, a multimillionaire if we are as successful as we expect to be."

Charles smiled wryly behind his glass. "That would make me a participant, a sort of partner," he said quietly. "Lashing down another kind of loose cannon."

"Let us think of the proposition in different terms, Mr. Johnson," said Yoshioka with a polite smile.

THIRTEEN

Christian Thyssen stalked into his office from the small private gymnasium he maintained in an adjacent room. Tall and athletic, he wore a gray sweatshirt, damp from his exertions, and a pair of black gym shorts. His office was furnished in a light, colorful, contemporary style, with mobiles hanging from the ceiling, bold abstract paintings on the walls, furniture crafted from exotic woods, and stainless steel chairs covered with leather. Scores of gaudy reef fish swam in big saltwater tanks. He had two computer terminals. The screen of one was alive with a constantly moving display of up-to-the-minute information from the securities and financial markets.

He walked to his desk and pressed a button. His secretary materialized immediately, a beautiful Teutonic blonde wearing a miniskirt. She carried a stack of mail, which she laid before him on his desk. He required nothing further from her and dismissed her with a faint smile and a curt gesture. She had sorted the mail as he required. He turned first to the mail she was not allowed to open.

Here was something he had been looking for, a fat envelope from New York. He sliced it open and pulled out the sheets inside. What he wanted to see was the report, but he glanced at the letter first.

March 5, 1987

Dear Christian,

Enclosed is the report from the investigator we employed at your direction. I think you will find his report most interesting. Please advise whether or not you want the agency to continue the surveillance.

We have disbursed $3800 to the investigative agency.

We hope to see you soon.

Sincerely,
Axel Hoch

Thyssen set the letter aside and began to read the report.

PUTNAM SECURITY AGENCY

March 3, 1987

Dear Mr. Hoch,

As requested by telephone and by your letter of authorization dated January 21, we have kept the subject Bert Stouffer under surveillance on a 24-hour basis, except for the time when he has been outside the United States. This report supplements and confirms our several telephoned reports.

The subject is a man of irregular habits, coming and going from his place of residence at odd hours. As per your instructions, we have not attempted an entry of his apartment. He is engaged, as you indicated, in the occupation of free-lance journalism, writing for a number of newspapers and magazines. This is the reason, apparently, for the irregularity of his personal habits.

Thyssen flipped forward. He was not much interested in Stouffer's personal habits nor his professional activities. On the third page he came to what Hoch found so interesting, thoughtfully marked in red:

We are able to confirm with certainty what we only suspected when we last reported to you on the telephone. The subject is carrying on a clandestine affair with a woman named Anne Catlett, the wife of the newspaper publisher F. Thad Catlett. As you may know, F. Thad Catlett has been confined to his home for about two weeks, suffering from some sort of collapse, described by the media as nervous exhaustion. During this period, Mrs. Catlett has assumed functional control of Catlett Communications Enterprises. She works in the CCE offices in the Pan Am Building every day and spends three or four nights a week in an apartment in Manhattan, which is leased by her husband. On two occasions we have observed the subject Stouffer entering this apartment early in the evening and remaining there overnight. On prior occasions, Mrs. Catlett visited him at his place of residence—during the day and never for more than an hour or two. In addition, they eat lunch or dinner together in various restaurants. We have observed them holding hands and otherwise demonstrating affection for each other.

During the last observed visit of Stouffer to this apartment, one of our operatives gained access to an office in a building opposite and was able to observe the living room of the apartment through binoculars. Stouffer and Mrs. Catlett were observed drinking, talking animatedly, and watching television. At the time, Mrs. Catlett was partially undressed—that is, she had removed her outer clothing. By the time an operative with a camera and telephoto lens could arrive, Mrs. Catlett had closed the curtains.

Thyssen was smiling cynically as he returned the confidential report to the envelope, unlocked a drawer, and carefully placed the envelope inside.

"A month," Anne told Thad. "That's what they said, a month."

"It's out of the question . . ." said Thad. "Out of the question."

"You think I'm doing so badly?" she asked.

Thad looked at Charles. "According to him, you don't need me back at all."

"The only matter that really could require your personal attention," said Charles with the majestic precision that sometimes impressed people and sometimes infuriated them, "is the very matter Anne is handling most capably. That is the matter of stroking States stockholders. She is every bit as persuasive as you could be, I believe. We have commitments from thirty-one percent of them."

"But the politicians . . . We've got Washington to deal with."

"That's another reason for you to do exactly what the doctors ordered," said Anne. "A month on the beach. In the Caribbean. The politicians will be less inclined to attack a man under doctor's care . . . a man who can't fight back . . . a man who must be represented by a harmless wife. . . ."

"Oh, to hell with congressional committees!" exclaimed Charles. "The nation could get along without Congress and be better off for it! It's your *health*, Thad, that we must consider. Four weeks on the beach. That's all. Just four weeks."

"I'm dying of boredom, you know," said Thad. "But . . . what the hell. I have an invitation from Thaddy. A few weeks in London. Some theater and opera. A bit of noodling among the monuments . . ." He paused, then declared, "Get me reservations for London."

He took up residence in the Park Lane Hotel, on Piccadilly, on the edge of Mayfair. Thaddy and Alan, who had met him at the airport and had driven him into town, arranged a light schedule for him, taking pains to make themselves available to help him all the time. Touched, he thanked them sincerely but assured them he really could take care of himself. He demonstrated it the next day by walking to the Westminster docks, taking the boat to Greenwich, and wandering through the naval museum and the Cutty Sark.

The next day Jennie arrived.

"Even here . . ." she said after they had cuddled in bed in the hotel. "Even here, we have to be secret. Let's go to Budapest, for Christ's sake . . . or Istanbul . . . or Timbuktu . . . any damn place, my only love, where we can be together. I love you, goddamnit Thad, and I'm ready to make any sacrifice."

He caressed her lovingly. "I've got it back, Jennie. I'm in control of myself again. I know what day it is and what time it is and—and I know every bastard who hates me is taking advantage of my absence!"

"So, let 'em! You and I . . ."

He drew her closer to him. "It's going to be thirty years soon, Jennie," he said. "*Thirty years!* I put my youth into this business. And my middle age. I'm fifty years old, Jennie! I can't walk away and say to hell with it."

Jennie rose from the bed and walked to the window. The window looked down on roofs and chimney pots; rooms on the Piccadilly side of the Park Lane Hotel overlooked noisy traffic. But she stood, stark naked, staring down on sooty tar.

"I have something to tell you, Thad," she said glumly. "My husband knows about us."

Thad sat bolt upright in the bed. "How did he find out?"

"He asked me out of the blue. I couldn't lie about it. I just couldn't. It would have been so—so *false!*"

Thad took both of Jennie's hands in his. "So he knows. . . . What was his reaction?"

"What do you suppose?" she asked bitterly. "What means the most to Martin Paget? 'Let us be careful not to make a scandal.' A partner at a large law firm loses points if he is involved in a scandal. And a scandal between his wife, a high-visibility congress-woman, and a headline name, like F. Thad Catlett would be . . . well, unacceptable. It would involve *publicity*! . . . unfavorable publicity. It would damage his fucking *career*!"

"Wouldn't it just. . . ." Thad muttered. "So what does he want? A divorce?"

"A very quiet one."

Thad lowered his eyes. "Anne doesn't know."

There was a long, awkward silence. At last, Jennie spoke in a voice so soft and gentle it was barely audible. But the words penetrated Thad like sword points. "I'm going to ask two questions. Please don't answer them. I'm afraid, Thad . . . afraid I may not want to know the answers. Anne owns half the stock in the business that you spent your youth and middle age to build. Do you intend to tell Anne about us? Would you risk half your kingdom, perhaps even a breakup of your empire, for my sake?"

Thad's voice was quiet but firm. "I'm going to introduce you to my son, Jennie."

He suggested the Sovereign, but Thaddy insisted he and Alan would prepare dinner in their studio flat. They sat on the stoop outside for an hour—Thad and Jennie, Thaddy and Alan—drinking beer the boys fetched from the adjoining pub, chatting with the neighbors, mostly young people. Thaddy—known in London as Frank—was a celebrated figure in the neighborhood. Then they climbed upstairs for the dinner: lamb chops and vegetables, a good vintage Bordeaux, fierce black coffee with their after-dinner brandy and cheese. Thaddy was cordial to Jennie. He showed her his studio and portfolios. Alan was awed to learn that a congresswoman was staying in the Park Lane with Thad.

After dinner, Alan took Jennie next door to the pub to see, as he said, the stained glass behind the bar. His real motive was apparent: to let Thad and Thaddy talk alone.

"I have tried to be understanding about your life-style," said Thad. "Now I need your understanding."

"I have no right to condemn you," Thaddy said.

"Condemn? . . ." Thad said. "That word has no place in this conversation. The word is *understand*. I didn't bring Jennie here to face judgment. I don't want you to condemn or approve our relationship. I had hoped to get your understanding."

"I have only one concern. What about Mother? I love her dearly. I don't want her to be hurt."

"I love her too, Son. I have no wish to hurt her. Do you understand that?"

Thaddy stared at the floor for a moment. Then he raised his eyes and looked straight at his father. "I believe you," he said.

The two men, father and son, embraced.

"Keep it quiet," Thad cautioned. "Publicity could be damaging. It is a measure of my confidence in you that I've brought Jennie to meet you."

"I know," Thaddy said. "I know."

With the tension broken, Thad and Thaddy relaxed. They talked about trivial things, and they poured more brandy. Both were a bit unsteady by the time Alan brought Jennie back from the pub.

"What I don't understand," Thaddy said to his father, "is this German connection. Tell me about your German partners. Who are those people?"

A fog had settled over Thad's mind, too. "Who owns anybody's stock?" he demanded. "IBM's? Exxon's? Dupont's? What obligation am I under to discover the identity and the moral quality of everyone who invests in CCE?"

"But who are your German partners?" Thaddy persisted with a tongue slightly thick from spirits.

"My German associates are selling debentures to *thousands* of investors. No one knows who all of them are. I don't know. Watson never knew everyone who owned IBM stock. We may have murderers and rapists. . . . Both CCE and IBM."

"I don't know much about business," Thaddy mumbled.

"We are going to build a communications conglomerate that will rival any in America," said Thad expansively. "Any in the world.

With the money those people are investing, we're going to outstrip Luce, Gannett, Knight-Ridder, Chandler, Murdoch, Turner. . . . We're going to have—"

"You're going to have nothing if the stations don't make enough to redeem the preferred stock," Jennie interrupted.

"We'll redeem it," said Thad. "We've got to think big. Big! I know how to redeem it. Don't worry about that. In five years, when we have to redeem it—"

"Thad! You're already obligated to redeem more than four hundred million. The States acquisition will boost your obligation to over a billion dollars!"

"But the assets appreciate, Jennie!" he chortled. "The four hundred million bought properties that are now worth more than half a billion dollars. In a year, States will be worth one hundred twenty-five percent of what it's going to cost us to acquire the network."

Jennie withdrew from the argument. She wondered whether Thad's collapse had damaged his judgment or sharpened it, whether he was a visionary building an empire or a tycoon demented by ambition. It was a subject fraught with clichés. But now . . . well, there was no point arguing.

With a noncommittal shrug, Thaddy also dismissed the subject. "Mrs. Paget," he said. "Would you sit for a portrait? Better still, would you sit for a set of nudes? I'd love to do them."

Startled, Jennie stiffened, then relaxed. She blushed. "Why . . ." She licked her lips. "I'm honored . . . uh . . . Frank. I'm flattered. I've never received an offer quite like that before."

"You are a beautiful woman, Mrs. Paget," said Thaddy soberly. "The pictures will be entirely private, of course."

In the mail at the Park Lane Hotel the next day, Thad received a package of clippings from New York. Among them was one from the *New York Times*:

Members of the academic community signed a protest last

evening against acquisition of the *Twentieth Century Review* by CCE, the corporate manifestation of controversial publisher F. Thad Catlett. A petition signed by 235 professors, associates, and assistant professors was sent to the executive offices of CCE in Manhattan, demanding that CCE withdraw its offer to purchase the financially ailing academic journal.

The essence of the protest was that Catlett is, first, the publisher of sex-and-scandal-oriented tabloids, and is, second, a "right-wing ideologue."

Mr. Catlett remains in seclusion, recovering from a nervous collapse. His wife, Anne Catlett, speaking for him, assured the academic community that CCE has no intention of altering the basic academic character of *Twentieth Century Review.* "We will be surprised," she said, "if subscribers notice any difference. Our idea is to prevent a respected and influential journal from dying."

Challenged on this by Professor Richard Ewing of Harvard, Mrs. Catlett added, "If Professor Ewing wants to invest a quarter of a million dollars to prevent the collapse of the journal, he is welcome to put up the money. If he can show that he can sustain the magazine, we will be happy to withdraw. Otherwise, my husband and I hope we will be able to continue to publish Professor Ewing's thoughtful and scholarly articles."

Smiling joyfully, the Reverend Billy Bob Calder extended his right hand to welcome the man striding onto the set. With his left, the televangelist urged his studio audience not just to clap but to shout and stomp. They did, obediently. The cameras swung around to focus on some beatific faces in the crowd—overweight young women with piled-high sprayed hair, men with shiny satin neckties, bewildered children—then back to the Reverend Billy Bob as he pumped the hand of Senator Eugene Borman and welcomed him to the Tower of Prayer broadcast.

"They're going to let you have it," said Bert. He was huddled with

Anne and Charles in the New York office, on Sunday evening, watching a television set tuned to the hour-long show known simply as *The Billy Bob Hour.*

Anne swallowed rye. "They're going to close his damned airbase, just the same."

"Not soon," said Bert.

"I don't need soon. Sooner or later."

In the studio-church in Birmingham, the crowd continued to applaud happily. The senator and the pastor sat down and beamed back at them, as if amazed at their fervor.

The studio was furnished as a combination talk-show set and electronic sanctuary. The Reverend Billy Bob sat behind a desk, with a couch to his right. This contained the grinning, overstuffed Senator Borman seated beside a smiling blond woman, the pastor's wife, who answered to the nickname Mrs. Billy Bob. She wore a red satin dress, with a tan suede vest and calf-high white boots. To the pastor's left was a stage with a lectern flanked by two small potted palms. A pleasing array of flowers, offerings from the congregation, formed a floral background both for the lectern and the sanctuary.

"Senator Borman! It's just so good of you to come all the way down here from Washin'ton to be with us for Sunday evening services. We praise God for your safe arrival."

"Thank you, Reverend Billy Bob. Thank you for the invitation to share this worship hour with you. Thank you for the opportunity to sit down with God's people."

For those who had not beheld Senator Borman before, he presented a disturbing apparition. Obese and rumpled, he was scarcely able to squeeze into his chair; and once wedged into it, he would balloon out like a cartoon caricature of a glutted politician. The eyes in his round face were small, or perhaps they only seemed small, encroached upon as they were by great cheeks. Chaotic wisps of thinning sandy hair completed the general picture of dishabille.

It was Borman's facial expression that was his most arresting feature—a look of baffled disgruntlement, of uncomprehending exasperation over the inability of others to see those simple truths that were so clear to him. He had a penchant for simple solutions to vexing problems—problems for which there were no solutions.

Reverend Billy Bob was handsome, with a Roman profile, a fixed smile, and a dramatic flair. His blue eyes, as clear and transparent as the sky above his native Alabama, compelled trust and confidence. Yet he displayed certain peculiarities that tended to raise the hair on the back of Bert's neck: an unfailing theatricality, a messianic urge, a master of imagery; the oratorical artillery, the brains, and the guile to create a great deal of mischief should a fortuitous conjunction of events arise.

But the televangilist's dominant feature was his voice. It was a voice of extraordinary resonance and power, sonorous but primordial, a voice such as is seldom heard on earth, such as one expects to hear call sinners to the Last Judgment.

"Among the greatest needs of mankind," Reverend Billy Bob began, "is communication. That's what this hour is all about— communication. We communicate with words, but it takes more than words to communicate God's message . . . uh. It's not just the words we use . . . uh . . . but the meanings; not just the phrases . . . uh . . . but the spirit; not just the sermon . . . uh . . . but the heart."

Senator Borman nodded silent but vigorous amens.

The reverend turned to Borman. "Now they're trying to revoke our means of communication. They're trying to strangle us! . . . to choke off our voice! They're trying to take away our television outlets! Isn't that right, Senator?"

"I'm afeared you're right, Reverend," Borman confirmed. "We tried to stop them. We thought maybe we could stop them. But now it looks like we cain't. I'm afeared we've lost."

Reverend Billy Bob's face clouded with a terrible wrath, a reflection supposedly of God's wrath. "No, Senator! It isn't over!" he declared, his voice breaking like thunderclaps. "Praise Jesus, we're gonna continyuh, we're gonna press on, we're gonna rally the Lord's people. . . . And in the end, we're gonna broadcast this hour to more people than ever watched it before. . . . Praise the Lord!"

The congregation erupted into shouting, stamping applause.

"He hasn't mentioned Thad by name yet," mused Bert. "Do you suppose he's listening to lawyers who warned him not to?"

"It's possible," said Charles, his brows knotted, his lips thinly pursed.

The reverend was on his feet now, thundering, pounding. His statements were crafted to skirt overt malice yet permit malicious inferences to be snapped up by his following, which swelled with empathetic frustration. Yet something overarching in his appeal spanned the chasm between him and his followers. He was seen by millions of fundamentalists across America as a mountain peak silhouetted against the lightning, the last bearer of the true flame.

He weighed in again. "There are many who want to shut out the Truth . . . uh . . . because they don't like to hear it . . . uh. There were many in ancient Israel . . . uh . . . who didn't like the Ten Commandments . . . uh. There were many in Jesus's day . . . uh . . . who didn't like the Sermon on the Mount. . . ."

The telephone in Thad's private office rang. Anne picked it up. Richard was on the line, calling from Cambridge. "Glad someone answered," he said. "I tried home first, but nobody answered. Grandmother said you might be there in the office. Have you got the TV on?"

"It's on. We're watching Reverend Billy Bob. Look's like he's preparing to crucify us."

"I'm glad Dad's in England with Thaddy. He shouldn't have to see this shit. Just look at them now!"

Anne turned and looked at the television set. Reverend Billy Bob had begun to sing, joined by his wife. The words were something about the promised land, all but impossible to understand. The cameras turned to catch people singing and weeping, tears coursing down their cheeks. Then the singing stopped, and the congregation fell silent in anticipation. The Reverend Billy Bob grabbed his microphone and Bible; he began to stride up and down the stage.

"Christ!" muttered Bert.

"We're being exorcised, Richard," said Anne. "Your grandmother may know something that breaks the spell. Something with bourbon in it, I imagine."

The Reverend Billy Bob was now in full cry.

"We face the powers of the demons . . . uh! Satan is among us . . . uh! The abortionists are among us . . . uh! The pornographers are among us . . . uh! The women's libbers are among us . . . uh! The boozers and addicts are among us . . . uh! The adulterers are among us . . . uh! The sodomites are among us . . . uh! The God-mockers are among us . . . uh! Oh, Lord, hear the lament of your people and deliver us . . . uh!"

The camera swung to the tear-wet faces of the congregation, then to the flushed face of Senator Borman, his features screwed into an expression of great gravity. He was rhythmically mouthing emphatic "amens."

"Lord, there is among us . . . uh . . . an idolater . . . uh! An adulterer . . . uh! A pornographer . . . uh! A God-mocker . . . uh . . . who seeks to take away this wonderful blessing of television . . . uh . . . to monopolize it . . . uh . . . for ungodly works! For sex and sin . . . uh! For nakedness . . . uh! For every kind of filth and lewdness . . . uh! Oh, Lord, hear the cry of thy *people*! Thou hast given us this miracle pulpit called television! Do not . . . uh . . . let the anti-Christ take it from us, oh Lord! Reach down, oh Lord, and smite the God-mocker with thy righteous hand! Oh, *Lord*!"

Anne let loose an audible sigh. "Richard . . . Don't let it bother you," she said into the telephone.

Richard laughed. He quickly stifled his laughter and explained to his mother, "I'm at Professor Harrington's house . . . with Betty. Professor Harrington just said, 'Pigs grunt; cows moo; every low form of life has its cry.'"

Charles was still staring intently at the television screen. "He's got a smart lawyer," Charles mused. "He still hasn't mentioned us by name."

"All he did was indict you," grunted Bert.

297

They were distracted by a new pitch from the television set, and Charles turned up the volume.

"Eighteen *million* people . . . uh! Eighteen million Christians—God-fearing, Jesus-loving . . . uh . . . *people*! That's how many . . . uh . . . watch this telecast! And with their prayers . . . uh . . . *all* of them praying . . . Praise the Lord! . . . God's people . . . uh . . . *Jesus*'s people . . . uh . . . will prevail!

"And we will smite the anti-Christ . . . uh! We will smite the sodomite . . . uh! We will smite the purveyor of lewdness and filth . . . uh! And we will keep the miracle of television in God's service . . . uh!"

Anne shook her fist at the television set. "Turn the blasted thing off, Bert," she said. "Enough is enough." She spoke into the telephone to Richard. "See what we're fighting?"

"I'm proud of you and Dad," said Richard. "Professor Harrington says to tell you to keep up the good work. Tell Dad, will you, when you talk to him?"

"Sure, dear. Call again."

Bert had leaned down to switch off the television set. He raised himself up slowly and faced Anne. "If you're going to make a stand at Armageddon," he said, "you need to know what kind of allies you have."

"You're going to give me more bad news from Frankfurt," sighed Anne. She tossed down the last of her rye. It was dark outside, and Manhattan was adorned in her colorful electric jewelry.

"Bruno Schmundt called," said Bert. "He—"

"Bruno . . . *Schmundt*? Who the hell is Bruno Schmundt?"

"A German policeman," said Bert. "He passed on a little piece of evidence. Just a tiny little piece."

"Why would a German policeman report a piece of evidence to you?"

"One of the secrets of investigative reporting is the art of swapping. I may uncover one piece of the puzzle; this policeman may uncover another. We exchange. He returned to VWH and checked the register again. He examined more closely the comings and goings on the day Colin Fleming was killed. The entry for Hanna Frank had been altered, he says. He was able to detect erasure marks. According to the entry, she was in her office at the time Colin Fleming was shot. But the actual time she signed in and signed out was erased. So we don't really know when she left the premises. She was probably telling the truth when she said she saw the murder."

Anne sighed. "She got around, that girl, didn't she? I'd like to see that videotape of her and Thad."

They left the offices in the Pan Am Building a few minutes after ten—Anne, Bert, and Charles. They signed out of the building at the top of the escalators and descended into Grand Central, which was still a human ant bed on Sunday night. They walked east, sifted through the hurrying ants, and emerged on Lexington Avenue. Anne and Bert waited until Charles hailed a cab, then they set out on foot to Thad's apartment.

As they strode uptown, Bert had an uneasy feeling and glanced over his shoulder. "I don't want to alarm you," he said in a low voice to Anne, "but I think we're being followed."

"I don't *think* so; I *know* we're being followed," said Anne. "As the wife of F. Thad Catlett, I have had some experience with surveillance. I usually know when I'm being followed."

"Let's stop and confront the son of a bitch."

"No. Just keep walking."

Not far behind Anne Catlett and Bert Stouffer, keeping close on their heels, was a husky, muscled young man named David Price. He was six feet two, with a wiry build, flattened nose, and pencil-line mouth, giving an intimation of the physical. He had just ended a college football career, without making the NFL draft. He walked with the confidence of a young athlete accustomed to being judged too formidable to challenge. So it came as a complete surprise, his face registering disbelief, when he felt a sudden harsh pain in his back. Someone had dared to hit him.

299

David Price whirled around, fists flailing. The next shock stunned him. For a moment the world was bright, then dark; then it spun under him. He staggered against some garbage cans and a brick wall.

"Gonna behave? . . . Or do you want some more?"

The man talking to him was not large. But his fist lay on David's jaw, and David felt cold metal. Brass knuckles. "Uhh . . ." he mumbled, realizing that the pain in his mouth was compounded by broken teeth, perhaps a broken jaw.

"Your wallet, sonny."

David pulled out his billfold and opened it to show that he was handing over all his money.

"I don't want your money. Just your ID."

Confused but intimidated, David pulled out cards—everything, including his driver's license, credit cards, his identification as a licensed private detective. . . . The man let most of the cards drop to the pavement, but he kept one. Sorting through the cards later, David would realize the man had taken his detective license.

Frank Dittoe caught up with Anne and Bert at the door of the apartment building. Tersely, he reported, "Putnam Security Agency . . . First-class outfit . . . Nice, clean-cut kid, too . . . Just learned his first hard lesson about the private dick business."

The next morning Anne placed a call to the Putnam Security Agency. After a bit of discussion, William Putnam came on the line. "Anne Catlett, Mr. Putnam. I hope your young man is not badly injured. This is just a friendly suggestion. . . . Get your people off our backs, Mr. Putnam. As you can see, we are quite capable of defending ourselves."

DO NOT, REPEAT, DO NOT GO TO FRANKFURT. PLEASE WAIT FOR CHARLES WHO WILL ARRIVE ON CONCORDE TODAY.

The Concorde pounced down on the runway at Heathrow before

the evening sun faded into dark. Charles maintained his aplomb through the indignities of British Immigration and Customs. He joined Thad for dinner at the Sovereign. Charles handed Thad a clipping from the *Washington Register-Herald.*

"Save my Airbase," Borman Demands of President

by Frank Siciliano

A question mark hangs darkly over the White House. This reporter put the unwanted question to the President at his press conference Monday night. Will he shut down Hork Air Force Base, a national monument to military waste? Over the past few weeks the cost of maintaining this obsolete and useless Mississippi airbase has been the topic of many newspaper articles and television reports. The question, it seems, was not unanticipated.

According to an authoritative White House source, Senator Eugene Borman, Mississippi Republican, telephoned the President at least six times during the week before the news conference, each time repeating his demand that the President declare his confidence in Hork and pledge that it would remain open.

Blackmailing the President

The ill-tempered senator, according to our sources, bluntly told the President that if his beloved airbase were closed, he held the political IOUs of several senators who would withhold their support of some elements of the President's legislative program. They might also hold up confirmation of judicial appointments.

"In all my years in the White House, I have never before witnessed such crude pressure applied to the President," our source said. The President, he said, was indignant.

301

Yet the President showed no sign of indignation at his press conference. He answered this reporter's question by saying he would leave the matter to the discretion of the Air Force. An Air Force spokesman said the matter is "being studied."

Charles waited until Thad had finished reading the story. "There's a more significant development," reported Charles, "that was omitted from the story. Senator Gallagher has again postponed hearings on Borman's bill."

"They can't hold the hearings until I'm available," said Thad with a shrug.

Charles frowned. "No, I don't think that's the reason. Something strange is going on behind the scenes. . . . Mrs. Paget called. She said Senator Gallagher's tone was final, as if he doesn't intend to hold hearings at all. I'm told Senator Borman got the same impression."

"But that doesn't make sense," said Thad. "Gallagher and Borman are closer than two 'coons in a hollow log."

"Maybe," said Charles. "But consider the facts: Borman and Gallagher are backroom buddies. Borman wants the bill expedited. It would be an easy favor for Gallagher to grant. But Gallagher is rebuffing his best friend in the Senate. I agree with you; it doesn't make sense. And listen to this: Mrs. Paget inquired about the bill. Senator Gallagher snapped at her. . . ."

"I wish she'd keep her distance from the whole business," interrupted Thad. "She could risk her career."

Charles changed expression, his eyes lowered, his face somber, his voice hushed. "I have late word for you from Anne," he said. "The younger Collins brother and the sister have abandoned Lucas Collins. They will vote to sell to us all the shares the Collins Trust holds in States Broadcasting. With those shares committed, we can exercise the options and take control of States."

"That's good news!" declared Thad.

"Yes . . . I guess."

"You seem to have reservations."

Charles drew a deep breath. "Thad . . . A private detective agency

302

put a tail on Anne. She was too alert for them. She spotted the same two men . . . alternately . . . about half a block behind." He smiled wanly. "She put Frank Dittoe on the case, tailing the tail. Frank knocked him senseless and lifted his identification. She was being followed, all right . . . by a private detective. . . . And private detectives do not follow people unless they are paid."

"Christ . . ."

"You haven't heard the worst. Whoever was following her made an unfortunate discovery," Charles went on. "We may be sure somebody will use this information some day, some way. Maybe somebody working for the born-agains. Maybe somebody working for Lucas Collins. Maybe—maybe somebody working for The Consortium."

"What did they find out?" Thad demanded.

Charles drew his lower lip in between his teeth, and for a moment he hesitated, scowling. "Thad . . . You aren't the only one who's involved in an affair. . . . Anne is seeing someone, too. She would tell you herself, but she's afraid it will come up in Frankfurt before you get home."

"For God's sake, who? What's it got to do with Frankfurt? Who is it, Charles?"

"Bert Stouffer."

"*Bert Stouffer!* Christ! . . . Has she told him everything?"

"No. Bert has spoken to me. He has tried to discourage her from discussing the business with him. He's an ethical man, Thad," Charles concluded simply.

"I hear he has been in Germany recently," said Thad.

"Yes. And he passed on to us what he learned. Someone at VWH falsified the records to make it appear Hanna Frank was in the executive office building when in fact she was in a hotel in Frankfurt, meeting Colin Fleming and witnessing his murder. Bert obtained a copy of the fingerprints taken from the body of Hanna Frank. Pittocco compared them to the fingerprints we found on the documents in your briefcase . . . the papers that were copied. Remember . . . you kept them clean of other fingerprints so you could have them checked when you returned to New York?" Thad indicated, with a nod, that he remembered. "They were her fingerprints, Thad. She handled all those documents. She copied the contents of your briefcase."

"I wonder if that's what she was delivering to Fleming."

"I doubt it. I don't think Colin Fleming was killed because he was carrying copies of the papers in your briefcase. There wasn't anything in those papers that should instigate a murder."

"What you are suggesting," said Thad, "is that we'll be walking into a pit of vipers when we return to Frankfurt."

"We could be snake-bitten if we're not careful," Charles agreed.

"Are you suggesting that I tell them to keep their money, that I am no longer interested in States Broadcasting Company?"

"I think the time has come for you to demand to know exactly where they get the money. One billion dollars, Thad. It's unrealistic to think these Germans and Japanese, wealthy though they have become in the postwar world, just reached into their pockets and pulled out a billion dollars. It could be Arab oil money. It could be South African gold and diamonds converted to cash. It could be profits from the drug trade. You need to know, Thad, whose money you're spending."

"We accepted financing from legitimate and respected interests. We're not obliged to investigate where they got the funds. All that matters is that we have complete control of all our properties. We have regained control of CCE. The Consortium doesn't own a share. The members are simply our lenders now."

"They don't see it that way, I can assure you. They mean to overextend you . . . to the point that they can control you."

Thad shook his head firmly. "They can't do that. We won't lose control. We haven't been that stupid."

"They are aggressive, Thad. They are not going to be satisfied with a passive partnership. They are—"

"I'm going to take over States Broadcasting, Charles. I'm not going to lose that opportunity."

*   *   *

When Thad and Charles entered the room with the parquetry floor, the first man to break away from a conversation and hurry to meet them was Dr. Kim Doo Chung.

"Ah, my friend! We have been deeply concerned about you. But you look fit."

Thad did, in fact, look well. He had lost weight. He had cut down his smoking, though his consumption of Scotch had not abated. During his stay in London, he had bought two suits from a Savile Row tailor, which fit his reduced size in Bristol fashion. His face, however, had not lost the pallor of illness, and gray streaks had crept down the sides of his head.

"While you were in London," said Kim, "I attended a preliminary showing of our film. You will be pleased with it, I am certain."

"I'm sorry I haven't caught up on that project yet," Thad replied.

"Your charming wife represented you," said Kim. "The picture opens in fifty theaters next week."

"I was surprised at how quickly the film was shot," said Charles. "These projects usually take longer."

Kim smiled. "I injected a bit more capital to expedite all elements of the project," he said.

Christian Thyssen strode up to shake Thad's hand. "It is good to see you," he said.

"And good to see you," said Thad.

"I understand you are fully recovered."

"And fully in charge," said Thad. "We are almost ready to take over States. Is the money in hand?"

"It will be," said Thyssen assuredly.

Before they sat down for dinner, Thyssen told Thad he did not expect to hold an after-dinner business meeting of The Consortium. "Also, I discouraged Friederich Hoffman from employing . . . uh . . . entertainers for tonight. If anyone wishes, we can arrange some later."

The dinner was excellent. Thad noticed that members of the

group deferred to Thyssen, more actually than they had to Wilhelm Hildebrandt. If there had been any question as to whether he or Papen, who seemed to have been his only rival, would replace Hildebrandt, that had been clearly settled. Even Kengo Yoshioka deferred to the young man from Berlin.

After the dinner the guests dispersed to their rooms. Thad was pleased enough with the prospect of a full night's sleep. He was undressing for a shower when he heard a knock at his door.

"Ah, Mr. Catlett," said Yoshioka when Thad opened the door. "I wonder if you would be so gracious as to come with me to a brief private meeting?"

"With?"

"Mr. Thyssen and myself."

He followed Yoshioka down the hall of the gasthaus to Thyssen's room. The young German was waiting, having set out bottles of Scotch and brandy along with a pot of coffee. His room was identical to Thad's—spacious, furnished with a couch and chairs around a coffee table and a bed and dresser at the other end. Thyssen had removed his business suit and was wearing a gray and maroon Dior jogging suit. Thad had come in shirtsleeves. Only Yoshioka remained dressed as he had been at dinner, in a trim double-breasted blue suit.

"Sit down, Thad," said Thyssen cordially. "Pour yourself a drink. Forgive our asking you to meet with us like this."

Thad picked up the bottle of Glenfiddich and poured himself a measure. With tongs he put two ice cubes in the glass. "What do you have in mind?" he asked directly.

"Bert Stouffer," said Thyssen. "This man Stouffer is prying into our business—yours and ours—looking for a way to score some sort of sensational journalistic triumph. He has become a problem with which we must deal."

Thad knew what Thyssen was driving at and wondered whether he would have the temerity to mention what the private detective had learned. He decided to let Thyssen talk. Thad shrugged and took a sip from his glass.

"Are you aware of what he has been doing?" Thyssen asked.

"I imagine you are better informed about it than I am," Thad said. "What has he been doing?"

"Prying," said Thyssen. "Into your business and ours. At first he wanted to know how CCE was funding the acquisition of television stations. He learned about the connection between you and Wilhelm Hildebrandt. Then he tried to find out who *we* are—we, The Consortium. He took a special interest in me. He learned of the BND. He has pried determinedly into that. Now he is conducting his own private investigation into the murder of Hildebrandt. He seems to be trying to make a connection between the deaths of Hildebrandt and Hanna Frank. Plus perhaps even that of the English journalist Colin Fleming. Three murders. If he can invent some link—no matter how imaginary, how fantastic—between those and our business arrangements, he can launch a sensationalist campaign in the press that can injure us enormously."

"By disclosing . . . what?"

"I am not concerned about what he could disclose, Thad," said Thyssen firmly. "I am deeply concerned about conjecture. If he makes wild guesses and publishes them—"

"From what little I know of him, he won't do that," said Thad.

"I am glad you are so confident," said Thyssen derisively.

"Anyway, what can we do about it?" Thad asked.

Thyssen sighed. "There happens to be a personal matter," he said.

"Uh—"

"Allow me to express it," said Yoshioka somberly. "We cannot, Mr. Catlett, help but be concerned by the fact that this Mr. Stouffer seems to be a close friend of Mrs. Catlett."

"How do you know that?" Thad asked bluntly.

Yoshioka began to flutter both hands. "Uh—"

"We've had Stouffer watched," said Thyssen.

Thad grinned, then laughed. "What did they charge you for the damage to the shamus?"

"What? I don't understand."

"Private detective," said Thad, chuckling. "So he was following

307

Stouffer? My wife thought he was following *her*. Wilhelm Hildebrandt urged me some time ago to hire a bodyguard. Which I did. He's been looking out for Anne lately, while I was out of circulation. She told him to get rid of the shamus, and I understand he carried out the assignment with quiet but efficient violence. Cost you a hospital bill?"

Thyssen allowed his chiseled features to assume a faint smile. "A broken jaw," he said.

"So you learned that Stouffer and my wife are friends," said Thad.

"We . . . cannot and . . . uh . . . do not . . . suggest," said Yoshioka painfully, "that Mrs. Catlett has disclosed any confidential information to Stouffer. In view of his determination to do us harm, however, the situataion is a difficult one. Do you disagree?"

"She knows nothing that is not available in the public records," said Thad. "We agreed, did we not, in February, that *I* would know nothing more about our investors than what we could afford to have me testify to before a congressional committee. And she knows even less than I do. As to the murders . . . I know nothing about them."

"There is also the question of Charles Johnson," Thyssen continued. "He and Stouffer are also friends. And I can tell you that Stouffer has taken advantage of that friendship."

"Be specific," Thad demanded sternly.

"Perhaps you have heard of the inquiry made in Tel Aviv," said Thyssen. "Stouffer obtained information from the confidential files of Israeli intelligence. To get that information, his own name was not enough. He used Charles's name—and yours. His contact did him the favor in the belief he was doing a favor for Charles Lodge Johnson and F. Thad Catlett."

"And how do you know that?"

Thyssen turned up his palms and raised his brows. "How do you suppose? When you are defending yourself against a snooper, you must snoop. He is not the only one who can do it."

"Our concern about Mr. Johnson is somewhat broader," said Yoshioka quietly. "We—that is, you and I and all the other members of our consortium—have a purpose. We are agreed as to the purpose. We wish to make a profit. We wish to afford the realistic business people of our countries a more effective voice in international affairs. It is important to us that the American people should hear our views."

"You are talking about propaganda," said Thad.

Yoshioka smiled blandly. "I should prefer another word."

"We do understand each other," said Thad. "Wilhelm Hildebrandt and I had a perfect understanding. I assume it continues."

"We are concerned," said Yoshioka, "with the question of whether or not Mr. Johnson also understands and whether or not he is committed to the same purposes to which we are committed. We have reason to doubt it."

"Charles is a man of high purpose," said Thad.

"And high integrity," said Yoshioka.

"Well, what are you suggesting? Do you want me to fire him?"

"Would you?" asked Thyssen.

"No. I am confident of his loyalty. But even if I had doubts, Charles knows too much to be cut loose."

Thyssen sighed heavily. "Thad . . . Some way you must separate Charles from Stouffer. Whatever you say, I can't help but feel that Charles is betraying us to Stouffer."

FOURTEEN

Thad emerged from the Pan Am Building in the April twilight. As he entered the pedestrian stream on Forty-fifth Street, he caught sight of Jennie. She was outfitted smartly in a belted camel-hair coat, a skirt just to her knees, high heels that emphasized her legs. As she paced up the street, her dark hair was caught by the wind and tossed recklessly. She neither slowed her pace nor reached for her hair. She was in a hurry to meet Thad.

Their timing was perfect. She spotted him coming out of the building, broke into a trot for the last few steps, and rushed into his arms. Because they were both public figures, they did not kiss. But their pleasure in seeing each other was complete.

They strolled back to Lexington Avenue and started north toward his apartment. Frank Dittoe, who had been standing apart in the forecourt of the Pan Am Building, followed fifty yards behind, watching for any suspicious faces or hostile moves. A block from the apartment building, he stepped up his pace and passed the pair

311

without a glance or a word; he hurried ahead to check out the entry. Jennie didn't even notice him. Thad had not told her about the tail on Anne and Bert.

Inside the apartment, he closed the curtains before he turned on the lights. She changed into a peignoir from the bedroom closet, left there untouched and unmentioned by Anne. He poured his usual quota of Scotch, They sat down in the living room, comfortable, relaxed, domestic.

"The word is that you're about to hand the born-agains *a fait accompli*," she said.

"I expect to win control of States Broadcasting."

"The battle is not over," she said. "You could enounter opposition at the FCC. You already own a powerful newspaper in Cleveland. Now you are about to gain the leading independent television station; States Broadcasting has a VHF station in Cleveland. I can tell you the FCC is going to be very uncomfortable about that. Bob McCluskey is uncomfortable about it."

"Have you identified yourself with me?" Thad asked. "I mean, in Washington?"

"Bob's my chairman, Thad. He's a friend. I told him you are a family friend."

"Jennie . . . Don't take up the sword for me. All you can get is hurt."

"I'll take my chances," she offered without concern.

"No. No, Jennie. You could kill yourself. You don't know everything. Anyway, I coordinate everything my troops do. I'm a commanding officer. You could charge into the face of the wrong enemy."

"Bob McCluskey's a straightforward guy," she said. "He's concerned about things like the Cleveland situation, where you would have an extraordinary impact on public opinion. He could care less whether the born-agains lose their 'miracle pulpit.'"

"Ken Asher is aware of the Cleveland situation," said Thad. "We're talking about selling the station there. In fact, you can tell McCluskey we'll sell it. He has my word on that."

"Seriously?"

"Yes, I'm serious. We're paying half a billion dollars for fourteen television stations. Do you have any idea how cheap that makes them? And do you know why we can buy them so cheaply? Because they're mired to the concept of 'family broadcasting.' . . . And chained to a management that won't even show reruns of *Policewoman*. These stations are worth four or five times what we're paying. Ken has a buyer who's willing to pay one hundred million for the Cleveland station if we decide to sell it."

"That's," said Jennie, "why you are willing to go into debt for half a billion."

"Exactly," said Thad. "I can sell off half a dozen stations, redeem the preferred stock, and still own eight stations. Or I can sell all the States stations separately, pay off the entire indebtedness of CCE, and own all my newspapers and ten television stations debt free."

Jennie wandered into the kitchen for the Scotch. "Thad . . ." she wondered aloud, "do you think your foreign investors will stand by and let that happen?"

"No. I don't."

"What will they do?"

"I don't know yet."

"Let me tell you something that troubles me. I suspect they have power in strange places," she said. "I suspect someone has brought pressure on Warren Gallagher. It must have been unbearable pressure. He's double-crossing a close friend. He's killing Borman's bill. As you know, Gallagher is allied with the political religious Right. It's strange . . . damned strange."

"Thank God for small blessings," said Thad.

"No. It may be premature to thank God. What if it leaked to the *Washington Post* that Gallagher had been threatened or blackmailed . . . or something we wouldn't even want to think about?"

"What do you mean?"

Jennie settled into a chair, placing the bottle of Scotch on the table before them. "Exactly what is the nature of the relationship between you and Dr. Kim Doo Chung?" she asked.

"The relationship, for better or worse, was fully and factually revealed today in the *Wall Street Journal*," said Thad, "—by my wife's dear friend Bert Stouffer.

He handed her a *Wall Street Journal* from the coffee table.

The Electrocutioner

by Bert Stouffer

It can now be revealed that the grotesque blood-and-guts film produced by F. Thad Catlett was backed with Korean money. Lucien Feinberg and Gary Burlew, respectively the director and screenwriter of that cinematic monstrosity, report frequent visits to their homes and offices and to the set by shadowy Oriental figures, sometimes just watching, sometimes offering suggestions, often bearing lavish gifts for the actors, screenwriter, and director.

A viewing of the film would explain why Seoul-connected Koreans would invest the twelve or fifteen million dollars that it cost to produce *The Electrocutioner*. The villains are all wooden Korean Communists, all capable of the most atrocious acts of cruelty and violence. The hero, played by the hapless Dino Bronte, lays them out like cordwood. If American troops do not remain to guard the 38th Parallel, the film implies, hoodlums like these will take over South Korea and then the world . . . for we cannot always depend on one-man crusades by heroes with oiled muscles.

Dr. Kim Doo Chung

It is no secret in Washington that Korean businessman Dr. Kim Doo Chung, who keeps an elegant mansion on Massachusetts Avenue and entertains more lavishly than any embassy, is a staunch advocate of the South Korean regime. Dr. Kim said he spoke only for himself, not for any government, group, or other interest. A spokesman for the South Korean embassy said Dr. Kim does not represent his government in any capacity. Since he is not registered as a foreign agent, it would be a violation of U.S. law for him to do so.

Dr. Kim, who has made millions in the real estate and construction businesses in his native land, is also a big investor in American enterprises. He is reported to be a confidential partner in many American businesses. He is, for example, an owner of 34.7% of the preferred stock issued by Grist Construction Company of Salt Lake City. Assistant Secretary of the Interior Ray Grist owns 25% of the common stock of Grist Construction—although the stock is in a blind trust during his tenure in government—and the rest of the stock is owned by his father and brother.

The story quoted confidential sources who said Dr. Kim "had bankrolled the Catlett film." Jennie frowned as she read it. "Thad . . . This man Kim is a sleazeball."

Thad, who had reached for the bottle, put it down. "He brought to The Consortium—that's what we call the group of investors who put this deal together—a lot of money. I said a lot of money. Not a lot of money, not if you figure it in percentages. But I can tell you this. . . . He's a pain in the ass. Everybody is unhappy with him."

Jennie sighed. "Thad, the Gallagher hearings on the Borman bill have been postponed. That's a polite way of saying the bill will probably die in the crib. I have an uneasy feeling that Kim is somehow behind this."

"Kim?"

"Kim. That place of his on Massachusetts Avenue is a whorehouse!"

"I suspected as much," said Thad, "though I saw nothing improper when I visited the place."

"What if Warren Gallagher killed the Borman bill because Kim has something on him?"

315

"Is that what you suspect?"

"Warren Gallagher loves to play poker and drink gin. He's considerably better at the former than at the latter. When he's full of gin, he . . . I hear Kim keeps a string of young girls available at the house on Massachusetts Avenue. What if—"

"Kim's capable of it," agreed Thad.

"From what I hear, he's more than capable of it," said Jennie. "He—"

Thad cut her off. "All I can tell you, Jennie, is that nobody in my company has participated in or approves of the kind of skulduggery you're talking about. I can tell you something more. The German and Japanese members of The Consortium are sorry they ever allowed Kim to join. He does not represent us."

Jennie leaned back into the corner of the couch. "Where," she sighed, "will it end?"

Anne lay in bed with Bert, in the master bedroom in the Greenwich house.

"I don't hate him, Bert. In a—a non-carnal sense, I still love him. He's the father of my sons. He really is a *good* man."

"Lord, I don't hate him either," said Bert. "I just think he's caught in the middle of a goddamned *conspiracy* . . . caught in a tangled web that's more than he can handle."

"He knows what he's doing. Don't put the man down, Bert. You haven't achieved what he has."

Bert withheld comment. What passed through his mind was better left unsaid.

"He's not insensitive," she said. "Look at this. That really hurt him."

She showed him a clipping from the *Los Angeles Times*:

From time to time, even a media genius is bound to trip over his shoelaces. Filmmaking is a special art. Success as the owner

316

of newspapers and television stations does not a film producer make.

How do we begin to describe this mess? Well, to start with, *Rambo* it ain't. And Stallone, Dino Bronte ain't. What is more, almost nobody gives a hoot in Hades about the South Korean police state.

Bronte, as *The Electrocutioner*, strives mightily in this film, first to show off his oiled muscles, second to attain a three-figure body count over Commie nasties. Yawn! Who cares? His muscles are a little long of tooth, and his baddies are paper dolls.

Rating: Minus 4. Minus 12 if you care about cinematic art.

—Brad Cooke

"Did *my* story about the picture hurt his feelings?" Bert asked.

"It made him angry," she said. "But not at you. He was angry at Dr. Kim. He knows that Kim sent men to Los Angeles to interfere in the making of the movie. He had tried to prevent it. But while he was sick, Kim did just what he had promised not to do."

"Will Thad react publicly to the Harding letter?" Bert asked.

She shook her head. "He'll ignore it."

The letter had been delivered to the CCE offices in the Pan Am Building thirty minutes after it was handed out to reporters at the Federal Communications Commission. It was addressed to F. Thad Catlett and signed Merrit T. Harding, Commissioner. The letter asked for a written commitment that the television stations of States Broadcasting Company would not be used to broadcast any "pornographic, lewd, suggestive, unwholesome" materials. The letter asked also for assurance that the stations would not be "withdrawn from community service, as by denying air time to religious programming and similar programming in the public interest."

Bert rolled off the bed and reached for his jacket, which hung on a chair in the bedroom. He pulled some folded sheets from his inside

317

pocket. "I've been editorializing," he said. "This will appear in a day or two. Here's a pro-Catlett column."

Anne read it:

When Carl Icahn bid for TWA, the Federal Aviation Administration didn't write him a letter telling him how to run the airline. The agency did not ask for a commitment that the famous entrepreneur obey the law. It was assumed he would.

What, then, is the motive behind the arrogant letter written by Federal Communications Commissioner Merrit Harding to F. Thad Catlett, who is engaged in an attempt to acquire States Broadcasting? Everyone knows that broadcasting pornography is unlawful—though Harding's fundamentalist friends may define pornography differently than Catlett does. CCE stations have never been convicted of broadcasting pornography. This means they are innocent, under the law, of the charges brought by certain televangelists.

Why, then, did Commissioner Harding write his incredible letter? It could have but one purpose—toadying to the demands of his friends on the "Christian" right. That this is the case is demonstrated by the second unwarranted demand in the letter, that Catlett promise to continue to broadcast religious and "similar" programming. Harding's letter is as crude as it is rude. We suggest Mr. Catlett tell him to eat it.

"Thank you, Bert," Anne said. "I know he'll appreciate it."

Bert cleared his throat. "I'm about to do something he won't appreciate. . . . I've got some more information from Germany."

"Damaging?"

He caught his breath for a moment. "Anne . . ."

She laid a gentle hand on his shoulder. "It's all right," she said quietly.

"What can I do?" he asked. "I can't close my eyes, plug my ears, and shut my mouth like the three monkeys in the parable. In my parable, there's a fourth monkey, with a telephone in one hand and a pencil in the other. . . . But I swear to you, Anne, I have never used anything I've learned from you."

"I think I have a sense of right and wrong," she said. "I honestly don't know of anything Thad is doing that's illegal or wrong. I wish he'd never met Wilhelm Hildebrandt. But if you could empty my mind on a table, Bert, you wouldn't find anything you could report."

"He has allowed his foreign associates to pull dollar signs over his eyes," said Bert. "His appetite for money has affected his judgment if not his ethics."

"Tell me something," she whispered. "In your . . . investigation, your looking into . . . everything, have you found out whose nightgowns those are hanging in his bedroom closet in the apartment?"

"No."

"Would you tell me if you did?"

"I hope I don't find out," said Bert.

In the apartment, Thad picked up the television controller and switched on WYRK-LI, which was now on scrambled broadcasting.

"Ah-hah," he said. "Timed right. Watch this, Jennie."

"My God, Thad!"

"Coup, huh?"

On the screen, the master of ceremonies of *Celebrity Strip* bawled an introduction: "The one! . . . The only! . . . None other than! . . . ROD . . . *GUNTHER!*"

The one-time heartthrob, forty-two years old but still trim, bronzed, with rippling muscles, still wearing the same boyish grin that had earned him millions, stood uncertainly mid-stage, forcing his stock-in-trade grin, glistening with sweat. The master of ceremonies pranced offstage and left him alone. Responding to the music and to directions from behind the cameras, he began to shuffle through a sort of dance, untying his necktie, unbuttoning his shirt to the waist, pulling off his tweed jacket.

"How in the world," whispered Jennie, shaking her head, "did you get Rod Gunther on *Celebrity Strip*? . . . To get him to do that . . ."

"He needs the money," said Thad. "Do you have any idea how much that phony snorts? Plus, every month he's got to come up with four alimony and six child-support checks."

Awkwardly, Gunther kicked off his shoes, pulled off his socks, and took down his pants. For a minute or two he shuffled around the stage in his sling underpants and unbuttoned shirt. Then, perceptibly responding to an off-camera command, he shrugged off the shirt and tossed it.

The studio audience screamed, the master of ceremonies trotted out, and Gunther forced a smile.

"I feel so—so embarrassed for him," Jennie said. "I hope that's the end."

"It is for the unscrambled stations," said Thad. "Not for the scrambled."

"Rod Gunther! . . . For God's sake!"

"They cancelled his series," explained Thad.

The master of ceremonies, beaming back at the animated audience, exchanged a few words with the sweating actor, gave him an amiable slap on the shoulder, and pranced off again. Gunther stood for a moment as if stricken. Then, agonizingly, he bent over and pulled down the underpants, standing naked before the cameras and the studio audience. For a tantalizing moment, the camera zoomed in on his flaccid penis, heavily swinging between his hips. The studio audience, watching the huge monitors, shrieked. Gunther smiled bravely at them, heaved a manly shrug, and began to stride around the stage. The light fantastic was beyond him, but he twisted his body and did a little hop, and the audience yelled with sheer joy.

"Really, Thad!"

Thad lifted his glass and gulped down a swallow of Scotch. "A hundred bucks says no cable show draws more viewers tonight. And when we rerun it in a couple of weeks, it'll draw double . . . thanks, in part, to the almighty howl we're going to hear from the Reverend

Billy Bob. We're rerunning it Sunday night. Reverend Billy will lose half his congregation. They'll stay home to watch Rod Gunther on *Celebrity Strip*."

"I think I'll take my stand somewhere between *Celebrity Strip* and *The Billy Bob Show*."

"At least," smiled Thad, "we'll find out who understands the public taste."

Jennie sighed. "Well, no one ever went broke underestimating the taste of the American people," she said.

As Rod Gunther fled through the curtain and the master of ceremonies bounced out to lead the applause, Thad switched off the television set. "Thank you, H. L. Mencken," he said.

Alone in his apartment, Bert Stouffer received a telephone call from Kennedy Airport.

"I can't tell you how pleased I am, Herr Westphal," he said. "Also, I can't tell you how surprised I am."

"I must see you as soon as possible," said the voice on the line. "I have booked a return flight, as I said I would do, ja? I'm not staying overnight, just flying in and out. My only mission is to meet with you, ja?"

"I will be at the airport in an hour," said Bert. "Where will I find you?"

"I see, to my surprise, a chapel in the middle of the airport. I should like to go there. I will wait for you there, ja?"

Bert could hardly believe it. The man had flown to New York from Hamburg on a Lufthansa flight that landed at two-thirty, and he was returning on a flight that departed at eight-twenty. The sole purpose of his trip was to meet an American journalist for a couple of hours. Bert had said he couldn't accept the man's story over the telephone, and the man had replied, "All right, I will fly to New York." The sound of his voice suggested he might be in his seventies. Bert wondered whether he had imposed an excessive burden on an elderly man.

321

The visitor from Germany was waiting in the interfaith chapel in the center of the airport, immediately recognizable. He was a small, fragile hunched man, wearing a black overcoat and clutching a walking stick between his knees as he sat, perched on a bench in a pew. His hat lay beside him, together with a small leather briefcase. His wispy hair was white, his pink face marked with brown liver spots. But his blue eyes were bright and sharp, and he smiled with enthusiasm as he rose to shake Bert's hand.

"Herr Westphal," said Bert respectfully, taking the old man's hand, anxious to grip it firmly yet not to squeeze so hard the delicate old hand might be hurt. Herr Westphal's hand was as pink as his face, and the skin had the same translucence; it was also smooth, not at all gnarled, and the returned grip was firm.

"Mr. Stouffer," said Herr Westphal, his glad smile sustained. "I am so pleased."

"You've had a long flight," said Bert. "You must be tired. Are you certain you should return tonight?"

"Dey take goot carc of me on the airplanes, ja?" said Herr Westphal, nodding. He spoke with an accent, yet effortlessly, with confidence. "I enjoy flying."

"Uh . . . well . . . do you prefer to talk here, or shall we go somewhere where we can have a little refreshment?"

"As you wish, Mr. Stouffer. I have had refreshments all the way across the ocean."

"Then maybe this is as quiet a place as we shall find for our talk," said Bert.

"And as private, ja?" said the old man.

They sat down side by side in a pew in the interfaith chapel. Though a few people occasionally slipped in and out, they were hushed, and Bert and Herr Westphal were able to confer quietly.

"You have stirred up much anger among the people I spoke to you about on the telephone," said Herr Westphal.

"They are neo-Nazis, aren't they?"

"No, I think dey are not," said Herr Westphal. "But what is a neo-Nazi? Who can be sure? But no. I am old enough to have had personal experience with the Nazis. These are just aggressive men . . . domineering truculent . . . and very, very angry, ja?"

"Angry?"

"Angry that dey are not in charge of affairs, ja? Angry that their opinions do not prevail in public councils. Angry that Germany is divided and powerless to reunify itself. Angry with defeat in two wars. And impatient! Oh, so impatient, Mr. Stouffer."

"And your—your connection with them, Herr Westphal?"

"Ah, that is of course the point, ja? As I told you on the telephone, my grandfather earned for our family a significant fortune, in the days of the Second Reich, the reign of the German kaisers. Our country has gone through many troubles. But through them all, somehow we managed to sustain our fortune and our position. In the last great war, I myself commanded twenty tanks, not Wehrmacht tanks, Mr. Stouffer, but Waffen SS tanks, ja? Yah. I vas an officer of the Waffen SS. Not those bullies in black uniforms of the Allgemeine SS, no—but still an officer of the *Waffen* SS. You understand the distinction, ja?"

"Soldiers," said Bert. "Not concentration camp guards. Soldiers. Nazi fanatics. Crack troops."

Herr Westphal nodded. "And dey committed war crimes, ja? I spent some time in a prison. Dey say I vas de-Nazified. You must know my background, Mr. Stouffer. You may choose not to believe what I say. You say we were Nazi fanatics. I suppose that is true. When I was thirty years old, I commanded tanks in battle on the Russian front. Do not expect me to apologize for that service, Mr. Stouffer."

"My mother was a Jew," Stouffer responded slowly. "But that doesn't make you a liar."

"Personally, I am sorry about two things," said Herr Westphal. "First, that we killed Jews. Second, that we did not succeed in holding the Russian barbarians out of western Europe, ja?" He shrugged. "But this is immaterial to our present discussion."

Bert nodded. "You mentioned Christian Thyssen in your phone call."

"Ah . . . Christian Thyssen . . . In my era, he would have been . . . myself, ja? A young man. Limited perspective. With a passionate love of his country."

"Truculent?" Bert asked.

"Truculent? Ja! But I think I was never so certain of my virtues as Christian is of his. The Führer claimed infallibility. I did not. I would guess Christian does."

"And the Bund für das Neues Deutschtum?"

Herr Westphal nodded. "Not Nazis, Mr. Stouffer. But unwilling to be limited by the usual standards of social conduct. I don't know how far they would go. I don't know what they would dare. But they dare a great deal."

"Murder?"

The old man frowned hard and shook his head firmly. "Not murder, no. I don't think they are capable of murder. But extortion, ja. That is what I have come to tell you."

"I'll listen and not interrupt," said Bert.

"At my age," said Herr Westphal, "I leave the management of my business to my sons, as my father left it to me. Our business is investment banking, Mr. Stouffer. Millions of marks . . . many millions . . . pass through our hands every week—funds invested by us on behalf of our clients. Of course, you understand the business. As investment advisers and trustees, we govern or influence the disposition of hundreds of millions of marks every year."

Sunlight through the stained glass of a chapel window fell on the old man's hands, turning them a bright blue.

"Mr. Stouffer, within the past several months, we have been subjected to improper pressures . . . pressures upon us to invest our clients' funds in certain instruments of debt . . . instruments issued by companies controlled by members of the BND. Do you understand what I am trying to tell you, ja?"

"You are being pressured," interpreted Bert, "to provide funds that will enable CATSERV to purchase States Broadcasting stock."

"So I believe," said Herr Westphal. "Dey come demanding."

"Exactly what kind of pressures are you talking about, Herr Westphal?"

The old man drew a breath. "None of us, Mr. Stouffer, have gone through life without committing indiscretions."

"Blackmail?"

"That is the American expression, I believe. It occurs in the form of suggestions that indiscretions may be disclosed, ja? . . . indiscretions one would wish would not be disclosed."

"Certainly not *your* indiscretions, Herr Westphal," Bert said.

The old man smiled wanly. "Ja, . . . Who else's? . . . Ja, my indiscretions. Most people have forgotten my Nazi affiliations. The BND has threatened to remind them. There was also a liaison some years ago with . . . I had a liaison with . . . what would you call her? . . . a nymphet." He shrugged. "I am too old to care what dey say about me. But my sons . . . Their wives. My grandchildren. My business associates."

"Blackmail," said Bert.

"Worse," said Herr Westphal. "I have not become so soft that I would submit to blackmail. I would call a press conference. I would tell all. I would accept the consequences. But I have been warned of other, more serious consequences. . . . Nothing specific . . . No one I can accuse . . . But it has been made clear to me that if I fail to cooperate with these angry young men, there will be misfortunes, accidents . . . ja?"

"That," agreed Bert, "is extortion, all right."

"I hope I do not exaggerate," said Herr Westphal.

Bert glowered. "Let's walk back to the terminal," he suggested. "If I can't buy you a dinner, let me at least buy you some wine or—"

"American whiskey," said Herr Westphal. "Bourbon. I have a small taste for it."

They recrossed into the terminal building from which Herr Westphal's Lufthansa flight would depart for Hamburg. Bert led the old gentleman into a restaurant inside the terminal and secured a window table where they could watch the departing flights.

Herr Westphal had brought documents. He laid them out meticulously on the table. Bert did not doubt their authenticity, though he could not translate the German. One set of documents purported to show that a veteran employee had been dismissed for investing a client's money in a fund that he, Herr Westphal, considered dubious.

"I know why he did it. It is part of a continuing pattern."

"BND?"

Herr Westphal nodded. "BND, ja . . . Blackmail, no . . ." he said. "Loyalty . . . A commitment higher than his commitment to our bank. He vas not blackmailed. He vas simply a believer."

Bert reflected for a moment over what he had learned. "Of course," he said, "Your bank would not be the only one. . . ."

"I have reason to believe," agreed Herr Westphal, "that even more severe pressures have been brought on others." So saying, he tossed back a shot of Jack Daniels, his benign face lighting up with a disarming smile, and he thumped the glass on the table—his signal for another. "Some of my friends are unwilling to speak."

"Hildebrandt?" asked Bert. "Was he the mastermind?"

"A man of my generation," said Herr Westphal. "A man with perspective. A man of restraint." He shrugged. "Since his death—"

"Christian Thyssen has taken over?"

Herr Westphal nodded. "So it would seem."

Bert signaled their waiter and pointed to the old gentleman's empty glass.

"I have seen all this before, Mr. Stouffer. The pattern is familiar. When we do not fight back, they overpower us."

"What are their aims, Herr Westphal?"

The old man smiled. "Power. What else? They seek power. And power today is won through control of public opinion. The successful leaders of our time understand that . . . on both sides of the iron curtain. . . . And you influence public opinion in one of two ways. You persuade people by the logic of your arguments and the force of your personality. Or you overwhelm them with propaganda. Christian Thyssen and his friends will use every device available to them. But in the end, they wish to flood the West with their propaganda."

"And what is their ultimate goal?"

"To manipulate events . . . To dictate policy . . . To control people," replied Herr Westphal. "Power is the driving force that brings together people of varying interests in the constantly evolving battle for control, ja?"

"And the end always justifies the means," said Bert.

Herr Westphal nodded. "For many people, the mere possession of power is an end in itself."

"Who killed Wilhelm Hildebrandt?"

The old man raised his white eyebrows and turned down the corners of his mouth. "He had many enemies . . . and many rivals. That's another thing about power. It creates opposition, ja?"

"And Hanna Frank?"

"Hanna Frank? I am sorry, I have not heard the name.

"Colin Fleming?"

Herr Westphal frowned. "The name is familiar." The frown quickly dissolved into a smile. "The English journalist, ja? You suspect someone killed the English journalist because he was close to disclosing something someone did not want disclosed." The smile broadened. "Journalists always believe such a plot whenever one of them is killed. Maybe he was seeing another man's wife. Maybe he owed gambling debts. The death of a journalist is not always martyrdom, ja?"

American Takeover May Be Funded
With Funds Extorted from European Businessmen

By Bert Stouffer

The source of nearly one billion dollars used by American media mogul F. Thad Catlett to finance the takeover of DunCast, Inc., then Runkle Broadcasting, then Conroy

Publishing, now States Broadcasting has remained a mystery that has stirred much speculation from Washington to Wall Street.

It is known that the money came out of a partnership formed in 1985 between Catlett and the late West German press baron Wilhelm Hildebrandt. It is known, too, that a number of other businessmen—German, Japanese, and maybe Korean—have contributed to the capital that was made available to Catlett. Among the investors behind the Catlett media empire, a few have been identified: the late Wilhelm Hildebrandt, Hans Dietrich, Klaus Schulenberg, Josef von Klauberg, Christian Thyssen, Kengo Yoshioka, Susumu Uchida, and possibly the shadowy Korean man-about-Washington, Kim Doo Chung. Still it has been difficult to account for one billion dollars. All these men are wealthy; some are presidents of major corporations; yet, they could not, according to financial sources, put their hands on one billion dollars.

Grand Extortion

A startling explanation of how these funds were raised has been brought to us by a senior German investment banker. Herr Franz Westphal, who flew to the United States to show us documentary evidence, explained that a German nationalist organization known as BND—Bund für das Neues Deutschtum—has engaged in widespread extortion and blackmail in high German financial circles to raise funds for various BND-controlled or influenced business organizations.

"It is not a new tactic," said Herr Westphal. "I am old enough to have seen it before." He referred to the strong-arm methods employed by the Nazis during their rise to power. He emphasized, however, that the BND is not pro-Nazi. Israeli sources confirmed that the BND is neither neo-Nazi nor anti-Semitic.

It is doubtful that F. Thad Catlett, beneficiary of BND's

tactics, has the least knowledge of them. Indeed, some investors may not know what other members of their group are doing. In a statement issued by his office, Catlett said all his financial transactions have been conducted with recognized respectable corporations engaged in legitimate and legal business activities.

Official German Reaction

A spokesperson for the German Federal Republic denied any knowledge of this extortion. Speaking for the Ministry of Economics in Bonn, he expressed skepticism at Westphal's story, citing his advanced age. He said the government "is aware" of BND and is "keeping a close watch on it." This is intriguing, in view of the fact that six months ago another official spokesperson denied ever having heard of such an organization as Bund für das Neues Deutschtum.

Billion-Dollar Question

Why would a consortium of German, Japanese, and Korean businessmen raise a billion dollars to invest in American television stations and a book publishing company? Perhaps they merely sought a substantial return on their investment. F. Thad Catlett has an outstanding record of turning failing newspapers into profit-makers. Similarly, the television stations he has acquired over the past two years have become far more profitable under his management—through his highly controversial "adult" programming. It may be expected that his new broadcast enterprises will become quite profitable.

Curiously, the German-Japanese-Korean consortium owns no equity interest in CATSERV or Catlett Communications Enterprises. Verlagsgruppe Wilhelm Hildebrandt acquired 40% of CCE in 1985, but the contract allowed Catlett to repurchase that interest in the event of Hildebrandt's death.

Hildebrandt was murdered in December—an unsolved crime—and Catlett repurchased all the stock. This leaves his foreign backers owners of a vast CCE debt but nothing else.

Informed Speculation

The informed speculation is that they would like to see a score of American television stations alter their editorial policies and become outlets for a nationalist-conservative political philosophy. Catlett's ongoing battle with the Christian fundamentalists, according to this view, would be relegated to a sideshow—a necessary battle that must be fought to switch these stations from "family" programming to mainstream American broadcasting. Then a conservative bias could be injected into the nightly programming favored by tens of millions of Americans. This conservative slant would offset the liberal bias that the consortium believes now dominates the media.

Did a foreign consortium invest a cool billion dollars in such a plot to infiltrate and influence the American media? There is evidence this is exactly what Catlett's consortium did.

Thad sat down on the edge of his bed in the master bedroom in Greenwich. Anne, stirred from her sleep by his movements, pounded pillows to make herself comfortable and pulled herself up to face him. He was glowering at the *Wall Street Journal*; he slapped angrily at it.

"Too much," he muttered. "Too goddamned much!"

She took the paper from his hand and studied the story. Though she had not yet seen the paper, she had already read the story. Bert had shown it to her in advance. He had told her about the cherubic little German gentleman, with the gossamerlike white hair, who had flown all the way from Hamburg just to speak with Bert. The old fellow had brought documents to back up his story, Bert had related.

"Too much what?" she asked. "Too much truth?"

Thad jerked up from the bed, strode to the window, and glared outside. Abruptly, he swung around to face her. "Did he write it here?" he demanded. "On my word processor downstairs?"

"No," she snapped back. "And he didn't get the story from me."

Thad charged back to the bed and drove his fist into the mattress. "Did he sleep in this bed? Did he wear my slippers? Did he eat at my table? . . . While he was investigating me?"

"Yes, he slept in your bed. But you're the only one who can identify all the other interlopers who have slept there."

"But of all men . . . Jesus Christ! Why *Bert Stouffer?*"

"How did you find out?" she asked coolly.

Thad heaved a long sigh, his body sagging as the breath left him. "Charles told me. He had to violate your confidence. He had to alert me that a private detective had followed you and reported it all to Thyssen."

"Whose nightgowns are those in the apartment?"

"Does it really make any difference?"

"I suppose not. It has come to that, hasn't it? But I am entitled to a woman's curiosity. You know about Bert; I should have equal . . . equal information."

"Are you in love with him?" Thad asked.

The sheet slipped down and uncovered her breasts; suddenly, it seemed she should cover them against the eyes of this man who stood before her in one of the bedrooms they had shared for almost thirty years. There he stood, the man she had married, still ruggedly handsome, unchanged by the years. He had just finished dressing; in full attire, he was always the model of a successful business executive—in clothes of fashionable color and cut. Today, he wore a dark blue suit, white shirt, tasteful silk tie, Gucci loafers. He glanced around for cigarettes. He had spent much of their thirty years together with his head enshrouded in cigarette smoke. Yet she had never known him to carry cigarettes in his pockets; he could not abide a bulge in his clothes. On the doctors' stern orders, she had thrown out all the cigarettes in the

331

house. Now he was searching agitatedly, distracted by the want of cigarettes.

Thad broke the silence. "I asked, are you in love with Stouffer?"

"I'm not sure," she said. "But it probably doesn't matter. I don't think he's in love with me."

"I'm sorry."

There was sympathy, not sarcasm, in his tone. She realized, with a start, that he saw no hurt to himself, only to her, from a blighted love affair.

"He learned nothing from me, Thad, about our business ventures," she said, "but I think he knows whose nightgowns I found in your apartment."

"He *doesn't* know," replied Thad.

"Are you in love this time?" she asked.

He nodded affirmatively. He stood there with his back to the window and nodded. That was all. He acknowledged he was in love with another woman.

"I was in love with Bill Shannon," she confessed.

"I was never in love with Megan," Thad responded.

"Funny thing, she was the woman Bert loved. They lived together before you broke into her life."

Thad shrugged. "I didn't know it."

"Are you going to tell me who the woman is you're in love with? I won't fight it. Really . . . I don't intend to cause trouble."

"You could hurt her badly if you did."

"I'm beyond hysteria, Thad."

"Okay. Jennie Paget. The congresswoman."

"Jesus Christ!"

"You really favor this pizzeria, don't you?" Bert commented.

Charles shrugged. "Why not? The food is excellent."

They were back at the little Italian restaurant not far from Charles's apartment. It was late in the evening. Charles had already eaten dinner with Kathy at home, but when Bert called and asked for a confidential meeting, adding that he had not had his dinner, Charles suggested they meet here. He sipped a glass or two of wine while Bert, his jokes about the place notwithstanding, devoured a plate of lasagna with a great smacking of lips. Save for three other people, they were the last customers of the evening, and the waiters were already stacking chairs.

"So . . ." Bert said, resuming the conversation that the waiter had interrupted, "your boss has done it again. Are you going to tell me what it cost?"

"It's no secret. Four hundred seventy-nine million dollars. Give or take a nickel."

"And when do you assume control? After a stockholders meeting?"

"The board of directors was graceful enough to resign," said Charles. "Except for Lucas Collins. He will remain—in a minority position."

"No, he won't," said Bert. "You haven't read your newswire. He announced this afternoon that he won't have any part of a corporation run by an atheist."

Charles was unperturbed. "So be it."

"But your troubles aren't over," said Bert. "The grapevine is buzzing with rumors that Dr. Kim Doo Chung brought improper pressures on Senator Warren Gallagher. . . . Scared hell out of him, I hear. It was too obvious, too crude, to be ignored. Some of the boys in Washington are looking into it."

"Thad Catlett holds Dr. Kim in utter contempt," said Charles.

"Catlett has every appearance of an accessory."

"Kim acts entirely on his own, without authority from Thad or anyone else."

"You'll never convince Washington of that."

Charles gazed out the window at the dark street beyond the restaurant. "Are you really convinced that your story about extortion was solid . . . that it involved more than an isolated incident or two?"

Bert leaned forward earnestly. "I'll tell you the truth. I fear for that

333

old man's life. . . . I mean Herr Westphal's. The story he gave me needed to be written. But I'm worried it may cost Westphal's life." Bert voice trailed off. "There are seasons when it seems a close call."

"Surely you exaggerate."

Bert shook his head. "Someone murdered Hanna Frank. It wasn't an agent of the East German government. The Communists may have wanted to eliminate Wilhelm Hildebrandt. But Hanna Frank . . . all her ties lead to Catlett's consortium. She handled the documents in Catlett's briefcase. We know that. Her fingerprints were found on the documents. Hard evidence. She was videotaped in bed with Catlett. She was implicated in a plot to blackmail Catlett and spy on him. Then something—or someone—scared her. Why else would she run away? And why would someone kill her?"

"Do you believe she met with Colin Fleming?"

"Yes, I believe it. It fits. Someone erased and altered an entry on the in-and-out log for personnel at VWH. This suggests there was some kind of connection between someone at VWH and the murder of Colin Fleming. Someone *knew* she was delivering stolen documents to somebody that morning. My guess is that they didn't know who. So they followed her. They saw a man with a briefcase go into the hotel and come back out, probably furtively. This was Colin Fleming. They may even have trailed him to Hanna Frank's room. Fleming was an amateur at this sort of thing, no match for the people on his tail. They probably killed him to recover the documents."

"Or maybe to prevent him from writing his story," suggested Charles.

"Provided that they knew he was a journalist. It's more likely they thought he was an agent for some unknown adversary. In all probability, they just didn't want to take any chances. They wanted to stop him from doing whatever he had in mind."

"Then who do you think killed Hildebrandt?" asked Charles. "And why?"

"I don't know. What I *do* know is that someone in the background of this whole VHW, BND, CCE connection is capable of murder."

"You can't write that. . . . Too speculative."

"The evidence is coming in," said Bert. "After my last story quoting Herr Westphal, I got another call from Germany . . . from Munich. I may go over there again."

Charles peered at him, frowning. "Do you think it's safe?" he asked. "Someone may be setting you up."

Bert shook his head. "I'm not sure."

Charles's frown deepened. "I wish I didn't believe you," he said quietly. "More than that, I wish Thad didn't believe you."

"Thad? . . ."

"He shares your suspicions. What's more, he knows about you and Anne."

"How is Anne? Is she all right? How did Catlett find out?"

"I told him," said Charles. "I didn't want him to hear it from somebody else, and he was about to. That private detective—the one Frank Dittoe put out of action—wasn't tailing Anne; he was tailing you. Christian Thyssen was behind it. Thyssen and his friends know all about you and Anne."

"Christ! . . ."

"I'm going to ask you a very personal question," said Charles gravely. "You're in love with Anne, aren't you?"

"How *can* I be, under the circumstances? It would be a conflict of interest, wouldn't it, for the reporter to fall in love with the wife of the guy he's investigating? Christ, I started out to write a story; now I find myself part of the story."

"You haven't answered my question."

"All right, I'm in love with her."

"Have you told her so?"

"Not in so many words."

"Well, I suggest you do," said Charles sternly.

Bert and Charles emerged, stretching and yawning, from the restaurant. Bert glanced up and down the empty street. "I don't suppose there's a cab within twenty blocks," he said. "I'd better walk toward Park Avenue. Better chance."

"We live only a block and a half from here," said Charles. "How

335

about a nightcap with Kathy and me? We can call a cab to pick you up."

"There are times," said Bert, "when I appreciate your Boston breeding."

They turned east, and the restaurant darkened behind them. It was a warm spring evening. The street, still wet from a brief shower, reflected the night lights amid patches of darkness. The balmy air was heavy with the sour smell of uncollected garbage.

"You know, I—"

Charles was shocked by an abrupt pain in his head, like an explosion of fireworks inside his brain. He staggered and lurched, then felt himself falling. His heart again! he thought. As he sprawled headlong on the pavement, he realized he had been struck from behind and was being struck again. A mugging! Instinctively, he hunched into a fetal position to protect himself. He was being brutally kicked, and he tried to roll away.

Cans banged. Charles saw Bert fall backward, slamming into some garbage cans. The man who was playing soccer with Charles's torso aimed a final foot at his face, then swung around and drove a fist into Bert. Through his own throbbing, excruciating pain, Charles could hear Bert grunting and moaning as two men beat him unmercifully. Irrationally, Charles tried to crawl away, to escape if even for only a few feet. Gagging on vomit, he looked up and saw what they were doing to Bert. Two of them. Pounding. Bert . . .

FIFTEEN

Kathy Welling felt better about herself. Her novel had not exactly set the literary world on fire; its sales had not reached the high altitudes. But it was out there in the bookstores in hard cover and soon would appear in paperback; it had achieved a British sale; it had even stirred some initial interest among Hollywood producers. That made her an author. That was most important to her. She didn't have to pretend any longer; she was a bona fide writer. She had plunged eagerly into a second novel. She was so excited about it, so confident she could do it, that she had not complained at all when Charles said he had to leave her alone for a couple of hours to meet Bert Stouffer. While he was gone, she had been pecking away at her typewriter, clad in bra and panties. She was pleased with herself; she had produced three acceptable pages.

The buzzer sounded. She ambled over to the intercom box, her mind still on the writing.

"Who is it?"

"Police officers," said a stern voice. "Will you buzz us in, please?"

She pressed the button to open the lock downstairs. She secured two chains on the door and fled into the bedroom to pick up a robe. She waited for the rap on the door, then opened it just a crack. The badge pushed through was authentic as far as she could determine—Sergeant Lawrence Rothman, NYPD. She released the chains.

There were two of them, Sergeant Rothman and a uniformed patrolman. Between them, they supported a staggering Charles. His head was bandaged. His eyes were bruised and swollen half shut. His nose was smashed in against his face and still oozing blood. They steered him to the sofa and helped him to sit down. His clothes were brown with blood.

"He wanted to come home," said Sergeant Rothman. "Insisted on it. . . . The doctors agreed."

"What the hell happened to him?"

"Muggers," grunted the sergeant. "Kids, looking to fund their crack. They worked him over pretty good. But he's lucky. His friend's in worse shape."

"Friend?"

"Bert Stouffer," Charles muttered.

"Right. He'll be in the hospital a while. Concussion. Broken cheekbone. Probably some internal injuries."

The sergeant started toward the door. "There's a painkiller in his shirt pocket. One tablet every two hours as needed . . . Instructions on the label. If you need help, call. Here's the number. It was Dr. Edmunds who attended him. The doctor thought he'd be as comfortable here as in the hospital."

As the door closed behind the two officers, Kathy rushed over to Charles. He had tipped his head back against the wall and was holding a blood-soaked cloth under his nose.

"Ice . . ." he muttered.

She scurried into the kitchen and brought back a bowl of ice and a clean kitchen towel. He sat up, wrapped several cubes of ice in the towel, and pressed it to his nose.

"Muggers? . . ."

He nodded. "Muggers."

The pills from the bottle in his shirt pocket made him drowsy. Kathy led him into the bedroom and, with some difficulty, deposited him on the bed. She pulled off the bloodiest of his clothes and sponged him off as best she could. He drowsed, slipping in and out of consciousness. She brewed some coffee. He swallowed a little, then slipped into a troubled sleep again.

By eleven, he was asleep. Kathy wandered aimlessly to her typewriter, slid into her chair, and stared blankly at the page she had been writing. Then abruptly, she grabbed the telephone and punched in a number.

"Mrs. Catlett? This is Kathy Welling. Charles has been hurt. He's asleep now here in the apartment. He wants me to believe he was mugged, but I don't believe it. Whoever attacked him also beat up Bert Stouffer. . . . I don't know who did it. I don't know why they hurt Charles and Bert . . . so viciously. . . . I don't know what to do. . . . The last thing Charles would want is for me to call Mr. Catlett. But I have a feeling he should be told.

At precisely 11:55 A.M. the limousine pulled up at the emergency entrance of Lehman Hospital and disgorged a grim Thad Catlett. Frank Dittoe was waiting for him. Dittoe silently slipped Thad a pistol, which Catlett jammed into the waistband of his trousers. He growled terse instructions: Frank would stay with Anne, and Thad would rush to Charles's apartment. He wasn't sure what he would find, but he would be ready. He patted the steel bulge under his jacket.

Frank's NYPD shield worked again. It got Anne and himself admitted to the emergency section, where they were allowed to see Bert Stouffer.

A battered and bandaged Stouffer lay in the center of a tangle of tubes and wires. Bert gasped and snorted in quick bursts as

339

he struggled to suck in breath through his swollen nose and mouth.

"Bert . . . It's Anne. Do you know me, Bert? . . . Bert?"

"Uh . . . Uh huh. . . ."

"You're hurt, I know. You don't have to talk. But the doctors say you'll be all right. I spoke to three doctors. You took a severe beating . . . just awful. But you're going to be okay, Bert. You're going to be all right."

His eyes were puffed slits, purple and red with pain, but they somehow focused. He struggled to wet his swollen lips. "Uh . . ."

"You don't have to talk."

"Uh . . . Anne . . . Please . . . Listen. Uh. Uh. *Love* you!" He coughed; it was a half gasp, half groan. "Anne . . . Love you . . ."

Anne sobbed, her eyes flooding with tears. The room and the bed swam in the dewy mist. "Yes, Bert. I love you, too. And, Bert . . . Thad knows. Everything will be all right."

He struggled for breath. "Cops . . . uh . . . wrong. Not . . . not mugged. Not . . . They said, 'Back off' . . . 'Back off' . . . Understand?"

"I understand," she said quietly. "We're stationing guards outside your room. Thad has ordered them. Guards. You understand? Frank and I will stay here until they're in place. Don't worry about anything. All you have to do is get well."

He raised a hand in a weak signal. "Herr Westphal . . . Warn him . . . Herr Westphal. They'll . . . kill him."

The warning came too late. Franz Westphal, seventy-eight years old, lay in his bed in his Hamburg home. He had been dead for six hours, but no one in the house knew it yet. He had died quietly, of an overdose of sodium pentothal injected in his arm.

Thad and Kathy decided not to waken Charles. They waited tensely in his living room. She had made coffee. He had refused

Scotch. He knew about Charles and Kathy. Anne had briefed him on the drive in from Greenwich; it was the first Thad had heard of Kathy Welling.

She had slipped into a gray skirt and navy blue T-shirt when the police had left. Still, she was earthy and unkempt, by Thad's surprised observation; not the sort of woman he had expected to see Charles Lodge Johnson take an interest in.

"He wasn't mugged," she said. "I just know it. . . . Somebody did this to Charles deliberately."

Thad had placed a transatlantic call. The telephone rang. The operator said she had been unable to locate Mr. Christian Thyssen in Berlin but that Mr. Friederich Papen, in Frankfurt, was on the line.

"Papen? Catlett. Look, somebody has done something unutterably stupid. Charles Lodge Johnson was attacked and beaten on the street tonight. Also Bert Stouffer. They were assaulted on their way home from a restaurant."

"I am not quite sure why you called to tell me this," said Papen. "I am naturally concerned about Charles, and it is too bad that the reporter Stouffer has been injured. But I hope you are not suggesting that any of our people have anything to do with it."

"Papen . . ." said Thad wearily. "I no longer am sure who has what to do with what. But it certainly is no coincidence that Stouffer was attacked only two days after his *Wall Street Journal* article appeared. Somebody has done something worse than stupid. Good lord! How do you think this is going to be received in this country?"

"Dr. Kim . . ." blurted Papen. "Do you think? . . ."

"It wouldn't surprise me. He already blackmailed a United States Senator, from all appearances. I'm trying to reach Christian. I suggest you spread the word to our people. The shit's hit the fan over here, Papen, if you know what that American expression means!"

"Yes, Thad. . . . I will circulate the word. In the meanwhile . . . uh . . . you sound . . . uh . . . distraught. Try to . . ."

"I know, relax. I tell you, this stupid violence is going to boomerang, with an explosion that could bring down our whole enterprise around our heads. Tell Christian to call me."

He banged down the receiver and turned to find Kathy Welling staring at him.

"What price glory, Mr. Catlett?" she asked.

"Trish . . . I don't give a damn if he's in conference with the Pope's wife," said Anne to Thad's secretary. "I want him on the phone *now*. It's urgent."

"Hold the line, Mrs. Catlett. I'll do what I can."

Trish knew he was on *that* line, his private line, and she knew whom he was talking to. She would just keep Mrs. C on hold for a minute. Then—

"Gallagher got a call from the White House," Jennie was telling Thad. "From the man. Not from some counsel. From the man. He was inquiring about the Borman bill. They've had a blizzard of mail from the rednecks. The president wants to know what's holding up the bill."

"What did Gallagher tell him?"

"That it's too late. That you've already gotten away with it. That you moved too fast for him. That the bill is pointless now. Which he obviously doesn't believe. And neither does the president."

"How did the *Post* report the attack on Charles Johnson and Bert Stouffer?" Thad asked.

"That they were mugged on a New York street last night. The *Post* just carried the wire story. Is there more to it?"

"My papers will quote the police dismissing it as a mugging. But my papers will point out that the circumstances are suspicious, that it looks like an effort to silence a journalist."

"By whom?" she asked. "Who are you accusing?"

"I can't accuse anybody. I don't know. I'm simply suspicious."

"I need to see you, Thad. I'm flying up tonight."

"Don't do it. Don't get involved in this. You should keep your distance."

"I'll just let myself in. I have the key."

"But . . . Listen, I have to get off the line. Something's come up. I'm getting an urgent signal from Trish."

Thad punched in the line with the blinking light.

Anne's troubled voice came on the line.

"Thad? Bert Stouffer was just taken back into surgery. Internal bleeding. They can't promise he'll make it."

Thad reached his apartment at eight-fifteen and let himself in. Jennie's raincoat was draped over a chair in the living room, the bedroom door was ajar, and he could hear the shower running. Frank Dittoe had accompanied him; Thad told Frank to mix himself a drink.

"Hey!" she said when he appeared at the glass door of the shower. "Strip your clothes off and join me."

"I need a drink."

She reached out with a dripping hand and seized him by the sleeve. "You need this more than you need a drink," she said. "Come on. Warm water. Naked woman. Beats Scotch."

For a moment, Thad was torn between Jennie and a jolt of Scotch. He was shaken by his visit to the hospital, where Bert Stouffer had just been wheeled out of surgery. The brutal assault had ruptured an artery, but the surgeons had managed to repair it. Their prognosis was now more encouraging. Thad had left Anne at Bert's bedside, where she had stayed since last night with one of Pittocco's men standing guard. She had told Thad there was nothing he could do for her; she would rather keep her own vigil.

Thad needed the drink, but he chose Jennie. The warm water, Jennie's embrace, her whispered words in his ear—it was the right therapy. The tension slowly drained out of him. As they clung together under the shower, the telephone rang urgently. Frank answered it. Thad explained to a startled Jennie that Frank, with an ugly pistol under his jacket, was sharing the premises with them.

"There's a good reason," he explained to her as they dressed, he in slacks and open shirt, she in jeans and sweatshirt. "Herr West-phal . . . the old German investment banker who talked to Stouffer. He was found dead this morning. Dead of a massive overdose of sodium pentothal. Someone invaded the old man's bedroom and probably held him while they injected the deadly dose in his arm."

"Thad . . . this is unreal. What's going on? What . . . who . . . are we *dealing* with?"

"I'm not sure. I'm trying to find out."

One of the calls that came while they were showering was from Josef von Klauberg in Bonn. Thad returned it.

"Yes, I do know about Herr Westphal," said von Klauberg. "In fact, that is why I called . . . to tell you. He was not robbed. He was murdered . . . executed."

"For God's sake, who is behind this?" Thad demanded.

"I wish I could tell you," said von Klauberg. "I can imagine what you are thinking. You must be wondering whether you are in business with a murderous gang. But you are not, I can assure you. Think of whom you have been dealing with, Thad. Wilhelm Hildebrandt. Hans and Ernst Dietrich. Kengo Yoshioka. I include myself. We are all prominent businessmen. We are known . . . re-spected . . . around the world."

"You didn't mention Christian Thyssen," said Thad coldly.

"A fortuitous omission," said von Klauberg. "I do not disagree that he lacks the experience and sophistication of our late friend, Wilhelm Hildebrandt."

"Since we formed our joint venture in 1985," said Thad, "I can count four murders connected in one way or another with Verlagsgruppe Wilhelm Hildebrandt and the associates we call The Consortium. First there was Hildebrandt himself. Then Colin Fleming, followed by Hanna Frank. And now Herr Westphal. On top of that, a journalist writing about our business has been attacked and beaten almost to death. . . . My own vice president, Charles Lodge Johnson, was injured in the attack on Stouffer. How many coincidences do you think it takes to create a suspicion?"

"I have been trying to reach Christian Thyssen all day," said von Klauberg.

"Meanwhile, I intend to act on my suspicion."

"Please," said von Klauberg. "Don't do anything foolish."

"Someone else has done something foolish," said Thad. "I hope to contain the damage."

As he cradled the telephone, Frank handed him another slip. Kathy Welling had called while he was in the shower.

"What's in the fridge? Can we grab a bite?" Thad asked as he reached again for the telephone.

Frank Dittoe grinned. "I've already checked out the pantry," he said. "Either we call out . . . or you take a chance on what an Italian cop can throw together with odds and ends and a box of pasta."

"I could use a cooking lesson," said Jennie. "Whatever accomplishments I might possess, culinary skill is not one of them."

Thad was already punching in the number for Charles's apartment. Charles answered in an uncertain voice.

"Are you functioning?"

"I'm functioning," said Charles. The words, strained through swollen lips, came out slightly slurred. "I've been functioning since about noon. I've called Washington . . . Put Frank Siciliano on the job . . ."

"Siciliano? . . . What . . ."

"Yes. . . . Had him call Immigration and Naturalization. . . . Wanted to know if any of our Germans are in the country. . . . One *is*. . . . He entered the States a week ago. . . . Landed at Kennedy."

"Who? . . . Which one?"

"Ernst Dietrich."

"Could he have been behind last night's incident?"

"I don't know. Could have been. My guess? We were probably attacked by hired gorillas. They were intent on hurting Bert Stouffer, not me. Heard one of them tell him, 'Back off. Back off.' That could have meant only one thing."

Thad was silent for a moment. "Unbelievable!" he muttered. Then he told Charles to give first priority to his recovery.

As Thad turned away from the telephone, he was distracted by the melodious ripple of laughter from the kitchen. Jennie and Frank were stirring up a concoction that permeated the apartment with a savory odor. He set forth to investigate. Frank had a great skillet on the range; he was sautéing onions and peppers in hot oil that bubbled and popped. Jennie was close by, barefoot, in faded jeans and ragged sweatshirt, overseeing the process and laughing at Frank's antics.

Jennie spotted Thad and abruptly left her kitchen duties. "I didn't know whether to laugh or cry," she explained. "Frank's cooking isn't really all that funny, but I decided to laugh."

Thad was in no mood to laugh nor cry. "I've got to notify Thaddy," he announced.

She nodded her acknowledgment and disappeared back into the kitchen.

"Thaddy, listen," Thad said when he heard his son's voice in London. "Everything's okay. I mean, your mother and I and Richard are all right. But I've got to warn you about something. It appears that one or more of my business associates in Europe has gone nuts or is a closet Nazi. Somebody beat up Charles last night, also a newspaper reporter who's been writing about our business. I don't think anybody's in real danger. But if you and Alan ever thought about driving up into the lake country or the moors and visiting a country inn, now would be a good time. I need a few days to bring everything to a head. It shouldn't take long. Meanwhile, I've got security men looking out for us here. I've got two assigned to Richard. I'll arrange for somebody to do the same for you in London if you can't get away."

"Are you serious?"

"Yes. I'm afraid so."

"I don't see how we can leave London right now. We've got—"

"Then I wish you'd cooperate with the bodyguards I get for you. I'll call a security service as soon as business opens over there. Better yet, you do it. Select the best and send me the bill."

"Dad, are you sure? . . ."

"Better safe than sorry. This isn't the first time. It's happened before. I had to hire people to protect you and your mother against union thugs when we lived in Pittsburgh. Part of the game. You do what I tell you, Thaddy. And cooperate with those guys. Richard is cooperating with his—buys 'em pizza. I don't want to have to worry about you."

Frank Dittoe bedded down in the living room. Thad and Jennie retired to the bedroom.

"You shouldn't be here tonight," he told her when they lay side by side. "I mean, if word about us gets out . . . well, you know what happened to Gary Hart."

"I've never been able to live a simple, comfortable life," she said quietly. "I guess I never wanted to. It could have been so easy, you know. . . . Just settle down in Scarsdale as the wife of an up-and-coming lawyer in a top firm. . . . Play golf. Tennis. Bridge." She shook her head. "Nor is that the life Anne would have chosen. As for *you* . . . You never played it safe."

"My mother and grandfather wanted me to become a lawyer," he confessed.

"You'd have been bored," she said. "Even Martin is bored by the paperwork. But it's part of the price he pays for his self-esteem and success."

Thad leaned over. "Jennie . . ." he whispered, brushing her lips with a kiss. "I'm glad you're here tonight. I'm just afraid you shouldn't be."

"I have my priorities in order, Thad," she said earnestly. "I'm not sure you do, but I do."

"Help me," he said simply.

She drew closer to him. "The first priority is for you to get some sleep," she said.

"Two things," said Trish briskly. "Frank Siciliano is on the line from Washington. And Charles has come in."

"He shouldn't be here! But bring him in. I'll pick up Frank. Which line? Six? Frank? What's up?"

"Something I thought you would want to know," said Frank Siciliano. "Dr. Kim Doo Chung has flown the coop. All the way back to Korea. He caught the shuttle out of National yesterday afternoon and took the Korean Air flight from New York to Seoul last night. The house on Massachusetts Avenue is still open, but only the caretaker appears to be there."

"Is it your impression this was an abrupt departure?" Thad asked.

"I hope to tell. He had appointments scheduled all day today. He didn't even call to cancel. Just took off."

"Was there a subpoena out for him?"

"Not that I know of. The *Post* broke the story of his departure."

"Curious. Okay, Frank. Thanks. Anything more, call me."

Thad turned immediately to Charles. Rising, he came around his desk to shake Charles's hand. "You shouldn't be here."

"My doctor would agree. I shouldn't. But it's important. Maybe I'm just too damned loyal."

Charles struggled to maintain his dignity, with a face bruised and swollen, lips blotched with dark scabs. Though his head was no longer wound in bandages, a thick yellowish pad was taped above and behind his right ear. He moved gingerly, wincing at every strain on his ribs.

"I'm serious," said Thad. "You should be home in bed."

"As I said, it's important. I want you to go to Lehman Hospital and see Bert Stouffer. We'll go together. . . . Uh . . . I talked to Anne this morning. She's going home at last, to take a bath and catch some sleep."

"What do you have in mind, Charles? Exactly what is it you want me to say to Bert Stouffer?"

Charles's jaw stiffened. "Whatever you wish. What I really mean is, I think you ought to listen to him."

"You're suggesting I should have listened to him before."

"No, Thad. *I* should have listened. He tried to tell *me*. Now we should listen together. He asked me to see him. We met in a restaurant just before we were attacked. He knows more than he has published . . . more than he has told me. I think we *must* see him. We must listen to him."

*   *   *

At the hospital, Frank Dittoe's tactics again were more effective than F. Thad Catlett's name. A frowning doctor eyed Dittoe's police badge and consented reluctantly to let them see Bert Stouffer. For ten minutes, he said. No more. And it damned well better be important.

Bert lay on a cranked-up bed, taking medication and nourishment through tubes and needles. His nose was smashed flat. His right cheekbone was broken. His mouth was a grotesque mass of cuts and swellings. His left arm was splintered. His left eye was swollen shut, and his right peered out with a hostile glint. He was painfully sucking broth into his mouth through a straw. When he saw Thad and Charles, he spat out the straw.

The nurse clucked but removed the jar of broth.

"You've met," said Charles to Bert. "This is Thad Catlett."

Bert tried to focus his eyes, without much success. He grunted.

"Tough business we're in," said Thad. "I got a working over once, many years ago. Union goons. Threw me down a flight of stairs."

Bert's eyes followed Thad as he edged around the bed and stood where he thought Stouffer might see him better.

"I have some bad news for you," Thad said. "I'm sorry, but you have to know sooner or later. Herr Westphal is dead. They got him the same night they assaulted you."

It seemed impossible that Bert's damaged face could register grief, but Stouffer somehow managed to do so. He winced perceptibly and choked as if he were about to cry.

"Apparently, your information was right," said Thad. "More right than we could have guessed."

"Hoo?" muttered Bert.

"What? . . ." asked Thad, straining to understand.

"Hoo . . . *How?* . . . Herr . . ."

"How did he die, Thad?" interpreted Charles. "What happened to Herr Westphal?"

"Someone shot him full of sodium pentothal."

"Uhh! Uhh! So— Sodium. Pwhh. Fame. *Fame.* Caw . . . Shit! . . ."

"Call?" Thad asked. "Call somebody?"

349

"Uh-huh!"

"Take it slow. Can you say who?"

"Off . . . Stan. Caw . . . Yoy. Yoy-ers. Funk . . . Funk . . . Funk-fer."

"Frankfurt," said Charles. "Call someone in Frankfurt? Right?"

"Uh-huh! Yoy-ers. Tan! Tan! Off!"

"Reuters!" exclaimed Charles. "Reuters. Stan Ross!"

"Uh-huh. . . ." Bert grunted weakly.

"Is it important? Urgent?"

"Uh-huh."

"Okay," agreed Thad. "We'll do it. And we'll be back in touch to tell you what we find out."

"Mmm-mm."

Thad rounded the bed again and started for the door. Then he stopped, paused, and looked down at Bert. "Uh . . . Anne will be back later. This evening, I think."

Bert strained through his half-open right eye to see Thad.

"Don't be concerned, Stouffer . . . about . . . uh . . . anything," said Thad. "Get your strength back. I'll check with Anne to see how you're doing. Anything you want to tell me, you can tell her."

Stan Ross was startled to receive a telephone call from F. Thad Catlett. It reached him at home while he was watching the television evening news. He did not know that Bert Stouffer had been attacked. But he did know that Herr Westphal had been murdered; he had also connected the death with Bert's story, which had reached him in Frankfurt.

"Bert can hardly speak," Thad said. "It's almost impossible to understand him. But he asked me to call you; he said it was urgent. He made the request after something we told him got him excited. I informed him that Herr Westphal was killed with an injection of sodium pentothal, and he suddenly got . . . well, he got as agitated as a man in his condition can get. He couldn't explain what had excited him. All he could communicate was that I should call you."

"Yes," said Ross. "I think I know what he was trying to tell you. He remembered something about the assassination of Wilhelm Hildebrandt. Not long after Hildebrandt was killed, the police found two other bodies. They were positively identified as two agents of the Ministerium für Staats-Sicherheit—the East German KGB. In the pocket of one was a key to the Volkswagen van that had been used in the Hildebrandt assassination. Both had died of overdoses of sodium pentothal, shot into their arms."

"That could be a link between the murder of Wilhelm Hildebrandt and the murder of Herr Westphal," said Thad.

"Possibly."

"Hanna Frank was shot with a nine-millimeter pistol, and Colin Fleming was shot with a nine-millimeter pistol," said Thad. "Do you know whether the police checked the ballistics? Were those two killings done with the same pistol?"

"Yes, the police checked," said Ross. "Not the same pistol."

That afternoon Thad sent cables to Christian Thyssen, Friederich Papen, Josef von Klauberg, Hans Dietrich, Ernst Dietrich, Klaus Schulenberg, Kengo Yoshioka, Susumu Uchida, Dr. Kim Doo Chung, and Park Il-Sung. The cables read:

I AM CALLING AN EMERGENCY MEETING OF THE MEMBERS OF THE CONSORTIUM TO ASSEMBLE IN MY OFFICE AT 7:00 PM (1900 HOURS) ON WEDNES-DAY, MAY 27. THE MEETING WILL BE HELD, AND DECISIONS WILL BE MADE IN THE ABSENCE OF MEMBERS WHO DO NOT APPEAR.

Two hours after the cables were sent, he received a reply from Christian Thyssen:

I MUST PROTEST YOUR ARBITRARY SUMMONS TO NEW YORK. NEVERTHELESS, I WILL ATTEND THE

MEETING. PLEASE PROVIDE AN AGENDA IN AD-
VANCE.

The House schedule would be light for the week, so Jennie remained in New York. She was touching up the apartment instinctively, as a woman in front of a mirror adjusts her face, when Thad arrived, acompanied again by the versatile Frank Dittoe.

"The recorder is on," she said. "I set it to pick up on the first ring. Let's relax and pretend for the evening that Alexander Graham Bell never invented the telephone."

Thad held up two fingers. "Just two calls," he said.

She had brought a bag full of groceries, so she steered Frank into the kitchen, and the two of them began assembling the ingredients for a meal. Thad, in the living room, telephoned Lehman Hospital and spoke to Anne. Stouffer was better. Thad asked her to pass on to Bert the result of his call to Ross. Then Thad telephoned his son in London. Thaddy was chortling as he answered the telephone. Two burly security guards had virtually moved into the flat with them. . . . "Eating and drinking everything we have."

Jennie and Frank broiled thick steaks and brought them triumphantly into the living room.

"Have to watch something on the tube," Thad said. "At eleven-thirty. We're supposed to be the subject of the Frank Evans show."

They ate. They talked. Frank amused them with anecdotes from his days on the New York City police force. At eleven, Thad and Jennie disappeared into the bedroom. They switched on the television and watched the news. At eleven-thirty, the *Frank Evans Night View* burst onto the screen.

It opened with the usual drama and urgency—a sepulchral summary of the controversies raised by CCE's acquisition of States Broadcasting. Then Evans began to interview people who had some opinion on the subject—all but one of them by remote television hookups to Washington, Birmingham, Detroit, and Los Angeles.

An industry analyst on the West Coast declared that Catlett

Communications Enterprises was overextended and would probably collapse from the sheer weight of its debts.

The Reverend Billy Bob Calder intoned that F. Thad Catlett was "a purveyor of every kind of filth and lewdness." From Detroit, the Reverend Henry Templeton, president of the Ministerial Association, said his organization had been invited to create a new schedule for religious broadcasting, fair to all denominations, on the Detroit station that CCE had just acquired. The purpose was to offer "*all* Detroit churches access to television," said the distinguished cleric. The Reverend Billy Bob broke in with a hostile question: Was the Reverend Templeton's church affiliated with the World Council of Churches? It was, confirmed Templeton. The Reverend Billy Bob laughed contemptuously. The World Council was a communist front, he snorted.

Evans turned to Senator Eugene Borman, who was wedged into a chair in the Washington television studio. "Senator Borman, you have sought to enact legislation to prevent the acquisition of States Broadcasting by CCE. . . ."

"Mistuh F. Thad Catlett has already acquired the States Broadcasting network, suh. My bill would force Catlett to remand the network to its former owners."

"Yes. Force them to give it up. And you have complained that your bill seems to be stuck in committee. In fact, there doesn't seem to be much enthusiasm for it on Capitol Hill. Are you giving up on the bill?"

"Frank, when you're doing God's work—and I sincerely believe that's what I'm doin' by offerin' this bill—you never give up. You just keep prayin' and pluggin'. God helps those who help themselves. We have the support of the people, Frank. And we're gaining support on the Hill. I also b'lieve the President wants this bill."

"Then—"

"But everybody knows Mr. Catlett is as powerful as he is evil. He has his friends in key places in the Congress."

"Do you refer to Senator Gallagher, who is reported to be holding up your bill?"

353

"Well . . . I'm not blaming Senator Gallagher. He's been put under terrible pressure. Catlett has other friends . . . important friends. For example, there's the congresswoman from N' Yawk, Mrs. Paget. I b'lieve she is an *intimate* friend of Mr. Catlett."

Thad reached for Jennie and drew her into his arms. Neither of them spoke. She rested her head on his shoulder and clung to him.

It was Charles's own prognosis that his stiffness and pain would recede faster if he walked; the exercise, he thought, would work the stiffness out of his system. On Friday morning he accepted, therefore, an invitation to lunch at the University Club with Robert Kline, who knew he had been hurt but had no idea how seriously. It was an ambitious walk, but Charles determined to try it. He could, after all, summon a cab if his body faltered.

He left the Pam Am Building at twelve-thirty, allowing himself half an hour for the walk—more time than he would need, even limping along and stopping occasionally to regroup. He walked west on Forty-fifth Street. Traffic was jammed as always; when it came to a standstill, he crossed to the north side. He rounded the corner onto Vanderbilt and walked along the narrow sidewalk past the food shops.

The walk ahead was blocked by a pallet stacked with cartons being off-loaded from the back of a truck. He stepped into the street and headed for the other side. A taxi was approaching but it was still beyond Forty-sixth Street; this should give him plenty of time to complete the crossing. He watched it coming, trying to make eye contact with the driver—the universal New York means of establishing right-of-way.

Suddenly, the cab accelerated. It bore down on him, its speed increasing. The adrenaline shot new energy into his injured limbs, and he sprinted for the west sidewalk. But the cab swerved toward him. Charles shrieked with terror the instant before it struck him. Hit by the right fender, he was thrown into the air; he crashed against the rear of a parked car and rolled across the sidewalk, his arms and legs flapping.

Gregg Islander, a black nineteen-year-old—one of the men who was unloading the truck—stared after the cab as it roared away and screeched around the corner onto Forty-fifth Street. "Man! Man! Did you see that?" he yelled. "That cab just run the man down!" He raced across the street to Charles and, kneeling over him, cried, "Man! Man! Are you alive? Man!"

Charles didn't hear him.

Thad arrived at Lehman Hospital a few minutes after one-thirty. Kathy Welling was already there, with Anne at her side. She had been visiting Bert Stouffer, and Frank Dittoe had called with the shocking news. A police sergeant, unimpressed over another hit-skip, another pedestrian knocked down by a wild cab driver, treated the incident as routine until he learned who the victim was. The name Charles Lodge Johnson didn't mean anything to him. The information that Johnson was a Pulitzer Prize journalist got the sergeant's attention, however. When he also discovered the victim was a top executive of Catlett Communications Enterprises— publisher of the *Sentinel-American*, owner of the three local television stations—the sergeant began bestirring himself. He placed an urgent call, and a watch commander—a uniformed captain— quickly arrived. The captain took very seriously Thad's assertion that this hit-skip was likely an attempted murder.

While Thad conferred with the police, Anne, herself distraught, tried to comfort the sobbing Kathy and hovered over the nurses' station, waiting for word from emergency surgery.

At quarter past two a doctor at last appeared. "I'm sorry, there is little we can tell you. His injuries are severe. He's in shock. We've surgically repaired what we can. He is not responding as well as we would like. It's going to be twenty-four hours before we will know anything. I wish I could be more positive."

Anne led Kathy to the third-floor room where she had rested during her own long vigil over Bert. Thad stayed outside the intensive-care unit, smoking furiously, pacing the halls, striding out the ambulance entrance, returning, watching the comings and goings. He was stunned, angry, fearful. He ducked into a telephone booth and called Asher. Then he called Jennie, who was hiding out in his apartment, unsure whether to return to Washington and face reporters.

Thad gulped down some coffee from a machine, munched on a packaged sandwich from another. Every few minutes he inquired about Charles.

The hospital personnel were sympathetic, but professional and impersonal. He was told that a nurse was monitoring Mr. Johnson closely and constantly, ready to respond to any emergency. Once he saw an orderly rush into Charles's room, pushing a cart. A bottle of saline solution had drained near empty, Thad was told; nothing alarming.

He was an impatient man, no good at waiting, he said to one of the nurses. She smiled tolerantly.

Anne and Kathy returned at four. They insisted he should return to his office; they would call him at once if there was any change in Charles's condition. Thad did not leave the hospital immediately. He stopped, instead, at Bert Stouffer's room.

"You know about Charles?"

"Umm-hmm."

"I've called a meeting of my business partners. They'll be at my office Wednesday evening. A confrontation."

"Good . . . luck."

After Thad reached his office, he telephoned Jennie. "Can you come here?" he asked. "We have work to do."

From the Associated Press

New York, May 2—Charles Lodge Johnson, vice president of Catlett Communications Enterprises, Inc., is in critical condition in Lehman Hospital today after being struck on a mid-Manhattan street by a taxicab shortly after noon yesterday.

356

Johnson, 48, won the Pulitzer Prize for his reporting of Boston and Massachusetts political corruption in the early 1970's. He became editor in chief of the *Washington Register-Herald* in 1973, shortly after that newspaper was acquired by F. Thad Catlett. In recent years, Johnson has served as a top executive in Catlett's rapidly expanding communications conglomerate. He has also been a close personal advisor to Mr. Catlett.

Police are investigating the circumstances which resulted in Johnson's injuries. At least one eyewitness has described the incident as intentional. Others say it was a typical city-street hit-and-run accident.

Charles Lodge Johnson was the victim of a mugging-beating only last week. Police are also investigating whether this incident was also deliberate.

From the Associated Press

New York, May 2—Congresswoman Jennie Paget, D-N.Y., acknowledged in a statement issued today that she is "a close and intimate friend" of F. Thad Catlett, president of Catlett Communications Enterprises, Inc. At the same time, Mrs. Paget denied she had "used her position as a member of Congress in any way whatever" in Catlett's behalf.

Senator Eugene Borman, R-Miss., brought up the relationship between the congresswoman and the controversial corporate raider during an interview on a television news program Thursday night. He has bitterly opposed Catlett's recent takeover of States Broadcasting Company. Catlett's newspapers have repeatedly accused Senator Borman of drunkenness and other misconduct as a senator.

In a statement issued from the offices of Catlett Communications Enterprises and published in the Saturday editions of all Catlett newspapers, Mrs. Paget described her relationship with Catlett as "warm and caring." She said it had never been a secret. Catlett has refused, she said, even to allow her to make inquiries on his behalf in Washington.

Mrs. Paget is the wife of Martin Paget, a prominent New York lawyer. Catlett's wife, Mrs. Anne Catlett, is owner of half the stock in Catlett Communications Enterprises and is a well-known photographer. Neither Mr. Paget nor Mrs. Catlett were available for comment.

All day Saturday, Charles's condition remained unchanged. Anne called from the hospital with the doctors' cryptic statements that Mr. Johnson's life signs had stabilized but that he remained unconscious. There was no reason, Anne insisted, for Thad to come to the hospital.

Thad stayed at the grindstone all day. He helped Jennie respond to press inquiries. He conferred twice with the lawyers who were working with Kenneth Asher. He began writing an article. He took telephone calls from everywhere. Then, in mid-afternoon, he shut off the calls. Jennie, meanwhile, returned to her home in Scarsdale to talk to her husband.

Thad stopped by the hospital in the evening. Anne had gone home. Kathy had gone home. The doctors had convinced them that nothing could be gained by their lingering in the hospital. They confided to Thad that Charles was somewhat weaker. They doubted, however, that there would be any significant change overnight.

"You mean, he won't die overnight?" Thad asked.

"No, not likely." It was a slow deterioration that might reverse itself.

Thad looked in on Stouffer and found him, fortunately, stronger. The swelling around his mouth had begun to recede, and he could talk.

Back at the apartment, Thad telephoned Anne. She was exhausted and intended to get her first solid sleep since violence had disrupted her life. She expected, she told him, to come to the Pan Am Building during the meeting with The Consortium Wednesday evening. It was her company, too, and she wanted to join in the confrontation.

Then Thad called Jennie.

"You wouldn't believe what's going on here," she said. "Calls. Visits. People raising hell. People offering advice. Martin is incommunicado. He's holed up in the Harvard Club."

"Then come back to the apartment. There's no reason for you to stay there," said Thad. "I'll send Frank out for you."

"No. Thad," she said firmly. "I was elected by these people, and I owe them a full accounting. Today I'll meet with my constituents and respond to their inquiries. Tomorrow I'll face my colleagues in Washington. I won't be in New York again until Wednesday, when you have to face your Germans. I'll be with you then. And I'll call. . . ." Her voice broke. "I'll call. . . ."

SIXTEEN

The conference room had been cleared and set up for the meeting. The great mahogany table was round, as Thad had always insisted conference tables in his offices must be; yet, it was obvious which chair was his—the one with the twenty-key telephone on the credenza behind it. The walls were paneled with walnut, but their dark color was relieved by four large abstract paintings in dramatic colors, lighted from the ceiling tracks. Charles Lodge Johnson had chosen the paintings and supervised their hanging. The large windows afforded a view of the city, but they were covered with blue draperies, since Thad considered the view distracting. Pots of coffee and tea steamed on the credenza. There was also an orderly array of bottles—wine, liquor, and mineral water—and a bucket of ice. Each place around the table was set with a pen-and-pencil set, a yellow legal pad, a printed report, a cup, a tumbler, and a wine glass.

Thad entered the conference room at seven o'clock, promptly. He was accompanied by Anne; they were followed by Kenneth Asher. Only five of the ten men to whom he had sent cables were present:

Christian Thyssen, who had taken the chair opposite Thad's, faced him across the table. He was handsome, cold as steel, with clear blue eyes and hair clipped short. He appeared, through some knack of carriage, to be menacing—a brusque young man, only thirty years old, to whom the others, nevertheless, deferred.

Ernst Dietrich, the forty-year old race driver whose father had given him a vice-presidency in a major industrial company. He was the tall, hard, pale Teuton. He sat on Thyssen's left.

Klaus Schulenberg, to Thyssen's right, a fortyish dark-haired man with great black eyebrows and gloomy mien.

Friederich Papen, Hildebrandt's successor at VWH, a ruddy, white-haired man who reminded Thad of an English butler.

Kengo Yoshioka, the sixty-three-year-old president of Videosonics, typically Japanese in his ageless appearance and unfailingly restrained manner.

Thad stopped to shake hands with each of the five and to introduce Anne to Thyssen and Yoshioka. Then he strode directly to his chair and sat down, with Anne on his right and Asher on his left.

"I've had no response from Dr. Kim Doo Chung," said Thad. "Does anyone know whether or not he is coming?"

For a moment no one answered, then Yoshioka smiled and said, "We may consider ourselves fortunate."

"He made an abrupt departure from the United States," said Thad. "Apparently he flew home to Seoul, and no one here has heard from him."

"The American newspaper press is making it very difficult for him," said Papen.

"I suppose you refer to stories in the *Times* and *Post* on his Washington . . . improprieties," said Thad.

"I think," said Thyssen with a dismissing tone, "that Dr. Kim Doo Chung will not appear for our meeting. Hans Dietrich called me and said he would not be coming, since Ernst is here to represent him. Josef von Klauberg elected not to come."

"My friend Mr. Uchida also asked me to extend his apologies," said Yoshioka.

"All right," said Thad. "I had hoped that Charles Lodge Johnson would be here. We—that is, Anne and I—left the hospital only an hour ago. Charles remains in critical condition. He has regained consciousness only briefly, and his doctors cannot assure us he will live."

"We are most sorry to hear that," said Klaus Schulenberg in his heavily accented English.

Thad nodded coldly. "Each of you has before you," he said, "a printed report on the present status of States Broadcasting."

That morning the medical bulletin on Charles had reported that he was stable again, but at a slightly weaker stage, a little closer to death but not sinking into it. He had regained consciousness briefly while Kathy was with him. She spoke to him, which seemed to do him good. So she was allowed to remain beside him. He had said nothing, just looked at her; but she could tell he recognized her.

Thad would remember the day as a whirl of meetings, telephone calls, hours snatched to work on an editorial, and Anne's calls from the hospital, which were always put through to him, no matter what he was doing. Late in the morning Christian Thyssen had called and asked Thad to meet him for lunch. Thyssen had said he wanted to talk privately with Thad before the seven-o'clock meeting. Thad had told him coldly that he was rushing to the hospital and was too busy to spare an hour for any kind of unscheduled meeting.

Word of the gathering of The Consortium had somehow leaked out, and television equipment had been set up by mid-afternoon in the elevator lobby, just outside the entrance doors to Catlett Communications Enterprises. Each of the arriving partners—men who hated the glare of publicity—had to push his way through a knot of determined reporters. The Germans had not concealed their irritation with this intrusion, and although Thad had not watched any television, the early-evening news broadcasts on New York stations included brief displays of grim-faced Teutonic impatience. This was followed by speculation as to whom these men were and whether the nation was about to learn more about the financial arrangements behind the controversial Catlett takeover of States Broadcasting.

Jennie had arrived at six, while Thad was at the hospital. She had stopped in Grand Central to telephone before coming up, and Asher asked her to wait at the phone booth. He hurried down and escorted her up in a freight elevator, depositing her in Charles's office.

Thad had stopped by Lehman Hospital to check on Charles. Kathy, drawn and exhausted, sat beside the bed. Charles, entangled in a cobweb of wires and tubes, slept. Or he may have been in a coma. Neither Thad nor Kathy could be sure. Anne accompanied Thad back to the Pan Am Building. They passed through the reporters' gauntlet with waves and smiles. Thad had managed to slip away for five minutes to talk with Jennie. Then he set his jaw and entered the conference room.

"I have used the credits you have extended," said Thad. "We now hold a controlling interest in States Broadcasting. The officers and directors have been intelligent enough to resign. We have begun to install new people where we need them, and we have already begun the revision of the broadcasting schedules of some stations. In short, we have pulled this one off, too. But it's the last one. I cannot tolerate . . . I will not tolerate . . . the criminal activity that has defiled everything we have done. I—"

"You have let your imagination run wild," Thyssen interrupted sullenly.

"Have I?" Thad shot back. "Charles Lodge Johnson lies near death. First he was attacked and beaten on the street, along with the

reporter Bert Stouffer. Then Charles was run down by an automobile that eyewitnesses say swerved to hit him. Both men were investigating a possible link between BND and earlier murders in Europe. Do you seriously expect me to believe these two men were injured by *coincidence?*" He shook his head. "Do you take me for a fool?"

"Mr. Catlett . . ." said Kengo Yoshioka. "Please. Surely you do not believe that we—"

"No, not *we*," Thad interrupted. "Not all of you. Not you, I imagine, Mr. Yoshioka. But someone in this room."

"Would you care to exclude anyone else?" asked Ernst Dietrich. "Why not narrow the circle of suspicion to one of us?"

"When did you arrive in the States, Ernst?" asked Thad curtly.

"This afternoon," said Dietrich.

"How long has it been since you were here last?"

"This is my first visit to the United States."

"You're a liar. You entered the United States through Kennedy Airport on Thursday, April 23, almost two weeks ago."

Dietrich banged his fist on the table. *"I entered the United States this afternoon!"*

"Really? Then show us the stamp on your passport."

Dietrich glanced furiously at Thyssen. "I refuse to be called a liar. I refuse to be cross-examined like a criminal on trial in an American court."

"If you don't want to be called a liar, then don't lie," said Thad. "If you don't want—"

"Is this why we have come to New York?" asked Thyssen. "To listen to wild accusations? You speak of criminal activity. Everyone in this room is highly respected. What evidence do you have?"

"I called you to New York," said Thad, "to advise you of my intention to redeem your preferred stock, pay off all other debt owed to your group, and terminate our relationship."

"You cannot do that," said Papen. "A billion dollars?"

"Actually," said Thad, "the total is eight hundred ninety-two million dollars. And I'm going to pay you off and boot you out."

"You can't," repeated Papen.

"Ken Asher will show you that we damned well can," said Thad.

Anne had heard what Ken was about to say. Thad had asked her to agree to it, and she had sought her father's opinion. Her father had telephoned her at the hospital to say he recommended she go along with what Thad planned to propose.

Asher rose slowly, with a sense of drama. He had earlier mounted a set of huge posters on an easel; deliberately underplaying the drama of the moment, he uncovered the first of them:

1985-1986 ACQUISITIONS

ASSET	PRICE	OFFERING PRICE
DunCast—WMOA-TV, WPAR-TV	$ 46,374,412	$ 62,000,000
WGMH-TV	$ 22,500,000	$ 30,000,000
WDHA-TV	$ 34,275,000	$ 40,000,000
Runkle Broadcasting	$150,000,000	$165,000,000
WYRK-LI, WYRK-NJ, WYRK-CT	$ 40,000,000	$ 70,000,000
Conroy Publishing	$135,000,000	$150,000,000
Totals	$428,149,412	$517,000,000
Financed by CCE	($ 15,000,000)	
Financed by Consortium	$413,149,412	

"Through careful purchasing, by resisting pressures to bid too high on some of these assets," said Asher dryly, "we acquired over a period of about eighteen months assets that appreciated immediately, simply by their passing into the hands of management in which the market had more confidence. By applying CCE management techniques and policies, we increased the value of all the assets. The figures given under the heading 'OFFERING

PRICE' are, we believe, realistic asking prices for these assets, should we elect to sell them."

Asher put the poster aside and uncovered another one:

STATES BROADCASTING

Cost of acquisition, funded by Consortium	$479,000,000
Offering price for selected stations:	
WNOH-TV, Cleveland (negotiated)	$121,000,000
WFRD-TV, Detroit	$125,000,000
WWPC-TV, Minneapolis	$ 85,000,000
WPPE-TV, St. Louis	$ 95,000,000
WOPR-TV, Nashville	$ 95,000,000
WIRN-TV, Birmingham	$ 50,000,000
Total	$571,000,000

"By selling off the six stations listed above, or some other five stations, CCE can redeem the preferred stock issued for the acquisition of States," Asher continued, affecting a businesslike tone. "As is apparent, by substantial trimming of its sails, CCE can achieve financial independence."

"You cannot do it," declared Papen, tapping the table with an index finger. "The terms of the preferred stock prohibit the sale of assets—"

"For less than their value," said Asher calmly. "CCE is specifically authorized to sell assets at a profit."

"You think we are fools," said Thyssen, leaning back in his chair and regarding Thad and Asher with a sneer. "But you will find we are not. We have analyzed your financial position very carefully. You *cannot* redeem our preferred stock. You think you can, but you cannot. We are in a position to squeeze you."

"Please, Mr. Thyssen," said Yoshioka. "It is unnecessary to speak in such angry terms."

"No, I think the time has come for plain talk," said Thyssen. "Let

367

us understand some facts. Your newspapers, Mr. Catlett, are supported by advertising. Since they are mostly tabloids, they rely on department-store advertising. What percentage of that advertising revenue, do you suppose, comes from stores that are owned, in whole or in part, by foreign investors such as ourselves? How many more of your advertisers have financial ties to us and will listen to our recommendations?"

"I suppose you refer to the BND," said Thad.

Thyssen shrugged. "Our members . . . Allies . . . Businessmen who are sympathetic with us. I can deprive you of sixty percent of your department-store advertising. Tomorrow. And the television stations. Take a close look at their sources of revenue. We can slash into that advertising revenue, too. Did you really think we were such fools as to put a billion dollars of our funds into your hands and leave ourselves no means of controlling you? Did Wilhelm Hildebrandt impress you as naive?"

Thad had lit a cigarette while Thyssen was talking; now he blew a thick white cloud of smoke across the table. "Who killed Hildebrandt, Thyssen? Who killed Franz Westphal? Who killed Hanna Frank? Who killed Colin Fleming?"

Thyssen snorted derisively. "You've become obsessed with questions like that. Why don't you leave police detective work to the police?"

"I did, unfortunately, until you tried to kill Charles. Until you attacked Bert Stouffer."

"Stouffer . . . Stouffer," muttered Schulenberg, searching for the English words. "He is an . . . *enemy.*"

"I wouldn't know about enemies," said Thad stiffly. "I have declined to classify people who disagree with me as my enemies."

"What about people who attempt to destroy you?" asked Thyssen.

"It has happened a hundred times," interjected Anne. "I mean, a hundred times at least in the past thirty years, people have tried to destroy our business, or some part of it, or us personally. I don't think we ever hated any of them."

"That is most noble, Mrs. Catlett," said Thyssen. "But let us be specific. Bert Stouffer—who is, of course, a close friend of yours—has sought to damage everyone in this room, if not outright destroy us. For what reason we are not sure. He is a Jew, I believe, and has a fixation about the possible resurgence of Naziism in Europe. He is also an obsessively competitive man, who hopes no doubt to win a second Pulitzer Prize. He has wheedled his way into your confidence. He appears to have had the confidence of Charles Lodge Johnson all along. He has gained information from the two of you for his self-declared war against us."

"What you are telling me, Mr. Thyssen," Anne replied icily, "is that you had a motive for a vicious attack on Bert Stouffer, followed by an attempt to murder Charles."

Thyssen slammed his fist on the table. "*Murder!* Who has been murdered? Stouffer is alive. Charles is alive. But why are we discussing these unfortunate incidents? We had nothing to do with any vicious attacks."

"Would any of you recognize Bert Stouffer if you saw him?" Thad asked.

Thyssen turned up his palms and chuckled. "Not if he came in here and sat down in my lap," he said.

"What if he knew some of you?"

Thyssen shrugged. "Shall we all adjourn to the hospital and see him?"

"That won't be necessary, Mr. Thyssen," said Anne. "You didn't kill him, and you didn't scare him."

As Thad picked up his telephone and pressed buttons, Anne left her chair and walked to the door of the conference room. She opened it and stepped out into the hall. In a moment she returned, helping Bert, who walked gingerly with a cane. She led him around the left side of the table to the chair beside Asher. Asher moved to the other side of Thad, and Anne sat down beside Bert.

"This is Bert Stouffer, gentlemen," said Anne bitterly. "Alive, in spite of you."

*   *   *

369

Bert had struggled for this moment. The doctors had said no, he couldn't possibly go to a meeting in the Pan Am Building on Wednesday evening; that would risk his recovery; it might set him back. But from the moment Thad Catlett had suggested the possibility, Bert had been determined to show up. And, *by God*, he was there.

He had waited in Charles Lodge Johnson's office, with the handsome and troubled young congresswoman Jennie Paget. Everything said in the conference room came through to them on speakers, as it did to the lawyers and other CCE officers listening in various rooms. Frank Dittoe—the ubiquitous Frank—had stationed himself at Stouffer's side. When Frank heard the cue, he had helped Bert limp along the hall two doors to the conference room.

Bert's face was flaming. Sweat stood on his forehead and on his cheeks. The doctors had not been entirely wrong. He was weak; he had overexerted himself. But he had dressed in a tweed jacket and dark brown trousers Anne had brought from his apartment, and his necktie was neat and knotted in place. Bert Stouffer was pleased with himself.

"You want a drink, Bert?" she asked gently.

He smiled. "Yeah. Gin."

She reached for a bottle and poured gin for him, on the rocks. He saw Catlett smile. The man was . . . odd. He was not what Bert had supposed. . . . Jennie Paget called him a fine man—back there, while they were waiting. Anne had said the same. And Charles. Bert was ready to buy it.

Catlett was talking. "Any of you ever see him before? Christian?"

"I never saw this man before in my life."

"Ernst?"

"He is Stouffer, you say?" Dietrich shrugged. "He could be a Hollywood actor for all I know. How do we know he *is* Stouffer?"

"I know you, you bastard," Bert muttered. "I wasn't absolutely sure until I heard the voice."

Catlett nodded at the German. "Don't plan on leaving after the meeting," he said grimly. "The police will be here."

"Insane!" yelled the German.

"What do you hope to achieve by this outrage?" asked the white-haired man two chairs to the right of Christian Thyssen.

"That's Friederich Papen," said Catlett. "He succeeded Wilhelm Hildebrandt at VWH. The one you recognize is Ernst Dietrich. And the man between Thyssen and Papen is Klaus Schulenberg. I guess you know all the names."

Bert nodded. Of course he did. It was always odd how people, when you at last saw them, were so different from the impressions you had formed of them over time. Thyssen in particular. He was so young. . . .

"Why did you bring this man into our meeting?" Papen demanded.

"I think we had better hear him," said Catlett. "Let me put it more directly. . . . We are *going* to hear him. Bert—"

Anne squeezed his hand, and Bert took a gulp of gin. "I wasn't willing to believe my conjectures until I learned of the death of Herr Westphal," he said. "That elegant old gentleman . . . Murdered."

Thyssen stared at Stouffer, hard and cold. Papen looked down at his hands. The other two Germans, Dietrich and Schulenberg, leaned back and regarded Stouffer with a mixture of contempt and apprehension. The Japanese—Catlett hadn't introduced him, but Bert supposed he was Yoshioka—had compressed his lips so tightly it distorted his whole face.

"The Bund für das Neues Deutschtum is not a neo-Nazi organization," said Bert. "It is not anti-Semitic. It does not wish to restore the Third Reich. It is just an organization of men who think they are infallible."

"You learned this from Israel?" asked Thyssen scornfully.

Bert shrugged. "From Israel. From Herr Westphal. From others of your countrymen. The only thing you have in common with Hitler, Herr Thyssen, is that you think you are inspired and incapable of error. That kind of certainty is a malevolent syndrome. You share it with Ayatollah Khomeini. With Charles Manson."

371

"You are deranged," said Thyssen through clenched teeth.

"We'll see who's deranged," said Catlett firmly.

Bert nodded at Catlett and resumed his narrative. He seemed to gain strength as he spoke. "The Bund für das Neues Deutschtum killed Colin Fleming," he said. "I can't prove everything I'm about to say, but the police investigation will eventually prove most of it. One piece of the puzzle I haven't figured out is whether Wilhelm Hildebrandt authorized the murder of Fleming—or even knew of it. I tend to doubt it. But Fleming had learned a lot about the organization. He was poking into it, getting too close to the truth. So the BND had him killed. Whether you ordered it, Thyssen, I don't know. I know more about Dietrich . . . that he's a competent street mugger and that I survived only because his accomplice restrained him. Yes, Dietrich would make a likely candidate for the killer of Colin Fleming."

"We'll discuss it at your trial for libel and slander," sneered Dietrich.

"Hanna Frank," said Bert, "had been stealing extra copies of the documents she copied for VWH. Every room at the VWH gasthaus was bugged; many rooms were monitored by hidden television cameras. Hanna entered the guests' rooms and photographed everything they were carrying: documents, their personal snapshots, everything. Wilhelm Hildebrandt may not have been a killer, but he was an extortionist. He was accused of blackmail as long ago as 1953. It was an element of his success, as a businessman and as the leader of BND. My guess is that he didn't know Hanna Frank was stealing copies of his blackmail materials. When Fleming's briefcase was taken after he was shot, the killer found Hanna's stolen materials in it. That doomed Hanna Frank."

"Speculation," muttered Papen.

"I don't know whether Hildebrandt ordered the murder of Hanna Frank—or even consented to it," said Bert. "If I were to hazard another guess, I believe she was killed without his consent or authority. I suspect that a bitter controversy over what to do about Hanna Frank resulted in the murder of Hildebrandt."

Yoshioka was now leaning forward. "Can you explain this, Mr. Stouffer?"

Bert nodded at the Japanese. "Those who know anything about the Bund für das Neues Deutschtum say it has become more doctrinaire over the years, more certain of its rectitude, more aggressive. The older members were more conservative, more cautious. They experienced defeat—some of them twice—and they were less willing to take risks. I acknowledge this is my own speculation, but I suspect Wilhelm Hildebrandt was murdered to make room for the younger, more aggressive leader that a growing faction wanted."

"Wilhelm Hildebrandt was killed by agents of the East German Ministerium für Staats-Sicherheit," said Papen. "That has been established."

"Not quite established," said Bert. He could feel the sweat dampening his clothes; he was conscious that his strength was ebbing. "It might have worked if the killer hadn't used the same unique method to murder poor old Herr Westphal. But because the killer repeated his MO . . ."

"MO?" asked Yoshioka.

"Method of operation . . . Because the killer repeated his MO, the investigation into the murder of Hildebrandt has suddenly been reopened. The German police are showing a new determination to find out what happened. The BND has agents inside the various police agencies, and they thwarted the original investigation. But no longer. I've spoken to police officials in Frankfurt. We've been exchanging information. I even called them from my hospital bed. I can tell you the Hildebrandt murder is at the top of the police agenda again."

"Two MfS agents . . ." Schulenberg persisted.

"Both were killed with injections of sodium pentothal," said Bert. "The key to the Volkswagen van was placed in one's pocket. They were known to the German authorities . . . easy to identify. I can give you the scenario that the police are piecing together. The East German agents were captured and injected with sodium pentothal.

They were probably interrogated while they were under the influence of the truth serum. When the interrogation was over, they were administered fatal amounts. It worked so well that someone used the same method on Herr Westphal."

"Are you finished, Herr Stouffer?" asked Thyssen in a voice of cold steel. "You promised information . . . evidence. Obviously, you have none. Like so many in your profession, you are a spinner of fairy tales."

"Herr Westphal left documents," said Bert. "He—"

"Bert!"

Anne seized his arm. Bert knew he was weaving; his vision began to blur; he felt his consciousness slowly fading. He grabbed his glass and swallowed some gin. The hard fumes revived him. "Documents . . ." he gasped. "There is evidence."

Thad watched with concern as Bert Stouffer almost fainted. Anne cared for him. Her gentle devotion was moving. Once . . .

"Mr. Catlett," said Kengo Yoshioka, carefully enunciating his words. "Do you believe these things are true?"

"Yes," said Thad. "I know enough to accept the premise if not yet all the specifics."

"Then we have been deceived," said Yoshioka.

"Yes," said Thad. "We have been fools."

"You *are* fools," said Thyssen, his voice still devoid of heat, "if you believe this. You can believe what you wish . . . if you are willing to accept the risk. It will take more than Stouffer's words to destroy us, and we will not sit by complacently while he aims his empty words at us." Thyssen threw out his right arm, aiming it like a rifle barrel straight at Stouffer. "He flatters himself. Why would anyone *bother* to attack him."

Thad crushed his cigarette in the crystal tray before him. He picked up the telephone, punched in three numbers, and spoke to the man who answered. "Roll 'em, Harry. Let 'em go."

Thyssen swung his arm around and aimed at Thad. "What was your word? *Boot,* you said. You are going to boot us out? We shall see, Thad Catlett. Tomorrow you will receive the first of the big advertising cancellations. *Tomorrow.* For your first lesson in humility. Who do you think you're dealing with? Do you really think you can boot us out? Do you think you can do what the governments of Europe cannot do? We are bigger than you . . . stronger than you, Thad Catlett. We know how to handle small annoyances."

"I want to show you something," Thad interjected. He opened a door of the credenza behind him and pulled out a small stack of newspapers. "These are a few advance copies of tomorrow morning's *New York Sentinel-American.* I just gave the order to roll the presses. A few hundred have already been printed. In a matter of minutes, thousands will be printed. They're being bundled and delivered to the streets. And there is no way you can stop them."

The men passed the newspapers around the table. All eyes focused on the front page of the *Sentinel-American,* then immediately became riveted on the editorial that dominated the page.

MY APOLOGY, AMERICA

Over the past eighteen months, Catlett Communications Enterprises, Inc., the owner of a powerful media combine which includes this newspaper, has invested more than eight hundred million dollars in acquisition and expansion. Many people have wondered where all that money came from. Except for mandated public disclosure, we have until now kept the sources of our capital essentially secret. The news stories that accompany this editorial describe how the money was raised, the motivation of those who have financed our expansion, and the criminal activities which some of them may have engaged in.

The accompanying news stories divulge all the information now available to us. We suspect even worse wrongdoing that we have not yet established.

Over the next few weeks, CCE will pursue a legal divorce from the consortium whose financial backing we, in good faith, accepted. We will disassociate ourselves from the people and organization you will read about in our news stories.

We also pledge to come clean with the American people, to disclose all that we learn just as fast as we learn it.

One thing more: I was responsible, and no one else, for the decisions and the blunders that led CCE into this financial entanglement. My wife, who is co-owner of CCE, smelled a rat and warned me not to associate our company with these people. I received a similar warning from my associate Charles Lodge Johnson. I foolishly disregarded their warnings.

All of us owe a debt of gratitude to the distinguished journalist Bert Stouffer, whose investigative reporting uncovered the scandal described in more detail on these pages. He does not work for our newspapers, but we will nominate him for the prize he has already won once, the top award in journalism—the Pulitzer Prize.

There is, of course, a larger issue—the stake we all have in the basic integrity of the media. A mere mistake, however garish, is one thing. If honestly made, if promptly and openly corrected, it should not damage public confidence. For the public, knowing its own failings, requires the media to be not infallible but only honest. Our readers rely on us for accurate information. When we pull a whopper, we have an obligation to our own credibility and to that of the media to explain it if we can. We can thus hope to atone for our sin and leave the credibility of the media as strong as we found it.

The mistake I made, though unintentional, was a betrayal of the public trust. It was my mistake alone. I apologize, America.

—F. Thad Catlett

The editorial was supported by news stories on the front, second, and third pages, stories that bore these headlines:

ONE BILLION DOLLARS AVAILABLE TO INFLUENCE PUBLIC OPINION IN UNITED STATES

376

BUND FÜR DAS NEUES DEUTSCHTUM
—WAS IST DAS?

* * *

GERMAN FINANCIAL TYCOON
THREATENS ADVERTISING BOYCOTT
AGAINST CATLETT PAPERS

* * *

MUGGING OR INTIMIDATION?
"BACK OFF!" GROWL ATTACKERS

* * *

EMINENT JOURNALIST REMAINS
IN CRITICAL CONDITION
Charles Lodge Johnson
Victim of Vicious Attack

* * *

SECOND JOURNALIST RECOVERING
Stouffer, Pulitzer Winner,
Mugged for Disclosures

Thad reached for the Scotch bottle. "Some of you," he said brusquely, "may be able to catch a plane out of Kennedy before this is widely enough distributed to cause someone to issue warrants for your arrest."

377

EPILOGUE

Saturday afternoon. July 4, 1987. Thad stood at the balustrade of his terrace, looking out over the wooded slope and Long Island Sound. In blue jeans and an Izod shirt, he smoked a cigarette, sipped Scotch, and scanned for the tenth time the story that would appear tomorrow in the business section of the Sunday *Times*. The reporter and analyst had written an accurate account of the straitened CCE.

CCE is selling all but three of the television stations it acquired by the acquisition of States Broadcasting, having to take into account capital-gains taxes on the profitable sale of a first group of stations. Stations in Detroit, Minneapolis, and St. Louis, valued at perhaps $300,000,000, are being retained. The company has sold—or is in the process of selling—stations in Miami, Tampa, and Louisville. It will retain three New York stations—WYRK-NH, WYRK-CT, and WYRK-LI—which were not part of the States Broadcasting network.

379

Former owner F. Thad Catlett expressed satisfaction that none of the stations had fallen back into the hands of Christian fundamentalist broadcasters.

The German investors, who engaged Catlett in a desperate corporate in-fight, have been bought out and no longer own any equity or debt in any Catlett corporation. Criminal charges have been brought against certain members of what was called The Consortium.

The minority shareholders of States Broadcasting, who were threatening to sue over the liquidation of almost the entire assets of their company, are being offered common shares of CCE as compensation. Twelve percent of the common stock of CCE has been set aside by Mr. and Mrs. Catlett for that purpose. Alternatively, the minority stockholders can sell their States shares to CCE for cash, an alternative that might cost CCE as much as $425,000,000. The sale of the Detroit station and perhaps other properties is CCE's contingency plan to meet such a demand for cash.

CCE might, in the end, be compelled to sell the remaining television stations and perhaps even Conroy Publishing. In that event, F. Thad Catlett would once more be the owner of seven daily newspapers, a weekly supermarket tabloid, and sixty-eight neighborhood newspapers. Since two of his newspapers—the *New York Sentinel-American* and the *Washington Register-Herald*—continue to lose money, he might be compelled even to give up one or both of them.

The communications tycoon out of Texas and Pittsburgh has suffered a near-fatal reverse. Those who know him, however, have little doubt that F. Thad Catlett will rise like a phoenix from the ashes. Interviewed in his Manhattan apartment, where he is slowly recovering from near-fatal injuries caused by a hit-skip accident, Charles Lodge Johnson, CCE vice president, called Catlett "unsinkable."

His mother was visiting the manor, dressed as he was in jeans and a golf shirt and deeply tanned from her summer days on the beach. "I was taught never to believe half of what I saw, a third of what I heard, and nothing that I read in the newspaper," she said, nodding at his advance copy of the Sunday-morning business section. She had poured herself a generous shot of bourbon. "Didn't I teach you that?"

"No. You taught me how to shoot rattlesnakes."

"You just plugged a few . . . German variety."

"Spare me," he said. "The truth is, your son had descended into the snake pit with them."

"Frankie," she said. "At age fifty, you just grew a little bit. Your gran'dad would have been proud. Yes . . . and your dad, too."

Thad shook his head. "They'd have called me stupid to get involved in the first place. If I remember, you don't get congratulated for pulling your truck out of the muck; you get laughed at for getting stuck in the first place."

"Uhmmm," she shrugged. "We all have to take our comedownances."

Thaddy had come home for the Fourth of July. He and Alan had flown over from London. Richard had driven down from Cambridge with Betty, who stood a little apart in almost-knee-length blue shorts and a white silk blouse.

Bert Stouffer sat on the balustrade and sipped a martini. He wore white tennis shorts, matching Anne's. They had played in the morning. Bert was still stiff, and she had beaten him, straight sets.

"Dad . . ." Thad turned. It was Richard who intruded on his father's solitude. "Dad, they're bringing Mr. Johnson in."

Thad left his glass on the balustrade, burst through the terrace door, and hurried through the house. The limousine was standing in the driveway, and Thaddy and Alan were helping Kathy hoist Charles from the car and into a wheelchair. Thad raced up to him and knelt in the gravel beside the wheelchair.

Charles was easily disoriented as Thad knew from his frequent visits to the hospital, then to the apartment; but now Charles reached for Thad and spoke clearly.

"Get up off the driveway, Thad. You'll damage your trousers. You've got Chateau Lafite for me, have you not? Anne promised. This . . . creature"—he glared at Kathy—"will not cooperate in offering me what the good health of a civilized man requires."

Charles's ability to speak was impaired. He spoke like a man who had just had his teeth extracted. The doctors promised that would clear up.

"Charles . . ."

Thad's eyes were wet.

"You going to cry? I'm going home."

Thad rose, chuckling. Anne rushed out and embraced Charles. Kathy took both Thad's hands in her own and sobbed, laughing at the same time. Thaddy and Alan settled Charles comfortably and securely in the wheelchair. The procession moved slowly into the house. They wheeled Charles out to the terrace where, as promised, a bottle of Chateau Lafite Rothschild was breathing for him.

"I have to tell you something," said Charles when he had tasted the wine. "It is not a good year. But . . . I would not pour it on the ground. Oh, yes . . . something else. The New York police department paid me a call this morning. . . ."

"Oh, honey, I'm not sure you should even mention it!"

Charles glanced at Kathy. "I still have the soul of a reporter," he said gently. "I can't withhold news."

"Charles . . ." she protested reprovingly. Kathy had begun to turn gray since the night Anne and Thad had seen her at the hospital. She was still the busty, fleshy girl Anne had first encountered in the apartment, but she had aged from Charles's double ordeal.

Charles proceeded with his account. "Thad, the intrepid investigators of the NYPD appeared at my place this morning—Fourth of July morning, would you believe?—to tell me they have arrested the taxi driver who ran me down. The man, it seems, has confessed. No one but a pitiable Hispanic lad who had, as they put it, 'done drugs' that morning. He was so high he didn't know his left from his right. It seems he swerved the wrong way."

"You mean a wrong turn of the wheel brought down the BND?" Thad asked incredulously, shaking his head.

"And just about ruined us," Charles added.

"Damn!" said Thad. He filled his glass with Scotch.

"Second thoughts?" Anne asked.

Thad lifted his glass. "None. . . . Here's to sunlight. May it ever reach into the dark corners of society. It is, after all, the best disinfectant."

"Please!" protested Charles. "No speeches. . . . Who chose this wine?"

"I did, you fraud," grumbled Thad.

"I must respectfully advise you—how can I put this delicately?—that you have a serious flaw in your social skills. I'm afraid you lack a distinguished taste for wine."

"I want you to know that my tastes were developed in the best damn saloon in Texas," retorted Thad. "Why, I . . ."

"Excuse me," said Anne. "More guests apparently. The doorbell rings."

They ignored her. Thad changed the subject. "When are you coming back to work?"

"And give up Kathy's spoiling?"

Turning serious, Thad said, "I've had to let a few people go."

"My God! Am I among them?"

"When the company consists of two people, Charles, they will be you and me."

Anne returned to the terrace. "Thad, you had better go to your den," she said mysteriously. "Someone to see you."

Thad stopped to squeeze her hand before he walked through the open French doors and into the house.

"Jennie!"

She rushed into his arms and pressed her mouth against his, so hard that it was painful. He clasped her to him, and they clung together for several minutes, squeezing.

"Anne called me," she murmured. Jennie was dressed in a white tennis skirt, an orange T-shirt, and white tennis shoes.

"How are you weathering the political storm?" he asked solicitously.

"I attend my committee meetings, service my constituents, vote my conscience, and scratch where it itches," Jennie said. "What more can I do?"

"I have faith in the American people and the American system," Thad replied. "If you are honest and open, the people will respond. You'll be reelected, Jennie. . . . You'll see."

"It doesn't really matter," she said. "All that matters is that I love you."

"I love you, too, Jennie."

Thad took her by the hand. "Everyone else is on the terrace. Anne. Bert. My sons. Thaddy's . . . friend. My mother. Charles and Kathy. People who love each other. And now we go out there with them."

Jennie nodded. "It sounds perfect. But I wish—I wish I knew how everything is going to come out."

"My mother shot a rattlesnake once," he said. "It was left on the ground for dead. At length, it began to stir and twitch. Then it slunk off unseen . . . to return another day, knitted back together and resuscitated."

"Are you saying that those German rattlesnakes might be back?"

"They'll be back . . . or someone like them."

Thad led Jennie through the house, out onto the terrace. Anne handed her a Scotch on the rocks.